THE MESSENGER
A ROB WALKER THRILLER BOOK I

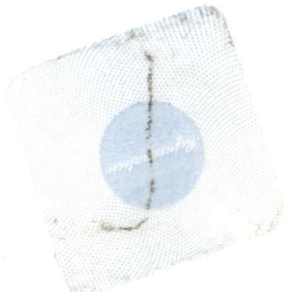

JOHN ETTERLEE

This is a work of fiction. Names, characters, places, and incidents either are the product of the author's imagination or are used fictitiously. Any resemblance to actual persons, living or dead, events, or locales is entirely coincidental.

Copyright © 2021 by John Etterlee

All rights reserved. No part of this book may be reproduced or used in any manner without written permission of the copyright owner except for the use of quotations in a book review. For more information, email john@johnetterleebooks.com

First edition, 2021
ISBN: 9798723055780

Independently published

www.johnetterleebooks.com

For my wife, Elizabeth, who is behind me in everything I do. Without her support, I wouldn't be where I am now. I love you! To Jose, New York City Police Officer and fellow Veteran who allowed me to use him as a character while offering his help and ideas. I really appreciate it! Last, but not least, to service members around the world in harm's way—none of us would be free without you. I wish I could still be with you. Keep on trucking!

"The only thing necessary for the triumph of evil is for good men to do nothing."

—Edmund Burke

ONE

Operation Inherent Resolve
Kunar Province
Afghanistan

Weeks before it happened, before she vanished from the New York City streets, Rob was thousands of miles away, fighting a war on foreign soil. He'd had little time to think about home, or anything else. Responsibility to his country and team took precedence over anything else, at least for the time being.

A chilly wind blew steadily through the Korangal Valley, also called the Valley of Death by American troops during the longest and most drawn-out war in the nation's history. It had become one of the most dangerous places in the world, marked by intense clashes between the US-led coalition and the Taliban. With its different tribes and no apparent laws other than those observed by a council of elders, the valley had been cause for hostility between the locals and the US military for years.

But that was in the past. Special Forces no longer needed

tribal approval to operate there. ISIL, or the Islamic State of Iraq and the Levant, set up shop within the surrounding mountains. It wasn't a matter of winning over hearts and minds. This time, the mission was straightforward: seek and destroy.

Beneath the gray, hazy sky, high grass and branches fluttered in the breeze beneath snow-capped mountains. Sergeant First Class Rob Walker, thirty-three, and his spotter, Staff Sergeant Kyle Branch, thirty, both with the 5th Special Forces Group, lay prone on that jagged mountainside, hundreds of meters from a suspected Islamic State stronghold.

Several years prior, ISIL had wreaked havoc in Iraq until the coalition had forced them out. But they were still attempting to spread their destructive message across the rest of the world. The US government knew they were hiding in small pockets across Afghanistan and parts of Pakistan. Well after the United States began its official withdrawal from Afghanistan, a small network of Special Forces and Special Operations Forces had stayed in the country to hunt down remaining ISIL fighters and provide firepower against the Taliban should a peace agreement fail to materialize. Here they were, doing what they did best.

Rob Walker was a third-generation military man. His father had served as a grunt in Vietnam, and his grandfather was a B-17 bomber pilot in World War II. Growing up on the streets of Brooklyn was rough, so his family understood why he left. He'd always felt destined to do bigger things while serving his country. And that he did.

Before joining the Special Forces, Rob was a sniper with the second battalion, 75th Ranger Regiment at Joint-Base Lewis/McChord. It wasn't a requirement to attend Ranger

School prior to joining the Special Forces. But many of those who earned that green beret tended to have special operations backgrounds. Rob was no exception.

He'd excelled in the Special Forces selection program, both physically and mentally. He was a team player. After graduating from the long qualification course, or Q-course as a Weapons Sergeant, they sent him to the Special Forces Sniper Course, where he finished in the top 1 percent of his class. Rob was noticed early on in his career for his superb marksmanship skills and raw talent. Adding training to that talent made him a sniper the enemy feared as he racked up nearly ninety confirmed kills in just a few years.

Like Rob, Kyle was a sniper with the Ranger Regiment for a time. He'd been assigned to the 3rd battalion out of Fort Benning, Georgia. But he'd always known he wanted to be a Special Forces operator. After serving a few years in the regiment, Kyle graduated from the qualification course, also as a Weapons Sergeant, and was sent to his team. Shortly after completing the sniper course, he and Rob were paired up as a sniper, spotter team. They became fast friends, bonding over their love for country and eradicating the nation's enemies.

Unlike special operations units like the Navy SEALs and Rangers, Special Forces had no dedicated sniper element for each team. The alpha-team captain would designate a qualified sniper and spotter who'd attended the Special Forces sniper course at Fort Bragg to perform overwatch or long range reconnaissance, sniper missions as he saw fit.

Rob and Kyle had positioned themselves at a distance to provide cover for the Special Forces team as they prepared to clear the remote Afghan village of militants and eliminate one of their top lieutenants. Special Forces had fought the Taliban and al-Qaeda for years. However, the Islamic State took savagery to a whole new level. They were brutal. The coalition could not allow ISIL to regroup and gain a foothold in Afghanistan after their defeat in Iraq and Syria. They were like a cancer that needed to be removed before it spread.

The rest of the US Army Special Forces team, Operational Detachment Alpha-595, or ODA-595, waited in position. Historically, the Special Forces, except for Operational Detachment-Delta, or Delta Force, didn't normally conduct direct action or high-value target raids like the Navy SEALs and the Army Rangers. Special Forces teams were mostly instructors to foreign military allies, going into battle with them when needed. However, the team was among some whose mission had recently changed.

On the other side of the valley, Rob looked through the glass of his M95 Barrett .50-caliber sniper rifle, its bipod resting sturdily on the flat rock surface amid the undergrowth. With a maximum effective range of eighteen hundred meters, that rifle was the optimal weapon for long-range targets in the Afghan Mountains.

Kyle studied the halfway point between their position and the target area through his Leupold Mark 4 spotting scope, noting the wind swaying the grass to one side. He called out the range while examining the scope's mil-reticle. "Distance to nearest building, five hundred and fifty meters."

Peering through his scope, camouflage Mechanix gloves on his hands, Rob grasped the pistol grip on his rifle.

"Roger that, five hundred and fifty meters," he replied as he started doping or dialing the elevation turret with his other hand.

Intelligence had received a tip from a confidential source

that ISIL leaders, or "Daesh" as they called them in that part of the world, had ordered the village taken over and a permanent terrorist training camp established. After taking most of the women as sex slaves for Islamic State fighters, ISIL ran off or killed the remaining villagers.

The team had also gotten a report that ISIL had a hostage, an American journalist who'd embedded with one of the Ranger battalions operating in the AO, or area of operations. Special Operations Command had given her the code name Scribe. Her rescue was a mission priority.

Rob held the butt of his rifle into his shoulder while he adjusted the tan sniper veil spread over his body.

"I don't see a damn thing," Kyle told Rob as he skimmed through his spotting scope.

"Yeah," Rob said in his New York accent as he scratched the side of his scruffy beard, his tan ball cap turned backward. "I wasn't expecting it to be this fucking quiet."

He spat a stream of Copenhagen to the side, keeping the glass right in his view. Kyle took another look as Rob moved his mouthpiece closer to his lips with his non-firing hand.

"Alpha-six," he said over the radio, feeling the light wind against the side of his face. "You see anything from over there? We got nothing at this location, over."

"Negative," Detachment Commander, Captain Wells, thirty-three, replied. "Nothing on this end yet. Hold position, over."

"Roger that, boss," Rob said, his trigger finger pointed straight over the trigger guard.

Captain Jonathan Wells had been a West Point cadet, graduating in the top 10 percent of his class. After serving in the Ranger Regiment for a stretch, he attended Special Forces selection at Fort Bragg. Upon his Q-course graduation and promotion to captain, Wells was sent straight to the 5th Special Forces Group and given his team assignment. Most of the team had already been together for a while, serving in Iraq and Afghanistan on numerous deployments. But Wells was surely gaining their confidence.

"Weren't they supposed to be here already?" Kyle asked Rob.

Rob removed his eye from the lens, momentarily glancing at his spotter and grinning, a fat dip of Copenhagen bulging in the side of his lip.

"Shit," he replied. "I forgot to call and set up the meeting."

"Funny," Kyle replied, laughing, "but I'm serious. Intel said the village was occupied."

"That's what they told us," Rob said. "When are they ever on point? It makes you wonder why they call it intelligence. Besides, when has a mission ever gone to plan?"

"You can say that again," Kyle replied while chewing on a piece of beef jerky.

Rob scanned the village below, shifting his rifle from right to left. He searched for any sign of movement through the oddly shaped windows and between the mud-brick buildings.

"You're right, though. Something's off. The place seems deserted. I don't like it one damn bit."

"Roger that," Kyle replied. "Think they knew we were coming?"

"I hope not. If this informant is trying to double-cross us, I will deal with his ass myself."

Kyle moved his spotting scope right. He noticed sand churning in the distance.

"Wait, I got something over here."

He zoomed the scope for a better look.

"What you got?" Rob asked as he turned his weapon toward the cloud of dust.

"Looks like three vehicles," replied Kyle.

Rob located them and followed their movement between the mil-lines in his scope reticle.

"It's them," he said. "See the black flags on the antennas?"

"Roger that, I see 'em."

Rob keyed the mic connected to his headset.

"Alpha-six," he said into the mic. "We got three technicals over here. An unknown number of occupants with mounted heavy machine guns approaching from the north. Please advise, over."

"Roger, Alpha-three," Captain Wells replied. "I got them. Just sit tight and let's see what they do. I repeat, hold fire. Wait for my signal. Then we'll crash their party."

"That's a good copy, Alpha-six."

Captain Wells and assistant detachment commander, Chief Warrant Officer Dylan Henderson, and team sergeant, Master Sergeant Brian Hobbs, took cover behind a low brick wall. The rest of the twelve-man team followed suit beside them a couple of hundred meters from the site.

The scout sniper team watched as three white Nissan pickups came to an immediate stop at the village's edge. As five men hopped from the vehicles, Rob caught something he wished he hadn't seen.

"Jesus," he said, watching a row of civilians, hoods over their heads and arms bound behind their backs, thrown from the bed of a truck and forced at gunpoint through the entrance to one of the buildings. "Are you seeing this?"

"Yeah," replied Kyle. "The fucking savages."

"Alpha-six," Rob said into the radio. "I see hostages. I say again. Multiple hostages, I count six being forced into the building. It looks like they are getting ready for an execution. I can't identify the Scribe, but it looks like ten, maybe twelve hostiles, including our star, Abbas. The civilians are in the way. I have no clear shot on him, over."

Adeel Abbas was the leader of ISIL in Afghanistan. His people and enemies alike called him the lion for his being ruthless with his chosen torture methods. No captive who'd ever been alone in a room with him had ever come out alive. He'd targeted civilians for a while, even ripping young boys from their homes and forcing them to fight for him. The team was there to remedy the problem. They had to deal with Abbas. JSOC, or Joint Special Operations Command, wanted his head on a platter.

Abbas moved around a lot, never sleeping in the same place twice. They had no idea when they'd ever have another chance at him. They had to deal with him now or risk many more civilian deaths.

Abbas was an Afghan. He was brought up in Kabul and highly influenced by al-Qaeda and a strict interpretation of Sharia law. But Special Forces command knew that most of the ISIL militants in Afghanistan were foreign fighters, with a tiny percentage being Afghan nationals. It was just as much a problem for the new Afghan government as it was for the Americans. Abbas grew to believe al-Qaeda to be too soft, thus turning his sights on ISIL as soon as they emerged. His brutal nature fit their ideals, and he gained rank rather quickly.

"I just lost visual on 'em," said Rob. "They've moved inside the buildings, over."

"God damn it," Wells replied. "Roger that."

Rob took another glimpse through the glass, squinting his non-dominant eye while surveying the space surrounding the trucks.

"Alpha-six," he continued. "They left two guys guarding the trucks over here. Let me send these assholes to Allah so you guys can proceed."

"Roger, Alpha-three. Send it. Make it fast."

Suddenly, the team heard a single gunshot from inside the house.

"Damn it!" Rob said as he aimed with his rifle. "Seems they've already started."

He breathed in and out calmly, watching the rise and fall of the reticle.

"Ready," Rob told Kyle as he held his aim.

On the spotting scope, Kyle called out the wind. "Wind, fifteen miles per hour from our three o'clock, full-value."

With no change to distance, Rob clicked the windage knob. The tip of his finger pressed against the trigger, and he squeezed off a round. The recoil of the large-caliber rifle bumped hard into Rob's shoulder, cracking as the bullet soared toward its intended target and splashed red mist against the vehicle's side. The enemy fighter's body plummeted to the earth, a baseball-sized hole left in his torso.

"Tango down."

He slid the bolt backward and ejected a single shell casing. Catching it in midair, he pocketed it. Rob rammed another round into the chamber with one forward motion, pushing the bolt knob down into its locked position.

Rob blinked his eyes to focus his vision, glaring back into the rifle scope. Seeing the red color splashed onto the truck's bed, the second militant wandered toward his dead partner lying on the dirt on the other side of the vehicle.

"I don't think so," Rob said under his breath.

Rob followed him through his scope as he strolled along in the dead man's direction. Finger over the trigger, he squeezed and watched as the high-powered round split apart the man's dome. The militant smacked his head on the tailgate and left a patch of blood dripping from it. Rob watched him drop to the ground hard.

"Fuck me. Somebody had to have heard that."

"Roger that," the captain said. "No time to wait. We're moving in."

"Watch your backs, Alpha-six. I can't cover you once you are inside."

Rob and his spotter observed through the glass. The rest of the team moved to the structure's side, hugging the wall beneath the window. He held the crosshairs on the front entrance. The wooden door came open, and a single fighter appeared, lighting up a cigarette in the doorway.

"Alpha-six, hold," said Rob. "Tango in the doorway."

"Roger," Wells whispered. "Holding position."

Rob touched the tip of his finger to the arc in the trigger.

"If I drop him, all his buddies are going to come pouring out like ants."

"Roger that," replied the captain. "Let's wait and see what he does."

Almost instantly, the hostile began walking to the corner of the house.

"Shit," Rob said as he panned the rifle left. "He's moving."

Just before the militant reached Wells's position, Rob pressed the trigger. A single shot tore through the man's torso, leaving a gaping hole in his chest and thrusting him backward against the wall before smashing face-down into a rock.

"He's down."

Rob guided his scope to the door.

"But there are more headed your way!"

A second man appeared in the doorway, and Rob dropped him.

"Take cover!" he yelled as he watched his team reposition behind a few large boulders. "They're coming fast!"

"Roger that, Alpha-three! We need to rescue these civilians!"

"Let's kill these bastards first, huh? Then we'll worry about getting them out of here!"

Wells and the rest of the team sent fire into the hostiles fleeing the house as Rob and Kyle looked on from hundreds of meters away.

"Fuck!" Rob yelled, watching one of the ISIL fighters appear, holding an RPG or rocket-propelled grenade launcher pointed in the team's direction. "RPG!"

"Allahu Akbar!" a voice echoed through the valley.

In no time, Rob took aim. As he squeezed the trigger, the RPG launched and shot through the air, exploding within a few meters of the team before the militant's body collapsed to the dirt.

"Shit!" Rob shouted into the radio as he looked for them through the large, fiery dust cloud. "You guys all right?"

Rob watched as the captain rose to one knee and continued shooting from cover.

"We're good, Alpha-three!" Captain Wells yelled between bursts of gunfire. "Just cover us!"

Hearing the constant fire from their position on the mountainside, Rob and Kyle knew they couldn't remain there much longer. The team was compromised. As quick as the captain could utter a single word, Rob engaged, ejecting shell casings and firing single shots into each militant. The team sent rounds into the sand-colored structure.

"Move, Alpha-six!" he said as bullets pinged off the surrounding rocks. "You're going to get pinned down! I'll cover you. Just move!"

Right then, he noticed an ISIL fighter clutching his AK-47 through the window, pointed in the team's direction.

"Big mistake, asshole," Rob said, squeezing the trigger. The man's covered head came apart by the weight of a .50-caliber rifle round flying at breakneck speed.

Suddenly, another truck appeared down the uneven dirt road, speeding toward the Special Forces team as they scrambled across the yard.

"We have a problem here, Alpha-six," said Rob. "Looks like a suicide bomber coming in hot!"

"You have a shot on him?" Wells asked over the radio. "I repeat, do you have a shot?"

"Working on it!" he replied as he followed the roof of the vehicle, partly obscured by the mountainous terrain.

The truck barreled around the curve, headed straight for the middle of the square, near to the team's location. Rob knew he'd only have one shot at it. He positioned his rifle toward the vehicle's grill and followed the truck as it grew closer.

Exhaling softly, he held his finger over the trigger. With a calm exhale, he squeezed. The bullet rocketed forward, striking the grill, and entered the center of the radiator, leaving a wet trail of antifreeze across the ground. The truck coasted down the hill and came to a slow stop in the middle of the square. Shifting the reticle and sliding another round forward, Rob fired once more into the windshield, killing the driver. His dead body slid sideways down the seat, a bloody mess left on the back glass.

The truck sat idling, white smoke rising from the engine. Then, without warning, a giant blast shook the entire area, the shock wave sending Wells and a couple of his teammates flying backward behind the hardcover.

"Fuck!" they heard Wells bellow, coughing and gasping from a mixture of smoke and dust filling the air.

"Alpha-six," Rob said, hearing his team grumble over the radio as he watched from his position. "That was close! You guys still in one piece?"

"Yeah," the captain said, spitting a glob of dirt from his mouth. "Yeah, we're good, I think. My ears are fucking ringing like crazy. Holy shit, that was nuts!"

"You should've seen it from up here," Rob joked as debris rained down on the team from above. "I'm glad you guys didn't get cooked in that inferno!"

Walker watched as Wells and Henderson stumbled to their knees and peeked around the corner at the vehicle, the ball of flames climbing high into the sky.

"Nice shot, man!" continued Wells. "Any closer, we would have been barbecue."

"Seriously," Chief Henderson said. "I don't know what we'd do without you."

"Dude, I'm buying you a whole fucking case of beer when we get home," Communications Sergeant, Javier López, told him.

"We can all hug and kiss later," Rob replied. "They are still inside. And I am pretty sure they won't come out quietly."

He glanced over at Kyle with a half-witted smirk as his

spotter patted him on the shoulder.

"Nice shooting, man," said Kyle.

Rob smiled and peeped back once more through his rifle scope.

As the smoke from the burning vehicle passed to the east in the increasing wind, a figure appeared through the doorway. Wearing a white robe and a thick bushy beard with a white *taqiyah* covering his head, the man walked into the center of the square, holding a pistol to one hostage as he held her in place. Rob studied his face closely through his scope. It was undeniable.

"Alpha-six," he said. "It's him. It's Abbas."

Rob moved his rifle in the team's direction and saw his captain glance out from his covered position.

"What the fuck is he doing?" the captain asked.

"I'm not sure yet," replied Rob.

"Do you have a shot on him?" Wells asked.

Rob stared at Abbas through the glass.

"Negative. No clear shot yet. He's using the hostage for cover."

As Rob watched and waited from his position on the hillside, Abbas spoke.

"I know you are out there, you American infidels!" he shouted in flawless English as he held his pistol to the woman's head. "We will continue to punish you and kidnap and kill your people and soldiers if you do not leave our Muslim lands, never to return! You have been killing Muslims for too long! You have bombed our women and children with your planes and drones! If you do not leave, you will face Allah's wrath and mine. Unlike you, I am not afraid of death. I welcome it!"

Neither Rob nor his spotter could hear Abbas from their

distant location on the rocky mountainside. But it didn't matter. They understood his intentions loud and clear.

Abbas wrapped his arm around the woman, pulling her tight to his chest. Rob held the scope on him, trying to find a shot. But her body was just too close for comfort.

Abbas snatched the cover from the woman's head, tossing it to the dirt.

"Is this what you're here for?" he asked. "I will kill her right here if you do not leave now!"

Recalling the mission briefing earlier that morning, Rob recognized her face as plain as day.

"Fucking hell."

Rob pressed the mic again.

"Alpha-six," he said. "Alpha-three confirming priority target has the Scribe, over."

"You sure it's her?" asked Wells.

"Roger that, Alpha-six. I have a clear view of her face."

Rob waited a moment for his team captain to answer.

"Hold tight," Wells said to Rob. "I have an idea."

Rob released the mic button and glanced over at Kyle.

"I get nervous every time he says that," he said.

Rob viewed through the scope as Captain Wells rose to his feet, revealing himself to Abbas and his henchmen in the building.

"Damn it," he said. "What the fuck are you doing, captain?"

Rob and Kyle watched as Wells slowly made his way toward Abbas.

"That's some cowboy shit right there!" Kyle said in his Texas drawl.

The captain held his M4 high in the air, then tossed it to

the ground a few feet away as Abbas's men directed their AK-47s at him.

"Just give me a half a second to take the shot," Rob said. "That's all I need."

He continued observing as his team captain stood there. Unable to hear the exchange between him and the ISIL lieutenant, Rob watched Abbas, hoping for a split-second of opportunity.

Then, out of nowhere, the captive journalist elbowed Abbas in the side. He lost his hold on her, dropping the pistol to the dirt as she dove away from him. Rob, already trained on his target, released a .50-caliber round at supersonic speed. It penetrated Abbas's neck just below the chin and tore his head clean off, leaving blood spurting out from the hole. The force of the shot jolted his body a few feet back as he crashed to the earth.

Abbas's bodyguards started firing in the team's direction, hitting Wells in the arm as he dove for cover.

"Fuck!" he shouted.

"You all right, boss?" Rob asked, watching the captain clench his left arm as he hit the ground.

"Yeah, I'm good," he replied. "Just a flesh wound!"

The rest of the team fired into the guards, dropping one to the ground as the journalist crawled under a nearby truck. The other was in Rob's crosshairs.

He sent a bullet tearing into the man's chest, leaving a baseball-sized hole as he collapsed. Sniper and spotter watched as Wells, winding a bandage around his bicep, advanced toward the woman as she screamed. The chief took the rest of the team to clear the house. Minutes later, they appeared with four civilians, minus one dead.

The team formed a diamond formation around the remaining hostages to protect them and wait for extraction.

"Angel-one," Rob heard Wells say over the radio as he popped and tossed a red smoke grenade into the square. "This is Alpha-six ready for extraction, over."

"That's a good copy, Alpha-six," the Night Stalker pilot replied over the sound of rotor blades beating the air. "Good to hear your voice, Captain. We're in the air and will be at your location in five mikes (minutes). Over and out."

With one more mission chalked up as a success, Rob and Kyle traveled down the slope to assist their team in loading the freed civilians as the MH-60 Blackhawk Helicopter emerged in the distance over the mountain skyline.

TWO

Bagram Airbase
Afghanistan

The whipping of helicopter rotor blades reverberated in the background, thrashing the air around them and spreading sand and dust across the desert ground. In pairs, Blackhawks and Chinooks rose from their helipads at the corner of the airfield. They soared high over the Special Forces Team barracks, a row of tan-colored tents that had been their home for the past six months. Beautiful snow-covered mountain peaks lined the backdrop of an otherwise dangerous place.

The airbase, twenty-five kilometers from the Afghan capital, Kabul, was enormous and had been home to Special Forces, Special Operations Forces, and even elements of the CIA for months at a time. Aircraft flew in and out of the airport around the clock, transporting troops and supplies to wherever they needed to be. Medevac choppers carrying injured service members arrived at random, bringing the wounded to the base hospital. Those stationed there had gotten used to the noise and the air raid sirens that detected incoming rockets and mortars on a nearly daily basis.

The green berets and other special units like Delta and the Navy SEALs got the golden treatment. And for a good reason. They conducted the most sensitive operations for the US government. Their missions were top secret, and disobeying OPSEC, or operational security, was unthinkable. Their budget seemed endless, with the capacity to get the best and most modern weapons and tools available.

However, with the massive withdrawal of conventional US forces, which had become the largest employer in Bagram District, the locals suffered economically. Those who made money working for the US government were now scrounging to get by. The situation had made it ideal for enemy forces to move in and take control of the population.

Rob sat on his cot, cleaning his sniper rifle and looking at a photo of his family that sat on top of an MRE, or meal ready-to-eat box, beside his bunk. Rob had never married. But he had a few past girlfriends who couldn't handle his leaving at a day's notice for months at a time. He was married to the team. They were his family away from home.

The only actual family Rob had were his mother and sister. His father had passed away from cancer when Rob was in school. Agent orange from his service in Vietnam had ruined his dad's health later in his life.

He worried about his family when he was away, especially his younger sister, Marianne. A rebellious teenager still in high school, she and her mom fought on a regular basis. Being away constantly, there wasn't much Rob could do about it. Though they grew up in Brooklyn, Marianne wasn't quite street smart. And Rob had lashed out at her many boyfriends when they mistreated her, breaking one guy's nose for grabbing Marianne's shoulders in an argument. To say he was protective would be an understatement.

He set the picture frame back down as Kyle walked through the door of the tent.

"Hey, brother," Kyle said as he placed his M4 onto the wood gun rack that hung above his cot. "You all right, man?"

"Yeah," Rob replied. "I'm good."

Kyle glanced over at the picture frame with the photo of Rob's mother and sister.

"Thinking about family?"

"Yep," he replied. "As a matter of fact, I am."

Kyle plopped down next to Rob on his bunk.

"Why don't you call them, then?"

"Because," Rob said as he glanced back at the photo. "My mom worries too fucking much, man. She keeps asking questions she knows I can't answer. I've told her time and time again. It's just easier to email her. Besides, I'll see them in a couple of weeks when we rotate back, anyhow."

Kyle nodded his head.

"How's your sis?"

Rob gave Kyle a ghastly look.

"I'm not sure, man. Every time I talk to mom, Marianne is out in the streets doing God knows what. I can't keep up with her. I just hope she isn't with some guy doing drugs somewhere, blitzed out of her mind."

Kyle patted his friend on the shoulder.

"Family's complicated, Rob. Kids do dumb shit sometimes. Hell, we've all been there. All you can do is the best you can, nothing more, nothing less. But try to put it out of your mind for now. You don't need the distraction, man. There's too much at stake out here."

Rob sprang to his feet, planting his dark combat boots on the plywood floor as he slung his rifle onto his back.

"Yeah," he said. "Yeah, you're right."

"Of course I'm right," Kyle replied. "Am I ever wrong?"

Rob smirked back at Kyle.

"Well," he laughed. "That could be up for debate."

"Oh, really?" Kyle asked. "How many times have I covered your ass?"

"Too many times, buddy," Rob replied, giving his buddy a high five.

"Exactly."

Rob reached into his assault pack to grab a can of Copenhagen. "What are you going to do when you get back to Texas?" he asked, placing a dip into the side of his lip.

"Well, let's see. I'm going to kiss my girlfriend, ride my horse, maybe get a little drunk, and pass out in the hay barn."

"Sounds like a good time to me."

"Yeah," replied Kyle. "Any time you want to come out, just say the word."

"Well, I'm sure it beats the crowded streets of NYC, anyway."

"You're always welcome, man," Kyle said. "You'd love my mom's cooking. Besides, there's something therapeutic about being one with nature. I could ride my horse all day long."

Kyle pulled a picture of a brown quarter horse from his pocket and presented it to Rob.

"That's my mare, Grace," he said. "I love her. She's never let me down. Sometimes I sit in the barn and talk to her for hours. She's like my best friend. Aside from you, of course."

"She's beautiful," Rob replied. "I may just have to take you up on that offer."

Kyle walked back to his bunk to grab a Gatorade as Captain Wells and Chief Henderson barged through the tent's door.

"Fellas," the captain said, "we've got ourselves a situation."

"Oh, hey boss," Rob said. "How's the arm?"

"It's fine, Sergeant," Wells replied. "Thanks for asking. It's not my first time getting shot, you know?"

Rob grinned back at the captain.

"At least they got the worst of it, right?" he asked. "So, what's going on, boss?"

"Just meet us in the team room in five, all right?" replied Wells. "We'll brief everyone there."

"Roger that, Captain," said Rob. "On the way."

As Wells and Henderson left the barracks tent, Rob and Kyle hurried to their racks to grab their stuff and head out.

"Come on, man," Rob told Kyle as he grabbed his weapon from the corner. "Let's not keep 'em waiting."

"Right behind you, buddy."

Kyle grabbed his M4 and the Gatorade bottle on his blanket and followed Rob through the tent door. Other members of ODA-595 sat in the briefing room tent, chatting with each other and waiting for the briefing to begin. Rob and Kyle made their way into the briefing room and took seats next to each other in the front row. As Rob set his weapon between his feet on the floor, Wells and Henderson entered through the door behind them.

"Gentlemen," Wells said. "We just got out of a meeting with Major Bradford."

Wells yanked the white screen down as Master Sergeant Hobbs, Operations Sergeant, switched the projector on.

"Apparently," Wells said, pointing to an image on the

screen. "We have another high-priority target in the AO."

Everyone in the room was quiet as they listened to the captain speak.

"Meet Ahmed Atallah," Captain Wells said. "Master at creating IEDs and leader of a cell of ISIL bomb-makers responsible for killing and maiming dozens of soldiers, Marines, and civilians, including children."

"Where's he operating, sir?" Rob asked.

"From here to Kabul," Master Sergeant Hobbs said from the back of the room. "He's been spotted in Khost and even as far away as Kandahar. But we have just gotten solid intel that he will be in a safe house here in Bagram tonight."

Rob gazed at Ahmed's picture enlarged on the screen.

"I know that face, Captain," he said, inspecting the grainy image. "I've met this man before."

"Yeah, I'm sure you have," Wells replied as he paced back and forth. "That brings me to the second part of the briefing. He's a former Afghan police officer. We've even worked with him before."

Rob thought to himself for a second, snapping his fingers.

"I fucking knew it!" he said. "We helped them push the Taliban out of Kandahar."

"You got it," the captain said. "But, obviously, he's since turned. Now he instructs ISIL recruits in all things bomb-making. The asshole even enlists kids from the local mosque, indoctrinating them in their twisted version of Islam. We have gotten information from local elders that some of their children have disappeared from the streets. They don't know where they ended up."

"Fuck," Rob said.

"That's right," Chief Henderson interrupted. "We are to

dispatch him and the rest of his terror cell, and recover any intel we can on their operations. We can't allow this bastard to kill any more Americans. This is now a top priority, coming straight from the Pentagon."

"Right," the captain confirmed as he glanced over at Rob. "Rob, you and Kyle will be on overwatch, watching from afar and covering us, per usual."

"Roger that, boss."

"But," the captain continued, "If you get a crack at him, take it. Our eye in the sky, courtesy of the CIA, has tracked Ahmed to one of the city's residential areas, a house at the southern edge of Bagram, so watch out for civilians."

"Got it, boss."

"The agency had said they would level the place with a hellfire," said Wells. "But, with the civilian populace, that would cause far too much collateral damage. That's where we come in. Let's get it done, gentlemen."

Rob and Kyle each pulled their rifles from the floor as Master Sergeant Hobbs interrupted.

"We are counting on you two. Do what you do. You are the best scout, sniper team I have ever worked with. Let's get these bastards!"

"Will do," said Rob.

"All right, guys," Captain Wells said. "Get some chow. We move out in two hours."

⋮⋮⋮

Two light M1161 Special Operations strike vehicles operating in blackout mode cruised down the dusty road, carrying the members of ODA-595 to their destination just outside of the city limits of Bagram. Machine gunners with NVGs, or night-vision goggles to their faces, scanned the area as they got closer to the bombed-out buildings up ahead. EOD, or explosive ordnance disposal, had just finished clearing the route of IEDs a few hours earlier.

Captain Wells halted the pair of trucks momentarily on the dusty road to allow Rob and Kyle to hop out and set up shop. The structure's silhouette barely showed through the only working light that lit up the square.

"That's your position, right over there, guys."

Wells pointed to one of the city's highest buildings.

The deserted apartment building appeared vacant and gutted, with missing and broken windows and piles of rubble from previous battles surrounding it. Remnants of a long war, from bullet holes in the walls to parts of floors, completely blown out, were clear.

"Roger that," Rob replied as he fastened his vest and tapped on his headgear.

Rob took the rest of his gear and rifle and hurried across the road with his spotter, sand-colored *shemaghs* strung around both of their necks.

The pair hustled into a field to the building on the other side. As Rob swung the rusty metal door open, cobwebs and piles of dust from past sandstorms filled the room. They propelled up the concrete stairs, seven floors up, to a room with a shattered window facing the center of a city square.

Upon entering, Rob took a quick look around the room for something to use while Kyle snagged his spotting scope from his pack and began setting it up on the tripod.

"Okay," Rob said as he pushed an old, wooden desk just under the windowsill. "This ought to do nicely."

He slid his body over the desk, legs spread in a V-shape

behind him, and unfolded the bipod mounted under his suppressed .300 Winchester Magnum M2010 sniper rifle. Rob inserted the five-round magazine into the weapon and tapped the bottom.

"On scope, Alpha-six," he said as he pulled the rifle into his shoulder

"Roger that, Alpha-three," the captain returned over the radio. "On our way. We'll be on location in two mikes."

Rob glanced into his night-vision scope, then peeked over at his spotter.

"All right," he said. "Your move."

Rob watched as Kyle pressed his face to the eyepiece.

"Okay," replied Kyle. "I've got seven hundred meters on the mosque."

Kyle was referring to a white mosque with a golden dome that sat close to the target building. He paused a moment, examining the mirage while gauging wind speed and direction through the spotting scope.

"Wind at ten miles per hour, one-quarter value."

"Roger," said Rob. "Distance, seven hundred meters. Wind, ten miles per hour, one-quarter value."

Rob dialed his scope for the correct elevation. With the breeze blowing at roughly 15 degrees, it should be a cakewalk for a seasoned sniper.

"Alpha-three," Rob heard Captain Wells say over the radio. "We're on the move, over."

"Roger, I see you," he said, following them through his rifle scope along the sandy pathway.

The team left the drivers and gunners to watch the vehicles, hidden in the field brush and standing by as they proceeded approximately half a klick, or kilometer, further to the target house. Not wanting to let anyone know they were coming, they crept forth through the dead undergrowth at the side of the road under cover of night. Trash blew gently across their path as they made their way ahead.

Ten minutes had passed by as Rob and his teammate observed civilians walking across and down the alleyways. Women wearing black burqas held children's hands as they retreated into their homes, unaware that anything was about to happen. Men smoking cigarettes stood in a doorway, conversing and sipping cups of chai. It seemed like a peaceful night in Bagram. But, abruptly, that peace took another turn. A man appeared under the low light in Rob's view. Immediately, every person within eyeshot disappeared from the street.

"There," said Rob. "It's him. I have eyes on the target."

"Where?" Kyle asked. "I don't see him."

"Check the doorway."

Kyle glanced through his spotting scope.

"Yep," he replied. "That's him, all right. Can't miss that ugly face."

"Alpha-three," Rob said into his mouthpiece. "I've got eyes on the target. Looks like he's out for some night air. No sign of his men yet, over."

"Roger, Alpha-three. Wait for my go-ahead. We are almost in position. I don't want to give these assholes the chance to escape."

"That's a good copy, Alpha-six," Rob replied. "We're standing by."

At once, two men appeared from the house, standing on opposite sides of Atallah and gripping AK-47s. It looked as though he assumed they could protect him, unconscious of the fact that they'd tracked him using human intel and satellite imaging across Afghanistan. There was no place he could hide. But it worked in the team's favor if they could catch him comfortably in his surroundings. That comfort would, at last, be short-lived.

As the scout sniper team kept their eyes firmly on Atallah, they saw as he flicked his cigarette into the sand below. Rob knew he didn't have much time.

"Hurry, Alpha-six. My window is rapidly closing."

There was a brief silence over the radio.

"All right, Alpha-three," Wells said quietly as the team stooped behind a car one hundred meters from Atallah. "We're in position. Take that motherfucker, now!"

"Roger that," replied Rob.

He held the reticle directed right at Atallah's back as he turned to reach for the door handle.

"Wind, no change," his spotter said, glancing through his scope.

Kyle wasn't bothered that they had only seconds to make that shot. He'd never seen Rob miss his target.

As Atallah made it somewhat through the doorway, his guards close behind, Rob squeezed the trigger. The round soared between the two guards, striking Atallah at the base of the skull, severing his brain stem and splattering blood on his men's faces as he toppled to the hard floor. The two enemy fighters dove into the building, leaving Atallah lying face-up in the doorway.

"He's down, Alpha-three," said the captain. "We're moving in."

Rob slid the bolt to the rear, discharging a single shell casing as he kept the glass on the men at the door. He drove the bolt forward as another cartridge entered the chamber. Squeezing the trigger a second time, he sent the shot flying into one militant, nearly decapitating him as the team engaged.

"Alpha-six," Rob said as he observed the structure from his position. "You've got an unknown number of hostiles moving in your direction, over!"

One at a time, he engaged men with his sniper rifle as they fled the dwelling. He and his spotter observed as the rest of the team began firing into the house. The militants continued coming, firing from the rooftop and windows down below.

"Fuck!" Rob said, releasing a magazine to the ground and inserting another. "How many of these assholes are there?"

Then, unexpectedly, PK machine gunfire erupted from the second-story window as the team went for cover behind a nearby building. Rob pivoted his rifle scope up to the machine gun's position as it pounded the wall in front of them.

"Alpha-three," Wells said to Rob as machine gun rounds shredded the building's side. "Would you kindly take care of this? We're kind of pinned over here!"

Rob pressed the rifle trigger, his bullet ripping into the gunner's chest, and spraying red mist on the wall behind him. The rapid gunfire ceased.

"He's down."

"Much obliged," Wells said, leading the team around the corner and toward the building, firing M4s into insurgents in the windows.

Rob and Kyle listened to radio chatter and watched muzzles flashing through the windows against their dark surroundings. Gunfire repeated through the square for a few minutes. Rob and Kyle observed the outside of the structure from their position in the building.

"I wish we could go down there and help them," said Kyle.

"I do too," Rob said. "But we are better from up here. Besides, who would watch our backs?"

"True. Very true."

Then, about as fast as it had begun, the gunfire abruptly ended. Rob watched the door for a couple of minutes, waiting for the team to exit.

"All clear," Wells said, holding an arm up to signal them as they moved out into the street. "We've recovered the intel. But there is a shitload of explosive material in there. I'll contact EOD. Alpha-three, you guys sit tight. We'll secure this place until they arrive, over."

"Roger that," replied Rob.

Before he could get up, Rob suddenly spotted someone moving in the dark beyond the team's location. Clutching an AK in his hands, the man was running in the team's direction.

"Alpha-three!" he yelled. "You got a tango coming from the west, over!"

Rob repositioned his sniper rifle, reticle following the lone figure as he dashed for the team. The militant got a shot off, striking Intelligence Sergeant, Sergeant First Class Terry Miles.

"Man down!" Chief Henderson yelled as the team moved for cover. "Sergeant Miles is hit!"

Rob squeezed the trigger, causing the insurgent to hurl forward as he ran, blood covering the surrounding sand in a bright red trail.

"Fuck!" Rob shouted, rapidly shifting his weapon to look for others. "You're clear! I repeat, all clear."

He and Kyle watched helplessly as team medic, Sergeant First Class Oscar Ramírez, rushed to Mile's side.

"What's his status, Alpha-six?" asked Rob.

There was quiet over the radio as they watched for signs of life.

"What's his status, over?" he asked again.

Suddenly, he and Kyle detected a raspy coughing through the radio.

"He's good," Wells replied, kneeling down by Miles as he lay across the ground, wheezing. "He's good, Alpha-three. The vest stopped it from penetrating!"

Rob gazed over at his spotter.

"Damn, man. That could've gone bad!"

"Yeah," Kyle replied. "Just be thankful you were on the long gun. I'm sure Miles is."

Rob watched as the captain and chief pulled Miles up off the ground to help him to the vehicles as they reached their location. Rob flipped the bipod under his rifle and clipped the sling to the black carabiner attached to the front of his vest as he watched the EOD trucks approach through the window.

"Let's move," he said to Kyle as he rolled off the desk, strapping his assault pack to his back. "We did what we came here to do. EOD can take over from here. Besides, Miles needs to get checked out at medical."

THREE

Two weeks later
Downtown, Brooklyn
New York City

The train pulled away as Rob, green duffel bag over one shoulder, stepped off the York Street Subway station platform through the crowd and up the stairs onto the New York City sidewalk above. Swarms of people hastened around him and filled the walkway as though they were hustling to get some place. Cars packed together at the stoplight, one at a time, as the green light turned to yellow, then red. He knew he was close to his old Brooklyn neighborhood.

It was the very place that he'd grown up. But Rob couldn't say that he missed it all that much. Life on the streets was hard on him as a kid, as it was for his family. It made him tough. But it probably would have destroyed him had he remained. Gangs and drugs ravished the New York City streets even back then. If he'd only known how bad it would eventually become.

Rob whistled urgently at a yellow taxicab that had pulled

up on the street near him. He picked up his pace and met the cab at the intersection just as the light changed to green, cars beeping from the rear as others picked up speed around them.

"Gold Street, please."

Rob swung the door open and hurled his bag onto the seat beside him. He tugged the bottom of his black T-shirt over his brown khaki pants and climbed into the back.

"You got it, Mister," the cabbie said.

As they rode away, Rob eyed his old neighborhood outside. It appeared so much more run-down than he'd remembered. Graffiti covered almost every building in their path, with youngsters standing on the street corners, surely up to no good.

"Is it that bad?" he asked the cab driver.

The cabbie just nodded his head.

Rob reflected on himself as a child. If it wasn't for a family friend named Joseph, who sort of stood in for his late father, he could have taken a different direction.

The car pushed on for a couple of miles. He pointed his head forward as the rain started coming down, seeing his mother's apartment building come into the picture in the background as they spun the corner.

"You visiting someone?" the driver asked.

"Yeah, my mother," Rob replied. "I'm only here for a few weeks."

The driver peered at Rob in the rearview mirror, noticing the Army duffel sitting upright beside him on the seat, his rank and name stenciled in black lettering.

"So, you military, huh?" he asked.

"Yeah, Army," Rob replied.

"Where are you coming from?"

"Afghanistan," said Rob.

The old man tipped his hat toward Rob in the rearview mirror.

"Well, thank you for your service, son. I served in Vietnam myself, First Calvary, sixty-nine to seventy-one."

"Welcome," Rob said, never one to boast about who he was or what he did. "To you as well, sir."

The driver ran his hand through his white, wavy hair and locked eyes with Rob once again.

"I will warn you, though," he said. "This place just isn't the same anymore."

"How so?" Rob asked.

"Drugs," the cab driver replied. "They are destroying this damn community. I remember when you could walk down the street without worrying about getting mugged. Now hoodlums sell that crap on every street corner. It's a goddamned shame. I thought it was bad when I came home from 'Nam."

Rob continued peering through the window at the city streets and decaying and neglected buildings around him as he listened to the old man. He knew it was bad. But nothing prepared him for just how bad.

"Well," the cabbie said. "Let's just say it's moving in the wrong direction. Watch yourself around here."

"Thanks, sir," Rob replied. "But I can take care of myself."

"I've got no doubt about that," said the driver.

As the building got closer, Rob snatched his duffel bag and seized the door handle.

"You can stop now. I can walk from here."

"You sure, pal?" the stranger asked, turning up the windshield wipers. "Rain is coming down pretty hard."

"Yeah, I'm sure. It's not that far ahead now."

"All right then, buddy," the taxi driver said as Rob tossed a few bills into the passenger-side window. "Be safe out there."

"You too," Rob replied, stretching his camouflage baseball cap tight over his head and slamming the cab door shut.

As Rob marched down the street to his mother's building, rain trickling off the front of his hat, he thought about what the cab driver had said. Was he exaggerating? But Rob's surroundings seemed to paint the same picture. Nearing the long front steps to the apartment building, Rob spotted a scraggly, homeless man lying face-up in an open tent. As he strolled toward the entrance, he tossed a couple of dollars into the opening and went on to the front door of the building.

Moving into the long hallway, Rob looked around, noticing the awful condition of the place. The walls were dirty, and the hallway reeked of mold and old garbage. It sure had seen better days. Shaking his head, he tightened the strap to his duffel and started jogging up the stairs, four floors up to his mom's apartment.

As he reached apartment 402, he knocked three times hard on the metal door and waited. It was a small three-bedroom, typical of a lower or middle-class Brooklyn apartment. The building was a little more disheveled than Rob remembered. Not wanting the streets to destroy him, he'd left home years earlier and never looked back. He'd sent money home to help his mom and little sis, social security disability for a back injury now being her only stable income. But the criminal element had swallowed the neighborhood whole. Section eight helped her cover most of the rental cost. She had very little money to save.

As he placed his ear to the door, Rob heard the television playing loudly from inside. He banged on the scratched metal door even harder, the noise echoing down the hall.

"Mom, open up!" he shouted. "It's me!"

The volume decreased. The door budged open slightly, the chain still attached. Rob's mother, Louise, fifty-three, peeked through the cracked door, still in her white nightgown.

"Mom," Rob said in a low voice. "Mom, it's me. Let me in."

"Hey baby," his mother replied, sliding the chain lock from the door. "I wasn't expecting you home."

Rob opened the apartment door the rest of the way.

"Well, I'm on leave, Mom. I thought I'd come home and surprise you."

"You have," she said, closing and securing the door behind him. "Come on in, honey. Come in. You want something to drink? Tea or something? Take the bag off and have a seat."

Rob removed the duffel bag from his back and tossed it into the corner of the small kitchen.

"Sure, Mom," he said, pulling up a chair at the dining table. "Tea sounds great, thanks."

Louise opened the refrigerator, poured a frosty glass of tea, and set it on the table in front of Rob.

"There you go, baby."

"Thanks, Mom," he replied, taking a sip from the glass.

Rob glanced at his mother, recognizing the dreary look on her face.

"So, how you been?"

Louise let out a deep sigh.

"I'm okay, Rob," she replied. "Things have just been a little rough around here lately, you know? But I don't want to bore you with that."

"What's up with this building?" Rob asked. "Looks like

they're letting it go. It sure isn't how I remember it."

"The last owner sold it some time ago," Louise replied. "And the new owners put nothing into it. They just let it go to hell."

"Why didn't you say something before, Mom?"

"I didn't want you to worry, baby," she said, her hands shivering. "You were doing important things over there. I didn't want to be the one to distract you. Besides, it's not your problem. It's nothing I can't handle."

Rob shot his mother a puzzled look as he glanced around the place.

"Why don't you use some of the money I sent to get a better place?"

Rob looked over at a bottle of Wild Turkey Bourbon sitting on the kitchen counter.

"Really? Is that where my money is going?"

"Honey...," she replied.

"Never mind, Mom," Rob said. "I'm sorry, don't answer that."

Rob had known for a while that his mother had a drinking problem. It started after his father passed from cancer years prior. She had a total breakdown and couldn't cope for the longest time. However, the last time he'd spoken to her, she'd told him it was under control. From the look of it, it appeared as though that wasn't entirely correct.

Rob set his glass of tea back on the table. He rose to his feet, snagging his bag from the floor, and headed down the narrow hallway.

"Is it okay if I stay in my old room?"

"Sure, honey," she replied, following close behind. "Of course you can. That's what it's there for."

He opened the last door on the left. The room had hardly changed since Rob had lived there. His New York Giants posters were still on the wall. His Louisville Slugger baseball bat was resting against the side of his old wood dresser.

"Wow."

Rob looked around at his old sports memorabilia all over the room.

"You've practically changed nothing."

"Yeah," she said, sitting at the foot of the queen-size bed. "I'd come in here sometimes and just sit here for hours and think about you, wondering where you were or what you were doing."

Rob put his bag on the floor next to the bed and sat next to his mother.

"Brings back some memories," he told her. "There were some good times. There were some bad, too."

Louise wrapped an arm around her son as he glanced around the room.

"Honey, I understand why you left. I do. I guess I just expected that after your father died, you'd be here to protect your sister and me."

"Mom—" he replied before she interrupted him.

"But I do understand."

Rob rose to his feet, opening his bag and pulling out a black T-shirt with a faded American flag across the front. Removing his hoodie, he slipped the shirt over his head. Rob's tattoo sleeve showed on his bare, muscular left arm. DE OPPRESSO LIBER, the Special Forces motto displayed in bright white letters under a skull as he tugged at the shirt's bottom.

"Speaking of my sister," he said. "Where is she? I thought

she'd be here to see me."

Louise hung her head as she hesitated to answer him.

"Mom. Where the hell is she?"

Louise stood and leaned against the doorway.

"The last time I spoke to her, she was with her boyfriend."

"And when was that, Mom?"

"A few days ago," she replied. "We got into an argument, and she left. It's gotten pretty bad since the last time you were here."

"Mom, she's only seventeen. She can't be running around doing stupid shit!"

"I know, honey," she said. "I know. But she just won't listen to me."

Rob pushed past his mother through the doorway.

"Who's her boyfriend now?" he asked.

But his mother didn't respond.

"Mom!" Rob said. "Who was she with? The same asshole?"

Rob could tell he was right by the look on her face.

"The one who hit her? Fuck, Mom! You know he's into some shady shit. Besides, he's in his damn thirties!"

His name was Mitch Buchanan. It wasn't the first time Rob had run-ins with the guy. He made a living in the drug game. Rob despised him. And he knew Mitch would only bring trouble for Marianne, a situation he didn't want his family anywhere near. He couldn't protect her while he was away. But it wouldn't stop him from trying now.

Marianne was his sister, and he loved her. But she was also a young, naïve, and easily influenced teenager. Rob spent his entire life defending her. He understood Mitch would take advantage of her, as he'd done to her many times before. The man was nothing more than a criminal.

The Messenger

Rob had recalled a bar that Mitch would regularly frequent on almost a nightly basis. The last time he caught him there with her, Rob had knocked out a few of his teeth. This time should be no different. Whatever happened, he was bringing Marianne home that night.

"I guess relaxing is fucking out," he said.

Rob spun around, grabbed his hoodie and the old baseball bat from the corner, and hurried down the hall toward the door, Louise close after him.

"Where are you going, Robert?" she asked as he unlocked the door.

"Where do you think I'm going, Mom?" he replied, moving in close to her. "She's in danger as long as she's with that douchebag!"

Rob fumbled through the keys that dangled from the key rack near the door.

"The car still run?" he asked his mother, jerking a set of keys from the wall.

"Yes, but Rob, please don't!" she said, clutching the back of his shirt. "You just got here!"

But he pushed her away, slamming the door behind him and tearing down the steps to the parking lot at the side of the building.

𝍫

The clock had just struck nine o'clock p.m. as Rob's classic 68 Mustang Shelby GT came gliding around the turn, coming to a squealing stop across the street from the corner bar, O'Malley's. The motor purred with all the power of three hundred and fifty-five horses under the hood.

The night sky was cloudy, a few raindrops trickling onto

the windshield as Rob shut the engine off and kicked the door open. His car was pure white, with two blue stripes running down the center and an all-black leather interior. It was the essence of a vintage muscle car. In need of a wash from sitting for an extended period, at least it still ran.

As Rob eyed patrons filing through the door one by one as their IDs got checked, he slipped the bat under his hoodie to hide it. He moved into the back, shuffling forward slowly for a few minutes as more people filled the line behind him.

"ID, please," the bouncer said to Rob as he reached the front of the line.

The bouncer was a tall, muscular African American guy, short haircut, and looked like he could handle himself in a fight. Rob, being a soldier himself, figured the guy to be ex-military.

Rob lifted his wallet from his pocket, flashing his military ID to the bouncer, whose muscles just about swelled through the sleeves of his black T-shirt.

"Army, huh?"

"Yep," replied Rob.

"Good shit, pal!" the bouncer said over the blaring music. "I was a Marine myself. Served in Kosovo and Bosnia back in the nineties."

"Thanks," Rob said, not in the mood for idle talk.

He had just one thing on his mind.

Distracted and neglecting to pat him down, the bouncer returned Rob's ID card and moved out of the way to allow him to enter. Rob continued through the door to the bar opposite the dance floor. He casually pulled up a stool as he relaxed, eyes fixed to the dancing crowd.

"What can I get you, hun?" a blonde bombshell of a

bartender asked from behind the counter.

"What?" he asked, not able to understand her over the booming music.

"What can I get you, sir?" she asked, drawing closer so he could hear her.

Rob leaned into her ear.

"Mojito, please," he replied.

"You sure you don't want to try one of our Irish specialties? It's what we're known for."

"No," Rob replied. "I'll stick to my rum, thanks."

"Suit yourself," she said. "Coming right up."

As the bartender began mixing the drink, Rob's eyes studied the room, watching for his sister and her loser boyfriend. But the club was so packed, he could barely see the other side.

The lady placed a full glass with straw onto a napkin on the counter as Rob retrieved Marianne's picture from his pocket.

"Can I ask you something?" he asked her, handing over the photo. "Have you seen this girl around here?"

The bartender checked the image for a moment.

"Nope," she replied, sliding the photo back across the bar. "Can't say I have. Who is she to you? Long-lost girlfriend?"

Rob looked down at Marianne's picture again.

"She's my sister."

The barkeep bent into him with a flirtatious manner, flipping her straight, blonde hair.

"Well, sweetie, I see looks run in the family. I'm sure she's got a boyfriend around here somewhere."

Rob took the glass from the bar and sucked down a large gulp through the straw.

"Tall white guy, long blond hair, and a scar across his face?" he asked, placing the glass back on the bar. "Does that ring a bell?"

Suddenly, her eyes got wide as she gazed at him in silence like she'd seen a ghost.

"You know him?" he asked, spotting the telling look on her face.

But she didn't utter a word.

"Look," he said. "I believe my sister is in trouble. Have you seen him or not?"

Instead of speaking, the woman's eyes diverted toward the club's upper floor and a private room in the back. Rob caught her movement, glaring up at the few people overlooking the dance floor from above. She didn't seem to want to mention his name out loud.

Rob picked the glass back up and downed the rest of his drink.

"Thanks for your time, miss..."

"Angela," she interrupted. "My name is Angela. But you can call me Angie."

Angela took a quick look around to make sure nobody was listening.

"That guy is bad news," she said. "But you didn't hear this from me, you understand me? I don't need any trouble."

"Don't worry about that," Rob replied. "We never even spoke."

Angela picked up a rag and began wiping the bar down after Rob.

"I always wondered where that scar came from, though."

Rob, grinning back at her, dropped a twenty into the tip jar on the counter.

"I gave it to him," he said over his shoulder as she watched him walk away.

He strolled around the wooden dance floor and up the stairs at the side of the club, random people drinking and bending over the metal railing, watching the drunken dancers below. As Rob made his way around the crowd of club-goers, he stepped from the staircase and noticed a single room at the very end of the floor.

Rob held the bat under his shirt and went to the other side, watching every patron as they drank and danced around him. On the way to the private room, a young, white man, obviously buzzed out of his mind, bumped into Rob.

Rob stopped, staring the boy down as he stumbled past him.

"Sorry, bro," the kid said, not quite able to speak coherently.

The boy's friend pulled him away from Rob and toward the stairs.

"You must excuse my friend, buddy," he said. "He isn't all there, if you know what I'm saying. Besides, we were just leaving."

Rob watched as the kid tripped down the curved staircase, and he continued to the private VIP room up ahead. Standing against the door, he knocked. But there was no answer. He would not give it another try. Without delay, Rob raised his brown, size twelve hiking boot. He kicked the door in hard, crashing it open with devastating force as it broke against the wall.

There was his sister, Marianne, drunk and passed out on the sofa, head propped on the man's lap.

"Mitch," Rob said, giving him a glare that should've been

all too familiar. "Hey, asshole."

Rob lowered the baseball bat from underneath his hoodie, holding it down by his side and gripping it tightly. The look on Mitch's face suddenly resembled that of a scared little boy. He'd never wanted to see Rob's face again.

"Well, well," he said to Rob, nervously placing his drink down on the glass table next to a drug pipe. "If it isn't GI Joe himself. I never thought I'd see you around here again. What the hell are you doing here?"

Rob moved in closer to Mitch, hovering over the table and staring. He snatched the pipe from the table and slammed it against the wall, shattering it.

"What am I doing here? What do you think I'm here for, you little prick? I am taking my little sister home. Hand her over, now!"

"Or what?" Mitch said, stroking the side of Marianne's head.

"Or you'll be eating through a straw from now on," Rob told him.

Mitch crossed his legs in his seat as he scowled at Rob.

"You don't know who you are fucking with," he said. "My men will handle you."

Rob didn't care to give Mitch another chance to speak. He raised the bat over his head and swung it down hard, smashing the glass coffee table into pieces and sending glass shards flying across the room.

"I don't give a fuck, asshole!" he shouted. "Next one goes right up against your head!"

Suddenly, the same African American man who'd checked him at the door appeared behind Rob, holding a forty-five caliber pistol to his back.

"Don't fucking move," the man said, poking a gun into the small of Rob's back. "Get 'em up, now!"

Rob released the bat to the floor and held his hands up as if to give in. But he wasn't about to do that.

"How much is this little shit paying you?" Rob asked him. "He can't fight his own fucking battles?"

Mitch just smiled.

"Shut the fuck up, white boy!" the bouncer said. "Before I put a bullet in your head for the fucking hell of it. Now move!"

Mitch shot Rob a shit-eating grin he wanted to beat clean off his face.

"What's the big war hero going to do now?" Mitch asked. "Looks like you're clean out of options, huh, big guy?"

But he wasn't prepared for what would come next. Rob reacted without hesitation, taking the gun barrel in his hand and twisting the bouncer's arm, forcing him to the floor and disarming him before he even knew what happened. Rob released the magazine to the floor and pulled back on the slide, catching the single cartridge as it fell.

"Fuck!" Mitch yelled. "What the fuck was that, you crazy bastard?"

Rob put the gun on Mitch, then kicked his buddy in the face as he held his arm, blood spurting from his lip across the floor and knocking him out cold.

"You're fucking crazy!" Mitch said, hands covering half of his face.

Rob took a brief glimpse at his sister. But she was out, too drunk and high to understand what was happening around her.

"Ah, but you knew that already, didn't you?" Rob asked as he furiously paced toward Mitch, now with the bat in hand. "You like taking advantage of young girls, you sick fuck? I'm a pissed-off warfighter with a lack of negotiating skills. And I don't mind taking it out on you! So you either give me my sister, or I will paint this room with your goddamned blood! It's your call!"

Rob was like a man possessed when he was angry. And he was ready to do anything he had to get Marianne out of there.

"I haven't forgotten what you did to me," Mitch said.

"Yeah? You want me to add another scar to the other side of your face?"

Rob grasped Mitch's shirt collar, touching his nose to his face. He held the forty-five caliber Beretta handgun against the side of Mitch's head, finger over the trigger.

"You know what I am capable of, you fucking dirtbag," he said in his ear. "Give me a fucking excuse to end you!"

Mitch held his hands up.

"Okay, okay, fine!" Mitch yelled, pressing himself deeper into his seat. "Take the bitch! I was going to throw her ass out, anyway. Just get the hell away from me!"

"Wise choice, you fucking punk," Rob said, pistol-whipping Mitch across the face and leaving an inch-long, gruesome gash on his cheek. "And if you ever call her a bitch again, I'll make sure you don't walk for the rest of your miserable life!"

Mitch cowered in his seat, shielding his face with his arms with blood dripping to his neck.

Rob picked his sister up, hoisting her over his shoulder and crossing over the man lying on the floor as she whimpered indistinctly.

"Motherfucker! This isn't over!" Mitch shouted, holding his face as Rob carried Marianne past the broken door and toward the exit, every person in the club watching them. "You don't know who you just fucked with, asshole!"

Rob hurried down the steps and faded into the crowd, busting through the front door on his way back to the car to take his little sister home.

FOUR

```
Louise's Apartment
Brooklyn
Next day
```

The old-fashioned clock sitting atop the brown wooden nightstand sounded loudly, bells ringing and awakening Rob from a deep sleep. It was a quarter past seven. He slowly opened his eyes and sat up in bed, wiping the sleep from his face with his finger. The piercing buzz from the alarm blared in his ears as he smacked the button to turn it off.

He swung his legs around the side of the bed, touching the hardwood floor to his bare feet. Stretching into the green duffel at his bedside, Rob took out a pair of jeans and a dark T-shirt from his pile of clothes. He gradually made his way down the hall to Marianne's room, looking in on her as she lay passed out on her single, metal-framed bed with a brass headboard.

He continued further toward the bathroom, swiping a towel from the closet, dropped his clothes to the floor, and hopped into the shower. Rob turned the knob and waited for the water to warm up. The scalding water rained down on his skin as he thought back to his team's previous mission. He missed those guys already. Being in the real world back home wasn't where Rob's mind was. It felt different to him, like he didn't fit in anymore. His job was more of a calling to him, something that most people could never fathom. Rob was the one percent of the one percent. It was the secrecy that he liked the most. Being a part of such a top-tier outfit was his purpose in life. It hadn't even been a few days, and he already wanted to go back.

But now, he was more worried about his sister. If she kept her lifestyle up, she would no doubt end up a statistic. Even though they hadn't spoken in quite some time, and she was more of the family's black sheep, she was still his sister. And he would do anything he had to do to protect her, even if she didn't want it.

A few minutes passed while Rob stood under the shower nozzle as if he was trying to wash something besides dirt away. He reached through the shower curtain, swiping the towel from the wall, and turned the knob off. Rob wrapped it around his body and stepped away from the shower, dripping water onto the blue bathroom mat by the tub. He dried his body off, rubbing the towel over his short buzz cut.

Rob pulled his jeans up over his boxers and slipped the polo over his head. He glanced at himself in the mirror, running his fingers through his medium-sized beard.

"I thought military guys couldn't have those," his mother said as she peeked around the corner of the doorway.

Rob smiled, glancing back at her in the mirror.

"They let us grow it out the way we want, so we look like the bad guys, Mom," he said. "We have to blend in."

"Oh, I see," she replied. "That's interesting. I have some

coffee on if you want some, hon."

"Sure," he said. "Sounds good, thanks."

Rob ran his hand down his damp hair and continued to the dining room. He sat down at the four-person table, pulling the chair in under him.

"Thanks," he said as Louise set a hot cup of coffee on the table in front of him.

Rob took a sip and pulled out his phone, checking a text message that had come in while he was asleep. It was his friend and spotter, Kyle: *Having fun at home?*

Rob texted his buddy back: *Not really, man. It's my sister.*

Rob paused for a few as he sipped from the mug. A couple of minutes later, Kyle replied: *Remember what I said.*

Rob responded before setting his phone on the table: *Yeah, yeah.*

Marianne unexpectedly turned up from her bedroom, still out of it from the night before. Her long, brown hair was messy, and her face was as white as a ghost. Whatever she'd taken, it still had a hold on her.

"Hey," she said to her brother, stumbling over the floor to the table.

Rob just nodded back at her.

"What the hell happened last night?" she asked as she took a seat across from him. "I don't remember anything."

Rob set the mug back on the table.

"What happened?" he replied. "You were out of your mind with that loser you call a boyfriend. That's what happened. What the hell? Why are you hanging around those people, anyway?"

Marianne braced her hands against the table.

"Those people are my friends," she told him, her mother

watching speechless from across the room.

"They are not your friends, Marianne," Rob said. "They are low-life thugs. And he is using you the same way he always has. I thought you'd be over this and him by now."

Marianne pounded her fist on the tabletop.

"Oh my God! What did you do?"

"What I had to do, little sister!" he returned, folding his hands under his arms. "You're going to end up dead if you don't wise up. If you don't want to listen to mom, at least listen to me."

Marianne glanced back at her mother and then to Rob.

"So, you come back from fighting a war God knows where and think you can order me around? I am almost eighteen. And when I am, I am out of here. You aren't my father. And neither you nor mom can control me or who I hang out with!"

Rob rose from the table and approached Marianne, pushing her arms down to her sides.

"You are right. Dad is dead. And I left. But that doesn't mean you get to run around doing dumb shit and trying to destroy your life. Mom is worrying herself sick about you!"

Marianne shoved Rob away from her, stomping back to her bedroom. She reappeared a minute later with a pink, flowery book bag strapped around one shoulder.

"I don't need this shit! You can't tell me what to do!"

Rob watched Marianne march toward the front door. He rushed in front of her.

"Where are you going?" he asked.

"None of your business!"

Rob braced against the doorway and blocked her from leaving.

"It is my business," he said. "You are my little sister. You are going to let these people ruin you. I'm not always around to protect you. But this time you've gone too far. And you're going to give mom a nervous breakdown."

Louise, leaning against the kitchen sink, tried to reach out for her daughter.

"Honey, don't you want to see your brother? He just got here."

Rob knew he couldn't keep his sister locked inside like a prisoner. If she wouldn't help herself, there was only so much he could do.

"Listen," Rob said to Marianne. "I will pay for you to go to rehab. I will help you get clean. I'll even get you and mom out of this dump and into a better neighborhood. I'll do whatever it takes to keep you safe. All I ask is that you stop hanging around these people!"

Marianne ducked under Rob's arm and gripped the knob, falling into the hall as she leaned on the opening door. He reached out to grab her, but she kicked against the wall, slipping from his grasp.

"Just leave me alone!" she yelled as she began darting toward the stairs.

"Marianne!" Rob's voice echoed down the hallway as he took off after her. "Marianne, stop!"

He chased his sister down the steps, to the lobby, and out the front door. He'd almost made it to her when he heard her whistle to hail a cab. She had the back door open before the taxi came to a full stop. As he reached for her, she slammed the door shut. Rob stood there, watching in frustration as the vehicle drove away.

"Damn it!" he said to himself.

Rob returned to his mother alone, afraid of what his little

sister was getting herself into. But it seemed there was nothing short of forcing her to stay that he could do about it.

⋮⋮⋮

Night had settled over downtown Brooklyn. The dark alley contrasted against the bright lights gleaming up and down the city street. The lawless were out in force, making a living at others' expense.

Three men stood against the hood of a black Chevy Suburban with tinted windows, parked in the dark, narrow alleyway beside O'Malley's bar. Holding a silver briefcase in one hand, the one in the center had a Marlboro cigarette between his lips as he lit it with the other. He kept his eyes locked on the street ahead.

His name was Mike Buchanan. He was a tall, rough-looking white guy with short, brown hair and a black Fedora hat, a red feather in the band. Mike wore a black trench coat and black patent leather shoes. He had all the hallmarks of a man in charge.

His gang ran the streets and the drug game in that part of town. Nobody dared to cross them. And Mike ruled his outfit with an iron fist, sending anyone who got in his way six feet under. But he never committed violence himself. He had people for that. They would do whatever Mike told them to do or suffer their own unmerciful results. He always had a hit squad on standby.

Mitch was among the men, a lower-level dealer in the organization. But he was also Mike's right-hand man and would do anything the boss ordered him to.

"They're late, boss," Mitch said as he glanced down at his shiny gold Rolex watch.

"Don't you think I fucking know that?" he asked, flicking the ash from his cigarette. "I'm not blind. Now, shut the fuck up. We'll give them a few more minutes, then we're gone."

They waited impatiently, gazing down the alleyway for the men to show. The area was ideal for what was going to happen, with only two ways in and out. If anyone other than who they were expecting showed up, they'd readily spot them.

Suddenly, a black Mercedes pulled around the corner.

"That's them," Mike said as they viewed the car getting closer.

The Mercedes-Benz came to a standstill in front of them, stopping a few meters away. The driver flashed his headlights twice.

"We're on," said Mike. "It's about fucking time."

Three Mexican men got out of the car, one carrying his own briefcase as they neared them. He held his hand up, stopping the other two men holding .45 caliber, nickel-plated pistols as he pushed forward.

The man stopped just five meters in front of Mike and his associates.

"You're late."

The Mexican snarled back at him. "Yeah, so? What are you going to do about it, ese?"

Mike glared at the Mexican as if he was looking right through him.

"Well," Mike said. "Since you can't fucking tell time, how about we get right down to business? We don't have all night."

The two cartel members behind him lifted their weapons and pointed them right at Mike and his men. Mike's men countered, raising their guns in return.

"You fucking kidding me?" Mike asked. "We can play that

fucking game. Or we can do what we came here to do. Otherwise, there's going to be a few dead people on this filthy ass ground before the night's over."

"Let us shoot these fuckers, boss!" said Mitch.

Mike grabbed Mitch by the collar of his Armani shirt and pushed him back.

"Shut the hell up!" he shouted. "The adults are talking right now."

Mike treated his men like dirt. But they feared him. Mitch, above all, got the harsh treatment. He never knew when to keep his mouth shut.

"Everyone, just put your weapons down," Mike added.

The Mexican in charge held his hand up, signaling them to stop. Mike didn't know his name, only his face, and nickname, the Lion. But the cartel evidently trusted him to do business for them in New York. He had a ruthless reputation. But Mike's temper was just as violent.

Mike's associates lowered their weapons.

"You got the stuff or not, motherfucker?" asked Mike.

Mike was referring to Fentanyl, a drug that was many times more potent than heroin. They would sometimes cut heroin with Fentanyl to enhance its euphoric effects. New York's addicts paid the price.

"You got the money?" the Mexican returned.

Mike held the briefcase out in front of him.

"It's right here, asshole," he said, cracking the case to allow him a peek. "Don't worry, it's all there."

The two prepared to make the exchange, each of their men with fingers on the triggers, just in case. Mike snatched the briefcase from the Mexican's hand, opening it to make sure everything was there. He closed it and fastened the lock, tossing the merchandise to Mitch.

"Don't touch that," he told Mitch. "Just put it in the back."

The Mexican walked back to his Mercedes, laying the money case out across the hood and opening it wide. He flipped through the stack of bills, counting it out in his head.

"Hijo de puta! You are short! Where is the other twenty grand? And don't play me, pendejo!"

Mike leaned his back against the car and lit another cigarette.

"That is the amount your boss, and I agreed on," he replied. "You have questions, take it up with him, asshole."

"I don't think so," he replied.

The Mexican wandered toward Mike and pulled his gun from its brown leather holster, pointing it at his head.

"The agreed-upon amount was one hundred thousand, not eighty, fucking bitch!"

Carelessly, Mitch jumped in between them.

"Hey, hey!" he said, flapping his hands in the air. "There's no need for that, man. I'm sure we can work something out! We're here for business, right? We can take care of this!"

"What the fuck are you doing, you idiot?" Mike asked him.

The Mexican withdrew his gun from Mike and aimed for Mitch.

"Are you fucking serious?" the man asked. "Who the hell is this guy?"

He glanced back at his men as they laughed at Mitch.

"You're a fucking nobody. Why in the hell would I listen to you?"

Mitch's gaze shifted over the Mexican's head toward the

street as he detected someone taking a wrong turn in their direction. She roamed near them, unaware of what she was walking into.

Mike peered back at Mitch, standing right behind him.

"Isn't that your fucking girlfriend, Mitch?" Mike asked.

"Nah," Mitch replied as he observed her getting closer. "Not a girlfriend, just a toy. She probably thinks she's my girlfriend. But I don't give a damn about that little whore."

"Didn't her brother come after you?"

"Yeah," Mitch said. "But I'm not worried about him."

"That's good," said Mike. "That's very good."

Mitch was overconfident in his words, however. He already knew that Rob wasn't a man to take lightly. But Mike had an old score to settle. He and Rob had once gotten into it over a girl, with the fight ending with Mike's broken nose. It happened just after high school, and Mike still held a grudge over fourteen years later. He may have just thought of a way to get back at his old friend.

As Mike watched Marianne amble toward the back of the Mercedes, one of the Mexicans raised his gun toward her.

"Put your weapons down, gentlemen," he told them. "I got this."

Mike propelled toward Marianne, clutching her by the arm.

"Hold up, young lady."

He planted a hand on Marianne's shoulder.

"Where exactly do you think you're going?"

Marianne's eyes met Mitch, and she pointed a finger right at him.

"Hey baby," she said in a drunken stammer. "I was looking all over for you!"

Mitch didn't even respond, only glancing at Mike and the cartel guys standing around him.

"Boss?" he asked. "You want me to take care of her?"

"No, no," Mike said, peeking back at Mitch while holding Marianne. "I have a better idea."

"She's seen too much, boss," Mitch said, stepping toward Mike.

Mike shoved Mitch back with his free hand.

"I said I'll take care of it!" he shouted. "Now back the fuck up!"

Mike glanced over at the Mexican in charge.

"How about we make a deal?"

The Mexican leader holstered his pistol.

"This better be fucking good, homes," he replied. "What you have in mind?"

Mike felt Marianne's face, running his finger over her lips and eyeing her short dress, taking a glimpse at her legs.

"The girl," Mike replied.

"What?" Marianne asked. "No, please!"

"Take the girl," he said. "She's worth that and then some."

The Mexican approached Marianne, holding the tip of her hair in his fingers as Mike held her in place.

"She a virgin?" he asked.

Mike glanced up at Mitch.

"Well, no," Mitch replied. "I kind of took care of that."

The Mexican rolled his eyes at Mitch.

"You dirty gringo," he said. "She's a fucking baby."

The Mexican placed his hand in the small of Marianne's back and looked into her eyes.

"But," he said, snapping his fingers at his men. "Still worth much over twenty grand, for sure. I think the boss will agree."

His men rushed to the other side, gripping both of Marianne's arms hard. They dragged her to the rear of the vehicle, some of her belongings falling to the ground.

"No!" Marianne shouted. "Let go of me!"

She struggled to break free from their control, pulling and jerking as hard as she could. But it just wasn't working.

"So, we have a deal?" asked Mike.

"We'll take her," he said. "But this is a one-time deal."

"Of course," Mike said.

"If you don't have our money in the future," the Mexican told him, "we will kill you where you stand, comprendes? My boss doesn't like surprises."

"Understood," Mike replied. "Loud and clear."

The men yanked the pink bag from Marianne's back and started tying her hands behind her as she tried to bust free.

"Help!" she screamed as one of them snagged a cloth and shoved it into her mouth to shut her up.

They popped the trunk, pushing her in like a rag doll and throwing the bag in with her before slamming it shut.

"Now shut the fuck up, bitch," one of them said.

The Mexican took the money case and handed it over to one of his men.

"Pleasure doing business with you," Mike said as the man climbed back into his fancy car.

Mitch took a seat next to the drug case as the Mercedes backed out of the alley.

"Let's see how he likes that. There's nothing like fresh meat."

"Somebody has to pay for this fucking cut on my cheek," said Mitch.

FIVE

Gold's Gym
Brooklyn

Metal clanking, people chatting, and music playing reverberated throughout the large, open gym as Rob got in a late-afternoon workout. He laid flat on that bench, sweat drenching through his white gym shirt and dripping onto the rubber gym mat beneath him. He breathed out and stretched his arms, pressing two hundred and seventy-five pounds of iron above his chest.

Rob was athletic from head to toe. He'd been that way ever since playing high school football. But now, he was in even better shape than back then. It was a requirement for his job. And he'd never waver from that obligation.

The Special Forces, just like other Special Operations Forces, took great care of their gear and themselves. Operating independently of regular forces, they were a cut above the rest. Nobody had to tell them how to do their jobs. They were on it 24/7. Rob was no exception. It was what he lived for. And everyone who knew him understood that.

"Come on, Rob," his workout partner, Anthony said as he stood over him. "You got it, man. You Special Forces guys are tough. Come on, pump it out!"

"Ugh...!" Rob bellowed, locking his elbows as he stretched the weight straight up for his eighth rep.

His veins seemed like they were about to pop out of his head. Anthony took the weight bar's underside, guiding it to him, the noise of metal on metal ringing as it came to a rest on the rack. Rob turned his legs to sit up, wiping his face with a towel. He took in a deep breath, drying the running sweat from his forehead. Reaching below him, Rob took his water bottle from the floor and tipped it back, swallowing a hefty swig.

"Your turn," Rob said, setting the bottle down on the top of his camouflage gym bag and flipping the white towel onto his shoulder. "Let's see you get it, tough guy."

Anthony Rossi was a high school friend of Rob's, graduating in the same class together. However, they'd taken different roads. While Rob heard the call to serve his country after 9/11, Anthony became a police officer. A beat cop back then. He was one of the first responders to answer the call after the Twin Towers' collapse in Manhattan in 2001. Now he was a sergeant in the Intelligence Bureau of the NYPD.

"Nah," Anthony told Rob, dangling his shield around his neck and shoving it under his shirt. "I need to go back to work, man."

"Come on, man," replied Rob. "We just got started."

"Sorry, bro. No can do. I have to go meet my partner at the precinct."

"All right, man," Rob replied. "Later, I guess. Go catch some bad guys."

"Yep," Anthony said, grabbing his phone from the next

bench over and placing it in his pocket as he went straight for the shower. "See you later, man."

Rob rubbed the sweat from his hands as he sat at the end of the bench, the outline of his ID tags showing through his damp shirt. His veins were almost bulging through his shirt sleeve as he stretched his arms up high over his head. Rob shifted toward the window, seeing as the cars outside drove by and down the street. Then, he heard his cell humming in his gym bag on the floor. He leaned over, unzipping the top, and reached for the phone in the side pocket.

"Hello?" he said as he brought the phone to his ear.

"Hello?" the caller replied.

But Rob couldn't hear him over the gym noise.

"Hello?" he asked again. "Who is this?"

There was only a faint sound coming from the other end of the line. Rob wasn't able to make out what the caller was saying.

"Hang on. Whoever this is, I can't hear you. Give me a second to get outside."

Rob snatched his bag from the floor and continued to the front door and out to the sidewalk.

"Hello? Who is this, and how did you get this number?"

Rob paused for a moment for the caller to answer.

"Yes, sir," the voice replied. "Is this Rob... Walker?"

"Yeah," Rob replied. "Who in the hell is this? What do you want?"

Rob knew he didn't recognize the voice. But, whoever it was, he seemed panicked.

"My name is not important," the mystery caller mentioned. "But I found a phone on the ground with this number in it."

Rob thought for a moment about what the caller had just said. There was only one person who'd come to mind.

"This phone... Does it have pink flower stickers all over the back?"

"Yes, sir, it does," the caller said.

"And you didn't steal it but called me?"

"I'm no thief, Mister," the man replied. "I am many things, but a thief ain't one of them."

"Sorry. It's just surprising. I meant nothing by it."

Rob could sense from the man's tone that something was wrong.

"There's more," the caller added. "I was walking down the street late last night, you know, minding my own business. It was dark. I heard a racket like a woman or a girl screaming. It didn't last long."

"What?" Rob returned.

"So," the caller continued. "I looked around the corner and saw these men forcing some poor person into the back of a car. I got out of there as fast as I could, man. And, when I came back, I found this phone on the ground."

"Did you see any faces, hers, or the men's?"

"No, Mister," he replied. "It was just too dark."

Rob moved the phone away from his mouth for a moment.

"Fuck!" he yelled, people around him staring.

He brought the phone back to his face.

"Did you call the police, then?" asked Rob.

"No, man," he said. "I'm sorry I didn't. I have my own problems with cops. But I thought somebody should know."

"Okay. Well, thanks for calling me. Can I meet you somewhere to pick up the phone?"

"Oh, no, sir," he said. "I'll leave it for you by the dumpster beside O'Malley's. I don't want any part of this. These people would kill me for sure!"

"So, you know 'em?" Rob asked.

Instead of answering, the phone fell silent.

"Hello?" Rob called out as pedestrians passed him on the sidewalk. "Hello?"

The caller had already hung up. Rob tried to dial back, but it went straight to Marianne's voicemail.

"Damn it, sis! What have you gotten yourself into this time?"

Who was this guy talking about? Rob thought to himself as he slid his phone into the pocket of his blue gym shorts. *What's he so afraid of?*

Did this fellow really see what he thought he'd seen? Rob just hoped his sister wasn't in any kind of trouble. All he knew for sure was that he needed to hurry down there and find out.

ııı

The late evening had only just turned to nighttime. Rob's GT turned onto the street in front of O'Malley's. It was far too soon for the place to be bustling, so he parked in the club's parking lot closest to the street. He looked through the passenger-side window and into the alley to the left-hand side of the building. Rob removed a tiny flashlight and a gun from the glove compartment and shoved them into his pocket.

He got out of the car, slamming the door closed, and zipped between cars sitting idle at the stoplight and to the alley across the street. He peeked into the small crack between the dumpster and the wall and found the phone lying on the ground, its silver case shining slightly beneath the streetlights.

The Messenger

At that instant, he knew his sister had gotten into something terrible. He just didn't know what. Like most teenage girls, she would have never left her phone behind. Unless, perhaps, she was attempting to leave a message.

Rob retrieved the flashlight. He walked down the side of the building and began combing every inch of ground, looking for clues about what happened or who Marianne was with. Then, as he glanced toward the ground, he saw a broken silver necklace lying on the blacktop. Rob picked the chain up and held it in his hand, noticing the small silver heart pendant attached.

It was then that Rob realized, without a doubt, that his sister had been there. It was too much to be a coincidence, and he knew it wasn't looking good. He looked to the ground, assuming there had been an encounter, and they forced her into a car, dropping the necklace in a struggle.

His first thought was to question the people working in the bar. He started marching toward the walkway and the front entrance. But before he could make it halfway, a shady character popped up before him. The gentleman, wearing a black suit and tie, white undershirt, and a Panama hat, strolled toward Rob.

The man had an unusual look on his face as he stared him up and down. Rob thought maybe he was one of the bad guys, his hand caressing the .40 caliber handgun on his side. But then he noticed the golden badge attached to the man's black leather belt.

"Who are you?" the man asked. "What are you doing back here?"

Rob stepped back with a baffled look, like the question surprised him.

"Who the hell are you?" Rob asked. "And last time I

checked, this was a public street."

"Well, that may be so," the man said, raising an eyebrow. "Still, the question remains."

"Rob Walker. Sergeant First Class Rob Walker."

Rob showed his military ID.

"US Army Special Forces."

The man glanced down at the ID card.

"What are you doing here?" Rob asked.

"I am Lieutenant Richard Miller of the Major Case Squad, NYPD," the man said. "I'm following up on a lead. That's all you need to know. And you're a long way from the front line, soldier. What you looking for back here?"

"I have cause to believe my sister was kidnapped from here," Rob mentioned. "I got a call from this guy. He wouldn't give his name. But he said he saw some men tossing someone into a car last night."

The lieutenant stepped in closer with a curious look.

"And what makes you think they took your sister?"

Rob glanced down at the necklace, then back at Miller.

"Because he made the call from her phone," Rob said, holding the cell phone out in front of him. "Evidently, she dropped it. I also found this necklace on the ground."

Rob showed the necklace to Miller.

"It's hers."

The lieutenant recovered a pen and a baggie from his coat, using the pen to place the necklace inside.

"And you are certain this is hers?" Miller asked, peering up at him.

"Of course I'm sure," Rob replied. "I gave it to her."

"You have any idea why she was down here?" asked the lieutenant.

"We got into an argument, and she ran off. Every time she leaves, she comes back to this fucking lowlife punk."

"This lowlife have a name?" he asked.

Rob went through the phone, pulling up a photo of Marianne, and gave it to the lieutenant.

"See the guy standing in front of the girl?" he asked. "His name is Mitch."

Miller's eyes focused on Mitch.

"Yep," Lieutenant Miller replied. "I recognize this asshole."

"You do?" Rob asked. "Who is he to you?"

Miller surveyed the photo.

"He's a dealer I've been watching for a while now," Miller said. "I've been trying to take down his gang for years. But his boss is careful. I haven't been able to get close. We even sent in an undercover. They got wise to him, and he disappeared without a trace. Mitch is a fucking idiot. But he's just a pawn. I want the head of the snake."

"He's a fucking moron," said Rob. "Somebody should have killed him a long time ago."

"What?" the lieutenant asked. "So you know the guy?"

"Yep," Rob said. "I met that punk in high school. He was a troublemaker even back then. I should've crippled his ass long ago."

Rob began flipping through the rest of the photos.

"This is my sister. She's just a fucking teenager. What are you going to do to find her?"

Miller glanced at the picture.

"We will do what we can. But I need to tell you, we have many missing person cases pending. And knowing who was most likely responsible for taking her, we have minimal resources and very little time."

"What the hell does that mean?" Rob asked. "You a fucking cop or not?"

"Yes. And it means that the chances of her still being in this city are slim, knowing who this gang's associates are."

Rob raised a fist and punched the side of the brick building.

"So you aren't even going to try?" Rob asked.

"Mister Walker," the lieutenant said. "We will investigate thoroughly, I assure you. But I have to be honest. I'm sure you can appreciate that. I think those who do business with this organization took your sister, although I have no proof. It's just a hunch from many years of working on these types of cases. It's not the first time I've dealt with these people."

"And who might that be?"

"Well," Miller said, "Los Lobos, the Mexican drug cartel."

Rob got into the lieutenant's face.

"Mexico? You are telling me they took her to Mexico?"

"I think so," replied Miller. "But, like I said, I have no proof. Yet, that is."

"How would you even fucking know that?" Rob asked the lieutenant.

Lieutenant Miller removed his hat and gave Rob the strained look of years of fighting evil in the streets.

"Call it intuition," Miller replied. "The gang is in bed with the cartel. They are the major supplier of narcotics in this area. Los Lobos recently moved up to sex trafficking. They ship young girls down, addict them to drugs, and force them to work in brothels or sell them off to the highest bidder. We've been working on 'em for years. How do you think the drugs get here? They don't just magically appear on the street."

"I'll go get her my fucking self!" Rob said. "If I wait for the law, she'll end up dead!"

"They don't just smuggle drugs into the US," the lieutenant said. "They run guns, girls, people. You name it, they have a hand in it. We've even set up joint task forces with the DEA, the ATF, and the FBI. We can never get close because everybody is so damn scared to rat them out."

Lieutenant Miller removed a business card from his wallet.

"Listen," Miller told Rob. "Here's my card. Call me if you think of anything. I promise you, Mister Walker, I will do everything in my power. But I want to caution you about taking the law into your own hands. You can't take these people on by yourself. It could backfire on you dramatically. You might be the one who ends up in jail or dead."

"This is my sister we're talking about!" Rob yelled.

Rob swiped the card from the lieutenant's hand and put it into his pocket.

"I understand, Mister Walker," Miller said as he continued further down into the dark alley. "I've been on these guys for a while. I got a tip they'd be at this location. And you seem like a capable guy. But please allow us to do our job. I'll be in touch."

Rob sat down on the curb beside the club. He felt numb, as if he'd seen it coming. Rob knew Marianne was a naïve teenager. He also understood how evil the world could be. He'd seen it firsthand. Time was not on his side.

"I'll take that fucking chance," Rob said to himself.

Rob was so enraged, he felt like beating someone. This was personal. She was his little sister. And he would burn an entire city to the ground if that's what it took to find her. He mainly didn't have the time or the patience to wait for an investigation that may or may not lead to her captors. No, he would take this on himself. And nobody in that city or elsewhere was going to stop what would come.

Never one to waste time, Rob barged through the front door of the club. It was relatively early, and the only people inside were the bartender and a few servers. He marched toward the middle of that room and let out a loud whistle.

"Listen up!" he erupted in a loud voice that rang throughout the bar. "My name is Rob Walker. My sister, Marianne, disappeared last night right here next to this establishment."

The club employees froze in their tracks, watching him in dismay.

"I am looking for two guys named Mike and Mitch, brothers. They are both gang members. If anyone knows either of their whereabouts, tell me now!"

Scared to speak up, nobody said a word. But Rob knew they were both regulars in that club. Someone had seen them.

"Anyone?" Rob asked. "Huh? Not a single one of you has seen them?"

That club became so quiet, you could've heard a pen drop.

"Fine," he said. "You all are a bunch of fucking cowards. You tell them both I am coming for them. There is no place they can hide that I won't find them. You tell them! And when I do, there will be hell to pay!"

Rob left the club in a frenzy. He was livid. Rob would find Marianne no matter who he had to destroy. But first, he had to handle the painful process of telling their mother. And an old friend owed him a favor—time to call it in.

SIX

```
88th Precinct, NYPD
Clinton Hill, Brooklyn
```

Rob waited in his old Mustang, parked in a row of spaces among patrol cars just off the street and down from the police precinct near downtown Brooklyn. He needed to have a conversation with his old high school buddy, Anthony.

Rob had gotten little sleep. Late the night before, he'd given the dreadful news to his mother, Louise. He was up most of the night, hearing her cry herself to sleep. She was distraught. And like any mother would do, her first reaction was to call the police. But Rob knew it would do no good. They were understaffed and entirely overwhelmed by the rising crime in the city.

She'd tried to stop Rob from taking his dad's old guns from the bedroom. Louise knew her son. And she understood he would do whatever he had to do to find out what happened to Marianne. She also realized that there was nothing she could do to stop him. Nobody could stop Rob when he'd made up his mind.

He'd been casing O'Malley's for a while before he went in. But he was pretty sure that Mitch wouldn't show his face after what happened. Mitch was a terrible person, but he wasn't a complete idiot. Mitch knew that would be the first place Rob would come looking for him. He would not make it that easy.

Rob had asked his friend to meet him when he could, without telling him why. He was hoping for a little help. Rob figured Anthony owed him that much for saving his ass from street hoods when they were boys. He'd been sitting there for just over an hour, not sure when Anthony was going to show up. Rob was in a rush to get to work. He didn't have time to be waiting around all day.

Rob was glancing through his rearview mirror when Anthony's black Dodge Charger appeared from behind. He waited as his friend reversed the car into the parking space next to his. He rolled his window down, leaving the engine running.

"Hey, man," Rob said to him. "Thanks for meeting me."

"Not a problem," Anthony replied. "You sounded pretty tense on the phone. What was so important?"

"Well," said Rob, "I have a problem, and I need a favor from a friend."

Anthony took a drink from the straw in his Starbucks Coffee cup and put it back into the cupholder.

"Why don't I like how sounds?" he asked.

Rob pulled up a picture of Mitch on his cell phone.

"Look," he said, passing the phone to Anthony through the window. "I just need to know everything you can tell me about this guy. His name is Mitch Buchanan."

Anthony glanced down at the photo.

"Where do I know this dude from? I know I've seen him before."

"He went to school with us," said Rob.

"That motherfucker?" asked Anthony. "Yeah, I remember him. If I remember right, he was a major douchebag. What do you want with him?"

"They took Marianne," Rob said. "And this asshole had something to do with it."

"What? Taken? Are you fucking kidding me?"

"Does it sound like I am fucking kidding?" Rob asked him. "Now, are you going to help me or not? I don't have the time to lose."

Anthony examined the photo one more time, rocking his head.

"I'd like to, Rob," he told him. "I really would. But I can't, officially. I could lose my job. Did you even bother to call the police? We have people who can handle this. Let me call it in."

Rob yanked his phone from Anthony's hand.

"Maybe you didn't hear me," he replied. "Drug traffickers kidnapped my sister! Now, if you don't help me, I will tear this city apart until I find out where she is. Then you guys will have a lot more work on your hands. And you and I both know that the NYPD is swamped. I don't have time to lose here. I don't have time to wait for an investigation or some bureaucratic bullshit. By then, she could disappear forever. I am asking for help from an old friend! Nobody needs to know."

Anthony knew Rob was right. Though he didn't want to admit it, they were all overworked. The chances of finding one girl that fast in a city of millions were meager, a million to one. And if they took her south, the case was even slimmer. Rob needed someone to interrogate. And there was nobody better than the one Rob had such a turbulent history with. No matter how far he had to go, he'd make him talk.

Anthony sat in silence for a bit, booting up the NYPD computer mounted above his center console.

"Fine," he said as he began typing on the keyboard. "Fine, I'll help you this one time. But I'm a cop, Rob. I can't be seen giving this to you. I know who you are. But on these streets, I treat you like everyone else."

Anthony removed a pen and a tiny notebook from his pocket and started writing.

"Damn. Your boy has a hell of a rap sheet. I'm surprised he's still walking around."

"He won't be walking any place for long," Rob replied.

"I'm just going to pretend I didn't hear that," said Anthony.

He tore the sheet of paper from his notebook and gave it to Rob.

"Is that what you need?" Anthony asked as Rob glanced at the paper, noting Mitch's home address written at the top.

"Yes," Rob said. "Thank you."

Rob put the vehicle into drive.

"I know it's just an address," Anthony told him. "And I don't know what your plans are. But you didn't get it from me. I've spent my entire career fighting corruption. Nobody can know that I helped you in some vigilante scheme. I can't condone it."

"I understand, friend," Rob replied. "Don't worry."

Rob didn't say another word. He just hit the gas, leaving a trail of skid marks and white smoke as he tore down the road and out of sight.

ııı

Later that night, Rob pulled up across the street from a

brownstone townhouse in the Crown Heights neighborhood of Brooklyn, just south of downtown. The car rolled to a standstill under a broken streetlight as he put the vehicle into park and killed the engine.

All the lights were off as he glanced at the house. Being the criminal that Rob knew he was, Mitch kept irregular hours, appearing home at odd times and out at all hours of the night. Like most gangs, they did most of their business in the dark. Rob had learned that early on from growing up on the same streets.

He waited in that car for what seemed like a couple of hours as he observed thugs hanging out on the street corner, slinging dope. Prostitutes waited along the road for their next client. It wasn't what some would call a pleasant area of town. The criminal part ran rampant in that part of Brooklyn, just like many other surrounding neighborhoods. But Rob didn't care about them, as long as they left him alone.

Rob continued observing as random hoodlums went up and down the city street. Like a flash, a silver Harley-Davidson motorcycle emerged from down the road. The driver reduced his speed to a crawl and stopped the bike just in front of the house's steps.

"Well, hello," Rob said to himself as he watched across the dark lot. "And who might you be?"

The bike driver shoved the kickstand down with his foot and left his black helmet hanging from the handlebars. It was Mitch. And it seemed like he was in a hurry, running up the steps to the house. Rob lingered there, viewing the front door as he waited to see if he would return. Mitch came out minutes later, backpack on, and hopped back onto the bike.

As Mitch zipped away from the brownstone, and down

the street, Rob pulled out to follow him. He figured Mitch was most likely on his way to a drug deal. But, this time, Rob would ensure Mitch didn't make it to his destination. He made a right turn into an industrial area of the city, and Rob pushed hard on the accelerator, his Mustang gaining speed rapidly as he charged up behind the bike.

He bumped the rear wheel, causing Mitch to slip and slide violently across the road. The bike struck the curb at full force, flipping him forward over the handlebars and thrusting his body into a stop sign, his bag landing a few feet away.

Rob hit the brakes, screeching as the car skid to a halt along the curb.

"Now I got you, jackass."

He snatched a rope from the car's trunk and cornered Mitch, lying barely conscious on the sidewalk. He flipped him over, hog-tying his hands and feet together and covering his mouth with duct tape. Rob lifted him over his shoulder and took him to the car, tossing Mitch into the trunk like a piece of trash as he grumbled incoherently. Rob snatched the bag up and took a peek inside, noticing what looked like a few kilos of heroin. He hurled the bag of drugs into the trunk with him.

"Let's see how you like that, dickhead."

Rob slammed the trunk closed and got back into the car. He hit the gas, running over the downed bike as he made his way down the street. As he drove, Rob began hearing banging coming from the back. He ignored his passenger's pounding as he continued to his destination. Mercy was not a luxury that Rob would grant Mitch this time. He was only out for two things: information and blood. If Mitch didn't know what he was in for yet, he would soon find out.

Rob drove for a few miles until he arrived near the Empire

The Messenger

Fulton Ferry Park, next to and underneath the Brooklyn bridge. It was the middle of the night, and not a single person in sight. He pulled onto the drive that looped around the park, stopping the car just shy of the East River. Rob took his baseball bat from the back seat and moved to the rear of the vehicle. Popping the trunk, he could vaguely hear Mitch's cries from under the tape over his mouth.

He picked Mitch up, grabbed the backpack, and toted him to a spot under the bridge, releasing him to the ground like a sack of potatoes. Rob held the bat down by his side, ripping the tape off and smacking Mitch across the face with an open hand.

"All right, fuck!" Mitch shouted. "What the hell do you want from me, you lunatic?"

"First," Rob replied, "I want you to lower your fucking voice before I scatter your brains all over this concrete."

Mitch didn't respond. So Rob raised the bat above his head like he was about to strike him. He stared a hole right through Mitch as he considered just killing him.

"Second, you know what I want, you fucking asshole. My sister, she's gone. And I know you had something to do with it, you little prick!"

"What?" Mitch asked. "I don't know what you are talking about, man. Okay? I don't fucking know!"

Rob raised the bat to eye level and then held it against Mitch's skull like he was about to hit a home run.

"I will only say it one more time, Mitch," Rob told him, lowering his voice in anger. "Then, I am going to knock your big, fucking mug out of the park. You understand what I'm telling you now? I fight terrorists for a living. You think I am worried about your ugly ass?"

"It isn't me you have to worry about," said Mitch. "It's my boss, and his boss, the entire organization."

Rob looked at him with a funny, disbelieving gaze. He didn't care about repercussions.

"You really think I give a shit, Mitch? If you tell me what happened to Marianne, I will let you go. Nobody will ever know you told me."

Mitch glanced at Rob like he was thinking about what to say.

"But," said Rob, "if you don't, I'll just kill you right here and stop wasting my time."

He lifted the bat above his head again.

"Okay, fine," Mitch said. "Fine, I'll tell you. But you have to promise to let me go."

Rob grinned at Mitch, knowing he was lying right through his teeth. He'd never planned to let Mitch go.

"I promise, Mitch."

"Okay," Mitch replied, his hands shaking. "We handed her over to the cartel. She's probably already in Mexico by now."

"Where, Mitch? Where did they take her to in Mexico?"

Mitch squirmed in place, unable to move his arms or legs.

"They can't find out, man. Those dirty ass fucking Mexicans will kill me."

Rob knelt down in front of Mitch, placing a hand on his shoulder like he was sympathizing with him.

"They won't, Mitch," Rob said. "They won't. Now, where did they take her?"

"Look, man," Mitch said. "I had nothing to do with it. All I know is they took her to one of their houses somewhere in the Sonora Desert. This sadistic motherfucker, an ugly ass Mexican with long hair and scars on his face. I don't know his name. But he and his men took her. That's all I know, I swear!"

Rob loosened his grip on the bat, still in his hands, as the end pinged off the ground.

"You did good, Mitch," Rob told him. "You did real good. See, that wasn't so hard, was it?"

Mitch gasped in relief. Not the hardcore gangster he liked to portray himself as with nobody to back him up, he'd come very close to pissing himself.

"I just have one more question, Mitch," Rob said. "Where can I find your brother, Mike?"

Mitch rattled his head from side to side. They had warned him of what would happen if he ever snitched.

"I can't tell you that!" replied Mitch. "He'd kill me for sure! He's my brother, but he's nuts!"

"I'll kill you if you don't!" said Rob.

Mitch was distressed and looked like he was about to cry. Rob held his head against the concrete wall behind him, pressing hard. His expression was a clear warning to Mitch, and he understood what Rob would do if he didn't give in.

"Okay, fine," Mitch said. "He'll kill me for telling you this. You can usually find him hanging out at the bar most nights."

"O'Malley's?" Rob asked.

"Yes, O'Malley's," he mentioned. "So, can I go now? I did what you asked."

Rob bounced to his feet.

"Sure, Mitch. Sure, you can go."

Rob's eyes saw nothing but red as they pierced right through Mitch. All he could think of was the man in front of him handing Marianne to the cartel. He had a feeling it was him all along.

"You can go," Rob said. "You can go straight to hell!"

With a gloved hand, Rob recovered a switchblade knife from his back pocket. Mitch must've thought he was going to cut him free. But Rob had other plans.

"Sorry, Mitch. But, I don't believe for one fucking second that it wasn't you. In fact, I think you had everything to do with it. And you've outlived your use to me."

"Wait, what? I thought you were going to let me go!"

"I lied!" Rob asserted. "After everything you have done, you really believed I was going to just let you walk? You are even dumber than I thought you were. I should've done this a long fucking time ago."

He released the knife blade, slicing Mitch's throat with one fluid move. Rob watched as Mitch slumped sideways to the ground, bleeding out fast and making a gurgling sound while slipping out of consciousness.

"That's for my sister, shit head," he grumbled as Mitch's life faded in front of him.

Rob dragged Mitch's body to the water's edge, using his foot to push him into the East River and hearing his corpse splash as it hit the water below. Rob removed the bag from the ground and chucked it into the river.

He washed the blood from his blade in the water, put it into his pocket, and went back to his Mustang. One down, many more to go. Nobody was going to slow him an inch. He just hoped that Marianne could hang on long enough. Rob was becoming a freight train with no means of stopping until he rammed right into his target at full speed.

SEVEN

Bushwick, Brooklyn

A blue Chevrolet Impala sat, parked at the curb in front of the Central Cafe on Central Avenue in East Brooklyn. Detective Lamar Bryant, an African American and fifteen-year police veteran of the NYPD, received a call early that morning from his boss about a murder near Ridge Wood. He'd been on the job since three o'clock that morning. It would be just another routine day of working overtime. Homicides in New York were up dramatically. The NYPD was doing their best to tackle the city's violent crime rate.

They believed the shooting to be gang-related. Lamar and his fellow homicide detectives were still on the case and waiting for the Crime Scene Unit to finish processing the scene. He and his partner, Detective Cliff Hartford, had only stopped for a few to grab a little pick-me-up on the way to the coroner's office. The two had been paired up for the last couple of years. Like Detective Bryant, Hartford was also a seasoned NYPD veteran.

They'd attended the police academy together a couple of decades earlier. Bryant had been a Homicide detective for longer. But because of their excellent working relationship and rapport, they'd asked their boss to be partnered up. But unlike Hartford, Bryant didn't come from a family of police officers. Everything that he knew, he'd learned on the job. Hartford's father and grandfather were both retired from the NYPD. Detective Hartford had taught him a thing or two along the way.

Detective Bryant snatched the two large paper coffee cups and dropped a ten-dollar bill on the counter to pay for both. The clerk slid the bill back across the table and smiled at them.

"No need for that, sir. We support our police here. It's on the house."

"Well, thank you very much for that, miss," he replied. "That is really kind of you."

The two plain-clothed detectives, service pistols on their hips, headed toward the entrance and back to the car. But as they passed through the glass door, Detective Bryant received a call from Homicide Captain Jacob Riggs. Riggs had been their captain for a couple of years after the previous one retired. He was a straight shooter and didn't have the patience for laziness or playing politics within his unit.

"Bryant," the captain said over the phone. "Listen, I know you guys are already working a scene. But I got a DOA (dead on arrival) over by Empire Park. Some random park-goer found him about an hour ago, floating facedown in the river. It looks like he's only been there, possibly overnight. You and your partner need to go as soon as possible and see what you can find out."

"Ten-Four, boss," Bryant replied. "We'll get on it right away."

"All right," Riggs said. "Keep me posted."

"Will do, boss," the detective replied.

Bryant hung the phone up, clipped it to his black leather belt, and glanced at his partner.

"What we got?" asked Hartford.

"That was the captain. There's a DOA over by the Brooklyn Bridge."

"Well, let's move then," said Hartford.

They both jumped into the car, and Detective Bryant hit the blue LED lights on the dash as they bustled down the street toward the murder scene. It took them nearly fifteen minutes to drive the usual half-hour route in the ordinarily heavy New York City traffic. When they arrived at the bridge, they had already roped the area off with yellow crime scene tape. Detective Bryant parked the vehicle at the side of the grassy area. They both got out of the car and approached the scene nearby.

"Detective Bryant, Homicide," he said to the uniformed officer, holding up the tape for his partner to duck under. "What can you tell me?"

"Ah, yes, sir," the officer replied. "We have a DOA over here by the water. He was found around seven o'clock a.m. by a gentleman walking through the park on his way to work. The guy found the body at the side of the pier. It appears his throat was sliced."

"Any witnesses, suspects? Anyone heard or seen anything unusual?"

"No, sir," replied the officer. "Nobody else has come forward. Apparently, the park was empty, except for the one who found the body."

"And where is he?" Bryant asked. "We need to speak to him."

"Of course," the officer said. "He's the one wearing the Yankees hat sitting over there on the curb."

"All right, thanks, Officer, uh, Jennings," Bryant said as he looked at his name tag. "We'll take it from here."

"Sure thing, Detective," Jennings said as he continued to guard the crime scene. "Let me know if I can do anything for you."

Detectives Bryant and Hartford moved to the river's edge, where the body was located. The crime scene unit continued working. Bryant pulled two sets of latex gloves from a box he'd brought with him and tossed one to his partner. Barry Doss, an African American crime scene investigator and older gentleman with gray, curled hair, examined the body as Bryant stooped down beside him.

"Looks like he was gashed pretty good."

"Yeah," Doss replied. "And there is no sign of water in his lungs, either."

"Meaning he was dead when he hit the water."

"Precisely," Doss said. "And the body had only been in the water for about seven or eight hours. Rigor mortis seems to have just set in. You're probably looking at about three or four hours before he was found."

Doss pointed to the victim's neck.

"See that knife wound?"

"Yeah," Bryant replied. "I see it. It looks pretty deep."

"It was clean," Doss added. "One swift cut to the carotid. But the killer didn't leave any other evidence behind."

"Any ID on him?"

"Yeah," replied Doss. "The responding officers found his wallet with his license in it. They put it in a baggie next to the other evidence over there."

The detective hunched over to pick the wallet up from the plastic-covered ground.

"All right," replied Bryant. "Thanks a lot. We need to speak with this witness."

"Not a problem," Doss said.

Bryant and his partner moved toward the witness, who was sitting alone close by.

"Hey, partner," Bryant said to Hartford, handing him the baggie. "Go run his ID and see what you come up with while I go question this guy. We also need to contact the medical examiner's office and try to notify his next of kin."

"You got it," he replied as he walked back to the car.

Detective Bryant addressed the witness.

"Excuse me, sir. I'm Detective Bryant, NYPD. I understand you found our deceased this morning on your way to work."

The man gazed up at the detective. He was a little unsettled and looked nervous about talking to the police.

"Relax, Mister," Bryant said. "You aren't in any trouble. We just have some questions."

"Yes, sir," the man replied. "It was so freaking bizarre. I was walking my normal route. I usually stop by the park on my way to work on Front Street every morning. Today was no different. As I was walking through the grass, I saw what looked like a shirt sticking out of the water."

"I see," said Bryant. "Go on, please."

"Well, I went over there to investigate and found a fucking body floating facedown. Man, I freaked out. That's when I called you guys. When they showed up, they told me to wait until I could speak to a detective. So here I am."

"Very good," replied Bryant. "You did the right thing, sir. And we appreciate your help."

"So can I go now?" he asked. "I am so late for work."

"Sure," Bryant said, retrieving a notebook and pen from

his pocket. "But before you do, could you please write your name and number here, so we can call you if we have any more questions?"

The witness seemed uncertain. But he began jotting down his information for the detective and gave the notebook back to him.

"Thank you, sir. We'll be in touch. You have yourself a nice day."

Bryant made his way back to the vehicle, a short walk away, as the man took off.

"You will not believe this shit," Hartford said to him as he stepped from the car. "The DOA was part of the Prospect Park crew, those assholes we've been trying to push out of Brooklyn."

"So he was a gang member?"

"It sure looks that way," Hartford replied. "His name is Mitch Buchanan, local dealer, hustler, and brother to the crew's leader. And he's got a sheet a mile long."

"Do we chalk this up to another gang hit?"

"Well, I wouldn't say that. This gang's usual MO is to shoot their victims in the head. Someone who knew what he was doing cut this guy. I think it was personal. And I also think this was the work of a professional. Gangs just normally aren't this clean. Someone with a knowledge of blades, someone who has killed before, sliced this guy. I don't think it was some random street hood."

"Good point," Bryant replied to his partner.

"So, what are you thinking?"

"Well," Bryant said. "I think we should give the Major Case Unit a courtesy call before we move forward. If he is part of that crew, knowing their involvement in extortion, kidnapping, and drugs, they will want their hands on this."

Across the city, Lieutenant Miller was getting ready to leave his house in Woodhaven, Queens, when he received Detective Bryant's call. He'd just woken up after only sleeping a few hours from a case he'd been working the night before. Miller was burned out from years of being on the job at all hours of the day and night. He was looking forward to his retirement in less than a year.

As Detective Miller verified the identity of the deceased, it instantly piqued his interest. Miller had bumped into him through past cases he'd worked on. He knew Mitch was nothing but a vile criminal, as were those he ran with.

"That guy?" he asked Detective Bryant over the phone, slipping his .40 caliber Glock 22 handgun into the shoulder holster under his sport coat. "We've been investigating that prick for at least a couple of years now. Somebody finally whacked his ass, huh?"

"Yep," Bryant replied.

Miller opened his car door and stepped in.

"Well," Miller said, "I can't say I'm surprised. It was bound to happen, eventually. You know how these guys are, Lamar, fucking scum of the earth. I say let 'em kill each other, less work for us."

Miller was well known in the department, considered a star and mentor by many. Nobody really questioned him or his motives, even his bosses. He had street credit in their eyes.

"Yeah, I know. Believe me. I just figured you'd want to know."

The lieutenant started his car as he held the phone with his chin.

"Yeah, yeah. Thanks for the call, Lamar. I really appreciate it. You have any suspects yet?"

"None yet," Bryant replied. "We just got it. But whoever killed him knew what the hell he was doing."

"How do you mean?"

"I mean, it looks like an assassin hit, not some hoodlum trying to rob someone. One clean cut to the carotid artery."

Something clicked in Detective Miller's mind. He thought about the recent encounter he'd had with one Special Forces soldier. Miller didn't mention that to Detective Bryant or anyone else. But he had a great memory. And the lieutenant recalled the name on the military ID that Rob had shown to him not long before. It couldn't be a fluke he was in that alley when Miller showed up. All he knew for sure was he needed to speak to him soon.

"All right, Lamar. Thanks a lot. You going to be there for a bit?"

"If you need me to," Detective Bryant said.

"Please," Miller told him. "I need to check something out first."

"Sure, Lieutenant," Bryant replied. "It's no issue. We'll be waiting for you."

Miller hung the phone up and put it on the dashboard. He started running Rob's name through the department laptop installed inside the car. It took a minute to pull up, and the findings showed Rob's next of kin, his mother, and her home address.

"Very interesting," he said to himself.

The detective backed out of the drive and pointed his vehicle toward downtown Brooklyn. He was thinking about what he was going to say to Rob when they were face-to-face.

He didn't want to hold him. As far as Miller cared, he'd unwittingly helped him rid New York of one of its depraved crooks.

The detective wasn't exactly corrupt. Over time, he'd just grown tired of the criminal trash he'd arrested walking because of some loophole in the system. And he knew they had a few crooked judges presiding over some of their major cases. But there was no way he could get away with accusing one of them without the evidence to back it up. Miller couldn't stand for it anymore. The more of these assholes who ended up dead and gone before he retired, the better. Plus, it saved him tremendously on paperwork.

Half an hour later, Lieutenant Miller rolled up in front of the large apartment building, parked on the street in front of the entrance, and stood by. He'd expected he would have to hold up there for some time. But, sooner than he'd predicted, he sighted Rob strolling down the sidewalk on his way to his car. The detective sped up, cornering Rob at the edge of the parking lot, and rolled his passenger window down.

"Mister Walker!" he said through the window. "A quick word, please, if you would."

Rob approached and leaned an arm against the open car window.

"What are you doing here, Detective? Are you following me?"

Miller just sneered at him.

"If I were following you, Mister Walker," he replied, "you wouldn't see me coming."

Rob shrugged his shoulders.

"So," Rob said. "What can I do for you, Lieutenant?"

"Well, for starters," Miller said. "You can get in the car.

We need to have a talk."

Rob stood there, arms folded with a questioning look on his face.

"Do I have a choice?"

The detective nodded his head.

"You always have a choice, Mister Walker," he said. "I just want to have a brief chat with you. No harm, no foul."

"Fine," Rob said as he climbed into the passenger seat. "What's this about?"

Detective Miller didn't immediately answer. He just drove the car a short way down the road to a vacant parking lot and stopped in the center, shutting the engine off.

"Detective," Rob said. "Are you going to tell me what this is all about?"

Rob figured he already knew why the detective was there. But he would never admit to anything. He knew that if they had anything concrete on him, the detective would have cuffed him already. Except Rob was much better than that. Snipers were taught not to leave evidence behind.

"Well, Mister Walker. We found the body of a local gang member washed up on the edge of the East River early this morning. The deceased's name is Mitch Buchanan. It looks like the killer knew what he was doing, too. In fact, he left absolutely no trail to follow. It was as if he'd just vanished. You wouldn't know anything about that, would you?"

Rob's display was stone cold, with absolutely no emotion. His poker face could bore right through even the most experienced man. He glanced over at the detective.

"Why would I?" he asked.

"I just thought maybe you'd heard something, is all," Miller replied.

"Nope," said Rob. "I'm afraid I can't help you, Lieutenant. But it sounds to me like the punk got what he deserved. It's dangerous out in these streets, you know? Anything can happen if you're not careful."

Detective Miller rolled the car windows back up in case anyone was within earshot.

"I'm not disputing that, Mister Walker. In fact, I couldn't care less. I'm even glad that someone put that bastard in the ground."

Rob couldn't believe what he was hearing. He'd thought for sure that Miller was there to arrest him or, at the very least, size him up.

"Why in the hell are you telling me this?" asked Rob. "Shouldn't you be out looking for my sister? My mom is worried sick. She's hardly eaten and hasn't slept in days."

The detective lit a cigar and took a puff, blowing a string of smoke into the air.

"Listen, Mister Walker," Miller replied.

"It's Sergeant Walker," Rob interrupted.

"Okay, Sergeant Walker. Look, I know you had something to do with the man's death. I can't prove it. But the fact of the matter is, I don't give a shit. If I were going to drag your ass to jail, I would've done it already. I am fed up with these assholes. If someone gets to them before I can, then so be it. I'm about to retire. After that, it's someone else's problem."

"Why are you talking to me, then?"

"Because, Sergeant Walker. We both know that the asshole had something to do with your sister's disappearance. We also know that she is not in the city any longer. Call it a courtesy call."

"And?" Rob asked.

"And," the detective replied. "As long as my name doesn't come up, we have no problem, period. That's it, that's the deal."

Miller removed a piece of paper from the glove box and slipped it to Rob. As he opened up the folded sheet, he was shocked. It was an address.

"What's this?" Rob asked.

"It's a stash house we surveilled in the past. You should find the one you are looking for there."

Detective Miller gazed up at Rob.

"Don't get caught. If you do, I will deny any part or even knowing who you are. And they will believe me."

There was a reason Detective Miller didn't speak to Rob over the phone. He didn't want the call traced.

"Why are you giving me this?" Rob asked him. "Are you trying to set me up for something, Lieutenant?"

"No, I'm not," Miller replied. "Let's just say I prefer it this way. You can do what I can't. Dead bad guys and less paperwork suits me just fine."

Rob couldn't believe that the detective was helping him. Why would he jeopardize his career? Maybe he knew something that Rob didn't. It didn't really matter, though. He wouldn't be able to stop him if he tried. Rob would not tell him he'd killed the man. And he would leave many more bodies in his wake before it was all over.

"Understood," he told the detective as he put the sheet into his blue jean pocket and lifted the hood on his gray hoodie.

That's all he had to say. Miller watched as Rob got out of the car and picked up a jog across the lot and down the street, a couple of city blocks back to his waiting Mustang. The detective had work to do. But he was going to stay out of that man's way, leaving Rob to get his hands even dirtier. It was as simple as that.

EIGHT

St. Augustine Church
Brooklyn

Though he hadn't attended mass in years, Rob grew up in a Catholic family. His mom and dad had always been devout to their faith when he was younger. However, his mother had stopped going soon after Rob's father passed. For a while, she was angry at God for her husband getting cancer. But now, she never missed Mass or a chance to confess her sins to her priest, Father Andrews. Rob knew she was on the verge of a nervous breakdown from everything that was happening. There was just one place she would be. That place was a beautiful and pristine Catholic church in Brooklyn, where the entire family had gone when Rob was a child.

He'd tried to ring Louise on the way, but the call kept going straight to voicemail. He needed to protect his mother. Rob had to assure her that everything was going to be okay. Although they'd had their differences, he still loved her. Rob didn't want Louise to succumb to the peril his family was now facing.

Rob stopped in front of the entrance and ran up the stone steps. He quietly opened the large wooden door. There, in front of the pulpit, he found his mother sitting in the front pew of the empty church, hands folded in silent prayer. The lovely crafted stained-glass windows and the openness inside welcomed all who wished to speak to God. But Rob wasn't there to pray.

He calmly made his way forward, approaching his mother from behind, her head bowed in her hands as he sat down behind her.

"Mom?" he called to her. "Mom, you okay?"

But she didn't respond, just continued praying to herself. Rob sat, watching his mother and not really knowing how to comfort her.

"Mom," Rob said. "Talk to me, please."

Louise slowly opened her eyes, her head still forward and her face red as if she'd been crying. She let out a moan as she spoke.

"You and your sister were christened and baptized here after you both were born," she said. "Your father was so happy that day. I was too."

"I know, Mom," Rob replied. "I know you were."

"Marianne was just as rambunctious as you growing up," Louise said. "Neither of you could sit still in church. You both were so active and hyper, I had a hard time quieting either of you down."

He continued listening to his mother as he put his arm around her neck. She glanced back at him with worry in her eyes.

"Rob, I know your sister has been caught up in some awful stuff. I know she doesn't make the best choices. Unlike you, she's made a total mess of her life. But she doesn't deserve this. Nobody deserves this."

Rob rested a hand on Louise's shoulder.

"Rob," Louise said. "Bring my baby back home. I don't care what you have to do. I don't care where you have to go. I don't care how long it takes. But, in the name of God, please bring your sister back here. She's just a baby!"

Louise saw the fierceness in her son's eyes for the first time as he stared back at her.

"Trust me," he replied, "God is going to want no part of what I'm about to do."

Without saying another word, Rob kissed his mother then marched through the front door like he was on a mission. He would wait for nightfall to loom over New York. Like vampires in the night, the city's criminals operated mostly in the dark. He'd stopped by his storage unit to pick up some of his privately owned weapons, his prized Remington 700 sniper rifle with a suppressor, and a .45 Glock pistol.

Later, as the evening sun fell, he dropped his car off blocks down the street on Riverdale Avenue and continued to the address on foot, not wanting anyone to identify the vehicle. He crept to the other side of the road, his rifle and pistol in a black, nondescript soft case on his back. Nearing an abandoned building across the street, Rob leaped into the air, gripping the bottom bar of the fire escape at the end of the empty shop, and pulled himself up. He climbed to the top and paused next to a top-floor window of the three-story building.

Rob attempted to lift the window open, but it was locked. He wore the same tactical Mechanix gloves with rubber-hardened knuckles he'd used in combat. Rob broke the glass with a single blow and headed through the darkened building right for the roof access on the other side of the room.

Rob was just doing what they trained him to do. But this time, he had little to go on. Rob didn't know how many people they had in that house, but he would soften the target and get rid of as many as possible before entering. He wanted to make his target fearful of what was coming for him. It was payback time. And there was no way Rob would allow Mike to escape.

Rob reached the building's rooftop and started setting up at the east corner facing the house as the clock hit ten past midnight. He flipped down the bipod on his rifle, propped it on the edge of the roof, and got into position. At that close of a range, it was child's play to him. All he had to do was point and shoot. And he knew they would never expect it.

"All right, you piece of shit. Where are you at?"

He surveyed the area surrounding the stash house through the glass. One man, possibly a guard, stood on the porch, and a single light was on in one of the upstairs rooms. Rob noticed shadows moving along the wall against the overhead light. Fortunately for Rob, he had a pricey mil-spec thermal optic attached to his rifle. The scope could show any heat signature, even through walls and other obstructions. He quickly swapped his night vision for his thermal scope, securely tightening it to the top rail. The Special Forces, mostly their snipers, used them during nighttime operations.

He moved the scope back to the guard at the door.

"Well, partner. Today is not your lucky day."

Rob settled his crosshairs over the man's heart. Without pause, he squeezed the trigger and let off a round. The suppressor made a light thump as Rob watched blood paint the screen door behind his target. He dropped against the top of the front porch chair, his lifeless body twitching on the ground as he took his last breath.

Rob held the rifle on the door, just in case any of his buddies had heard the fall. As suspected, a single individual opened the door, jumping back and startled, his dead buddy just a few feet away. Rob inched the rifle scope up, pressing the trigger again and sending the man falling back into the doorway. His bloodied back slammed hard against the porch, arms flopping down on the wood by his side.

Rob waited for a moment, but nobody else showed up in his sights. Guessing them to be upstairs, he veered his rifle back to the second-floor window.

The thermal optic showed the full outline of a man through the black curtain. He appeared to be wandering toward the window. As soon as he dropped him through the glass, Rob knew it would alert them to his presence. But they wouldn't yet know who it was. Nor would they be able to determine his position on the building. After all, they were thugs, not trained killers.

"Fuck it," Rob said as he held the tip of his finger over the curve of his rifle trigger.

He sent a .30-caliber bullet soaring toward the window. The round pierced the glass, shattering it and striking the man at the center of his forehead. It thrust his body rearward and out of sight as he sank to the floor.

"Good night, you son of a bitch," said Rob.

Someone inside had heard the glass break. The place livened up as people started scurrying downstairs and through the back door. Rob had sent them running for their lives. He broke down his rifle, inserted it into its carrier, and cocked his .45-caliber pistol. He made his way through the top floor of the building and hurried back down the fire escape, hopping to the ground into a kneeling position. With his gun at the ready, Rob sneaked across the empty street, creeping to the front and taking cover at the side of the front door. One at a time, he snagged each body by the feet, dragging them off the doorstep and around the corner.

Rob returned to the door, his pistol out in front of him, preparing to engage anyone who emerged. But nobody was there, just an empty and dilapidated drug house. The brown carpet was foul-looking, and the walls had graffiti and marks all over. The place looked inhabitable. But that wasn't its intention.

"Come out, Mike!" Rob yelled out. "It's just you and me now, old friend! Your pussy friends left you!"

Rob inched up the stairs.

"Come on, Mike!" he said. "I just want to talk!"

But there was no response. Rob turned the banister at the top of the steps and into the nearest bedroom.

"You can't hide from me! Come out, come out, wherever you are!"

Rob heard a creak from the floor coming from down the hall. He followed the noise, not making a sound. He moved to a doorway at the end and caught movement in the corner of the darkened room as he peeked in. Rob switched on the tactical flashlight attached to the underside of his gun barrel. He found Mike hiding in the corner of the room behind a wooden bookshelf.

"There you are," Rob said, displaying an ominous grin. "I figured you'd be hiding from me, you fucking coward. You're not so tough now, are you?"

Rob held the pistol toward his feet. Abruptly, Mike lashed out, running toward Rob at full force to tackle him. But he sidestepped just in time, tripping Mike to the floor beside him.

"Ah, you don't have to be like that. Now you leave me no choice, Mike."

Rob kicked Mike in the face, dazing him as he started tying his hands and feet behind his back with a long piece of para-cord. He heaved Mike over his shoulder and started carrying him out of the house and down the street.

"Where the fuck are you taking me?" Mike asked him. "You won't get away with this!"

"Oh," Rob replied, "I think I will. Don't you worry, though. We're just going for a brief drive, just you and me."

They came to Rob's GT, parked at the side of the street. He shoved a piece of cloth into Mike's mouth and hurled him into the trunk.

"You know what's funny?" he asked Mike, knowing he couldn't answer. "Your brother Mitch begged for his life too. He betrayed you, Mike. And he acted like a little girl all the way to the end."

Rob stared into Mike's eyes like he knew what he was thinking. He wouldn't permit him a moment's peace any longer.

"Have a nice ride, motherfucker," he said, slamming the trunk down.

ııı

Rob drove out to an abandoned waterfront power plant, a place the city had been pledging to tear down for years. The decaying, multi-story brick building hadn't been in use for decades and sat in an empty lot, rotting away from years of neglect. He knew nobody would disturb them or come looking for Mike out there. Nobody would hear them. It was the ideal spot for what was about to take place.

He pulled into the rear and backed the car into a large, broken bay door opening in the back of the building. Broken glass and trash littered the inside, and cobwebs and grime filled the surrounding space. Nobody had touched the place in a while, except for some drug addicts. Hypodermic needles were spread all over the floor in the corner and on top of an old, filthy mattress.

Seizing a large bag from the car, Rob got out and walked near the trunk. Popping it open, he pulled Mike from the back and dragged him by his tied feet to a spot in the center of the room. Rob recovered a chain from the bag, tossed it over a pipe above his head, and began securing Mike's arms as he held him up, his feet almost touching the ground. The floor was wet from leaky cracks in the roof above.

Rob returned to his car, removing an electrical device and a battery from the back seat.

"This should do fine," he said. "What do you think, Mike?"

Mike made a faint noise that Rob couldn't decipher from under the rag. He yanked it from his mouth.

"What was that, asshole?" he asked while fastening the device to the battery terminal on an old table he'd moved for the occasion. "I couldn't hear you."

"What are you going to do with that?" Mike asked.

Rob only laughed.

"I think you should be more concerned about what I am not going to do with this, Mike," Rob replied. "I have seen this technique in action more than once over the years. Trust me, it is pretty horrific. Try not to shit yourself."

Rob began stripping Mike down to nothing but his

underwear, ripping the shirt and jeans away from his body, and tossed them out of the way as Mike hung helplessly from the chain. Rob started adding the cupped suction clips to Mike's bare chest.

"Man, you don't have to do this!" Mike screamed. "Please, I'll tell you anything you want to know!"

But Rob ignored him. Instead, he emptied a bottle of water over Mike's head.

"I know you aren't the brightest person in the world," he told Mike, "but I'm sure you know that water and electricity don't mix."

Rob turned the device on and tapped the positive and negative ends together, seeing sparks shooting out from the ends.

"Well, it looks like we're in business now," Rob said.

"No!" Mike yelled as Rob attached both ends to Mike's chest.

He vibrated, bellowing as loud as he could for it to stop. Rob held on a bit longer.

"All right," Rob said as he removed them. "Now that we got you all warmed up, where the fuck is my sister, jackass?"

"Wh-What?" Mike stuttered, whimpering from the volts that had just shot through his body. "What a-are you t-talking about?"

"Not good enough!"

Rob connected the device again. But this time, he kept it on even longer, watching as Mike squirmed wildly.

"You're only making this harder on yourself," Rob told him.

Mike continued stirring and screaming from the intense electric current coursing through him. He couldn't control himself, and his white boxers became wet right before Rob's eyes.

"Well, look at that. If only your boys could see you now!"

Rob turned the electricity off.

"Had enough yet, tough guy? I've seen guys much harder than your pitiful ass break from this. And, believe me, you aren't a hardened warrior. You're nothing more than a pathetic criminal, preying on those weaker than you. But this is what happens when you fuck with the big boys!"

Rob clutched Mike by his jaw.

"I can go all night, Mike," he said. "But you can't. Now, I know you had something to do with Marianne's disappearance. Tell me where she is being held, and it'll save you a lot more pain!"

"Who fucking ratted?" asked Mike. "Who told you where I was? My brother?"

"Your brother is dead, you bastard. And you're going to end up just like him!"

Rob raised his arm, smacking Mike across the face with an open hand. Blood splattered from his lip and left red splotches on the dirty concrete floor.

"I am losing my patience, Mike! Where the fuck is she? This is the last time I'm going to ask you!"

Rob reconnected the clips near Mike's nipples.

"I see how it's going to be," he said. "You just need more convincing. Okay, I can do that."

"No, no, no!" Mike shouted.

He turned the juice back on, and Mike was powerless to curb his body's response, flipping and flopping like a hung fish out of water. Rob sat in a nearby chair, watching as Mike came near to his last moment of life.

"How about that, Mike?" he asked as he unhooked the clips. "That jog your memory a little?"

Mike rocked his head back and forth, not able to hold it up straight.

"The next one will kill you, Mike," Rob told him. "You can save it if you just tell me where she is."

Rob moved an ear closer as Mike mumbled.

"What was that?"

"Pen and paper," Mike said, hardly able to string a sentence together.

Rob went back to his car to fetch a pocket notebook. He removed a pen from his pants and gave them both to Mike, loosening the rope around one arm. He began sketching on the paper, and Rob wondered if Mike was trying to rebuff him. But then he gave the notebook back, and Rob glanced down at it.

"SONORA DESERT," it read.

Rob looked down and noticed a circle around a roughly sketched square with an address below and a crooked road drawn next to it. It was a map.

"This is it, Mike?" Rob asked as he tightened the rope on his wrist. "This is the place?"

Mike just bent his head and made a faltering noise that was unintelligible.

"Very good. I believe you, Mike."

Mike had a look of relief on his face, like he thought Rob would surely let him walk.

"But you sold an innocent child, you bastard!" Rob said. "My flesh and blood! Did you think you were going to get off that easy? You don't deserve to breathe, asshole. You deserve to suffer!"

Rob took a bag of frozen fruit from his bag, now just a melted mess.

"New York City has probably the biggest rat problem in any metropolis in the United States," he said.

Rob ripped the bag open, and a foul stench came out. It was days old.

"And they love fruit."

Rob peeled Mike's underwear off slightly and emptied the gooey, sour-smelling mess of fruit down his crouch, liquid seeping down both thighs. He turned his nose away from the awful smell.

"Man, that's some nasty shit," Rob said as he finished dumping the bag and tossed it to the side. "By the time they find you, they'll have eaten just up to your knees if they start at your feet. If they start on that little prick of yours, well, your bowels and the rest of you will spill out like one big buffet. There's a reason I'm telling you all this, Mike. I want you to understand what's happening to you."

Mike whimpered in place, too weak to move much or scream. But it was apparent that he was panicking and fearful of the inevitable.

"You'll probably die first from thousands of volts coursing through your body. But you'll be nothing more than a fried, bloody pulp when they find you."

Rob smiled bitterly at him as he returned to the device.

"I have to go now, Mike."

Mike watched in horror as Rob turned the electricity to the highest setting. He tried to scream but couldn't muster another sound. Rob left Mike hanging, thrashing around uncontrollably in a last-ditch effort to break away.

Rob hopped into his car, and a trail of smoke rose behind

him as he spun his rear tires, peeling away from the building. He whipped out into the street. The skyline of the borough Rob had once called home rose behind him as he glanced into his mirror. He had one thing on his mind: destruction. Those who'd taken his sister were going to pay dearly for their crimes.

Rob turned on the radio, and a breaking news report interrupted the rock music playing.

The body of a suspected gang member was found in the East River over the weekend. Police are offering a 5000-dollar reward for any information that leads to a suspect and a conviction. Officials say that it resembles a professional style hit, the kind used by the Italian Mafia at the height of their power in the city, and is most likely gang-on-gang violence as they battle for territory in downtown Brooklyn. Stay tuned for more updates. Lee Jackson, WNYL.

Rob smiled and twisted the dial to change the station. A sign that read "LEAVING BROOKLYN" passed by as he crossed over the Verrazzano-Narrows Bridge toward New Jersey on his way south. It would be awhile before anyone found Mike's body. But Rob could rest a little easier knowing that he got what he deserved. Mike's reign in the city had come to a merciless and painful end. Now, Rob had much bigger fish to fry.

NINE

```
Denton, Texas
Three days later
```

Rob passed the Denton City limit sign as sprawling ranches and open farmland came into view over the hill. Countless rows of cornstalks and wheat fields bordered both sides of the two-lane road as Rob zoomed past them. Horses and cows grazed on acres upon acres of fenced, green pastures. Silos and windmills seemed to set the tone in America's heartland as they dotted the landscape.

An unmistakable sense came over Rob. It assured him he wasn't in the busy and overpopulated streets of New York City any longer. He'd accepted an open invitation to visit his buddy and spotter, Kyle. But he didn't think it would be so soon or under this type of desperate circumstance.

He plugged Kyle's address into the GPS on the dash. His home was only a few miles away. So Rob picked up the pace in a push to finally get to where he was going after many driving hours. He had thought about calling on the way, but that type of news was better delivered in person. Rob felt a mixture of numbness and fury, but he would not allow his anger to mar his judgment.

Rob turned onto a long, dirt driveway. White wooden fencing formed large horse paddocks on both sides as he stopped to check the address on the mailbox. He had the right place. Rob continued down the drive, noticing a gigantic red barn with a cupola to the property's right. A large, round hay bale and a round pen were situated toward the front of it. A big, white farmhouse with a wrap-around style porch sat to his left.

As he came to a stop just shy of the horse barn, Rob observed a character in faded jeans, a blue plaid shirt, and a black cowboy hat and boots. He was riding a trotting brown Quarter Horse mare down the hill and across the pasture, other horses grazing around them.

"Whoa, girl!" he heard Kyle say to his horse as he pulled back softly on the reins. "Whoa. That's it. Good girl."

Rob watched as Kyle made his way to the paddock gate to the left of the double barn doors and hopped from the saddle.

"Good girl," he said to his horse as he patted her gently on the backside. "Go on, girl. Go play."

The horse began walking toward others in the middle of the paddock. Rob got out of the Mustang as Kyle approached him through the large, metal tube gate. Kyle wrapped the gate chain around the fence post to secure it.

"Rob!" Kyle yelled across the yard. "Hey, man, I wasn't expecting you so soon! I was just out taking Grace for a trail ride around the property."

"She's a nice-looking horse!" Rob yelled back.

"Thanks, man. She's my girl. Maybe we can find the time to go riding sometime."

"I'd love that," Rob replied.

As Kyle neared him, he stretched his hand to shake Rob's.

"It is good to see you, buddy!" Kyle said. "How the hell have you been since we got back?"

Kyle noticed the grim look on Rob's face.

"Not great, man," Rob replied, spitting the rest of his dip onto the ground. "Not great. You mind if we talk inside?"

"Sure," Kyle said. "Of course. No problem."

Rob accompanied his friend up the porch steps and through the front door of the house. Kyle set his hat on a coat rack in the foyer and led Rob to the living room.

"Have a seat, man. You want something to drink?"

"Sure, thanks."

Kyle went to the kitchen counter and poured them both a shot of Jose Cuervo, setting the glasses on the hand-crafted, dark stained coffee table in front of the sofa.

"Nice life you have out here," Rob said, downing his tequila in one gulp. "It seems pretty peaceful."

Kyle took a seat next to Rob.

"It's a lot of work," replied Kyle. "But the key thing I have learned growing up around horses is, if you take care of them, they'll take care of you. I have a few scars from being thrown when I was a kid. I learned that the hard way."

"Nice," Rob replied, not able to think of a more definite answer.

"Rob," Kyle said. "I know you. I know you didn't just come all the way down here to talk about horses. What's going on?"

Rob placed his shot glass back on the table in front of him.

"I need your help. I'm getting ready to go to war."

"What?" Kyle asked. "What the hell are you talking about, man?"

Rob removed his ball cap and ran a hand over his face and hair. Kyle could tell he was upset.

"There's no easy way to say this," he replied. "It's my sister, Marianne. She's been taken!"

"Taken?" Kyle asked. "What do you mean, taken?"

"I mean abducted, man," Rob told him. "She was kidnapped in New York and taken south by a fucking cartel. And I need your help to get her back!"

"You are fucking bullshitting me, right?"

"Do I sound like I am bullshitting you?" Rob asked. "If they hurt her, I swear to God I'll never forgive myself!"

Kyle downed his tequila, setting the glass on the end table.

"Okay, just calm down for a second. How do you know who took your sister or where they went?"

"It's a long story," replied Rob. "Let's just say I had a little help. But I knew the guy she was running with was a low-life. He always has been. I think it was a drug deal gone bad, something like that. Wrong place, right time. These people are fucking evil."

Kyle sat and thought to himself for a moment.

"So you know who was responsible?"

"I do," Rob replied. "They are both gone now."

Kyle looked away for a moment like he was thinking about something. Then it hit him.

"Wait a second," said Kyle. "I just heard on the news yesterday about two gang bangers from New York being killed in a hit. They said one was tortured to death and found electrocuted and hanging from the ceiling, a bloody mess. Are you saying that was you?"

"It was," Rob replied. "Those bastards sold her, man, like a fucking piece of property. And I need to get down there and get her out of whatever fucking hole they got her in!"

Kyle pressed his head into his folded arm and glanced back up at Rob.

"Jesus," Kyle said. "What about the law?"

"The law can't touch them down there. You know that. And we both know the Mexican police are corrupt as hell. Many of them are even in bed with the cartels. I have to do this, Kyle. With or without your help. The longer I wait, the more danger she's in, and the less chance I'll be able to find her. I can't do that to my mom. She's scared as hell right now. And this might just kill her!"

"Okay," Kyle said. "Just let me think."

He could tell that Rob was troubled, naturally.

"You have a lead?" Kyle asked.

"Yep," Rob said. "I got it out of the prick just before I killed him."

"How do you know it's the right one? He could've lied to you, hoping you'd let him go."

"I don't," said Rob. "But it's a starting point. Even if we tear that place apart, I'm not coming home empty-handed."

Kyle poured them both another drink, getting up and setting the bottle back on the bar that divided the kitchen from the living room. As they drank their shots of tequila, Kyle got an idea, something he'd prepared for a rainy day.

"I want to show you something," he said as he stood from the sofa. "Follow me."

Kyle guided Rob through the hall, down a staircase that pointed to a basement. As he opened up the door, Rob was in awe of what he was looking at. It was a shooter's paradise. From submachine guns to pistols, shotguns, and rifles, every type of weapon imaginable was hanging from the black pegboard on the wall. Large gun safes and green ammo-filled cans lined the surrounding wall.

"Holy shit," Rob said. "You have a fucking arsenal in here!"

"Yep, I like to be ready..."

"For fucking World War Three?" Rob asked.

"If need be. We're going to need these if we plan to save your sister."

"So you're going to help me?" asked Rob.

"Of course I'm going to help you," he replied. "We're a pair, man. And you're my best friend. I can't let you go in there alone. Who would watch your back?"

"Thanks, brother. I was hoping you would say that."

The two friends settled in for a long night of preparations and planning. Not only did they have to worry about finding the place—how would they get all the weapons and ammo they needed across the border into Mexico without being discovered by the law? But it's not as if they'd never infiltrated before. They'd find a way. Kyle knew just who to call for help.

⫲

The following morning, the men had set out just after sunup, gear and equipment loaded down in the bed. Rob was edgy, concerned for his sister. But he trusted Kyle knew what he was doing. He was counting on it.

"Where are we going?" Rob asked as Kyle drove his lifted F-250 pickup over the dusty road, past oil rigs and fluttering plains outside San Antonio, Texas.

It was now a little after noon, and they'd almost made it to their destination hours south of Kyle's hometown.

"We're going to see a friend of mine," Kyle replied. "His

name is José. He's a US citizen born in Mexico City. But some of his family came here illegally. Several just made it alive. Some died in the desert. But he knows a lot of the routes and tunnels that the Border Patrol and the Mexican police haven't found yet, the ones coyotes use."

"He won't talk?" asked Rob. "And you trust him?"

"Damn right, I trust him," Kyle said. "He's an old friend. Plus, he despises the cartels. Cartel members killed his younger cousin, Miguel, when he stumbled into one of their drug operations out in the Chihuahua desert. José has a vendetta against them. He'll help us for sure."

Kyle skidded to a stop on the gravel in front of a charming little three-bedroom, ranch-style house in the middle of nowhere. He put the vehicle into park and shut off the engine.

"This is the place," he said to Rob. "I hope he's here."

They both exited the truck, and Kyle grasped the chain-link fence gate at the opening of a stone pathway to a white, wooden porch.

"Hola, amigo," José said as he opened the screen door to meet them in the yard, wearing a white cowboy hat with a large, silver belt buckle and worn cowboy boots. "What you doing in my neck of the woods, hombre?"

José was an older gentleman, sixties, with semi-long wavy, gray hair past his shoulders and a finely trimmed beard and mustache. He looked like a cowboy right out of old Mexico.

"Hey, friend," Kyle returned as they shook hands. "This is my buddy and teammate, Sergeant First Class Rob Walker."

"How you doing, Sergeant Walker? Thank you for your service, son."

Rob grinned back at José.

"Please, call me Rob."

"Nice to meet you, Rob," José said. "Any friend of Kyle is a friend of mine."

José stood there, arms folded and wondering why the surprise visit from his old friend. Kyle had never shown up unannounced.

"So," José continued. "To what do I owe the pleasure?"

"Well," Kyle replied. "It might be best if we continue this conversation inside, if that's okay."

"Sure, it's okay," José said. "Come on in."

José ushered the two men to the living room, just past the front door, and showed them to the sofa.

"Have a seat. Can I offer you boys anything? Tea, whiskey, or something?"

"Patron, if you have it," said Kyle.

"If I have it?" José asked, laughing as he marched toward the corner bar in the same room. "Of course I do! A Mexican without tequila is just posing as one, my friend."

Rob looked around the room, noticing the Mexican decor spread around the house and an old 44 Largo repeating rifle displayed above the white brick fireplace. Paintings that depicted long past Mexican Wars, including the Mexican war of independence from Spain, hung from the wall around the living room and hallway. There was no mistaking that José was proud of his Mexican heritage. But one thing he was not proud of was the violence and turmoil the drug cartels and corrupt government officials had been causing for decades in his country.

José gave them each a glass full.

"So, you going to tell me what you guys are really doing down here?"

"Well, José," Kyle replied. "My friend here has a problem.

We were hoping you could help us out."

"I might," he said. "Depends on the problem."

"Well..."

Rob interrupted Kyle before he could finish his thought.

"It's my sister, Marianne," he told him. "She was picked up in New York by members of the Los Lobos cartel and taken into Mexico. I have a location. But I don't know how solid it is."

"The Los Lobos Cartel?" José asked. "Fuck. Those sons of bitches are ruthless, man. I am sorry to hear that. But why did they take her? Do you have any idea?"

"Yeah, I think I do," Rob said. "She was hooked on this fucking loser drug dealer up in Brooklyn. The gang he was with did some business with the cartel. I think she saw something, maybe walked into a drug deal going down. I'm not really sure of the specifics. But I know they took her."

"Juan Luis," José said. "That filthy pendejo. He's in charge of Los Lobos. Anyone who challenges him ends up dead."

"How do you know that?" asked Rob.

"I wasn't born under a rock. I'm from Mexico, amigo. I've had relatives murdered by his enforcers. The guy is a fucking maniac. Anyone who crosses him or his men ends up lost, probably dumped out in the desert or the sea somewhere. And the police don't do a fucking thing about it."

Rob took a quick gulp from his glass.

"What are you saying?" Rob asked him.

José paused for a moment.

"I am saying that if you want to go to war with them and find your sister, you must deal with him. But first, you have to go through his men. And, believe me, he has a lot of protection. And you can forget about the Mexican law. With few exceptions, they are not on your side. It is best you just avoid them altogether."

"Believe me," Rob said, "I plan to."

Rob glanced back at Kyle, knowing they were probably thinking the same thing.

"What about our guns and stuff? How do we smuggle them in without being detected? Where are these tunnels located? And who will we most likely cross paths with along the way?"

José rose from his chair and walked to the kitchen to grab a map from the drawer. He returned moments later, laying it out it across the table in front of them.

"See that spot right there?" he asked, circling in red ink a spot in the Arizona border region.

"Yep," Rob replied.

"That's it. The law on neither side has found it yet."

"It's in Arizona?" asked Rob. "I thought there was one here in Texas."

"It's the only one I know of so far," José said. "This is your safest bet."

"How come you never notified authorities about it?"

"Because, Mister Walker, I worry about my family. I don't want to be in the cartel's crosshairs."

"Good reason," said Rob. "Well, looks like we have a drive ahead of us."

"Who might we run into?" Kyle asked.

"You may run into a few runners or smugglers. They'll think it's odd you are sneaking into Mexico. Even if you spot any smugglers, they'll only be those who they paid to cross, not the cartel. They don't run their own drugs. They pay mules to do that for them. And they are too fearful of talking, particularly to Americans, and absolutely not to law enforcement. But, if you sense they made run and rat you out, kill them on the spot."

"Of course," Rob said.

"Your biggest concern will be not getting caught with the weapons," José continued, "so discretion is of the utmost concern. So you should move at night until you reach a safe house about fifty miles from the border. I don't know where the tunnel will lead. So be careful when you pop out. And, if anyone, especially the police, tries to search you, elude them at all costs. If not, you'll end up in a Mexican prison. Believe me, as a gringo, that is not a place you want to be."

Rob had already thought of that. They'd brought a couple of large camouflage rucksacks with them for the occasion, the very ones they'd used in battle. Rob's .300 Winchester Magnum long gun and his ghillie suit were his most valuable cargo. He figured he'd need them in the immense and expansive desert of Mexico.

"Sounds like a walk in the park," Kyle joked, knowing that it would be far from it.

"Anything else?" asked Rob.

"Yeah," José said, producing a news clipping from the end table drawer beside him. "Kill Juan. That fucker has ruined so many Mexican families and killed so many young Americans with his drugs. If you see him, put that bastard in the fucking ground with two shots to the head! Understand? I'll get you guys as far as the tunnel and point you in the right direction. After that, you're on your own."

"Oh, we'll get him," Rob told him. "And anyone else who gets in the way of finding my sister."

TEN

Douglas, Arizona

José left his old white Ford Aerostar Van by the side of the sandy road next to a patch of desert brush and cacti outside of the Arizona border. The town sat only a couple of miles from the Mexican-American border wall. It had been a long twenty-four-hour car ride west across desert plains and through steep, rocky canyons.

Tumbleweeds followed the wind over the road in front of them as they got ready for a hike. The place was secluded, a small, one-horse town of just over seventeen thousand people. Residents there had been used to living with a steady influx of illegal immigrants who made up a sizable portion of cheap labor in the mines, the area's largest industry.

But illegals weren't the only ones who'd made it across. The tunnel was among many built by the cartels in the early 2000s to smuggle drugs over the border. So far, they'd remained undetected. Nobody in that tiny town, easily reached by the cartel, would speak out against them. But everyone who lived there understood what was happening. The Cochise

County Sheriff was assassinated there ten years prior for reporting their criminal activity to the Feds. They never found his killer. Nobody had come close to narcing on them since for fear of a similar fate.

The cartels wouldn't just kill people they deemed enemies. They'd come after entire families. They were evil. And the Los Lobos Cartel leader, Juan Luis, had the Mexican Police in his hip pocket. It looked as though they were untouchable by the law and the system. But the cartel had yet to meet the likes of a pair of vengeful US Army Special Forces Operators.

The boys jumped from the vehicle, dressed inconspicuously in cargo pants, athletic T-shirts, and baseball caps, and filled their canteens from an igloo jug full of water. They seized their equipment carrier cases from the back of the van, strapping them to their backs. During the long drive, Rob and Kyle had spent most of that time getting their weapons ready, cleaning, and loading magazines with ammunition. They knew they'd be prepared for action by the time they arrived.

The men left the vehicle and followed José through the barren wasteland. The heat bore down on them as the temperature soared upwards of ninety-five degrees Fahrenheit. Rob wiped the dripping sweat from his eyebrows as they pressed through a scorching desert, toting over thirty-five pounds of gear. He paused for a moment to take a drink from his green, two-quart Army canteen.

As they crossed over the hill, José pointed to the front.

"There. It's right over there."

But they couldn't see anything ahead but dead shrubs and a tall cactus. The hole was hidden well. Rob and Kyle followed José down the slope until they came across a square patch of dead bush. José crouched down, sliding his hand between the dried-up scrubs until he gripped something beneath it. The metal made a grinding noise as he dragged the hatch across the ground and kicked the cover with his foot. There it was, an opening with metal steps that descended into the earth.

"It looks like nobody has used this one in a while," José said. "We would see tracks all over the place."

"Yeah, I noticed that," Rob replied.

"Maybe they dug another one," said José. "The cartels have many tunnels just like this. Some found, some not. You better believe when they find one, they have two or three more to take its place."

"I can imagine," said Rob.

"Anyway," José said. "There's no sense in waiting around here to be seen. You boys better head down."

Rob put a hand on Kyle's back and gingerly nudged him toward the hole.

"After you."

As Rob followed his buddy, suspended from the ladder, José clenched his right hand.

"Listen, hombre, remember what I said. Kill that motherfucker, for all of us. And good luck finding your sister. I will say a prayer for your family and for her and your safe return. But be careful. I don't know where this tunnel will lead you. Remember, you got nothing from me."

"Thanks, amigo," Rob said as he stepped down. "Will do. And thank you for your help and the ride. I owe you one."

"As long as you kill that man, you don't owe me a damn thing."

Rob removed a green chem light attached to the slots on the side of his ruck as his boot met the dirt thirty feet beneath the surface. He snapped it on, giving them the little light they would need to move around in the tunnel darkness.

The hole was only five and a half feet high. With both men nearing the six-foot mark, they'd need to crawl on their hands and knees the hundreds of feet to the other side of the border. But that should be a pinch for two men in better shape than most.

"All right, man," said Rob. "Looks like we're going to have to hug the dirt."

"Right behind you, partner," replied Kyle.

Rob hit his knees and lowered himself to the earth, his belly rubbing the ground as Kyle trailed behind him. The men inched hundreds of feet to the other side of the tunnel. Dirt and grime gathered across the front of their clothes as they pushed on, not sure of how long they'd need to crawl or where the tunnel would lead them.

As they neared the end, Rob touched his hand to the end of the hole.

"I think this is it."

Rob held the light up, locating another metal hatch above his head. Not sure if anyone was on the other side, he took the bag off his back to retrieve his suppressed .45 Glock from inside the top pouch.

"Good call," Kyle said as he snagged his.

Rob stuffed the gun into the back of his pants and tugged his shirt to conceal it. He used his hand to knock the dirt from his clothes. He reached up and forced the hatch open just enough to allow him a look. Rob picked up voices coming from the other side.

"Looks like someone's house," he whispered to Kyle. "Get ready for contact."

"I always am," replied Kyle.

Rob took a quick glimpse to ensure nobody would see them rise from the tunnel, not yet sure what they were dealing with or who they would run into. He opened up the rest of the way, and Kyle accompanied him to the corner wall of what looked like a utility room, letting the metal down softly to the floor. Rob took his sidearm and peeked around the corner.

"There are two, maybe three men in the living area. Get ready."

Rob could just see the men from his location, and he couldn't tell whether they had weapons on them. But they weren't going to take any chances.

"Let's do it," he said.

The men readied their guns and turned the corner to the living room. The occupants hadn't discovered them yet as they sat around, drinking beer and shouting at a football match on television. Rob and Kyle cornered them from behind.

"Don't fucking move," Rob ordered them. "Hands up, now."

"Who are you?" one of them asked as he held his hands in the air. "Why are you in my house?"

Rob kept his gun on the man while Kyle watched the other two.

"Any of you speak English?" asked Rob. "I speak little Spanish."

But none of them responded. One by one, Rob pointed his Glock at each of them.

"I'm only going to ask one more time. Do any of you speak English?"

One man slowly raised his hand.

"I do," the Mexican replied from the other side of the room.

"Okay, well," Rob said. "Now we're getting somewhere."

Rob stepped to the man, holding the barrel of his pistol against the side of his head.

"Are you guys with the cartel?" asked Rob.

He gazed up at Rob as if he couldn't believe the question.

"What?" the man replied. "No. Fuck those pendejos! We have nothing to do with them. Those fuckers are crazy, gringo!"

Rob poked the gun harder into his temple.

"No? Really? Then why is there a fucking hole in your laundry room?"

The man dropped to his knees and seemed as if he was about to cry.

"What is your name?" Rob asked as he stood over him.

The man was scared and nervous, trembling like a leaf.

"I'm Antonio, Mister... Don't hurt me, please!"

"Well, Antonio, you have precisely three seconds to answer me. Then we will kill every single one of you."

He peered up at Rob, unmistakably terrified.

"Mister, they made us do it! The cartel threatened me and said they would kill my entire family if we didn't go along with it. But we have nothing to do with them, I swear! Those guys are fucking animals!"

Rob glanced behind him, seeing the startled look on each of their faces. Realizing that they weren't gangsters, he lowered his gun.

"Look, Antonio," he said, "I believe you. And you never saw us here, got it?"

Antonio bowed his head.

"Yes, Mister. Whatever you say."

"If I find out you lied to me," Rob said, "or told anyone you saw us, we will come back here and finish you all. I don't care if it's your fucking mother, not a word to anyone."

Antonio didn't reply. He just bent, shivering.

"Do you understand what I'm telling you, Antonio?"

"Sí!" he shouted. "Yes, yes, I understand."

"I'm glad we could come to an agreement," Rob said. "You three have a nice day, now."

He and Kyle slipped through the front door, packs over their shoulders and leaving the Mexicans to wonder what the hell had just happened. Trusting no one in Mexico, they would tell no one why they were there. They knew they needed to get the hell out of there as soon as possible. José had suggested an empty house that he sometimes used when visiting relatives. He'd given them permission to use it so long as it wasn't damaged. They would need a place to stay and prepare as they planned their next move.

Rob continued down the front steps, searching the yard for something they could use to hightail it out of there. He located a couple of old dirt bikes sitting under a canopy next to the small, tan adobe-style house.

"Over here," he said to Kyle, pointing at the bikes.

"Perfect," replied Kyle. "Let's get away from here."

The two mounted the dirt bikes, kick-starting and revving the engines. They rode away in a rush, gliding across the ground and kicking up dust and dirt on their way down the bumpy, unpaved stretch of road.

A forty-five-minute bike ride later, on an empty path void of any other soul, they entered the road on the map. They found the house up ahead as the motorbikes bounced from the road over the hill on the two-car-wide dirt road north of the Sonora Desert. Steep red canyons lined the backdrop, facing the flat and dry desert below them.

The light breeze sent litter and dust across the road in front of them as both men moved across the sand beside a rusty chain-link fence surrounding the unoccupied house. Stacked tires and old car parts were scattered across the surrounding yard. It mirrored a typical lower-class Mexican home, ideal for an indistinct hideout. They couldn't hide that they were both gringos in a country where they didn't speak the language, but they knew how to blend in. As long as nobody knew their real purpose, they would remain incognito.

Rob pushed the kickstand down with his foot, hopping off next to the crooked front yard gate. He glanced down at the map José had given him, noting the red circle around the address.

"This looks like the place. I think it'll work for now. But in a few hours, we have another long trip through this fucking desert again. We'd better get some rest."

Rob and Kyle knew they wouldn't be staying there for long. José had given them a list as a starting point, with the assurance they wouldn't involve him or disclose his identity. They had some people to talk to and some questions to be answered.

⁂

The Los Lobos Cartel boss, Juan Luis, got out of his sparkling black Mercedes-Benz. Guards circled him on all sides as they accompanied Juan to the inside of an old, plain-looking motel. It was situated just outside the city of Culiacán, the capital of Sinaloa, Mexico. With a flashy new gray Armani suit and white snakeskin boots, Juan was the embodiment of money. The cartel controlled the motel, as they did many other businesses in the region. But it wasn't open to the public. It was one of many of its kind they had used to house their working girls.

Everyone feared Juan, even rival cartel bosses. He'd grown

a reputation over the years of being cruel. If anyone in the organization snitched or did anything he believed unfaithful, Juan would have them hacked up and left for the wild animals.

As the most prominent cartel boss in Mexico, Juan also had much of the law and politicians on his side. And he had the cash to pay for it. He'd slip them dinero to look the other way when the murder rates went up. It allowed him to continue expanding his operations and taking over vast swaths of territory, even from other cartels.

The last cartel war ended with Juan and his men butchering hundreds of enemies and civilians. The killing was a way of life for him. And he would do anything to maintain his grip on power, even if it meant killing members of his own family. Nobody got in the way of his money. If they did, they were handled accordingly.

Juan addressed a line of girls they'd freshly smuggled into Mexico from the United States. He looked each one up and down as he walked down the line in front of them. One of those girls was Marianne Walker. She was doped up pretty bad and was utterly incoherent. She couldn't sit up straight and didn't even realize where she was.

Juan glanced down at her face and breasts.

"Excellent," Juan said as he stroked the side of Marianne's hair. "You are lovely, my dear."

Marianne stared up at him, brown hair masking her hollow eyes. She was too far gone to speak. She'd become a tool, another means for the cartel to make more cash. Sex workers for the cartel were nothing more than property. And once they were incapable of performing, they disappeared. Another girl could undoubtedly take their place. But Juan took an interest in Marianne.

Juan drew a hand back and whacked Marianne hard across the face, knocking her down to the floor and leaving a red hand mark on her cheek. She lay on the ground, groaning and too feeble to move.

Juan whispered in one of his men's ears. The guy jerked Marianne from the floor and ordered her into a nearby room. He tied her to the bedpost and shoved a white rag into her mouth so she couldn't squeal.

"Where did we get this one?"

"Boss," one of them said. "She came from New York. Mister Buchanan failed to deliver some cash, so we took her instead."

"Impressive," replied Juan. "We should be able to make a ton off her. Did you kill that fucking dickhead, Mike?"

"No, boss," he said. "But we heard somebody else did. They found the body yesterday morning."

Juan took him by the throat.

"What did I say about those who cross us?" asked Juan. "What the fuck did I tell you? It does no good if someone else kills him. We are the ones to fear. You should have killed him yourself. I can't be fucking everywhere!"

"Boss!" the man moaned under Juan's grip.

Juan pressed even tighter.

"Why didn't you kill him? Answer me."

He let go of his neck, leaving him gulping for air. Juan brandished his .45 Desert Eagle from his suit coat pocket, directing it at his head.

"You know what happens to those who disobey me!"

"I know, boss," he said. "It won't happen again. I promise!"

"It better not. Or you'll be the one I dump into the sea. Do you fucking understand me? You do what I tell you to do!"

"Yes, boss. Yes, I'm sorry!"

Juan placed the gun back into his coat. He balled his fist, punched the man in the stomach, and watched him hunch over, trying to regain his senses and spitting up on the floor.

"Now," Juan said as the man tried to stand up straight, holding his abdomen. "Get these girls ready to work. We aren't making any money with them sitting around!"

"Right away, boss."

As Juan and his men began walking back to his car, he received a call on his cell.

"What?" he asked. "I'm kind of fucking busy right now!"

"I know, boss, I know. But I thought you would want to hear this!"

"Hear what?" asked Juan.

"Our associates in New York, boss."

"Yeah, what about them?"

There was a brief pause on the line.

"Well, somebody killed them both right after the deal went bad," the caller said.

"And?" said Juan. "So they're both dead. What does that have to do with us? Gangs kill each other all the time, especially in New York."

"You don't find that strange, boss? Maybe the killer knows the girl. Maybe he's coming for her."

Juan just chuckled.

"You serious? Come after us? He would need a whole fucking army to do that. Nobody comes for us, cabrón. We go after them."

"All right, boss," the caller said. "I just thought you should know."

"Well," Juan replied, "I don't give a shit about those assholes.

Let them kill each other. We can always find others to take their place. Thanks for wasting my fucking time!"

He pressed the end button on the call and tossed his phone onto the seat as he climbed into the back of the car.

"Come after us? That's the fucking dumbest shit I've ever heard!"

Juan signaled for one of his associates to join him in the car.

"Javier," he said. "Get over here!"

Javier was the man Juan had put in charge of his sex trafficking operation. He was one of the few people Juan trusted. And Javier would do anything to make the boss happy. The last thing he wanted to do was to get on his nasty side.

Javier rushed over and sat next to Juan in the back of the car. Juan glanced up at his bodyguards, requiring some privacy.

"Leave us! We have business to discuss!"

His guards scampered away as Juan closed the door behind them.

"What is it, boss?" asked Javier.

"Well, Javier," Juan replied. "As you know, we've been working on developing our operations overseas. I have a few buyers lined up in the international market."

"Really? That's great, boss."

"So far, it seems like Prince Ashir, the one from Dubai, is going to be our biggest spender."

"I bet he has deep pockets!" Javier said.

"Very deep," Juan said. "He'll be here in a couple of weeks to sample the merchandise."

"Great, boss," replied Javier.

"And I think the new girl would be perfect for him, so don't use her up. I don't want to spoil the bitch before he gets here."

"Sure, boss. Whatever you say. I'll make sure of it."

"Good," Juan told him. "Now, get to work. I have other matters to tend to."

ELEVEN

```
Coahuila, Mexico
```

After a day-long drive down twisting roads and rough, off-road trails, Rob and Kyle shed their gear at the Hotel Jiménez, just on the town's outskirts in northern Mexico. Though mostly sparse and desert, Jiménez was met in areas by luscious trees and greenery.

The men were back on the road, headed down to the Santa Cruz Restaurant, a family-owned spot in the center of the small town. They were specifically looking for the whereabouts and details of the Los Lobos cartel's human trafficking ring. But Rob and Kyle both knew going in that they would have trouble getting people to talk. The cartel, the most notoriously violent in all of Mexico, dominated out of fear. They would put a hit out on anyone they believed had double-crossed them. Police officers, soldiers, politicians, grandmothers, it didn't matter. There was no community in Mexico, America, or elsewhere they couldn't touch. They even had operations in the Philippines and Europe.

Distribution hubs had been set in secret in towns

internationally to distribute smuggled drugs or other cargo to local gangs for sale on the streets in cities like Los Angeles, Chicago, and New York. Nobody, not even the DEA or Mexican authorities, had been able to shut them down. Many Mexican officials were terrified to speak against them. It had long become a nightmare for governments to handle the massive rise of people who'd overdosed on highly potent and addictive drugs such as Fentanyl and heroin.

The cartel's new MO, sex trafficking, had already crushed many families across the United States and Mexico. Both young and older female family members faded into obscurity, leaving no trail behind. It was a tragic situation for those who'd never see their wives, sisters, or daughters ever again. They had no one to turn to. Now, Rob's sister was their latest victim.

Guns concealed under their clothes, the pair left the motorbikes in front of the small, white building and went inside. They took seats at a table in the center of the room and waited. Glancing down at a menu written in Spanish, Rob could make out bits and pieces of what he was looking at.

The establishment had the feel of an old mom-and-pop kind of place. In fact, it was. A sign that read "Maria's" hung outside above the double-door entrance. The restaurant had a warm and welcoming feeling. But the men weren't just there to taste the delicious food.

A server approached, holding a pen and pad, and set pairs of silverware and napkins on the round table.

"Puedo tomar su pedidos, caballeros?" she asked.

But neither had any idea what she'd said.

"Permiso. Ustedes hablan español?"

"Muy poco," Rob replied.

"I'm sorry, sir. I didn't realize you were Americans. What I said was, may I take your order?"

"Yes, María," Rob replied, glancing at her name tag. "Two burritos, no habanero sauce, lots of sour cream, and a bottle of Montejo, please."

"Yep, same for me," Kyle said to her.

"Excellent, gentlemen," she replied. "Your beers will be out soon."

"Gracias," Rob said.

She grabbed their menus from the table and returned to the kitchen.

Rob began looking around the room, noticing how empty it was. In fact, there were only four patrons, including them, in the whole place. But he and Kyle weren't there by chance. They were looking for someone, a kid José had alluded to on the long ride to Arizona, who purportedly had family who worked for the cartel. His name was Jesús García. José knew little more about him. But his older son, Pablo, used to hang around him before José put a stop to it. That family was terrible news by association. At least, in his mind.

As the waitress opened the double doors, carrying two bottles of beer and a basket, Rob's eyes met a young kid washing dishes in the back. He had long, straight black hair, a tattoo on his left arm, and wore a dirty, white apron.

Rob waited for Maria to set the beers and a basket of tortilla chips on the table.

"There you go, sirs," she said to them. "Food will be here in a minute."

"Gracias, señorita," replied Rob, his eyes still glued to the kid.

Rob put a chip in his mouth. He glanced up and noticed a kid working behind the kitchen. Rob nudged Kyle in the side to get his attention.

"Look," said Rob. "The one washing dishes. I think that's him."

Kyle followed Rob's head movement toward the other side of the room. "You sure?"

"He matches the description José gave us. And he's the only kid I see in here."

"You think he's related to the waitress?"

"I don't know," Rob said. "Could be. He said this place was family-owned."

They began eating their food while periodically peeking up at the kid to make sure he hadn't left. A few minutes later, as they threw back the rest of their beers, Rob saw the boy exit through the back door. He got up, tossing a twenty-dollar bill on the table.

"Let's go have a chat."

The men proceeded through the front door and moved around to the back of the restaurant. The kid was taking a break, smoking a cigarette, and playing a game on his phone as he sat back on top of a stack of milk crates.

His eyes met Rob's as they turned the corner past a large dumpster. The kid appeared stunned, as if he thought they were going to rob him.

"Excuse us," Rob said as they approached. "Are you Jesús? Jesús García?"

He looked Rob up and down.

"Who wants to know?" he asked in English, glimpsing up at Rob.

"We do," he said. "I'm Rob, and this is Kyle."

"You are a long way from home, gringo. What are you doing down here?"

"We just have some questions for you, Jesús. About El Carnicero."

Jesús's jaw dropped as he gave them a blank stare. Rob could tell he knew who he was referring to. Instead of answering, he quickly bound from his seat and started running at full speed down the alley and across the street.

"We just have some questions, Jesús!" Rob shouted as they took off after him. "Why are you running?"

But he didn't slow a bit. Jesús tried his best to lose them, dodging and looping around cars and between businesses and houses.

"Stop running!" Rob said as he and Kyle raced across the road. "We're not going to hurt you!"

Rob bolted as fast as he could, slowly gaining on him. As Jesús turned another building corner, Rob caught up with him. He dove straight ahead, hitting Jesús on his back and knocking him to the dirt, leaving scrapes underneath his torn shirt.

"Damn it, kid! I told you we wouldn't harm you. What the hell are you running for?"

"You don't understand, Mister," Jesús replied as Rob hovered over him. "Nobody talks about that around here. Nobody! I care too much about my life!"

Rob knelt on the ground beside the boy.

"Listen, son. We aren't here to hurt you. We just have some questions. They snatched my sister up from the States. We are pretty sure they had something to do with it."

Jesús sobbed into his hands, tears running down both cheeks.

"They killed my sister, Ana," he uttered. "She was only

twelve! Some of my cousin's work for them. If I talk, they will kill the rest of my family and me!"

"Trust me, Jesús," Rob added, touching him on his shoulder. "They will never find out. We can and will handle it. No harm will come to you or your family. I just need you to talk to me and tell me everything you know about them."

"Yeah? Who is going to protect me? You and what army? There are so many of them!"

"Listen," said Rob. "I gotta save my sister. We are going to bring hell down on these people. They will harm no one ever again. But we need your help. Is there someplace we can speak in private?"

"You promise to leave me out of it?"

"Yes, Jesús," he said. "We promise."

"If they find out, I'm as good as dead. The restaurant is my family's livelihood. They'll burn it to the ground and dump our bodies in the desert."

The boy wiped the tears from his face and then brushed the dirt from his beige pants.

"We aren't here to put you in danger, kid. We are here to stop it. Give us a little, and we'll do what we have to. Nobody will know. But we need somewhere to start."

"Bueno, fine," replied Jesús. "Follow me. I don't want anyone to see me with you."

Jesús got up from the ground and directed them to a small home nearby and across the street. If he was going to tell what he knew, he needed to make sure nobody else was within hearing distance of them. They could trust nobody when it came to the cartels. Some would turn in their friends to save their own skin. That was an unfortunate, well-known fact in that part of Mexico.

Rob and Kyle knew Jesús was scared to death of the cartel. He had every right to be. He'd admitted they'd forced his cousins to work for them. That was a terrible position to be in. If the cartel had caught wind that two outsiders were in town questioning people, Jesús's people would surely be in danger. They couldn't let that happen. The men didn't want innocent people to die. But they needed to speak with these cousins. It was the only lead they had. If they were going to find out more about their operations and bring themselves closer to finding Rob's sister, then so be it. They needed to know who Jesús's relatives reported to. There was always a lower-level boss in each syndicate. Like a Fortune 500 company, they managed the cartel as a business, a very violent one.

One by one, they'd bring down each one until they found where the sex slaves were held, starting at the bottom and working their way up. Punishment was on Rob's agenda. He wanted to look them in the eyes and make them feel all the suffering they had caused so many innocent people. Jesús mentioned the location of one of his cousins. His name was Carlos. The guy worked out of a local tire shop, not very far outside of town. But they weren't just selling tires. They used the shop as a front to smuggle drugs into the United States by hiding them in the tires and driving straight through the border checkpoint. Border patrol seized some.

But the majority slipped right through the crowded, understated checkpoint and made it to their destination. The ones who didn't make it ended up in jail, the cartel washing their hands of them. They wouldn't speak to the law, so the border patrol could never put the runners and the cartels together. With the poor Mexican economy, they could make much more money as drug mules than they ever did at their day jobs.

Rob and Kyle were getting ready to head that way. But in the middle of the afternoon, they weren't about to make their presence known with witnesses around.

"We need some new wheels," Rob said to Kyle as they made their way down the road on foot. "These bikes are just too damn loud."

They'd left the bikes behind, wandering through a parking lot to search for a car they could lift.

"Hey, what about this one?" Kyle asked as they came upon an old and slightly beat-up gray Ford Focus.

"Yeah," Rob replied. "That should do nicely."

To his shock, the driver's side door wasn't locked. Rob reached in, opening the rest of the doors, and tossed his ruck onto the backseat.

"Give me your pack," he said to Kyle.

Rob snatched Kyle's ruck and tossed it behind, and hopped into the driver's seat.

"Can you hot-wire this thing?" asked Kyle.

"Yeah, I think so. Give me a second."

Kyle ran around to the passenger side while Rob jammed his knife to break the lock pin. He whipped the gun from his pants and pounded a few times on the end of the blade, breaking the pin. Rob removed the plastic panel from the steering column, exposing the bundle of wiring. He pulled the red wire out and, with the knife, removed the insulation at the tip.

"Come on!" he said as he let go and touched the wires together repeatedly. "Work, you bastard!"

But nothing happened.

"Try the other one!" Kyle said.

Rob yanked on the green wire, cutting off the end. He connected it. Suddenly, the radio came on as the engine turned over and starting humming.

"Ha!" he said. "Now we're in business."

They closed the doors and raced out of that parking lot before anyone could see them. They arrived in the late evening, and Rob stopped the car along the road across from the shop. Jesús had given them a description of Carlos's car, a candy apple red convertible Pinto with a white top. He obviously hadn't bought the car with money he'd made working in a tire shop.

Almost two hours went by. The sun had gone down. They talked about random things while waiting for Carlos to appear. Then Kyle spotted someone exiting the shop under the pole light.

"Hey, there he is."

They watched as Carlos jumped into his car, switched the hydraulics and the headlights, and kicked up debris as he tore out into the roadway.

Rob pulled out onto the street a couple of hundred meters behind him.

"Let's see where the prick takes us."

They followed behind Carlos as he took a left onto another two-lane road farther out into the desert. Ten miles down the road, Carlos swung the car right into the driveway of a single-wide trailer. The place was trashy, an old type of mobile home one would expect to see in a run-down trailer park. Rob passed the trailer by a couple of hundred feet and swerved off the road into the bush. They left the car, guns ready, and made their way across the street and toward the property.

"Keep an eye out," Rob said. "We don't know how many are in there."

"Roger that," replied Kyle.

The men skulked across the ground, staying low so their silhouettes wouldn't show in the bright moonlight. Rob held up a fist at the end of the desert field, halting them in place to take a quick look at the house. Then he spotted a single man taking a piss behind the back porch of the rusty trailer.

"He's not alone. Come on, quietly. Let's get this over with."

Rob pressed on, and Kyle followed him to the front door, glancing into a large window at the side of the rickety porch.

"Shit," said Rob. "It looks like a lab. They got a meth operation or something going on here. A single shot or spark could blow this place sky-high."

"What do you have in mind?" asked Kyle.

"Let's shut it down for good. That'll get El Jefe nice and pissed off."

He gripped the doorknob and started turning it slowly, grabbing his gun with his other hand. He bumped the door open, and they entered quietly. As Rob peeked through a curtain hanging from the doorway, he found two men hovering over the lab in the next room.

Rob inched his way forward, and Kyle faced the opposite direction in case of any surprises.

"Don't fucking move. Get your hands up and don't even think about trying anything."

"Qué pasa?" one of them asked. "Quién eres tú?"

Rob was astounded to see that they were just boys, probably still in their teens. But one of them tried to make a break past them. Rob snatched him by the shirt collar, shoving him back into place.

"I said don't move!"

"I don't think they speak English," Kyle said.

"Just watch them while I look around," Rob told him. "If they move, slice them."

He started going through the trailer, room by room. But as Rob wandered down the hall, a familiar face popped up through the back door. Rob held his piece on him.

"What the hell, man?" asked Carlos. "Who the fuck are you? What are you doing here?"

"I'll be asking the questions, Carlos. Now, get in there with the others."

Rob forced him to the other room and made him sit on a dirty white lounge chair nearby.

"Now, Carlos," Rob said. "I have a few questions for you, and you're going to answer them. Or I'm going to be really pissed off. Trust me, you don't want that."

"How the fuck do you know my name?"

Rob took him by the mouth and pinched.

"I said I'm asking the fucking questions! Now, who do you work for? Give me a name!"

"What? I can't!" he yelled. "I can't tell you that!"

Carlos tried to flee, but Rob clutched him by the shirt and shoved him back down in the seat. He got down in front of Carlos and pressed his K-Bar knife to his cheek.

"You will, Carlos. If not, this will be your metal coffin. We aren't fucking around. You get what I'm saying to you? And if you try to run again, I will slit your throat. You won't make it to the door. So don't play games with me!"

"I just can't! Why do you want to know, anyway? I don't fucking know you!"

"Indulge me, Carlos," Rob said. "You want to live beyond

today? Or do you want to end up in ashes scattered across the fucking ground?"

"Vete a la mierda!" Carlos yelled, hitting his hands on his legs. "Why does it matter to you?"

Rob put his finely sharpened blade to Carlos's neck and pricked it to make it bleed.

"Let's just say that I have a personal stake in it. Tell me about the cartel's human trafficking operation."

"What?" asked Carlos. "I know nothing about that. I'm just a meth cook!"

"Who does, Carlos? Your boss? Where can I find him?"

Carlos froze in silence.

"If you don't answer me, this is going to end poorly for you and your buddies here. I'm giving you a chance. Tell me, or we will just finish you all right here and leave you to fucking rot."

Rob glanced back at Kyle, who still had his knife on the other two. He put more pressure on the blade, letting blood trickle down Carlos's neck and onto his shoulder.

"Five..." Rob started counting.

"Four..." he said, pressing the tip of the blade further into his skin.

"Three..."

"Two..."

Rob leaned into his neck with his body weight.

"One..."

"Okay!" Carlos screamed. "Okay, fuck. I'll tell you!"

"Smart kid," Rob said as he lowered his weapon. "Now, where can I find him?"

Carlos panted, touching the bloody slit as his head sagged.

"I am dead if he finds out I talked."

"You'll be dead a lot sooner if you don't. Tell me what I need to know, and I'll let you loose."

"His name is Eduardo Hernández, okay?" Carlos said, shaking in fear. "He lives in a villa in San Pedro, near Monterrey. But he always has guards around. You will never get past them!"

"That's a good boy."

Rob pulled a lighter from his pocket.

"We'll worry about the guards. And don't worry, Carlos. You can just tell them bandidos robbed you. Or that a rival cartel tried to kill you. I really don't give a shit."

Rob released his grip on Carlos. The three looked alarmed as he took a piece of paper from the table.

"What are you going to do with that?" Carlos asked.

Rob lit the piece of scrap paper on fire.

"You're fucking crazy!" shouted Carlos.

"I'd get out of here if I were you," Rob told them. "Unless you want to be cremated."

They all flew from the trailer as Rob flung the paper onto the littered counter. He and Kyle darted through the front door behind them.

"I think you guys are going to have to find a new line of work," Rob said as he crossed the road and ducked.

The table abruptly went up in flames. They stared as the fire rose high into the ceiling, consuming everything in its path. The lab detonated, and a massive blast erupted and sent pieces of torn metal and broken glass flying everywhere. Carlos and the others saw as their meth lab burned to a crisp, flames spitting out from the tangled windows and torching the surrounding metal.

Rob shoved Carlos back.

"Get the fuck out of here before I change my mind and

shoot your ass for cooking this shit!"

Carlos appeared dazed and confused, trying to make sense in his head of what just happened. But Rob wasn't playing with him. He sent two warning shots into the air.

"Go! Run!"

Carlos and his buddies took off in a rush, running through the dark field behind them. Rob couldn't wait to meet this notorious drug boss and one of Luis's lieutenants they'd heard about. He was just getting started.

TWELVE

San Pedro
Monterrey, Mexico

The pair crawled to the top of that hill, hundreds of meters from the presumed mountainside villa of Eduardo Hernández in the Monterrey suburb. Rob had removed the folded 300 Winchester Magnum sniper rifle from its case and screwed the suppressor to the tip of the barrel. They had a bird's-eye view from their nest high above. With his ghillie suit on, Rob flipped the bipod down and removed the lens covers from the high-powered rifle scope. Kyle, a couple feet to Rob's left, adjusted his Leupold spotting scope. Also a trained sniper, Kyle had his long gun set and ready nearby. They'd need the added firepower if they were going to handle Eduardo's muscle.

Rob knew that as soon as they nabbed him, the entire Los Lobos Cartel would be gunning for them, if they weren't already. But he was used to it. As a lethal Special Forces sharpshooter in Afghanistan, the Taliban had placed a fifty-thousand-dollar bounty on Rob's head. He'd killed many al-Qaeda and Taliban leaders over the years. So Rob wasn't particularly concerned about that. His only worry was finding his sister, even if it killed him. He would send her back home to their mother.

"On the glass," Rob said to his spotter as he glanced through the reticle. "Call it."

Kyle held his right eye to the lens and focused.

"Eight hundred meters at the fountain," he replied.

Looking through the spotting scope to adjust for wind, Kyle noticed the trees around the residence blowing from their two o'clock.

"Wind, twelve miles per hour, half-value."

"Perfect," Rob said, using formulas in his head he'd long memorized as he began clicking the windage and elevation turrets.

The mansion sat in the center of the spacious property with a giant water fountain out front and Saint Francis's statue by the high, double-door entrance. Trees bordered each side of the long, paved driveway with a tall, concrete wall circling the boundary. A wrought-iron gate was at the front between two stone pillars with a guard shack next to it. The place indicated someone who had the wealth to pay for his protection. But Eduardo didn't yet realize precisely how much he needed it.

Rob glanced around the sizable estate, noting and counting in his head how many men were posted outside.

"I've got two men at the gate," he told Kyle. "Two by the door, and five more spread around that I can see. It looks like they're all carrying Uzi submachine guns."

"No telling how many are inside," Kyle said.

"I don't see our man yet, though," said Rob. "Remember, we need his ass alive, at least until he tells us what we need to know."

The cartels were remarkably well armed. But they couldn't hit what they couldn't see. With a well-disciplined Special Forces Operator behind the long gun, they'd never see it coming.

Rob trained his weapon on the two guards at the gate.

"I'll deal with these assholes first."

"Hold one," Kyle told him, detecting something coming from the left. "I've got a vehicle coming at our nine o'clock, a black Range Rover."

"Yeah," Rob said. "I see it."

The vehicle pulled up to the gate and slowed as the gate guards readily moved out of the way. They opened up the entrance to allow them to pass through.

"They didn't even check it. That's got to be Eduardo."

The Rover moved around the circular drive and stopped just in front of the white pillars that made up the house's entry. Four guards stepped from the vehicle. One held the back door open for a gentleman wearing a black silk shirt, shiny black boots, and gold aviator sunglasses.

"I believe we have a winner," Rob said. "God, he looks gaudy, like a damn eighties episode of Miami Vice."

"Money buys poor taste, I guess," Kyle replied.

The men saw the guards surround Eduardo as they entered the home. Rob turned his rifle toward the two at the gate.

"Get ready."

Kyle moved the spotting scope to his right and positioned his rifle to his front, suppressor already attached.

"Remember," Rob continued, "we do this together."

"Roger that, partner," said Kyle.

Rob set his aim for the guard to the left of the small guard shack. Kyle took the one on the right.

With his finger over the trigger, Rob took in a deep breath while glancing through the glass. He touched the cold metal trigger with the tip of his finger and readied himself to execute.

"Three, two, one, now."

At the same moment, both men sent rounds flying into the gate guards' bodies, causing both of them to tumble back where they stood, blood splashing out and dotting the black metal gate.

"They're down," said Rob.

Kyle focused his glass on the drive right behind the gate.

"I have a rover over here. Get him before he finds his buddies."

"He's mine," said Rob.

Rob shifted his rifle until the third guard came into view. Before the man could reach the gate, Rob let go of another 7.62 mm round that hit him in the neck and almost severed his head, flinging him off the drive and into the pristine grass.

"Tango down," he said.

But then, out of nowhere, a window opened, and an M249 SAW (squad automatic weapon) machine gun popped up and began firing up at the side of the mountain in rapid succession.

"Shit!" Rob yelled as they snatched their gear and rolled behind the hill. "Someone must've seen the body!"

"Sounds like a fucking SAW!" Kyle said over the piercing sound of rounds pounding the hills in front of them. "I never thought I'd get shot at by one of those! They can't see us, you know?"

The M249 SAW was a light machine gun used by the US military. It fired the 5.56-millimeter cartridge, the same one used in M4 and M16 rifles. Unlike those, it was belt-fed, fired on automatic, and could shoot up to one thousand rounds per minute. However, extended firing with no break would melt the barrel after turning it a bright red. The drug lords had them smuggled, among many other firearms, into Mexico from the United States to arm their drug wars with other cartels, the Mexican Army, and police. You could say that the US was unwittingly arming them.

"Yeah," Rob replied, slipping further down the hillside, "but they could get lucky. It would never be that easy, anyway."

Kyle followed Rob down the hill and back to flat ground.

"I guess we're going to have to do this the hard way," Rob said.

Kyle followed as Rob snaked down the back and to another hill close by. He crawled up and laid his rifle out front. It was an evasion tactic employed by many snipers, pulling back out of sight and changing positions to keep the enemy guessing.

"There we go," he said. "At this range, they won't be able to spot us ghillied up."

The gunner had stopped firing, probably thinking he'd either killed them or scared them away. But they had no idea who they were dealing with. Nor could they hear the shots from the compound.

Rob set his eyes on the gunman, who was still in the window behind the machine gun.

"I got his ass."

He squeezed the trigger and watched as the round shot forward with incredible power. It tore straight through the man's head and left it a bloody mess as his body crashed against the wall behind him. His corpse slid down, leaving a bloody trail down the wall.

"Lights out," said Rob.

"Don't look now, brother," Kyle said. "But we have six more moving through the gate."

Rob turned his scope and caught the men whisking through the gate in their direction. He fired, striking two of them with one shot as the round pierced the first man's chest and exited through his back.

Both men saw as the four other guards moved to cover behind the wall.

"Well, shall we?" Kyle asked.

Rob ejected the bullet casing from his rifle and dropped the magazine, replacing it. He retrieved the M4 beside him and put the sniper rifle into his bag, settling it on his back.

"Yep," he replied. "Let's go get this motherfucker."

They crouched and started advancing down the front of the hill. Kyle paused for a moment.

"Wait," he said. "I have an idea."

Rob waited for him to continue.

"They don't know there are two of us," Kyle said.

"You're probably right," Rob told him.

"So," Kyle said, "you go down there with your hands up and pretend to surrender, and I'll get them as they get closer."

"That could work," Rob replied. "But if they shoot me, I'm blaming you."

Kyle hid behind a tree as Rob advanced onward, his hands held high. They guessed the guards wouldn't kill him until Eduardo could get his hands on him. Rob just hoped that assumption was correct.

"I give up!" Rob said to them.

All four men emerged from behind the compound wall, holding submachine guns on him.

"You stupid gringo!" one of them yelled in Spanish.

"You're going to get it now. Don't fucking move!"

Rob held up in place, acting scared.

"Who hired you, ese?" another man asked in Spanish. "The Caro Quinterro (Sinaloa Cartel), or Vicente Carrillo Fuentes (Juárez Cartel)? You can tell them they ain't getting shit from us. But the boss is going to have some fun with you, asshole!"

The men proceeded toward Rob while Kyle kept a watchful eye on them. Then, as soon as they walked past the gate, practically in single file, Kyle opened fire. None of them even had the chance to fire their weapons. They collapsed to the ground on top of one another right in front of him.

"Fuck, man!" Rob said. "I can't believe that actually worked!"

Kyle met Rob in the driveway.

"Come on," said Rob. "Let's snatch him before he runs away like a pussy."

They hurried for the door. But as Rob gripped the knob, he realized it was bolted shut. He moved to a window on the right side and broke it with the butt of his rifle, sending pieces of glass everywhere. They climbed in.

Rob and Kyle began scouring the large house, finding no other guards on the floor.

"First floor, clear," Rob said before he started climbing the shiny marble staircase to the second story, Kyle by his side. "Watch out. There could be others up here."

They reached a large bedroom, each man facing opposite directions. Rob opened the door somewhat to take a glimpse.

"It's weirdly quiet in here," Kyle said.

"You can say that again," replied Rob. "I counted nine guards, including the gunner. Maybe that was all of them."

Rob passed in front of the bathroom door on the other side, holding his ear to it.

"I hear some heavy breathing in there. What do you think?"

Kyle simply shrugged his arms.

"Fuck it," said Rob.

He kicked the door as hard as he could with his right boot, breaking the latch and sending it flying back and tearing a hole in the wall behind it. Eduardo Hernández, cartel lieutenant, held a .40 caliber gun in his right hand and pointed it at Rob.

"You both will fucking die!" Eduardo yelled. "Guardias, guardias!"

But there was nobody there to heed his call.

Rob squeezed off a round that went right through his hand, causing him to release the gun to the ground. Rob kicked it across the floor.

"You bitch!" Eduardo screamed as he held his hand tight, blood dripping down his palm. "That is my shooting hand!"

"You won't need it anymore," Rob said, jerking him by his shirt. "Now, move, asshole!"

They escorted Eduardo down the stairs and outside to his car and ordered him into the back while Kyle kept his gun on him. Rob began tying his hands and feet with rope.

"Perhaps you should have hired more security," Rob told him as Eduardo saw the bodies littering the ground.

"Where the fuck are you taking me?" Eduardo asked. "You know my men will kill you for this."

Kyle struck him hard in the face, and he winced in pain, clenching his jaw.

"Shut the fuck up!" Kyle told him, shoving him deeper into the backseat and holding a gun to his head.

"Oh, look here," Rob said as he put the Range Rover into gear. "The keys are already here. And don't you worry about where we're going. We're taking you to a nice little spot in the middle of nowhere where nobody will disturb us. It'll just be the three of us."

Rob shot out of the drive and into the roadway, driving Eduardo a few miles outside of town to a dirt trail just off the main road. Kyle held his pistol on Eduardo for the roughly ten-minute car ride. Rob pulled off the road and up a car-wide path, stopping half a mile in.

He got out of the car, lugging Eduardo from the back, and shoved him to the dirt. Rob cut a piece of para-cord from a spool and began tying Eduardo to a Palo Verde tree.

"What the fuck do you want, you motherfucker?" Eduardo asked, spitting in Rob's direction. "My boss will hunt you like an animal for this!"

"That not very nice," Rob said as he wiped the spit from his arm. "But I'll allow you to redeem yourself. Tell me about your sex trafficking business."

"I don't know what you are talking about, you fucking gringo!" he yelled.

Rob thrust a sharp kick into his gut as Eduardo wailed in agony.

"What the fuck?" Eduardo asked, hunching over in pain. "What do you want from me?"

Rob squatted in front of him, wielding a long K-bar knife from under his ghillie top.

"I want you to be honest with me, Eduardo," Rob replied. "Tell me about it. My little sister was snatched by you assholes. That makes it my business. I'm going to kill each one of you one by one. But if you cooperate, I promise to make it quick."

Eduardo glared at Rob with eyes full of contempt.

"I'm not telling you shit! Who the fuck are you guys, anyway, with your fucking ragged ass camo suits? You think you're in Iraq or something?"

Rob grinned back at him.

"Simple. We're the executioners. And this is a message for your boss!"

Rob gripped the knife handle hard and wedged it into Eduardo's chest, watching the blood spurt from his wound onto the dry ground. Rob moved closer to his face.

"We're coming for all of you, every fucking one of you assholes. There is nowhere you can hide."

They watched Eduardo heave for air as he took his last breath, his head dipping forward to his chest.

"Check that bastard's pockets," Kyle said.

Rob moved a hand into Eduardo's pants, yanking out a folded piece of paper and a cell phone. He saw it needed finger recognition to unlock. Rob grabbed the dead man's hand and pressed his finger to it.

"How much you want to bet we just found a gold mine?" Rob asked. "Let's get the hell out of here. We'll leave him for the fucking coyotes."

Rob swiped his knife and began sawing Eduardo's finger off in case they needed it again. The men hopped into the Range Rover, leaving Eduardo's dead body still tied to the tree. They needed to return to the villa to get rid of the guards' bodies. But now they had the contact list of a Los Lobos Cartel lieutenant. It was sure to contain something of significance to them.

THIRTEEN

```
Culiacán
Sinaloa, Mexico
```

Juan Luis lounged on the brown leather sofa between two beautiful women, a blonde and a brunette, clad in skimpy bikinis in his mansion's living room. Juan's arm stretched out around each one while watching his favorite football team on TV. He'd been cursing at the screen between fondling the girls and taking shots of expensive Don Julio Tequila.

Juan lived the high life and had built an empire thanks to his organization's involvement in just about any illegal trade imaginable. Juan had been untouchable in Mexico for the longest time. There wasn't a single soul in the country who didn't know who he was. Some silently cursed Juan. But others lauded him as a hero for the poor. Though he was evil, he gave a lot of his money to the impoverished. Many believed Juan to be a Robin Hood of sorts for those who lived in the Mexican slums.

But there was a high cost to his power. He'd ravaged many lives, whether it was his extensive drug business or his

The Messenger

involvement in the sex trade. Juan was the devil in disguise and had no compassion for his enemies. He'd gotten his nickname, El Carnicero (the butcher), for always having those he killed or had killed sliced up into pieces and fed to the pigs.

Many people wanted him dead, particularly his rivals and those whose families he had torn apart with his savage nature. However, when the government was as wicked as the criminals they were supposed to lock up, it became a desperate plight for those who ended up on the wrong side. Nobody ever had the balls to stand up to Juan or his criminal enterprise.

"Boss!" one of his men blurted out as he barged into the living room. "Boss, we have a problem! We have a big fucking problem!"

Juan glared back at him.

"What is it, Raúl?" Juan asked. "I told you not to disturb me! Can't you see I'm fucking busy?"

"I know, boss," Raúl said, catching his breath. "I know. I'm sorry. But this is important!"

Juan shot a flirty look at the women by his side.

"I will decide how important it is, Raúl."

Juan began kissing one woman, moving his tongue along her cheek and feeling the goosebumps on her exposed legs with his hand.

"Somebody's messing with our business," Raúl interrupted.

Raúl appeared agitated. And Juan realized then that maybe he should stop enjoying himself, as this might be something he'd want to hear.

"Shit. You heard him, ladies. Leave us, please. Business calls."

The women pouted as they rose to their feet. Juan

smacked each one on the ass as they walked off toward the pool patio just outside.

"We'll continue this party later, girls."

Juan pointed Raúl to a nearby chair.

"This better be important for you to interrupt my favorite football team, Raúl," Juan said, watching through the glass as the girls removed their bikinis and dove into the swimming pool. "This is the only time I get to myself. You know that."

"I'm sorry, boss," Raúl said. "I really am. But this just couldn't wait."

"What couldn't wait, damn it? Spit it out!"

"Somebody blew up one of our meth kitchens, boss."

Juan's demeanor turned.

"Can you be more specific?"

"It's our operation in Jiménez. Somebody came and burned it down!"

Juan placed a hand on his chin and crossed his legs.

"What do you mean, they burned it down?"

"I mean burned, boss. It's all gone!"

"And our men?" asked Juan.

"They made it out," he replied. "But they destroyed the lab!"

"You sure it wasn't an accident, Raúl? That fool Carlos is in charge of that. I probably should've had that idiot killed a long time ago."

"I'm sure, boss. Carlos gave him up. He said the guy threatened to kill him if he talked. But he's more scared of you. He said there were two guys there asking questions."

"Did you ask him if he knew who's responsible, so we can take care of it?"

"I did. Carlos is outside."

"He's here?" Juan asked. "Bring him in, then. I want to know more about this mystery man who's trying to fuck with us."

"There's something else, boss," Raúl added. "Eduardo is missing."

"What? He's missing?"

"We went to his place, and it was just empty. I tried calling, but his phone was off. Nobody can reach him. I'm worried something is wrong."

"Fuck!" Juan yelled. "Motherfucker! All right, I'll deal with that in a minute. First bring that fucker Carlos to me so we can have a little talk."

"Right, boss."

Saying that Juan could be a little unstable would be an understatement. And everyone knew that when he said he wanted to have a talk, it was nearly always much more than that. Someone would be penalized for pissing him off.

Juan took a Cuban cigar from the case on the glass coffee table, cut the tip, and lit it as Raúl left Carlos in the doorway to the room. Shaking in place, his knees tapping against one another, Carlos was intimidated. He'd never been in a room alone with the boss before. And he figured Juan wasn't calling him in to give him a pat on the back.

"Come in, Carlos," Juan said. "I won't bite you."

Carlos slowly made his way into the room. His head sagged, too nervous about making eye contact. He stood by the table, staring at the ground.

"Come on, have a seat right here."

Juan stood and shoved him into a chair across the table from the sofa. He sat back down, crossing his legs.

"So," Juan said as he took a drag from his cigar. "Tell me

what happened. I want to know everything."

Carlos just sat in fear, not able to look at him.

"Carlos," Juan said. "Look me in the eye. If you don't talk to me, I'm going to be very upset. Trust me, you don't want that. Now speak!"

"These two guys, b-boss," Carlos stammered. "They came busting in, asking all kinds of questions."

"What sort of questions, Carlos?"

Carlos thought carefully about what to say next.

Juan poured a shot of liquor and set it down in front of him.

"Will this loosen your tongue a little, Carlos?"

Carlos took the shot glass and swallowed it down.

"Boss," he said, touching the cut on the side of his neck. "They held us at knifepoint and were asking about the girls and stuff. They asked about you and about the drugs. I don't know what they wanted. But one of them said something about his sister, I think."

"What about his sister, Carlos?"

"Just that she was taken, boss," he replied. "That's all I know. Oh, and he said he's from New York."

"And the other one?" Juan asked.

"Nothing, sir. He didn't say much, just pointed his pistol at us."

Juan set his cigar down in the ashtray.

"Then what happened?"

"They made us go outside, and they lit the kitchen on fire. The man said they would kill us if we talked. We lied and said we wouldn't. We would never betray you, boss. That's the honest to God truth!"

Juan rose, walked to the other side of the coffee table, and stood over Carlos.

"You did good, kid," he told him. "Relax. I'm glad you came to me. I am."

A sense of relief came over Carlos, like he'd just dodged a bullet. But he'd thought too soon. Juan would not let him just walk. He didn't want the weak in his presence, let alone working for him.

"Except," Juan said.

A swift jolt ran through Carlos's body.

"You shouldn't have let some fucking gringos walk in there and push you around! And for that, there are consequences!"

Juan raised his shiny, silver 357 Magnum Desert Eagle from the side table and pointed it at Carlos's head.

"You fucking pussy!" he shouted. "You let two guys, two Americans, come in there and walk over you? Is that the people I have working for me? I told you to protect that place with your life. Now open your mouth!"

"Boss!" Carlos pleaded with Juan. "Please, don't, boss! I'm sorry!"

"I said open your fucking mouth, now!"

Juan jammed the pistol into Carlos's mouth, knocking out a couple of his teeth and leaving blood trailing from his lips to his chin.

"Ugh!" Carlos yelped, trying to scream.

He couldn't get much out with a gun barrel over his tongue. Juan put a hand over Carlos's forehead.

"This is what happens when you fuck with my money!"

Juan rammed the gun even further in and pulled the trigger. The penetration of the powerful magnum round went up through the top of his throat. It scattered his brains all over the curtain as it blew out half of his head, leaving Carlos motionless in the chair with blood splattered on the marble floor.

Hearing the deafening blast from the living room, Raúl hurried in to see what was going on.

"Boss? Is everything okay?"

"It is now, Raúl," Juan said. "It is now. Clean up this fucking mess. And get rid of his body, somewhere nobody will find him!"

"Right away, boss," Raúl answered.

Juan snatched the phone from the table and dialed Eduardo's number. But instead of ringing, the call went straight to voicemail.

"Eduardo, it's Juan," he said in a voicemail message. "Everyone is looking for you, brother. Where you at? Call me back right away!"

Juan ended the call and dialed a second number.

"Marco," Juan said as he picked up. "Yeah, it's Juan. Listen, I have another job for you. I'm going to give you some info. I need you to find two Americans for me."

Juan listened to Marco for a time.

"Yes," he said. "I need you to find them, figure out why they are here, then kill them. I think one of them might be the brother of one of our new girls."

Just before he was about to hang up, Juan recalled something else Raúl had told him.

"Oh, and Marco. Nobody has heard from Eduardo. It's not like him to not answer his phone when it's me calling. So I would start there."

Marco Torres was a cartel hitman. He was the man Juan called when he needed to get rid of someone. Marco ran a hit squad for the cartel, Los Ántrax. Inspired by the Anthrax infection, the name was symbolic of the violence they spread across Mexico and other places, wherever business took them. Working as enforcers for the Los Lobos cartel, they were, in essence, a security force. They were engaged in extortion, kidnappings, and assassinations of rival cartel members, Mexican authorities, and politicians, to name a few. But they also acted as security for high-ranking cartel members, like Juan. To them, it was just another job. But it was anything but. Marco would find that out soon enough.

Once upon a time, Marco was a Mexican police officer. The cartel had paid him off as they did many others. But Marco figured out soon that he could make a lot more money if he worked for them full-time. Being a former detective, Marco was skilled at locating people. And he'd never messed up a contract. Marco didn't expect this time to be any different. First, he had to find them. But this one may just prove much more complicated than any job he'd ever done in his fifteen years of working for Los Lobos.

"You've never let me down. Don't start now. I pay you way too much money to fuck this up!"

"Okay, I'm on it," Marco replied. "It'll get done."

"I want you to make them feel pain before they die," said Juan. "Leave an example for everyone!"

Juan hung the phone up and set it on the glass table. He glanced at the leather seat, still covered with Carlo's blood.

"Raúl!" he yelled. "I thought I told you to clean this mess up!"

Raúl ran into the room in a hurry, carrying a towel, and knelt beside the chair.

"Sorry, boss," he said. "We had to load the body into the truck."

"Make sure you leave him outside for the fucking animals. I want nothing left of that fucking rat!"

"Will do, boss."

"And Raúl, when you finish, don't come back in here. Don't bother me for the rest of the night unless someone is dying. Got it?"

Juan got up and stepped through the sliding glass door to the pool area. He left his gun on the patio table and ushered the girls to the hot tub, dropping his pants to the concrete beneath his feet.

"Well, ladies," he said as he removed his shirt and tossed it onto a lounge chair. "Where were we?"

Juan climbed down into the hot tub between the two girls. He grabbed a small baggie from the side, flicking powder between one of their breasts. Juan took a one-hundred-dollar bill from the cup holder at the side of the tub and snorted a line of coke from her tanned skin. He wiped the excess powder from his nostrils with his finger and put his arms around them.

"Now it's a party."

Comfortable that Marco would take care of pressing business for him, Juan didn't give it a second thought.

FOURTEEN

On the road

Rob drove over the Coahuila State line, dip bottle rattling in the center console. He pulled the vehicle into a deserted area off the side of the two-lane road past the Mesa de Piños Mountain peak. A few miles outside the city, that mountain countryside was an impressive sight to see. It would have been a nice place to visit under ordinary circumstances, but the men didn't have time for that, at least not until they found Marianne.

They knew she was somewhere in Los Lobos Cartel territory. But where? The area was so vast; it was like searching for a needle in a million haystacks. They needed a tip, a clue, something to point them in the right direction.

Rob began going through Eduardo's cell phone, getting into his contacts and latest text messages, searching for something, anything that might prove helpful to them.

"You see anything?" asked Kyle.

Rob continued thumbing through the long list.

"I see a bunch of names. Nothing else, no places or addresses."

There was so much information inside the phone that it seemed like it would take forever to go through it all. But Rob stopped cold as he looked at one message.

"Wait, a minute. There's a text here from someone named Ángel, Ángel Ruiz."

"So, what's it say?"

Rob scrolled down to read the contents. He knew some Spanish, not enough to hold a conversation. But he could pick up bits and pieces here and there.

"It looks like he said something about a meeting," Rob said. "And he mentioned a place. It says tonight, ten p.m. sharp, at Manuel's Cantina. I can't make out the rest."

Rob started looking up the location on his phone.

"That's in one hour," Kyle said. "They don't know Eduardo is dead yet."

"Let's hope not, anyway," Rob replied.

"Sounds like some kind of bar," said Kyle. "I wonder what the meeting is about."

Rob placed the phone into the glove box.

"Well, I guess there's only one way to find out."

Rob slammed the accelerator hard, heading for the meeting spot. They drove for half an hour, neither man hardly uttering a word. They didn't need to. Both of them knew what they were getting into. They would have each other's backs, regardless if anything happened.

As they neared the bar entrance, Rob reduced speed and took a right into the parking lot.

"This is Eduardo's car," said Rob. "I don't want them to see it, thinking it is him."

Rob drove around to the rear of the building and parked the car a reasonable distance away in the gravel parking lot, so they wouldn't be noticed.

"Just act casual," he said as they got out of the car. "We're just two white gringos having some drinks."

The men wandered around the building and through the front door. As they entered, all eyes in the room diverted toward them. Since they were the only foreigners in a bar of locals, it was quite expected. They acted like they didn't notice and went right for the bar counter, each pulling up a stool.

The barkeep had a bewildered look on her face as she watched them take a seat. They didn't get many non-locals in the place.

"Americans?" the lady asked.

Rob and Kyle seemed somewhat out of their element in that place.

"Guilty," Rob replied. "We're just down here, taking in some sights. It's beautiful countryside you have here."

The bartender smiled at them. Rob thought she was stunning with her light brown skin, shiny jet-black hair, and a pretty smile. But he couldn't let that distract him.

"We don't see many Americans in here. What can I get you two?"

"Two beers, please," Rob said.

"What kind?"

"Surprise us," he replied.

The two weren't there for the beers. They were there for information, playing it by ear.

"All right," said the bartender.

She grabbed them both a bottle of Pacífico from the cooler and set them over napkins on the counter.

"Gracias," Rob said to her.

"De nada, señor," she replied.

Rob twisted the cap and took a quick sip from the bottle.

"That's good stuff," he said as Kyle swallowed a large gulp of his.

Rob started hearing chatter coming from the other side of the bar. He peered into the mirror on the wall behind the counter. Rob saw a group of Mexican men sitting in the corner, talking among themselves, and a lone police officer in uniform who'd appeared to be watching them from a table in the corner.

Rob flagged down the bartender again as she stocked the bar.

"Excuse me," he said. "But I was just wondering, who owns this place?"

But she didn't answer, just glanced up at the same group of men. Rob realized why the meeting was being held there. The cartel owned the bar. It made perfect sense. It also explained why they met in such a public place. Everyone knew who they were. It wasn't like they were hiding their identities. They surely didn't need to worry about anyone calling the police.

Rob and Kyle remained at the bar, listening in on the conversation, what little they could make out. But it seemed to be just random chitchat. One man harassed the waitress, pulling at her short skirt and trying to grope her breasts. Rob turned his head, eyeing the guy down as he tried to grab her. The man was not keen on being stared at.

"Hey, gringo!" he shouted across the room. "You have a fucking problem, ese?"

Unbeknownst to them, the man was Felipe Ortega, one of the big players in the cartel's drug game. He was there to meet with Eduardo to discuss business. Rob didn't entertain him with a response. Instead, he snubbed him and faced forward, taking another sip from his beer. He glanced up at the security camera above the TV behind the counter, gesturing toward it for Kyle to see.

"I think he wants to talk to you," Kyle said.

"Hey, white boy!" Felipe yelled again. "I'm talking to you, fucker!"

Felipe got up from the table and marched toward them.

"Is there a problem, boy? I should shoot you in the fucking head for looking at me like that. Nobody stares at me like that! You got a death wish, vato?"

Things weren't going how Rob thought they would. It looked like they might have to devise a plan fast.

Felipe cornered Rob and put a hard grip on his arm. But Rob didn't hesitate. In a sharp turn, Rob took his wrist and twisted, springing up at the same time and overpowering him to the floor.

"I was looking at the girl, asshole," Rob told him. "She looks like someone I know."

The bartender dipped behind the counter, knowing that Rob had crossed a line. Rob released Felipe's arm, and he fell back to the floor, gripping it with the other.

"And, by the way," Rob added, "don't touch me again."

Another of the cartel members got up from his chair, and the rest followed him.

"You want to die, cabrón?" he asked. "This is our house. Disrespecting us is a good way to get your ass killed!"

The police officer, who'd remained quiet the entire time, suddenly locked eyes with Rob and hopped from his chair.

"You need to leave, now, both of you," he said. "We don't need or want trouble from outsiders!"

"No, fuck that!" Felipe shouted. "Shoot this motherfucker!"

Rob backed up a little.

"My apologies," he replied with his hands up. "It was just a reflex. I'm a little paranoid, you know? Not much sleep lately."

The officer poked his gun into Rob's face.

"It better be. And if I see you two in here again, I won't hesitate to arrest you!"

"All right, man," said Rob. "We're just leaving, anyway."

The man lowered his weapon and watched as Rob and Kyle returned to the counter.

"And don't fucking come back here!" he shouted.

The two grabbed their beers and left. As they exited the bar entrance, Rob saw the officer's police car to the far left, number GP-074 on the bumper's right side.

"Well, that was eventful," Kyle said as they crossed the parking lot and climbed into the car. "What are we going to do now?"

"We're going to follow them," replied Rob. "I think when they realize Eduardo is a no-show, they'll go straight to his place. We're going to make sure they don't make it."

"Why not just kill them right there?"

"Because," Rob answered. "I don't want to leave witnesses."

They waited for close to an hour for the gangsters to leave the bar. Then, a bright beam of headlights appeared past the building as the rain drizzled from the cloudy night sky.

"Hey, they're leaving," Rob said.

Kyle jerked his M4 rifle from the back and rolled the window down.

The black Chevrolet Tahoe pulled out and took a left onto the two-lane road. Rob edged out behind them, maintaining the gap to keep from being spotted. He waited for them to reach the secluded wilderness a few miles down the road. Minutes later, Rob built up speed.

"Get ready," he told Kyle.

Rob spotted a bridge up ahead of them that ran over a narrow river below. He hit the gas harder. Kyle switched the safety off his weapon as Rob swerved to the left to speed up beside the driver.

"Shoot that motherfucker, now!"

Kyle let a round go as the men in the backseat glared in their direction and began shooting pistols through the rear window, bullets tearing holes into the vehicle. They returned fire as Rob swung the Range Rover back to the left to avoid being hit and sped up.

The Tahoe abruptly swerved right as the driver's body fell limp, blood coating the windshield in front of him. Another man tried to move the driver's body to slow the vehicle, to no avail. The Tahoe smashed into the guardrail, scraping its right side as the front right tire jumped over the metal. Rob slowed somewhat to allow it to pass, then stepped up his momentum, striking the SUV hard on its rear bumper.

As the back end jumped the railing, the Tahoe flipped to the right. It tumbled down the steep embankment, overturning on its top, and came to a rest upside down by the water. Rob hit the brakes on the Rover and skid to a stop at the side of the road.

"Come on," Rob said as he bounded from the vehicle. "Let's get down there!"

They raced around the bridge railing and down the grassy hill that led to the bottom of the steep ravine. Two of the men were dead. The other three were crying in pain, lying upside down on the roof above the back seat. One of them was attempting to crawl through the shattered rear window, blood flowing from a deep gash to the top of his head. He had a sharp laceration from a piece of metal lodged in his thigh.

Rob looked beyond and spotted a leak coming from the fuel line above the man's head. He snatched the guy by the arm and dragged him from the car. Rob loosened his grip, releasing him to the ground.

He knelt on the ground beside the man, clutching his face in his hands.

"Your friend, Eduardo. Well, I'm afraid he's gone, worm food. And you're going to end up with the same fate if you don't answer one question."

The man looked up at Rob, his left eye sealed shut from the impact.

"Who the fuck are you, gringo?" he asked.

He was out of it and bloody, hardly able to muster up a conversation.

"Who I am is not important," Rob replied. "What I want is something else altogether. I want to know about your sex trafficking operations. Who runs it, where they keep the girls, everything."

He groaned in pain and tried to wipe away the blood running down his arm. Rob reached into the man's pocket and got an ID.

"So, Ricardo," Rob said, glancing down at his driver's license. "Are you going to cooperate with us? Or do you want to end up like your friend? That's a nasty leg wound. You won't make it far on that thing."

"Fuck you, puto," Ricardo replied. "I'll never talk to you. I'd rather die than betray the organization."

"That's the second time you've said 'fuck you' to me," replied Rob. "It's not very hospitable. But, I guess your wish is my command."

Rob snagged his legs and dragged him backward, leaving him lying against the door of the Tahoe while his buddies fumbled around in the back seat, trying to get free. Rob retrieved the rest of the man's belongings, including a cell phone.

"You won't be needing this anymore," Rob told him.

"Go to hell!" Ricardo yelled, trying to squirm away from his unavoidable fate.

But he wouldn't make it far.

"You first," Rob replied.

Rob and Kyle backed away from the vehicle as Rob sparked Ricardo's own cigarette lighter and tossed it onto the Tahoe. The fuel line caught fire and went up fast. As the men made their way back to the top and to the roadway, the Tahoe burst into towering flames. It exploded, charring everything and everyone around it and inside to a blackened crisp. They left the men to die in the blazing vehicle.

"What now?" Kyle asked Rob as they got back into the stolen car.

Rob thought for a while. Then he remembered the mystery police officer who'd confronted them back at the bar. Rob knew the officer had something to do with the cartel. He must. Why else would he try so hard to protect those men?

"Don't worry," Rob said. "I have a plan, the beginning of one at least. But first, we need to get rid of Eduardo's car."

FIFTEEN

```
San Pedro
Next morning
```

Marco had just finished searching Eduardo's villa, including his house and every inch of the surrounding garden. He'd found bloodstains on the ground and out into the grass.

It looked to him like some kind of fight had taken place there. But where were Eduardo and his guards? It was as if they'd just vanished. As Marco roamed down the path to the front, he found another red blotch on the wall by the gate. Following the trail down to the ground, something shiny reflected from below it. He bent over to pick it up. It was a bullet fragment.

Marco studied the size of the round. He knew it was too large to be a handgun.

Fuck, he thought. *This is from a large-caliber rifle. But where did it come from?*

Then, with a hand over his eyes to block the sun, he peeped up at the only bluff facing the compound that had the best vantage point of the entire area.

He pushed the gate open and picked up a jog around and up the back of the steep hill. As he made it to the top, he noticed something distinct. The grass was matted down like someone had been lying there. Searching the surrounding area, he found zero additional evidence, no bullet casings, nothing. He snapped a picture and went down the hill to his waiting car.

Marco left the property and turned his vehicle onto the road in front of it. Further down, he began scanning for anything that he might find off the road just down from Eduardo's place. He'd just passed by a dirt trail seldom used by anyone. It didn't lead anyplace but out to the woods. Seeing tire tracks in the dirt, he reversed the car and made a hard left.

As he progressed up the hill, Marco saw something up ahead. Something or someone was propped up against a tree about fifty feet off the trail. He halted the vehicle and hopped out, leaving the engine running.

"Motherfucker!" he said as he got closer. "Eduardo?"

Flies and maggots covered his body. Eduardo was hardly recognizable. His face was battered, and dried blood caked the side of it. It looked like wild animals had gotten to him. No telling how many days he'd been out there. But Marco noticed what was left of his taste in clothing. It had to be him.

Marco pulled his cell out to phone the boss.

"It's Marco, boss," he said as he watched the flies circle Eduardo's corpse. "Eduardo, he's gone, dead. I searched his house, the grounds. I found him out here tied to a fucking tree. It looks like they beat him pretty bad before they killed him. Boss, they left him out here like a goddamned animal!"

"Fuck!" Juan shouted from the other end of the line. "So, what the hell are you standing around there for, then? Find them!"

"I'm on it, boss," Marco replied. "But I found a large-caliber projectile used to kill the guards. Whoever this man is, he's an excellent shot."

"So get fucking busy, Marco! I want you to send an undeniable message. Nobody comes to our home and fucks with us. Do what I pay you to do!"

"Yes, sir," Marco replied.

There was a brief silence on the line.

"Hold on, Marco. I got another call."

Marco held the line open as he started going through Eduardo's pants. But everything was missing.

They must've taken his stuff, he thought.

Juan returned moments later, sounding even more infuriated than he was before.

"Marco, you there?"

"Yeah, I'm here, boss."

"Damn it!" he said. "I've just been told that two gringos were at Manuel's last night while they were waiting for Eduardo to show up to the meeting. They got into a dispute in the bar, and then they left. The bartender, Adriana, said they started asking her questions."

"That can't be a coincidence, boss. It looks like they dumped Eduardo's pockets. I found nothing."

"That means they took his phone. He'd go nowhere without it. So they probably knew about the meeting. And now they are missing as well. Nobody's heard from them since."

"I don't like this, boss."

"Get over there as soon as you can, Marco," Juan told him. "See what you can find out. Maybe they left some breadcrumbs behind. I'll send someone to collect Eduardo's body. Find those assholes before they cause any more fucking damage!"

"Yes, sir," Marco replied. "I'll head that way right now."

"Oh, and Marco," Juan said. "I changed my mind. Don't kill them yet. Bring them to me. I'll show them what it means to be Los Lobos."

"I'm on it, sir."

Marco hurried to his black Mercedes G-class and rode off toward Manuel's Cantina. He was going to find out what the Americans wanted. It was apparent they weren't just random tourists. Marco continued driving down the mountain roadway. But as he whisked the car around the curve, he found blue lights ahead and smoke billowing from under the bridge. Multiple police cars, lights twirling, a fire engine, and an ambulance circled the hillside.

Marco tapped his brakes and came to a stop on the shoulder.

"What the hell?"

Marco bounced from the vehicle on the opposite side of the road. He darted across until he saw an overturned car down lying on its roof down below. Black and gutted, burned remains filled the inside. The emergency crew worked to remove the lifeless bodies from the wreckage. They were so unrecognizable that the only viable means of officially identifying them would be through dental records. But Marco didn't need to see that.

He made his way further down for a better look. It was undeniable. Though the car was smoldering and black inside and out, he knew who it belonged to. Marco retrieved his phone to call the boss. He placed the call on video.

"Boss," he said as he held the phone out. "I'm afraid I have worse news."

"What is it now, Marco?"

Marco faced the camera toward the vehicle so Juan could see what he was looking at.

"Fuck!" Juan yelled. "I don't fucking need this shit right now! Those guys were preparing to make a deal that would've netted us millions more in profits. Now they're dead?"

Marco said nothing. He knew better than to disrupt the boss when he was angry. And this was the most irate he'd ever heard him.

"Listen to me carefully, Marco," Juan said. "I want these fuckers. And I want them bad. Find them and deliver them to me!"

Before Marco could answer, Juan had already hung up. He snapped a photo of the car with his phone. Marco made his way back to his car to get to the bar. He took off down the road in a fury.

He arrived in a couple of minutes, just in time for the place to open. As he rolled into the front lot, he saw Adriana step from her car and move through the entrance to open the bar. He went straight in after her.

"Hey!" Marco called out as he let the door swing shut behind them. "Excuse me!"

"We're not open yet," she told him. "You've got another thirty minutes."

Marco jumped into her path.

"I didn't come here to drink," he said. "I am here on business."

He pulled up Juan's contact information on his phone and showed it to her.

"He sent me," Marco said. "You're more than welcome to call and ask him. But I don't think it'll go so well for you, my dear."

Adriana glanced at the name on the phone.

"No, no. I'm sorry, sir. I didn't know who you were."

Marco placed the phone back into his back pocket.

"Well," he said. "Now you do."

Adriana wasn't about to get in Marco's way. She didn't want a surprise visit from Juan. His violent nature terrified her immensely. She didn't know who Marco was, but whatever he wanted, she would give him.

Marco leaned against the counter, watching her shy nervousness show right through her pretty brown eyes. As Juan's right-hand man, Marco had a commanding presence about him. He carried that authority with him wherever he went.

"Can I get you a beer, Mister?" she asked him.

"Yes, you can," he replied. "And I have a few questions I'd like to ask you."

Adriana placed a cold bottle of beer on the counter in front of him.

"I understand there were some Americans in here inquiring about the place," he said. "Tell me about them." Marco shot her a bitter grin, his gold front tooth glinting beneath the yellow bar light.

"Oh, those guys," she replied. "One of them asked who owned the bar. I didn't answer him. But then he and Felipe got into it. I thought Felipe was going to kill him. But that gringo put him on the floor like it was nothing."

"Did he, now?" asked Marco.

"Yeah. It happened so fast."

"And the other guy?"

"He said little," she said. "But they were undoubtedly together."

"And they let those two Americans just walk out the front door?" asked Marco. "Show me to your security footage."

Adriana led Marco beyond the bar counter through a bead curtain and down a long hallway to a secured room at the back of the building. She entered the key to unlock it. As she opened up, Marco approached the security setup and monitors with cameras covering the whole interior and both entrances outside and into the parking lot.

"Excellent," he said as he took a chair in front. "Show me the footage of when they came in."

Adriana pulled up the tape from the night before. She fast-forwarded it, freezing it after Rob and Kyle walked into the bar.

She hit play.

With no audio on the tape, Marco watched as Rob spoke to Adriana.

"That's where he asked me who owned this place," she said.

Rob stared up at the camera. He wasn't even trying to hide his face. To Marco, it appeared as if he was taunting him.

He continued watching the recording as Felipe confronted Rob.

"Motherfucker," he said as Rob brought Felipe down to the floor.

He didn't want to say it in front of Adriana, but now he was really wondering who these guys were. Only a skilled person could put Felipe on the floor like that. But he couldn't understand why they let them walk. Now they were all dead. He wouldn't have the chance to ask.

Marco resumed the video as Officer Ramos intervened, pointing his gun and forcing them out.

"Why didn't they fucking kill these men?" he asked

himself. "It would've saved me a lot of trouble, and them too, obviously."

He continued fast-forwarding the tape to the point when the cartel men gave up on the meeting and left. Marco located the black SUV as it appeared behind them on the road out front.

He paused it.

Examining closely, Marco could just make out the model of the vehicle they were in. Then he saw the number on the plate.

"That's Eduardo's car!"

Marco pulled the security tape and put it into a plastic bag he'd found on the table.

"Thanks for your help," he told Adriana. "Not that you had a choice."

Marco hustled back to his car and tossed the bag into the passenger-side seat.

He called the boss back using the Bluetooth in his Mercedes SUV.

"Hey, boss! I got 'em on the security footage from the bar. Their faces are on this clear as day!"

"And what did you find, Marco?" he asked.

"They got into a scuffle. The man put Felipe down so effortlessly. Ramos got in the way. Then they just fucking let them walk. I don't get it, boss!"

"All right," Juan replied. "Finish these assholes, Marco. They have caused enough damage. I don't want this to come back and bite me!"

"I thought you wanted me to bring them in, boss," replied Marco.

Juan had a reputation for being unpredictable. And he

changed his mind often. But now they were killing his men.

"Just do what I fucking tell you, Marco!" Juan yelled. "Or I'll find someone who will!"

"I got it, boss," Marco said. "I'll handle it."

SIXTEEN

Police Precinct
Monterrey, Mexico

They sat at the side of the four-lane street in front of a small Mexican takeout restaurant, eating tacos and watching the locals go about their daily routines, working and haggling with patrons at the nearby strip mall. Away from the city center, beaches, and upscale resorts, it wasn't a prime tourist destination. But they got the occasional American passing through that part of town on their way elsewhere. Monterrey was crawling with cartel members and crooked cops on their payroll.

Rob's eyes were glued to a newspaper he couldn't read, and he was hearing people around him whom he couldn't understand. But the paper covered his face well. He didn't want to spook the man before they could talk. It wasn't by accident that they were across the road from the police station. They were waiting for a particular officer to show. And so far, it was the one and only option they had. Rob knew much of the police force and departments in Mexico were dirty, whether they were coerced or just did it for the money.

So far, Rob had gotten little in the way of information. And he was losing his patience. Somebody was going to talk. They waited around for most of that morning, watching every person who came in and out of that place. But Rob figured he had to leave sometime.

"Hey, bro," Rob said to Kyle while they had a few minutes to talk. "I just wanted to tell you how much I appreciate you being here with me."

"Of course, man," replied Kyle. "Why wouldn't I?"

"No, I mean it, man. I couldn't do this without you. And Marianne is going to know that when we find her."

"Don't worry, Rob. We'll find your sister. She knows you. So do I. I'm sure she's just waiting for us to come to her rescue."

Hopefully she's not hurt, Rob thought.

Rob just hoped that Kyle was right.

He recalled the last mission they were on together. He'd thought about how scared those people were when they freed them. The more he reflected, the more irritated he got. Rob could only wish that, wherever Marianne was, she wasn't suffering.

This mission wasn't sanctioned. The two men were on their own. But Rob had little time to wonder what would happen when it was all over. He would give his life to protect his family, what little family he had left. And, if required, Rob would go to prison for it.

They were sitting outside, near a white Toyota Tacoma pickup they'd stolen from a motel parking lot earlier that morning. Rob was just finishing up his food and drinking the last bit of beer in his plastic cup. Rob covered his face with the paper, his eyes peeking over the top of it. He spotted a gentleman in uniform, walking away from a group of police officers through the vast complex's entrance, surrounded by a ten-foot concrete wall with barbed wire on top.

"Heads up," Rob told Kyle in a quiet voice so nobody around would hear. "There he is."

Rob folded up the newspaper and placed it on the table as they waited for him to leave. The officer reversed his police cruiser and took off down the street.

"Let's go," said Rob.

The men hopped into the truck and waited for the officer to move a little further away. Rob pulled out a couple of cars behind. He followed the police car for a few miles until he pulled left into a drive-through taco stand. Rob stopped and waited on the other side of the highway.

Not five minutes later, the cruiser pulled out onto the road, continuing in the same direction. Rob backed the truck out after a car came between them a couple of hundred meters from the vehicle. He trailed the officer until he turned the car into an overgrown, thick patch of grass. It had once been a parking area for the boarded-up and graffiti-riddled buildings nearby.

Rob swung right and pulled up beside the officer's car. Ramos gave them an odd look as he observed the men getting out of the truck. Rob tapped on the driver's-side window.

"Yeah?" Officer Ramos asked in Spanish, a taco in one hand and rolling the window down with the other. "What can I do for you, gentlemen?"

He looked closer, realizing the men weren't Mexican.

"If it's not an emergency," he said, "dial nine-one-one. As you can see, I'm on my lunch break."

Officer Ramos caught Rob's movement as he reached for

his waist, and he tried to beat him to it.

"I wouldn't do that if I were you," said Rob. "I think I'm a little quicker on the draw, Officer."

Staring at the barrel of Rob's .45, Officer Ramos slowly put his half-drawn revolver back into its holster. Rob lowered his weapon to his side.

"Wait a minute, hombre," the officer said, overtly nervous. "I have seen you before."

"Yes, you have," replied Rob. "You were the one who kicked us out of Manuel's. That wasn't a very nice thing to do, you know?"

It annoyed Officer Ramos, not yet knowing why the men were stalking him.

"What do you want with me?" he asked. "I'm a police officer. You know I could just arrest you?"

"Yeah," Rob said as he snatched his arm from the steering wheel. "You're a fucking crooked cop, is what you are. I hate dirty cops, specifically ones that contribute to hooking kids to drugs and holding them as sex slaves!"

Officer Ramos attempted to fight with him, but he couldn't break free from Rob's firm grasp of his wrist. He tried to snag the radio mic with his other hand. Rob lifted his suppressed handgun and shot into the radio, sparks shooting from it as the lights went out.

"I don't think so, amigo!" Rob told him.

Rob reached into the window and unlocked the door before Ramos could roll it up, the glass pinning his arm at the top.

"You motherfucker!" Rob yelled.

Kyle yanked the door open and jerked Ramos out, his taco lunch flying in the air, as the officer's head smacked onto the ground. They dragged him across the weed-covered pavement by his legs. Rob removed the officer's gun from his duty belt and tossed it.

"What do you want from me?" the officer asked. "They will come looking for me when I don't show up! I'm a fucking police officer!"

"Shut up," Rob said, shoving a handkerchief into his mouth. "Give me your cuffs."

Ramos just gawked up at him. Rob swung and gave him a swift blow to the gut.

"I said, give me your fucking handcuffs!"

Ramos removed the cuffs from the back of his belt and tossed them across the ground. Rob picked them up, holding his arms behind his back and securing them tight around the officer's wrist while Kyle bound his feet together with a zip tie from his back pocket. Kyle helped Rob lift Ramos up, and they chucked him into the rear floorboard of the pickup.

"Don't try anything stupid," Rob told him. "Or you'll be dead before we even get to where we're going."

ııı

They'd just got finished stripping the officer of everything but his pants. Inside an old, abandoned, and derelict building they'd scouted in advance, Kyle re-fastened the cuffs to secure Officer Ramos and hung his arms high above him. Rob grabbed Ramos's wrists and fastened the cuffs to an old, rusty metal hook. It seemed the empty building had been used as some sort of abattoir in the past. The place had been falling apart for some time, with leaky holes in the roof and rats scampering in every dark corner. They knew nobody would look for him in there for quite a while, and Ramos did too.

Rob set an old metal chair he'd found under the officer,

his feet just touching it as he draped from the chain. He removed the rag from his mouth.

"Now, we have some questions for you, Officer Ramos. And you're going to answer them. If you don't, you will end up in a lot of pain. You understand me?"

"Fuck you!" he screamed, spit spurting from his mouth. "They will come to find me. And when they do, they will kill you!"

His desperate voice seemed to ring through the vacant building.

"Nope," Rob said. "I don't think so. And you have that all wrong, Officer. I'm not the one who is fucked here."

Rob placed the rag back into his mouth and punched him hard in the stomach as the officer closed his eyes and let out a muffled grunt.

"You hear that, Officer?" asked Rob. "You hear that? Nobody is coming to save your ass. It would be in your best interest not to piss us off!"

Rob strolled to the other side of the room and picked up a long metal pipe from the corner.

"Here's what's going to happen, Officer Ramos," Rob said, holding the pipe out in front of him. "I'm going to ask some questions. Every time you don't give me an answer, we're going to beat you with this thing. I would think long and hard about what you do or say from now on. It is up to you whether you walk out of here alive."

Rob handed the piece of metal over to Kyle.

"Now, Officer," Rob said as he plucked the rag from his mouth. "Tell me about your relationship with the Los Lobos Cartel, what you do for them, and everything you know."

"What? Is that why you brought me here? I don't know

what you are talking about!"

"Really?" Rob asked. "That's what everyone keeps saying. It's getting fucking old!"

Rob signaled Kyle as he popped the rag back in.

Kyle swung the pipe, striking the officer hard in his midsection, causing him to make puking sounds as he bent forward from the blow. Rob pulled the rag out yet again.

"Answer my question, Officer Ramos. How are you involved?"

The officer didn't answer. He was more scared of the cartel getting a hold of him. But that would soon change.

"Kyle," Rob said.

Kyle hit him again, this time even harder. Ramos's cries were faint. But he looked as though he'd try to puke at any moment.

"Next one goes straight to your head," said Rob, extracting the rag and dropping it to the floor. "Answer me, Officer, or you won't survive the next few minutes. I could split your skull open with this thing!"

Kyle took the metal and rotated it toward Ramos's head in slow motion, like he was warming up at a baseball game.

"Listen to me carefully," Rob said. "These pricks you work for took my sister. That means I don't give a damn whether you live or die. All I give a fuck about is finding her. So, do yourself a favor and talk to me. If not, I'm going to let my friend here hit a home run on your ugly mug!"

Rob raised his Glock and put it in the officer's face.

"Of course, I could just shoot you. But I think the other way is more fun, don't you?"

Officer Ramos shivered erratically, but not because he was cold.

"You're scared," Rob said to the officer as he took a piece of fat on his stomach and twisted it in his hand. "That's good. You should be. Now talk!"

"I can't," Ramos said, closing his eyes. "There is nowhere on this earth I can hide if I talk to you. Nowhere! These animals will find me and kill me, my family, everyone. I am not safe!"

Rob replaced the rag violently.

Kyle guided the metal bar back and scuffed it against the side of Ramos's head. It snapped him hard to the side and left a thick cut above his ear. Rob kicked the chair out from under his legs and struck him in the ribs, watching him swing by his arms.

"I told you. And it's only going to be worse the more you resist!"

The blow had dazed the officer, prompting him to briefly forget where he was. Kyle raised the pipe again.

"Okay, okay!" Ramos squealed, blood dripping down from his hair as he fought to breathe from the blow to his rib cage. "I will talk, okay? Just please stop beating me! I'll do what you ask!"

"That's the spirit," replied Rob, sliding the chair back into place with his foot. "Way to be a team player. So, tell us what they pay you for, Officer Ramos."

"I'm going to die for telling you this."

"What do you think is going to happen if you don't?" Rob asked.

"Okay, fine, damn it. The cartel mostly just pays me to look the other way. There are many police officers like me."

"Yeah, I figured that," Rob said. "And?"

"And we are outgunned and outnumbered. You don't know what it's like living here, Mister. There is no way we can compete with them. So we don't even try. We don't make a lot of money as officers. So we accept dinero from them in exchange for letting them operate. If we don't, they kill us and everyone we care about."

"So you don't even consider all the innocent people they hurt in the process?" asked Rob.

"I do, Mister," Ramos replied. "Believe me, I do. But I don't have a choice! The cartels have their own fucking army! They can buy just about any weapon known to man. What can we do?"

Rob picked up a chair in front of him and sat.

"How far up does the corruption go? To the top?"

"Yes!" Ramos replied. "The Mexican police, the national guard."

Officer Ramos was referring to the newly formed Mexican National Guard, which took the place of the disbanded Federales, or federal police, in 2019.

"Politicians are even in on it," he said. "Many of them receive kickbacks from the cartels. They have even donated lots of money to political campaigns. Their influence is endless!"

Rob felt afflicted by what he was hearing. But he wasn't surprised. Everyone knew about the corrupt Mexican system.

"Tell me about their sex trafficking. You know about that, too, right?"

The officer's head popped up, but he didn't respond right away. By the look on his face, he knew more than a little.

"It's terrible, Mister," he replied. "What they do to those girls."

"Tell me about it. Where do they get them? Where do they end up? How can I find them?"

"The cartels have recently extended their business to include trafficking," Ramos said. "They make more money. I don't know where they end up. But I know they find the girls from all over, the US, Central America, South America, Europe... all over the world."

"And how do they get them?"

The officer let out an anxious gasp. They had warned him countless times not to talk about the organization.

"Let it out, Officer Ramos!" Rob yelled. "I'm starting to believe you. I wouldn't want to have to bash your head in. But I will if you don't give me more!"

"Fine, fine, okay," he said. "They send people to these places to scout for young girls. Sometimes they just snatch them up. Sometimes they promise them jobs or whatever. They drug the girls and turn them into prostitutes, some auctioned off."

Rob folded his arms as he sat there, contemplating what the officer said.

"Where do they take the girls, Officer Ramos?" he asked. "Where can I find my sister?"

"I don't know! I swear on the Virgin Mary, I've told you everything I know!"

Rob motioned for Kyle to give him a hand. They raised the officer's body above the hook and sat him on the seat, his arms and legs still bound.

"Interestingly enough," Rob said, "I believe you."

Officer Ramos had a look of pure relief. But he wasn't out of the woods yet.

"So here's what's going to happen," Rob told him, inserting the key into the cuffs and loosening the cord around his legs. "You're going to help us."

"I thought that's what I was doing," Ramos replied.

"No, I mean, you're going to help us," Rob repeated. "You are going to set up a sting operation so we can follow them, and then you're going to stay out of our way, and I'll let you live. If not, well, you know the rest."

"You want me to set them up for you?" he asked. "Are you crazy? I'll be dead before I can make it home."

"Not if you do this right," Rob replied. "And there's no need to worry about the ones from the bar. We killed them already."

Ramos looked dismayed.

"But the organization doesn't have to know it was you," Rob said. "You'll wear a wire. We'll be watching and listening from a distance until we make our move. I will warn you, if you fuck us over, this will seem like a party. You think the cartel is bad? Wait until you see me furious!"

"But what if they search me?" asked Ramos.

"Well," Rob said, "we'll deal with that if the time comes."

"Who the fuck are you guys?" asked the officer.

"Everyone wants to know," replied Rob. "Let's just say we are trained for war. Leave it at that."

"Fine," Ramos said, realizing he had little choice. "I'll do what you say. But if it goes wrong, I need your reassurance and protection! I won't last without it. And please get me a bandage for my fucking bloody head!"

"You got it, Officer," he said. "No problem."

Rob picked the cloth that was in his mouth from the floor and gave it to him.

"Here. Hold this over it. That should do until it's stitched up. And, if they ask, you just got into a little accident, okay?"

Rob and Kyle both knew they couldn't guarantee Officer Ramos's safety when dealing with the cartel. But Rob would do anything if it got him one step closer to Marianne. He didn't care if they had to start World War Three.

SEVENTEEN

El Milagro, Mexico

Officer Ramos stood by in his private vehicle, a 2015 KIA Sorento SUV parked at the side of the remote road a long way outside of his jurisdiction. Wearing ordinary clothes, he looked like any average citizen. The situation was anything but typical, however. It was the last place Ramos ever wanted to be. But Rob had left him no choice. He could have just killed the man. However, Rob figured they could get good use out of him.

He'd picked that town for a reason. Ramos didn't want anyone to see him meeting with the cartel in a populated city like Monterrey. Parked on the edge of a dirt pathway just off the blacktop, he stared into the night and counted down the time on his watch.

A couple of hundred meters away, Rob and Kyle perched on top of a small, bushy hill. The mountainous background silhouetted against the clear moonlit night sky behind them. The peaks seemed like they were right on top of them. But they were miles away. From their position on the foothills, they could see anyone coming far away in either direction. It was the perfect spot to lie in wait. They held tight with Rob's Remington 700 sniper rifle out front and binoculars lying next to Kyle as the agreed-upon meeting time neared.

They had wired Officer Ramos up, and Rob and Kyle could plainly hear him breathing fast and deeply. But he couldn't listen to them. They didn't want to risk giving him away by putting an earpiece into his ear and ending the meeting before it even started. Rob wasn't heartless. He'd felt a little sorry for the guy. But the choice Ramos had in benefiting from the cartel's business had remained to be seen. Rob just hoped he'd stick to the plan. Ramos knew what was at stake. He either walked the line, or someone was going to kill that officer before the night was over.

A few minutes later, two pairs of bright headlights, one with off-road lights on top, appeared down the curve between the two mountain peaks.

"Game on," Rob said to Kyle. "I see lights coming in fast."

"Yeah, I got 'em," Kyle replied as he glanced through the binoculars. "Let's just hope he doesn't fuck this up."

"Don't worry," Rob answered. "If he does, we'll deal with him."

Rob followed through his night-vision as the convoy got closer to the meeting spot. He could hear Officer Ramos's breathing becoming more labored the closer they got to him.

"He sounds scared shitless," Rob said.

"He should be," replied Kyle. "He's surrounded by people who could kill him without a second thought."

Rob and Kyle saw as the vehicles drifted to a standstill fifty meters from the officer's KIA.

"I see three vehicles," Rob said. "An Escalade out front, a

Suburban, and a black Hummer in the rear."

It looked like a standoff as they waited for the occupants to exit their cars. Then Ramos blinked his headlights twice. Slowly, four men got out of the first car, with three surrounding the other. They'd left the cargo light on to light up the road. But one of them stood out from the others.

"Is that Juan?" asked Kyle.

"I don't think so. Fuck! I thought he'd be here."

"So who is this guy, then?"

"I have no idea," Rob said. "But he looks like someone important."

They paused as the four men stopped midway between the cars, waiting for Ramos to exit his vehicle. Far enough away to avoid being detected, Rob dialed a number on his phone. It rang four times.

"Hey, José," he said as he picked up. "I need you to translate for me."

"Translate what?" he asked. "What are you two up to down there?"

"Give me a second, okay?" Rob said. "Just hold on."

Rob stared through the green-tinted night-vision scope as Ramos waited motionless in the car, too rattled to move.

"What the hell are you waiting for, Ramos? Get out of the damn car."

"What?" José asked from the other end of the phone.

"Nothing, José. I was just talking to myself."

The KIA door cracked open, and Ramos's feet hit the ground. He started shuffling anxiously toward the cartel members, showing his hands and trying not to display any sudden movement. The last thing he wanted was to startle them. Slowly, they met face-to-face. Ramos stiffened in place.

Fernando had a reputation for shooting first and asking questions later. And Ramos knew what could happen if he was even marginally suspecting of him.

"All right," Rob said into the phone. "Get ready, José."

Rob removed his right earpiece and held it to the phone.

"Okay," Rob heard their leader say in Spanish. "You got us all the way out here. What the fuck was so important?"

The guy wore a long gold chain, shiny boots, and a half-buttoned silk shirt that exposed his hairy chest underneath. All the cartel bosses had the same lame taste in clothing, it seemed. But he wasn't who Rob and Kyle had expected. And they were still waiting to find out who the mystery man was.

Officer Ramos stood quietly.

"What's the matter?" he asked Ramos. "Cat got your tongue, Officer?"

"Sorry, sir," Ramos replied. "I was expecting your brother."

"Well, you got me, hombre!" he said. "My brother is busy. He doesn't have the time for the likes of you!"

"What did he say?" Rob asked José as he held the phone with his chin.

"It sounds like he's Juan's brother," José said.

Rob and Kyle continued monitoring the meeting.

"Someone killed some of our men," Fernando told him. "Eduardo was among them. You wouldn't know anything about that, would you, Officer Ramos?"

"No, sir," Ramos answered. "I can't say I do."

"Well, we've got you on tape talking to the Americans in the bar. You're telling me you know nothing?"

"I-I would never!" Ramos said, stuttering. "I would never betray you or the organization like that! They seemed a little too curious, so I gave them a warning and told them to leave.

They had no business there, anyway."

The man pulled out a large pistol and directed it at Ramos. His men followed suit behind him.

"I'm sorry, Fernando! I didn't know! I had nothing to do with it. Please, I'm telling you the truth!"

Cartel bosses could be jumpy when they were suspicious. Officer Ramos only hoped he wouldn't kill him. Fernando was Juan's brother and the leader of Los Negros (the black ones), a wing of the Los Lobos Cartel charged with countering other gangs and government security forces. They were known to use the Mexican Mafia and the MS-13 gang to carry out their killings. Los Negros was the cartel's paramilitary unit. And they violently opposed the Mexican Army and the National Guard.

"I believe you, Officer."

There was no telling if Fernando was being serious or not. It was better for Ramos if he said as little as possible. Fernando could be finicky with his men and his money.

"Now, back to my original question," he said. "What are we doing here? And don't call me by my name again, or I will fuck'n shoot you and leave you out here! You understand me?"

"Yes, sir! I'm very sorry, sir!"

Fernando signaled his men to lower their guns. He gazed at the officer, staring him up and down.

"I'm waiting."

"Yes, sir," Ramos replied. "I came to deliver a warning."

"A warning, huh?" Fernando asked, laughing with his men. "This should be interesting."

"It's the national guard, sir," said Ramos. "They are planning a big operation. They know about your business with the girls. And they plan to seize the drugs and whatever else they find."

The Messenger

Fernando stepped closer to the officer.

"Are you serious? That's what you got me all the way out here for?"

"Yes, sir. I didn't want to tell you over the phone."

"I got cops," Fernando told him. "I own cops. They don't have the muscle to take us on! Believe that, Officer Ramos."

Rob called on José, waiting on the other line.

"Translate, José," he said. "Please."

"He advised Fernando that the national guard is onto them, that they are planning to make a big bust. Fernando is making light of it, saying they could never take on the cartel. He also spoke of someone killing their men. Was that you two?"

"What do you think?" asked Rob.

José cleared his throat.

"All right," Rob said. "So he's sticking to the plan."

"Is it bullshit?" asked José.

"Of course it's bullshit, José," Rob said. "We're hoping to stir them up like fucking ants, so they'll lead us right to the mound."

Rob and Kyle held their sights on the men in the road.

"Come on, Ramos. Get him to say it."

Rob had coached Officer Ramos on what to say to Juan, now Fernando. They were hoping for him to reveal a place, an address, or anything they could use to find out where the cartel was keeping the girls. The closer they got to them, the closer he'd get to his sister.

"What if I have some girls lined up?" Ramos asked Fernando. "To make amends. What if I deliver them to you? They're young, too. They would probably make you lots of cash."

Fernando scratched his chin with his shiny gold ring and popped his knuckles.

"Officer Ramos," Fernando replied, "you know I do not discuss business matters with you. We pay you to keep your fucking mouth shut and stay the hell out of our way like all the other pigs!"

"Yes, sir," Ramos said. "I know, sir. I just meant it as a sign of good faith. I deliver the girls, and you make more money. I don't need or want anything in return."

Fernando's eyes seemed to pierce right through Ramos.

"What's your fucking angle, huh? Are you snitching? You trying to set us up?"

Rob watched as Fernando bent down into Ramos's face, praying that he wouldn't find the wire underneath his shirt.

"What did he say, José?" asked Rob.

"Ramos is trying to negotiate a deal to deliver girls to them," replied José. "It doesn't sound like he's going for it. He seems wary of him."

Fernando and his cronies laughed at the officer. Fernando glanced back at his men, then at Ramos.

"You have some giant cojones, Officer!" Fernando told him. "I like that. I do."

His men pointed their guns back at the officer.

"But it can also get you killed!" he said.

Ramos shut his eyes and covered his face, pleading with Fernando not to kill him.

"I just want to make things right with you, sir," Ramos replied. "That's it, I swear! I respect you too much to fuck with you. Everyone knows not to fuck with you!"

Fernando gave a half-smirk as he holstered his gun.

"Well, I can't argue with that, Officer Ramos," he said. "I

will show you where you can drop them off. But, I swear hombre, if you are fucking with us, I will come to your house and kill your wife and children while you watch. Then I will kill you slowly, entiendes?"

"Yes, sir," Officer Ramos said. "Loud and clear, sir."

Anything less than respect from Ramos would bring suspicion on him. He knew that going in. If Fernando found out he was playing him, Ramos would never walk away from that meeting. But if he didn't play along, he had Rob to worry about. It was hard to tell which was worse.

"You get that?" Rob asked José over the phone.

"Yep. He's threatening to kill Ramos and his family if he crosses them. Fernando said he will tell him where to drop the girls."

"Hey, I have to go, brother," Rob said to José. "Thanks for the help. We'll talk later."

"All right, good luck," he replied.

Rob hung the phone up and put it into his breast pocket. Officer Ramos went for his car. Fernando Luis and his associates moved back to theirs. They seemed in a rush to get somewhere.

"Good boy," Rob said, though he knew Ramos couldn't hear him.

Rob began breaking down his rifle and hung it over his shoulder.

"Come on," he said. "Let's go meet up with him."

The men hurried to the old pickup parked down the hill behind them. They were on their way to the agreed-upon rendezvous point. Officer Ramos was lucky to be alive. Rob thought for sure they'd kill him. The meeting had gone off without a hitch. And now Rob was about to turn up the heat.

EIGHTEEN

El Carmen, Mexico

Rob used the information, a tiny blip on the map that Fernando had given Officer Ramos. But it wasn't an address. It was a set of coordinates that pointed them to a position on the desert flats facing hilly terrain outside of the tiny, mountainous town of El Carmen.

Using a GPS, they'd pushed for most of the day to arrive and scout the location. Neither man had slept much in the past couple of days. Rob dozed off at the side of the two-lane road by a truck stop down from the sparsely populated town of just over four thousand people.

But they weren't going into town. Coordinates had led them to an old depot, settled off the beaten path in the heart of open country. The place was mostly hidden from view, with nothing more than a trail in the dirt pointing to it. The roof of the building was almost visible from where they sat in the truck.

Kyle lifted his head and jabbed Rob in the side with his elbow. He rubbed his eyes as the sun settled over the flatlands, canyons just noticeable on the horizon. Rob opened his eyes and took a quick look around, yawning as he watched semi trucks pass them by with the loud zip from their large tires.

"Damn, I had the worst fucking dream. How long was I out?"

"A couple of hours," he replied. "Think you got enough beauty rest?"

Rob grinned as he turned the truck keys to start it.

"Let's hope so. I dreamt that they'd sold Marianne. It was fucking nuts, man."

"What?" Kyle asked. "Did you at least kill him?"

"Yeah, I killed him," replied Rob. "A record shot for me, just under a mile."

"Well," Kyle said, "let's just hope it doesn't come to that."

Rob packed his dip can and put one in the side of his mouth to wake himself up.

"You ready?" he asked, spitting a stream of Copenhagen into a water bottle.

Kyle grabbed the door handle.

"Hold on a second. I need to take a piss."

Kyle got out of the vehicle and did his thing on the side of the road while Rob waited. A long stream of urine gushed by the open door.

"Damn," Rob said. "How much water have you been drinking?"

"Enough," replied Kyle. "You should see what happens when I drink too much beer."

Kyle zipped his pants up and climbed back in.

"Now I'm ready."

"All right," Rob said. "Let's do this."

Rob pressed tentatively on the gas. They traveled down the highway for a bit, then Rob drove off into the open meadow, bumping and rocking as they made their way across, a cloud of chalky dust trailing behind them. He stopped the truck nearly a mile from the spot, and they hopped out to hoof it the rest of the way.

They snatched their weapons and gear from the truck bed, stepped into their ghillie suits, and located a decent overwatch position. The men slipped across the field like mice, between bushes and under cover of darkness. They advanced until they reached an ideal spot with a good view of the full warehouse yard.

Rob set up the long gun while Kyle took a quick glimpse through his binoculars.

"You see anything?" Rob asked.

"No, not yet," he replied. "Just a truck parked by the building."

"Yeah, it looks pretty quiet," Rob said as he peeped through his night-vision scope. "This is the location he gave him. I hope it isn't a fucking dead end, or, even worse, a trap."

"I don't think so. I think we're just early to the party."

It was still relatively early in the evening. The men figured they were probably in for a lengthy wait. They settled between the withered brush as the light breeze flowed over the plain. Fighting through his tiredness, Rob kept alert, peering into the glass every few minutes.

Four hours went by as they kept each other awake by random chitchat. They weren't really talking about anything in particular, just past missions and wherever else they'd rather be. Rob thrust his body up and bent on the ground and moved a bit to keep his legs from falling asleep. But as he leaned forth to stretch his limbs, they spotted a semi-truck hauling a large trailer driving down the road toward the target building.

"Well, hello," Rob said. "What do we have here?"

Rob guided his right eye to the front of the lens.

They observed as the truck braked just shy of a ramp that led to a high bay door in front. The driver left his vehicle running and climbed down from the cab to meet another fellow who'd just exited the warehouse door.

"So it wasn't empty," Kyle said.

"Doesn't look that way," replied Rob. "Let's see what that bastard's carrying."

The driver appeared to hand the man some kind of document. The unknown gentleman led the other to the trailer, and he reached for the container door at the back of the truck. He opened up and pulled down a set of metal ramps. Four more men marched down, pulling a row of young girls connected like they were on a chain gang. Most couldn't walk straight, pulled along by the men with a chain attached to their wrists and ankles.

"What the fuck?" Rob said. "Am I seeing what I think I'm seeing?"

They looked like cattle being herded through a corral.

"Yep," Kyle said. "It looks like a place to store their girls, or, in this case, cargo."

Rob shut his eyes for a second and touched his forehead to the ground.

"Damn, I thought we'd seen the worst of humanity. But this is some sick shit."

"Yeah," Kyle said. "I don't see Marianne, though."

"I don't either," Rob said. "She's been gone for a while. These girls look like they were just snatched up. But I'm willing to bet someone down there knows where she is."

Rob looked over at his partner.

"Listen, we do this quietly. We need to find my sister. But

we should save these poor girls, too. If they know we are coming, they could kill them all."

"Roger that, bro," Kyle replied. "We grab one of these assholes and make him talk."

"Yep," said Rob. "But, whatever we do, we can't give them a chance to kill them. We go in swift and silent, my friend. They won't know what hit them."

⦙⦙⦙

Rob planted himself behind the glass again, legs straight behind him, and pulled the butt of the rifle into his shoulder. He watched as the men led the girls into the warehouse and shut the door after them. They'd left four guards roaming the grounds and an unknown number of men inside.

"What do you think this place is?" Rob asked.

"Honestly," Kyle replied. "From what I see, it looks like it's storage. Instead of storing cargo, they're keeping girls. I think they keep them here, possibly drug them, get them nice and fucked up, and send them somewhere else."

"Sounds about right," said Rob. "Let's get rid of these fuckers so we can get to them before that happens. It's a shame. They're all someone's fucking daughter, man."

Kyle peeped through his binoculars. He located two guards on each side of the building.

"Let's wait for this truck driver to move out of the fucking picture," said Rob. "Then we drop 'em."

They viewed as the driver climbed back into the cab of the truck, smoke rising from the exhaust as he turned it around and left down the path the same way he'd come in.

"All right," Kyle said.

He started setting up his rifle next to Rob's.

Rob felt the tip of the trigger with his finger and exhaled.

"Okay," Kyle said, flipping the bipod down and raising the dust cover from his scope. "On your go."

Rob watched as the closest man, three hundred meters away, roamed to the edge of the sandlot and lit a cigarette. He blew a string of white smoke into the air as Rob set up the shot. With suppressed weapons, nobody would hear from that distance.

Exhaling smoothly through his lips, Rob squeezed the trigger. Kyle followed up with a shot a millisecond later. Each target collapsed to the dirt with a red mist splattering the back through gaping exit wounds. Both men were dead before they hit the earth, a single cigarette still smoking on the ground beside one body.

"Tangos down," said Rob.

He swiveled his rifle to the other side.

"Let's fucking drop these guys before they find their dead buddies."

But as Rob regained his focus on the other targets, he saw one of them walking in that direction.

"Damn. I think he's seen them."

The man darted toward his dead friend. Following the target through the scope, Rob pressed the trigger. The man fell headfirst, sliding across the sand and leaving a bloodstream over the dusty ground.

Kyle had the other in his sights and was about to engage. He made the shot and struck his target in the chest, leaving a large exit wound in his back as he fell.

"Fuck, that was close," Rob said. "I thought he was going to give us away."

But neither Rob nor Kyle realized the Mexicans had radios

on them. And one target had contacted the men inside just before they killed him. A light appeared from inside the building as the door swung open. Ten men popped out of the warehouse and started moving fast through the field, holding American M4 rifles.

"Shit," said Rob. "There's too many of them. And we don't have time to move."

Short of taking off, there was only one thing they could do. Both Rob and Kyle slid their weapons and binoculars under their bodies as they spread over them. They buried their heads in the dirt between the brush and remained as still as they could. Each took pieces of dead foliage nearby and dropped them over their ghillie suits. It was a learned skill, something they'd trained for in sniper school.

They remained still as the sounds of chatter and footsteps got closer. In a matter of seconds, the men were just about on top of them. Rob could see a beam of flashing light in his peripheral vision as it flashed behind them. Chills ran down his body. He could almost feel their hot breath on his skin. He'd just hoped that one of them didn't roam too near and trip over them.

Rob edged his right arm under his body to the front of his vest, gripping his .45 pistol in case he needed to shoot. He was careful not to be clear in his movement and give their position away. The men shouted in Spanish in every direction, trying to figure out what had just happened. They aimed their weapons into the dark, cursing at every slight of wind. Rob knew they hadn't heard the shots. They were expecting to find someone fleeing the scene. They weren't focusing much on the ground.

But as soon as they'd appeared, they left frustrated in the other direction to search the opposite side. Rob could hear one of them cursing up a storm as they poked through the bush. He lifted his head slightly and peeked out.

"Damn," he whispered to Kyle. "A few more feet, they would've been standing right on top of us."

"Got that right," Kyle replied. "That was too close for comfort."

The cartel men were just outside of the warehouse, searching every piece of ground. They looked puzzled and irritable, shouting at each other. But they had no clue who killed their men or where the bullets had come from. Rob took advantage of the confusion. He instantly brought his rifle back up.

"Come on, partner," he said to Kyle. "Let's get 'em before they go back inside."

Rob discharged the empty shell casing from the chamber. He inserted another magazine, riding the bolt forward and pushing down on the bolt knob. He took aim and began firing systematically, one round at a time continuously until his five-round magazine was empty. The men scattered, firing their weapons indiscriminately in all directions. They were oblivious to the fact that a sniper team was on the prowl, hiding in the shadows among the vegetation.

Rob dropped his magazine to the earth and inserted another. He and Kyle fired into the group at the same time. They observed one by one as each of the men tumbled to the ground beneath them, not able to hear the shots. Rob and Kyle put them in the dirt before they knew what had happened. By the time they finished, many bodies were spread over the area in front of the warehouse.

Rob snatched his pistol, slung his rifle, and made his way ahead.

"Come on. Let's go."

Pistols ready, they crept across the field to the building's entry, crossing over dead bodies along the way. But one of them was still moving, trying to crawl across the ground to retrieve his weapon. He groaned painstakingly as Rob stood over him, removing the ghillie hood and pointing his gun downward.

"Who... are... you?" the man asked, blood spurting from his chest and coating his shirt.

"I'm the man who's going to kill you," Rob told him. "And the rest of your sick fucking friends."

Rob pressed the trigger, and his .45-caliber projectile ripped into the man's head, dispersing its contents across the now red ground. He fell silent. Rob continued forward, gripping the metal knob, and yanked the door open. He peeked in and saw something he'd never wanted to see in his lifetime.

The place was dingy. The foul odor of sweat and urine mixed with the desert heat filled the interior. There were two long rows of metal boxes in the middle of the room, each containing many girls who'd become demoralized with every sound and movement.

"Fuck," Rob said as they moved inside. "I wouldn't treat a rabid dog this way!"

They hurried to the center, watching out for other guards. Rob peered into the cages. Most of the girls were too strung out on drugs to talk. Only one was coherent enough. However, she appeared too terrified of their presence.

She was a pretty young girl with long, straight black hair. But she had bags under her eyes like she hadn't slept in weeks.

"Por favor... No!" she said as Rob got closer to her.

She couldn't have been over eighteen years old.

"No, no, miss," Rob replied. "It's all right. We're just here to help."

Rob lowered his gun and placed it back into the holster.

"See?" he said, displaying his hands to her. "I've put my gun away. Those evil men aren't coming back. We will not hurt you."

"No, no, por favor!" she said.

Whatever the cartel had done to her, it paralyzed her with fear.

"Do you speak English?" he asked. "Looks, miss, I have no weapon. We are here to get you out."

The girl calmed down a bit, nodding her head to address him.

Rob glanced down, seeing the locks on the gates.

"Good," said Rob. "Do you know where I can find the keys? Tell me where they are, and I'll let you out of there. We aren't these monsters. We are the good guys."

Kidnappings were a way of life, happening in almost every corner of Mexico. And these girls were not used to anyone being their savior. The cartels ran the streets and preyed on the poor. They were alone. Nobody had ever come to their rescue.

The girl said nothing, only facing the door.

"Stay here and watch them," he told Kyle. "Be right back."

Rob rushed outside to search the dead guards. As he fumbled through each of their pockets, he found a large key ring hung from one of their belts. He snapped it off and dashed back inside. Rob tried each padlock, eventually reaching the right key. He started unlocking the cages, all six of them, one by one. Most of the girls couldn't move. Many of them didn't even know where they were. But the one that Rob had been trying to talk to spoke up.

"Thank you, Mister," she mumbled. "I thought we would never be free again."

Tears flowed down her dirty cheek as she glanced at the others.

"You're welcome," he replied. "I'm sorry you had to go through that. What's your name?"

"Isabella," she said.

"That's a pretty name," Rob told her. "How did you end up here, Isabella?"

She looked like she was about to break down right in front of him as she thought back to the moment they took her.

"The narcos, Mister," she replied. "They come to our home, follow us from school, wherever they find us, it doesn't matter. They took me from my mother's front yard in the middle of the day."

Rob just listened. He felt sorrow for her and those like her.

"It pays to be an ugly girl in Mexico," she said.

"What do you mean by that?" asked Rob.

"I mean, they only want pretty girls," she replied. "They make more money from us. Many of us hide in the cornfields and other places, hoping they don't find us. But, somehow, they always do. They even kill families trying to protect their daughters."

"Listen, Isabella. My name is Rob. My friend and I are looking for my sister, Marianne."

He showed her a picture on his cell phone.

"Have you seen her? They took her, like you, from my home in New York. I have to find her."

"No, Mister. Sorry, I haven't. But I pray to God that you find her. It's terrifying what they do to us. I was so scared. All of us were!"

"I know," said Rob. "Thank you. They will pay for what they do to girls like you."

Rob could tell she was letting her guard down some, realizing they were no threat to her.

"Let's get them the hell out of here!" Rob told Kyle.

With Isabella's help, they started loading the girls into the back of a cargo truck left at the side of the warehouse. But one of them appeared unable to move, lying alone in the cage's corner.

"Hey, sweetie," he said. "Nod if you can understand me."

But she didn't acknowledge him. There wasn't even so much as a head movement. Rob knew that they had doped her up like the rest. But she looked to be on the brink of death. She appeared to be in her early teens. And Rob was hoping her frail-looking body wouldn't give way to the narcotics in her system.

He boosted her up over his shoulder and carried her through the door as Kyle helped load the rest. They would do their best to save her. Maybe she would remember something that would help them find the rest of the girls, and, at last, Marianne.

"Go, hurry," Rob told Isabella as she climbed into the cab of the oversized cargo truck. "Get out of here!"

As exhaust from the vehicle shot into the air as she put it in drive, Rob and Kyle whipped out in the other direction, leaving a dust cloud rising behind them.

NINETEEN

Santiago, Mexico

Rob settled at the foot of the squeaky, queen-size bed, dripping gun oil onto his rifle bolt and sliding it back and forth to lubricate it. The morning sun had just peeked into the faded window drapes in the small room of a cheap, one-story highway motel. He'd been up since four o'clock a.m., observing that young girl and waiting for signs of life.

But she had moved little all night. A makeshift IV dangled from a wire coat hanger hung from a small nail in the wall above her head. They loaded it with Narcan, dripping much-needed fluids into her veins to counteract the drugs in her body.

Rob had cross-trained as a medic and a first responder, as many of his fellow Special Forces operators did. Out of habit, he'd carried a medical kit in his pack. Rob had administered Narcan before, but only to counter the respiratory-depressing side effects of morphine he'd injected injured soldiers with on the battlefield.

Rob wiped the excess oil from his rifle with a clean cloth.

He set it up against the wall in the corner as Kyle appeared from the bathroom after a hot shower.

"Anything yet?" Kyle asked, drying his head and face with a towel.

"Nope," Rob replied. "Nothing yet."

Kyle took a seat next to Rob at the edge of the bed as he slipped on a T-shirt.

"I'll tell you something, man," he said. "These assholes are going straight to hell for what they do to these poor people."

"It's not just these people," Rob replied. "It's also every American city with junkies and dealers on the corners. They don't care about the lives they destroy, as long as they stay fucking rich."

"Yeah. You're absolutely right."

Rob grabbed one of his rifle magazines from his ruck's side pocket and started refilling it with ammo. He reflected for a moment, glancing up at his friend as he dumped the remaining ammo from the ammo box onto the bedsheet.

"I remember sniper school, man," Rob said, pushing rounds into the magazine one at a time with his thumb. "How they taught us not to see the enemy as human, how to get rid of the emotion that came with killing, so we could do our jobs. It became like a reflex, a reaction. To take lives, you have to, or it will eat away at you."

"Yeah," Kyle said. "I remember all too well."

"I remember my first sniper mission," said Rob. "I buried any feeling of guilt deep inside. Like they taught us, I saw the enemy as objects to get rid of, not human beings. It worked. When I killed those people, the only thing I felt was the recoil from my rifle. And ever since then, I've done it with little thought."

"I know, man," replied Kyle. "I know what you mean."

"That's what these guys are to me," said Rob. "Objects, obstacles to run the fuck over. And we're going to tear their house down until there's nothing but fucking rubble left. I want them to know the grim reaper is coming for their asses. There is nowhere they can hide from us."

Rob finished loading the rifle magazine and slid it back into his pouch. As he lowered the pack onto the carpet, he felt a slight movement from behind him. He scanned down and saw the girl's feet twitching.

"Hey," he told Kyle. "She's moving."

Rob moved around the bed and sat on the chair beside her. He grasped her hand softly. The girl's body moved more. As her eyes cracked open, she slowly tilted her head to the side. Seeing Rob's outline through her fuzzy vision, she gasped as she tried to sit up. But she was too frail to lift her body.

Rob gripped her arm to keep the IV from being ripped out as she tried to turn away from him.

"No, no," she cried in Spanish. "No, por favor!"

Like many young girls in Mexico, strangers horrified her. Anyone who got close to her could be a kidnapper.

"We aren't going to hurt you," said Rob. "Calm down, please."

But she started thrashing around, trying to muster up enough strength to get out of bed. Rob held her arms down by her side. The girl turned her head, liquid flowing from her mouth to the side of the bed. Rob took a clean towel and began wiping it up, propping her head with a pillow.

"It's okay," he said, watching her cough up the rest. "You're okay."

Rob wiped her mouth with the towel and felt her forehead.

"Listen. We are here to help you. Maybe you don't remember, but they captured you with a group of other girls. We got you out of there and away from those men."

The girl was scared and didn't trust them. She didn't trust anyone but her family.

"No!" she screamed again in Spanish. "Eres un secuestrador! You kidnapper!"

Rob didn't fully grasp what the girl was saying.

"You speak English?" he asked her.

"Si! Yes, I do. What you want with me?"

Rob lifted a Velcro patch from his rucksack and showed it to her.

"Look, we are US Army Special Forces. We are trying to help you!"

The girl glanced down at the IV in her right arm.

"US Army? Why you here? Why is a needle in my arm?"

Rob flung the patch on top of his pack.

"They drugged you," he said. "This will get rid of the fentanyl in your system."

The girl put her face to the pillow as she cried. Rob took her hand.

"What is your name, sweetie?" he asked.

The girl was reluctant to answer him.

"My name is Rosa," she replied, rubbing her wet eyes. "Rosa Vásquez."

"Good," said Rob. "That's a beautiful name. I'm Rob. And this fellow here is Kyle."

Rob gave her a piece of a sandwich he had wrapped up on the TV table.

"Come on. You need to eat something."

She took the piece of meat and bread and started nibbling at it.

"Do you remember anything you can tell us about the men who took you?" he asked. "Anything at all?"

Rosa attempted to sit up in bed.

"Can you help me, please, Mister?"

Rob and Kyle each took an arm and pulled her upward, piling two pillows behind her back.

"There you go," Rob said. "Now, is there anything you remember?"

She seemed hesitant to talk about it, looking at Rob with terror in her eyes.

"Please," he said. "Anything is helpful."

"It happened fast," she said, sniffling. "I was walking home from school. These men, they pulled up in a van, grabbed me. The last thing I remember is being tossed into a box with other girls. They chained us up and threw us in like dogs!"

"Fucking pigs," said Kyle. "All of 'em."

Rob retrieved a picture of Marianne, showing it to her.

"What about this one? Did you see her?"

Rosa held the photo in her hand.

"No, I don't think so."

Frustrated, Rob took the image in his hand.

"Wait," she said, snatching it back.

"What is it?" asked Rob.

"She looks familiar."

"Really? Do you remember where you might have seen her?"

"Yes, sir," she replied. "I saw a photo. They were talking about how much money they could make with her."

"Do you know where they took her?" Kyle asked.

"No, Mister. I'm sorry, I don't."

"Where was this at?" Rob asked her.

"It was in Mexico City, sir," she said. "That's where I'm from and where they took me. I remember being chained and put into a dark container. They put a needle in me. I remember nothing else. Then I woke up here."

Rob glanced back at Kyle.

"Mexico City, huh?" Kyle said. "That's a good place to start."

Rob wiped his hands with a baby wipe and put on a pair of latex gloves. He delicately removed the IV needle from Rosa's arm and left the bag hanging. Rob opened his medical kit and applied a piece of sterile gauze and tape over the tiny hole.

"Come on," he said, wrapping his arms around her and helping her shift her frail body to get off the bed. "We're going to take you home. I'm sure your family is worried sick about you."

♦♦♦

In Monterrey, Marco had been busy tracking a lead on the men's whereabouts. Unknown to them, Fernando suspected Officer Ramos from the very start. But it wasn't just their last meeting that had him wondering about him. They'd believed him to be a mole all along.

There was a big push from the Mexican government's higher echelons, who'd made an agreement with the US. They wanted to get tough on crime in the country and rid their departments of corrupt police officers. An arrangement between ICE (Immigration and Customs Enforcement) and Mexico's National Guard had developed. The United States

Federal Government had partnered with Mexico to reduce the amount of narcotics and sex trafficking victims that crossed the border. In return, they would tackle the problem of unlawfully smuggled American firearms into Mexico.

Higher-ups in the police force had found Officer Ramos out. But instead of imprisoning him, he'd agreed to remain undercover and feed them intelligence. But being doubted by the cartel wasn't great news for him. Marco had also been secretly looking in on Ramos's meeting with Fernando, unaware of Rob and Kyle's presence. Marco followed him to his home in downtown Monterrey shortly after. The cartel wasn't taking any more chances on him. He simply knew too much.

Marco had broken into Officer Ramos's home by smashing a window. Now, he was standing before him, blade in hand, while Ramos's wife and daughter watched in horror, tied up together in the corner of the dining room.

"Please, no!" the officer's wife screamed. "Please, don't hurt him! We'll give you money, whatever you want! Just don't kill my husband!"

Ramos's young daughter cried hysterically next to her mother as she pleaded with Marco not to kill her husband.

"Bitch, like I fucking need your money," he said.

Marco stared at the officer's wife with a bitter smirk. Then he glanced down at Officer Ramos.

"You didn't even have the fucking cojones to tell your own wife, did you?" he asked. "Fucking pathetic."

Marco glared back at the woman as she looked at her husband.

"What?" she asked. "What is it I don't know? Tell me why this is happening!"

The Messenger

Marco approached and crouched on the ground beside her.

"You see," he said, "your husband has been working for us, Mrs. Ramos. And he's been a very bad boy."

A tear rolled down her cheek as she looked on in disgust.

"Is this true?" she asked Ramos. "You've been working for these people?"

"I wanted to tell you…" he said. "Please, forgive me,"

But Marco interrupted him, standing over the officer with the knife to his neck.

"Enough, you fucking people!" Marco shouted. "I don't have time for this sentimental bullshit. He betrayed us. Now, he must pay the price!"

Marco reached around with that blade and slit the officer's throat, whose body slumped over to one side as he quickly began bleeding out on the dining room floor. He spit on the body.

"Fucking puto!" he said.

Marco ripped away Ramos's blood-soaked shirt and wiped the blade on his pants leg. As mother and daughter sobbed in the corner, Marco went around the puddle of blood and stood over them. They each covered their faces as they cried hysterically.

"Please, no…" the wife said.

But it was too late. Not wanting to leave witnesses, he snatched his pistol from the back of his pants and shot them both once in the head. He left the bodies and wandered through the front door and out to the yard, draping the shirt from the mailbox as a warning to all who passed by, especially the police.

Marco jumped into his vehicle nearby and sped down the

road as fast as that Suburban would go on his way to the warehouse. A twenty-minute ride later, he pulled up to the front of the building. He tapped the brakes hard, kicking up a fine dust into the air, and skimmed to a halt. The door swung open, and his brown cowboy boots hit the ground.

The first thing that Marco noticed were bodies, lots of bodies left across the ground in front of him. He knew it was them. Nobody else would have the balls to do such a thing.

"Fuck!" he said to himself. "How could this happen?"

But that was just the beginning of his trouble. Marco skipped over the corpses in his way and advanced through the front door of the place. He couldn't believe what his eyes were seeing: nothing, absolutely nothing. The whole place was totally bare except for a few open cages.

"Shit," he said. "Juan is going to be pissed."

Marco dialed Juan's number, contemplating what he was going to say to him.

"Tell me good news, Marco," Juan answered. "Have you dealt with our problem yet?"

"Not exactly, boss," he replied. "Ramos is dead. But somebody has seriously fucked with our operation in Los Fuentes."

"What do you mean, fucked with, Marco? Speak plainly! I don't have time for this!"

"I mean, they're dead. They are all fucking dead, boss!" Marco told him. "And the merchandise is all gone. There is nothing left!"

Marco could hear on the line as Juan threw his phone to the floor.

"Fuck!" Juan screamed. "Two men! You can't find two fucking men?"

Juan cursed loudly as he stomped around. He returned to the phone a minute later and jerked it from the floor.

"Listen to me very carefully, Marco. I don't care what you have to do. I don't care if you have to tear an entire city apart to find them. You find them now. If you aren't capable, I will find someone who is. And I will kill you for the trouble, got it? I am losing my fucking patience!"

"Yeah, boss," Marco replied. "I got it, loud and clear."

"You'd better!" Juan shouted. "This is your last fucking chance!"

But in Marco's head, he was cursing him right back. He hung up on Juan before he could say another foul word to him.

"Fuck you too," he said to the empty line. "You question my fucking competence?"

Frustrated, Marco went back outside to search for anything that might tell him what happened to their men. He crouched down and turned one body over, removing the AK-47 from beneath him. It was clear from the size of the exit wound that he'd been shot with a large-caliber rifle. Marco had long guessed that they were dealing with trained sharpshooters. And, judging by the shot placement, they were skilled. The random formation of these men on the ground told him they had no idea where the shots had come from. With nowhere to run, they never stood a chance.

But, if they were after the girls, assuming any of them could talk, Marco could think of one place they might go. The cartel had people all over, those that fed them information for a little slice of the pie. They were mostly poor, young kids who would do anything to make quick dinero for their families. They were kind of like police informants, but on the opposite side of the coin. The cartels used them because they were desperate. And during desperate times, some would do the unimaginable. It's how the cartels repressed people, even purchasing phones for them.

Marco placed another call on his cell.

"Hello?" a fourteen-year-old kid answered, out of breath.

"Hey, Raúl. How are you, kid?"

"I'm good, sir," he said. "I'm just playing football with the neighborhood kids."

"That's good, Raúl," Marco said. "That's fantastic. Listen, I have something for you."

Raúl went quiet.

"Yeah?" he asked.

"Yeah," Marco said. "I'm going to send you a photo of a couple of men, all right? I need you to spread it around town. Tell anyone who sees them to notify you right away. Then, you contact me. It's that simple. Can you do that for me? I'll pay you more money for this one, okay?"

Marco waited for Raúl to answer.

"You with me, Raúl?" he asked. "Do we have a deal?"

"Yes," Raúl replied. "I mean, yes, sir. I will do it."

Raúl's family was dirt poor. There was no way he was going to say no. Like others, he was afraid of the cartel. His family needed the money. His parents could barely put food on the table. They couldn't even afford to buy him and his sister's clothes or send them to school. It restricted the kids to staying home and making money however they could, it seemed. Everyone in Mexico City knew what was happening to the children. But the cartel was just too overpowering to take on unless they wanted a bloodbath.

"Good," Marco said. "I knew you'd be a good sport. I'll text you the picture after I hang up."

The Messenger

Marco ended the call and headed to the back of his vehicle. He popped the hatch and reached for a long black hard case and opened it. Made in the USA, a .338 Lapua Magnum sniper rifle capable of tearing someone's head off at over fifteen hundred meters rested inside. The gun could rip right through standard body armor. The Los Lobos Cartel had an immense weapon smuggling operation, arming themselves to the teeth with mostly US weapons. And nobody, even the powerful US government, could stop it. Once they made it to Mexico, it was fair game.

"I can play that too," Marco said to himself, loading the rest of the two hundred and eighty-five-grain rounds into the magazine.

That long gun fired a round that traveled at just over three thousand feet per second. For the right marksman, it was deadly accurate. He raised the rifle and took a quick peek through the glass. You could say it was a hunting rifle of sorts, but not for killing animals. He hunted men. Marco had trained as a sharpshooter for the police department in Mexico. And he was about to get warmed up.

TWENTY

Mexico City

They dropped Rosa off at the end of a long road a quarter of a mile from her house by a row of similar-style buildings. It was a typical, humble, one-room home in Iztapalapa, one of Mexico City's lower-class urban neighborhoods in the city's southeastern part. Graffiti decorated almost every structure and concrete wall around them. It wasn't considered a nice area of town, even by the locals. Barbed wire lined the tops of some barriers that surrounded many of the homes to ward off trespassers. Bars were fixed to almost every window. But those who lived there were used to the crime.

Rosa's mother was out front, hanging clothes over the line to dry. Rob almost teared up as they watched the girl gallop down the street. Her mother glanced up as she reached into the clothes basket and saw her daughter darting toward her. Rosa ran fast and almost tumbled over her own feet. Hysterical, her mother dumped the clothes basket to the ground. She ran with her arms wide open to meet her daughter by the high metal gate. Rosa's mom was astounded to see her, thinking they had lost their precious daughter permanently.

Rob and Kyle looked on from a distance as Rosa and her panic-stricken mother locked in a warm embrace. Rosa couldn't contain her emotion and the glowing smile on her face. They'd seen her glance back at them one last time, just before the rest of the family rushed through the front door to meet her at the bottom of the small brick porch. It was a happy ending for one little girl.

"I wish they all could end up like that," Rob said.

"Yeah," Kyle replied. "Me too."

The men hadn't planned to stay, and they didn't want Rosa's family to know who'd rescued her. They just wanted to make sure she got home safely. And now that she had, they could move on to pressing business.

Rob whipped the car in the other direction and sped away toward the opposite side of town.

Rosa had mentioned the name of a local bar on the long drive to her family home. She'd said that many of the older neighborhood teenagers hung out there since Mexico's legal drinking age was eighteen. But they did more than drink. It was a local hangout spot for some of the Los Lobos errand boys. They were just kids. But they carried guns and worked for the cartel, doing odd jobs and scouting for young girls to take off the street. Mexico's capital city was a target-rich environment for them. And they looked the part, sporting gold chains and driving cars and motorbikes they never could have afforded otherwise. Everyone in the city knew who they were. They didn't hide it. But nobody messed with them for worry of facing the cartel. That was enough to silence just about everyone.

Rob and Kyle rocketed down the one-way street, through

intersections and past multi-colored apartments and businesses. When they pulled into the lot, they noticed a large sign at the top of the building that read La Organización, or "the Organization." The bar was one of many cartel-owned establishments. Eyes would be on them as soon as they entered the bar. They were gringos, outsiders to most. To the cartel and to Juan Luis, they were now a mark.

Rob slid his Glock into his jeans and went directly for the glass front door, Kyle right behind. As soon as they walked into the place, heads turned to the open door. The locals were skittish, uneasy, and not trusting of strangers. Not taken back by anyone, Rob and Kyle ignored them. They each took a stool by the bar counter. Rob waved down the bartender.

The man approached them, a troubled look on his face. Everyone who lived around there knew it was a cartel joint. And having two white guys in the bar and in that part of town was unusual and troubling to him.

"American?" the bartender asked.

Rob gave him a slight sneer.

"You know, you're not the first person to ask us that," Rob said to him. "Yeah, we're American. And we'd like two beers, please."

"Gringo," the man replied. "Do you have any idea where you are?"

Rob took a quick glance around the room.

"Yep," he said. "I know exactly where we are. Two beers, please."

It was clear to the bartender they didn't want to heed his warning. He just shook his head and set two beer bottles on the counter. Rob tossed a few bills into the tip jar.

Tourists didn't go to that part of the city. Just by looking around, they could tell it wasn't a very welcoming place. It was a slum, and crime prevailed in the neighborhood. It wasn't just pickpockets and burglaries on the rise. Murder and kidnapping had become routine. The King of Mexico City, the Los Lobos cartel, had dominated all the other criminal empires in that city and the rest of Mexico with their inhuman nature.

Rob tipped his head back, taking a long gulp from his bottle while glimpsing at the bartender. He peeped down at his name tag.

"Listen, Roberto, I have a question for you."

Roberto didn't want to talk to him. He didn't want to answer questions from a couple of white guys, but it wouldn't stop Rob from asking. The barkeep just quietly stared at him.

"Look, partner," Rob said.

He retrieved his picture of Marianne.

"Have you seen this girl?" he asked, placing the image on the counter in front of him. "They took her from my home and brought her down here."

Roberto didn't dare say a word. He knew people were watching, people who had a direct line to the cartel.

"No hablo inglés, Mister."

"Well, you sure did a couple of minutes ago."

Rob leaned over the bar and got closer to him.

"Listen, Roberto," said Rob. "I'm in a foul mood and all out of patience. Have you seen this girl or not?"

He still wouldn't answer. Rob grabbed him by his shirt collar and snatched him down, slamming his head into the bar counter.

"I will ask you one more time!"

Everyone in the room heard Rob. Roberto tried to look up, blood spilling from his lip onto the shiny countertop. But

Rob held a steady grip on him.

"Have you seen her or not, asshole? It's a simple fucking question!"

Rob drove Roberto's head harder into the bar and began smashing it down. Blood started dripping from his nose. Suddenly, a young Mexican kid strolled through the back door of the place. As he came around the room from the back of the building, he saw them.

It was Raúl. And while Rob pounded Roberto, Raúl froze in his tracks, remembering their faces right away from Marco's images.

"I know you know something, asshole!" Rob shouted in Roberto's face. "I'll fucking make you talk!"

He noticed the kid out of the corner of his eye and swung his head. Rob locked eyes with the kid. Raúl dashed past the bar and through the front door.

"The kid!" Kyle said to Rob. "Get the kid!"

Rob let go of Roberto, leaving his face bleeding, and they both ran for the street to chase Raúl down. The kid moved as fast as he could go down the sidewalk as Rob and Kyle scrambled after him. He looked back, seeing them gaining on him, and took a left through an alley between two buildings. Raúl ducked into a restaurant, almost knocking a couple of patrons to the floor. He burst into the kitchen, barely missing kitchen staff as he broke through the back door.

"Sorry, sir," Rob said, skirting around a restaurant customer. The kid had bumped into a table. Rob almost crashed into him as he made his way after Raúl.

Rob bolted through the back door. He looked left and saw Raúl rounding the corner, heading across a hotel parking lot. Rob and Kyle picked up the pace, sprinting full speed as they caught up. Raúl shot between parked cars and out to the street, passing in front of a moving vehicle, almost striking him down in the busy intersection. Raúl vanished behind a building. Rob and Kyle turned the hotel wall corner, expecting to see him up ahead of them.

They slowed to a fast walk.

"Where the fuck did he go?" asked Rob.

"I don't know," Kyle replied. "That slick bastard. He can't be far."

They wandered past a parking garage, looking for Raúl. As they arrived at the entrance, Rob scanned to his left and found Raúl huddled against the wall behind a bush, a cell phone to his ear.

Raúl saw them, and he made a break for it through the structure, trying to lose them. But Rob wasn't playing games. He rushed Raúl before he could gain much ground and dove headfirst, clipping him in the back and knocking him over. The phone slipped from Raúl's hand and tumbled across the ground. Kyle snatched him to keep him from getting away and pinned him to the ground.

"Why are you running, kid?" Rob asked. "Huh? What do you know? You better start talking before I get even angrier than I already am!"

Kyle handed the kid over and began watching the entrance for witnesses.

Raúl's eyes showed bitterness and fear as he scowled up at Rob. But he was going to get it out of him.

"Listen, man," Rob said. "I'm not into beating the hell out of kids. But I'm close to not giving a shit! Answer my question. Why did you run from us?"

Rob reached into Raúl's front pants pocket and pulled out

a picture. It was the picture Marco had given him of Rob and Kyle at Manuel's.

"Where did you get this?"

Rob withdrew his gun and stuck it in Raúl's face.

"Listen, kid," he said. "I don't want to. But I will. Now, you tell me about the cartel's sex trafficking in this city, or I will put one between your eyes. I know they use kids like you to do their dirty work. Don't make me do this."

Rob grasped Raúl's chin hard with his left palm and poked the gun into his head. Raúl knew Rob wasn't messing around. He was just a teenager. Raúl didn't know if Rob would really shoot him or not. But he didn't want to find out.

"Okay, Mister!" Raúl said. "Okay! Please, don't shoot!"

Rob lowered his weapon.

"You have something to tell me, son?" asked Rob.

Raúl's face turned bright red. Now, he seemed nothing more than a scared young boy.

"They make us do it!" Raúl told him. "They pay us. But they threaten to kill our families if we say no. I didn't have a choice, Mister!"

"Pay you to do what, kid?" Rob asked him. "What do you do for them?"

"To find the girls, Mister. We are lookouts."

Rob set the gun beside him on the floor as he knelt down near Raúl. He realized that the boy was afraid. He was probably just trying to help his family. That was the cartel's poison. They turned hopeless, impoverished youngsters into criminals. Like cancer, they spread across Mexico without compassion for any human being.

"Where do they take them?" asked Rob. "The girls, where do they go?"

"Um..."

Raúl thought for a moment.

"What's your name?" Rob asked.

"Raúl, Mister."

"Okay, Raúl. Where do they take the girls?"

"You'd better answer him, kid," Kyle told him. "I've seen him when he's mad. It isn't pretty."

"Um..." Raúl said. "The big house... Yeah, the big house with the big blue door, Mister."

"And where is this big house with the big blue door?" asked Rob.

"Near the park," he replied. "Near the entrance to the park."

"Which park, Raúl? There's more than one park in this city."

"American Park, Mister!" he said. "Yeah, the American Park!"

Rob glanced behind Raúl and noticed the phone not far away. He went to snatch it from the ground. The screen was cracked, but it still worked.

"I think he was calling his cartel buddies on us," Kyle said.

"Who were you talking to?" Rob said, holding the phone in front of Raúl's face. "Were you trying to sic the dogs on us?"

Rob checked the phone for Raúl's last dialed number.

"Well, let's just see, shall we?"

The phone rang, and Rob waited, switching it to speaker. A few seconds later, a deep voice answered the line.

"Raúl?" the voice said. "What you got for me, kid? It better be good."

"Marco!" he blurted out. "They caught me! I'm sorry, I tried to run away!"

Raúl was nothing more than a child. He thought for sure that Marco would forgive him.

"That's not the answer I was looking for," Marco replied to the kid. "And what did you tell them?"

"He said nothing, jackass," Rob said, trying to save the kid. "Not a damn thing. He's been a good little cartel soldier."

They could hear Marco's heavy and heated breathing on the line. He was utterly silent for a while. Then he broke the silence.

"And to whom am I speaking?" Marco asked.

"The name is Rob Walker," he replied. "Who are you, asshole?"

"I am the man who's going to hunt you down like an animal," Marco told him.

"Oh, yeah?" Rob asked.

"Bring it on, shithead," Kyle said.

"You see," Marco said. "I am the one they call to take care of certain problems. I am a fixer of sorts. Like everyone else, you should fear me. I am hired to get rid of trash like you."

"Oh, really?" asked Rob. "Well, dickhead. You've got my sister. I'm going to get her back. And we're going to bring your house of cards crashing to the fucking ground!"

Marco chuckled at him.

What Rob and Kyle didn't realize was Raúl had gotten through to Marco. He'd already been on his way to intercept them when they found the kid. Marco had a view of the parking garage inside from the roof of another building close by.

"The kid looks scared, Mister Walker. Don't hurt him. He's just a boy."

Rob realized that Marco was watching. He didn't have an unobstructed view of them, but the kid was in his line of sight.

The Messenger

"Show yourself, and maybe I spare him!" Marco said.

Rob had been trying to scare the kid into talking. He didn't really want to see him hurt. He knew Raúl had just been following orders.

"Move, kid," Rob said to Raúl. "Duck behind the wall, now!"

But it was too late. A shot rang out from beyond the parking garage. Striking Raúl in the face, it split his jaw apart. The impact scattered parts of his face and head across the floor and flung his body back onto the cold concrete surface.

"That happens to those who cross us!" Marco roared through the phone. "You will pay the price!"

The line went dead. Rob glanced at Raúl's body, his arms stretched out to the side in a puddle of blood.

"Damn it, kid. I wasn't going to do anything that bad."

Rob wasn't a monster. He never wanted to go around bullying kids. But he had no mercy for those who took advantage of them.

"I know," Kyle said. "But we have another problem here."

Rob secured his long gun from its carrier, extending the foldable buttstock. He carefully inched out just enough to view Marco's presumed position and braced the weapon onto the hood of a nearby car. With no time for scope adjustments, he'd make the shot on the fly. Rob spotted the small outline of Marco's head just above the rooftop wall. But before he could fire, the crack of another shot sounded through the air and put a hole in the hood to the left of Rob's rifle barrel.

Rob dipped behind the car next to Kyle.

"This guy is irritating me!"

Rob placed his sniper rifle on the concrete and hit the floor.

"Come on," he said to Kyle. "This is not a good position. We can't stay here!"

Kyle followed Rob's lead as he started low-crawling through the garage to the other side, both their chins dragging across the ground. They made their way to the other entrance, bobbing up behind the wall and out of Marco's vision. Both men hugged the wall and began circling the outside of the parking garage, dashing across the street and staying out of Marco's view.

A few minutes later, they approached the outside of Marco's suspected position. Rob and Kyle crept onward to the six-story building's interior and headed up the stairs. But as they broke through the roof access door, weapons ready to engage, they found the place empty.

The men began looking around the rooftop. But it seemed they'd just missed him.

"Where the hell he go?" Rob asked, searching behind every corner and crevice. "This is where the shot came from. I'm sure of it!"

"I don't know," Kyle said. "But I think he's fucking toying with us. It won't be the last time we deal with this asshole, I'm sure."

Rob knew Marco didn't have a decent shot on them from up there. Instead, he'd killed Raúl. Maybe that was his plan all along. But they understood one thing quite clear: they had another sniper on their tail. And one or more of them would end up in the grave before it was all over. As for Raúl, he was just one more pawn in the cartel's deadly game. But his death wasn't in vain. Raúl had given them a tidbit of information to go on before he died.

"Come on," Rob said. "Let's get the hell out of here."

TWENTY-ONE

```
Polanco
Mexico City
```

The afternoon daylight heat blazed down over the city as Rob and Kyle sat on a bench on the near-empty park's outer edges. It was an area the cartel had frequented. Mexico City was the kidnapping capital of the country. Parents were too skeptical about letting their kids run around, afraid they'd vanish like so many others had. Many had gone missing over the years. It was a big problem. Most had given up hope, not trusting the rotten Mexican criminal justice system.

Under the shade of park trees, the men had an excellent view of the neighborhood houses opposite them across the roundabout. They were onto something, watching the house with the blue door that Raúl had told them about right before he died. They'd forced Raúl, like a myriad of other children the cartel had used over the years. And Rob was sure that pure evil waited behind that big door.

The men lingered in that spot all afternoon, watching as the cars passed by them one after the other. Pedestrians were noticeably lacking, most preferring to stay away from that part of town. Although people wouldn't talk about it, the cartel had control over that city. Even the police, the ones who weren't corrupt, wouldn't fight back. Rob and Kyle had other plans. They were on a mission to destroy their sex industry from the inside out. But first, they had to get inside that house.

Rob knew they couldn't just stroll through the front door. They'd be safeguarding the entrance very closely. As the sun retreated behind the city buildings overlooking the residential area, someone caught Rob's eye. It was a pair of men, and they looked to be going for that door.

"Hey," Rob said to Kyle. "Check it out."

They saw as the men reached the house and knocked three times on the blue painted door. A second later, the door slot slid open. There was a brief conversation, and the character behind the door opened up just enough to allow them in. Rob and Kyle waited to see how long it would take before the mystery gentlemen reemerged.

Almost twenty minutes later, the men finally exited the home, marching down the street in the opposite direction they'd come from.

"Let's do this," Rob told him. "Follow me."

Rob picked up a slow jog across the street, slightly obscured behind a line of trees around the circular roadway so the men wouldn't see him. Kyle followed close after, and they got down behind several parked cars and waited for the men to gain a little distance.

"What's the plan, Rob?" Kyle asked.

"The plan?" Rob replied. "We're going to grab these assholes. They're going to help us get in."

They moved alongside the vehicles parked on the curb

until Rob saw the men turn right onto a side street between two buildings. Rob hugged the wall as he peeked around the corner. This time, the two men made another turn into a dead-end alley and past a row of dumpsters.

Rob picked up the pace, charging down the path to cut them off. Moving up along a tall privacy fence, he lifted the suppressed Glock from his waistband.

He gave Kyle a hand signal.

The duo scooped up behind the two men as they prepared to enter one door, guns pointed outward.

"Don't move," said Rob. "Get your hands up, both of you, and turn around."

The two men slowly raised their hands and turned around, facing the wall.

"No hablo inglés, señor," one of them said.

"No habla, huh?" Rob asked, sticking his gun into the man's face. "What if I shoot you right now? Or you can help us and live. It's not a tough choice."

The Mexican's facial expression changed. Rob put the barrel into his eye, watching him flinch.

"Oh, yeah," Rob said. "You understand English just perfect, don't you?"

The other man spat in Rob's direction, just missing his face. Kyle reared back and whacked him across the cheek, knocking his head back. Rob grabbed him and shoved him against the wall.

"Gentlemen. You can help us, and we'll be on our way. Or we can just kill you here and put your bodies in the dumpster like pieces of trash. What's it going to be, amigos?"

Rob took the man's head in his hands, holding his gun to his throat.

"Give me an answer. Or we're going to kill you and your friend, right here!"

"What do you want, Mister?"

"You're going to get us in that house," replied Rob. "Right about now!"

They each took hold of one, and Rob ordered them back to the street, concealing their guns under their shirts.

"Walk! And don't think of trying to run or make a sound, or you'll be dead before you even cross the fucking street."

The Mexicans probably believed they'd be let go once they'd done what Rob had told them to. Knowing they worked for the cartel in some capacity, he'd let them think that. His hand on the pistol hidden under his shirt, they followed the men down the sidewalk back to the place they were at before. Once they reached the doorstep, Rob and Kyle braced themselves against the wall, facing each other.

"Just tell them you need to talk," Rob whispered. "Don't fuck up or even think about giving us away."

He pounded on the door. Moments later, the peephole thrust open.

"What do you want?" the figure behind the door asked in Spanish. "You forget something?"

"Yeah," he said. "We need to talk. It's important."

They heard the large lock being turned. Then the door came open. But before the man could close it behind them, Rob inserted his foot in the doorway to block it. He took the inside edge of the door and flung it back, flattening the two men on the other side to the floor, their Uzi submachine guns falling from their hands and clanking off the floor. Rob and Kyle recovered their pistols, eliminating the men on the ground before they could move. Rob raised his gun again as the other two tried to flee to the opposite end. He mowed them both down before they could make it down the hall, their bodies plunging forward and sliding across the smooth tile floor. Rob latched the door behind them.

He bent down and picked up one of the Uzis.

"On me," Rob said.

Kyle followed Rob as he made his way down the corridor, peering into every room and around each corner. But the floor was empty. Everything looked quiet. But as they advanced forward, they found a locked steel door at the back of the house.

"You got your lock pick kit on you?" he asked Kyle. "This door is too heavy to kick in."

"Of course I do," Kyle replied. "I never leave home without it."

Kyle reached into his pocket and lifted the lock pick, giving it to Rob.

"Perfect. This should do the trick."

Rob began messing with the lock. A couple of minutes later, it was released. He bumped the door open gingerly and peeked through the crack, the only light coming from a dim bulb casting a yellow glare onto the white wall next to a stairwell.

"Looks like a basement. We have another floor down here."

Kyle laid his hand on Rob's shoulder.

"Right behind you."

The men moved on to the top step. They heard a commotion coming from down below. It was an unknown number of men talking among each other and cursing a fight on TV. Rob and Kyle continued, descending the stairs one step at a time until they reached the bottom, moving into a shadow in the corner. Rob knew it was a cartel stash house when he saw the stacks of money along the right wall, wrapped in plastic.

"I can't believe they can get away with this shit in the middle of the fucking city," Rob whispered.

"The government's in their hip pocket," replied Kyle.

Rob peeped out for a moment. He counted six rooms, including a living area that he could not see inside. But he could hear the men babbling in Spanish. With the television blaring, it was no wonder they didn't hear the noise from above.

Rob and Kyle turned to the edge of the wall. A single man, noticing them out of the corner of his eye, tried to grab his own gun from the table. Rob beat him to it, pressing the Uzi trigger and watching his lifeless head smash into a plate full of food on the table. Blood spilled from his neck onto the plate as his arms dangled from the side of the table.

Before Rob could engage the second target, Kyle had already dispatched the other two. A fourth skulked on the other side with his hands out.

"Don't bother calling for help," Rob said. "Your pals upstairs are dead."

Rob began to hear a moan emanating from down the hallway.

"Watch this fucker," Rob told Kyle. "I need to check this out. If he moves or screams, kill him."

Rob went on down the hallway until he reached the first room. Rob saw a young girl, mid-teens, lying on a slim mattress on the ground in a pool of her own vomit with a needle sticking from her arm. He went to her bedside and felt her neck for a pulse. Barely alive—her pulse was weak. Without medical help, she'd most likely die.

Rob stood and continued to the next room. He looked in, and in the dark corner, could see an even younger girl lying dead with dried blood oozed down her arm and a needle on the dirty floor. Rob moved in and felt her body. But, dead for some time, her body was cold to the touch. He took a glimpse into the other rooms down the way. These rooms were considerably larger. Several little girls lay there in files of single metal beds, out of their minds on something, and tied to the bedposts, so they couldn't leave. Their ages ranged from twelve to eighteen. But Marianne was nowhere around.

He marched back into the main area, snatching the Mexican by his throat.

"You like doping up young girls, you motherfucker? What the fuck is wrong with you people?"

The man tried to speak but couldn't under the weight of Rob's heavy hand. Rob loosened his grip a little.

"You have something to say to me, you little pussy?" Rob asked.

The man held a hand over his neck, straining to regain his breathing.

"The young ones make more money," he said, coughing to clear his throat.

Rob set a hand on the man and began beating him, slamming the back of his head against the wall and making it bleed.

"Tie his ass to the fucking chair," Rob told Kyle. "We're going to have a little fun with this asshole."

Kyle began binding the man's arms and legs to the wood chair. The deafening sound coming from the TV was making Rob even angrier. He struck the TV glass with the butt of his weapon, shattering it, sparks shooting out as the noise ceased.

"You know the best part about this?" Kyle asked the Mexican. "Nobody will hear you scream from down here!"

Rob stretched into his pack and got a multi-tool with attached pliers. He kept the tool over the man's right hand and held Marianne's picture in front of him.

"Do you know her?" he asked.

"No, Mister, I do not."

Rob started fooling with the pliers as he thought about what he was going to do to him.

"What is your name?" asked Rob.

"Javier, why?"

"Okay, Javier. I'll ask you again. Have you seen the girl? Answer me, or I'll start removing your fingers one at a time."

Javier just shook his head from side to side.

"No, Mister. I swear!"

"That's what everyone keeps telling me," he replied.

Rob gripped the pair of pliers over Javier's hand and started squeezing his fingers, watching him cry like a little girl.

"Not so tough now, huh?" Kyle asked him. "You can't handle someone your own size. You have to fuck with someone's daughter!"

Rob let go for a moment.

"Have you seen her? I can keep going, Javier. We're just getting started!"

"No!" Javier screamed as Rob took a tighter grip on his hand. Rob squeezed. This time, he didn't stop. Javier's finger popped as Rob's grip on his hand broke the bone in two. Javier squealed like a stuck pig.

"If we keep going this route," Rob told him, "you won't have any fingers or toes left!"

Rob put all of his strength into it. He separated Javier's finger from his hand and dropped the bloody mess to the floor. Blood pooled on the table in front of him.

"One finger down, nine more to go," Rob said. "Then I continue to your toes. It would be wise of you to be honest with me, Javier. I'm not someone you want to anger. Now, have you seen her or not?"

Rob glanced back at Kyle.

"Hold him down for me," said Rob.

Kyle placed a death grip on Javier's arm. He couldn't budge. Rob stood over him, preparing to break every single bone in his hand.

"Okay!" Javier said, blood oozing from the metal table to the floor. "Okay, no more, please!"

Javier sat still, in shock and staring down at his bleeding hand.

"I'll tell you what you want to know!" he yelled. "Just please stop!"

Javier's hand was nothing more than a bloody glob on the armrest. Rob had severed a nerve, and Javier could no longer feel it.

"Yeah?" said Rob. "What you got to say to me now? You think I'm playing with you?"

"Okay," Javier said. "Okay, that girl."

"Yeah?" Rob asked. "What about her?"

Rob scared Javier to death. He knew he was fucked, but he wanted the pain to stop.

"She was here, okay?" Javier said. "But the boss took her."

Rob set his gun down by him on the table where he could reach it.

"What does that mean, Javier? Why did he take her?

Where the fuck can I find him?"

Javier hesitated before answering.

"It means that he plans to sell her," he replied. "And I will never give up the boss!"

Rob felt his heart drop into his stomach.

"Sell her to where, who? This is my fucking sister!"

"To the highest bidder," Javier said. "Lots of dinero."

"Tell me where to find him, you motherfucker!"

In an instant, a flood of rage-filled adrenaline rushed over Rob. He snatched his gun from his pants and cocked it.

"No, please," Javier said. "I told you what you wanted to know!"

"But you won't tell me where to find your boss!" said Rob. "Now you can join the rest of your friends in hell. I'm coming for all of you bastards. Every single one of you who had anything to do with my sister's abduction faces the same end!"

Rob took the gun and stuck it into Javier's mouth.

"Don't worry," he told him. "Your boss will join you soon."

Rob squeezed the trigger, sending a shot into his mouth, blowing out teeth, splitting his brain stem, leaving pieces of brain and a bloody stain on the wall behind him. Javier's body fell back in the chair, limp. Rob reached for a landline phone sitting on the end table and dialed. With what little Spanish he knew, he hoped somebody on the other end gave a damn about those girls.

"Emergency services," the voice on the other end said in Spanish. "What is your emergency?"

"Shots fired," Rob said in broken Spanish. "Please come quick!"

Before the operator could react or ask questions, Rob had

already hung up the phone.

"Let's go," Rob told Kyle. "I don't want to be here when they show up."

Rob swiped Javier's phone from the counter. They vacated the house and headed back across the park as sirens wailed a few city blocks away.

TWENTY-TWO

Toluca, Mexico

Rob opened his eyes as the dawn beamed in between the semi-closed curtain in a motel just outside of town. It was one more sleepless night for him.

He'd had another terrible dream that night. This time, they had executed his sister right in front of him. He'd woken up with cold sweats in the middle of the night, not able to rest for more than a few hours at a time. He glanced at the clock on the nightstand as it hit six forty-five. He removed the blanket and hung his legs off the side of the bed. Rob rose and went to the coffeepot sitting on the motel dresser. He'd set it to run the night before. Rob poured himself a cup, mixed in a little sugar, and turned on the flat-screen TV on the wall. The morning news was on. As he sat at the foot of the bed and slurped from the Styrofoam coffee cup, something familiar caught his eye.

As the Mexican correspondent spoke to the camera, Rob saw the gurneys being hauled away, covered with white sheets behind her. Though he couldn't understand her, Rob could read what she was saying by the English captions below.

Breaking news as police in Mexico City have uncovered what looks like a sex trafficking ring. Officials aren't ruling out a cartel hit as they have recovered multiple bodies from the scene. They found a few of these poor girls dead, some barely alive, as the emergency crew tries to determine what they were given. However, it was a dire situation in that basement. Girls were chained in place and unable to move, even to use the restroom. Detectives are still working the scene to find out who was responsible for the killings. We'll update you as more information comes in. Coming to you live from Mexico City, I'm Alejandra Rodríguez, Channel 4 news.

Rob was all out of information to help him find his sister. And it frustrated him. Rob knew they took her. And he knew from what Javier had told him she was being sold. But that was all. He needed someone who understood the inner workings of the Los Lobos Cartel.

"What the hell?" he heard Kyle say from the bed across the room as he woke. "Is that...?"

"Yep," Rob replied. "It sure is."

Rob knew what Kyle was pointing out. It was undeniable.

"Fuck," Kyle added. "Let's just hope they actually investigate instead of bowing to the fucking cartel."

"Here," Rob said, reaching onto the dresser for another cup. "I made some coffee."

He handed the cup to Kyle across the bed.

"Thanks, man. I need to wake my ass up."

"Yeah, you do," said Rob. "We have shit to do."

Rob continued watching the news. In the background, he

recognized a detective he'd seen before. From the tape on his black ballistic vest, Rob could just decipher his name. "Pérez," it read in white.

"Get dressed," Rob told Kyle. "We have a stop to make."

Rob had seen Detective Pérez on the news before. But he'd previously read about him on an American news website, talking about his struggles to fight the cartels and bribery in the police ranks. By interviews the man had given, he appeared to be knowledgeable of the drug cartels. They needed to speak to him. But would the detective try to arrest them? Or would he help? They would soon find out.

Rob threw on a short-sleeve shirt and some khakis and placed his gun in the back of his pants. He grabbed his coffee cup to refill it.

"Let's go, bro. We need some answers."

Rob and Kyle both hurried to the vehicle parked right outside of the room. He cranked it up and headed toward Mexico City, just over an hour away.

"I can't believe we're going back there," said Kyle.

"Neither can I," Rob replied. "But we need information, something we are fresh out of."

Kyle took a sip of coffee from his cup.

"How do you know he won't try to jail us?"

"I don't," Rob said. "But, if he does, you know what to do. I'm hoping that we can make him see it our way. If not, then I guess we fight our way out. It's our only option right now."

"Fuck me," said Kyle.

Kyle raised his cup and dabbled a little rum into it from a mini bottle.

"Well," he continued as he tilted the cup. "Here's to hoping."

The Messenger

The drive was quiet. Rob had thought about what he was going to say to the detective. But things could go wrong in the blink of an eye. Whatever happened, though, Rob and Kyle could not allow the Mexican police to arrest them. That would truly put a barrier on Rob's ability to save his sister. They'd have to play it by ear. Going to the police was not something Rob had thought he'd do. However, with limited knowledge of the cartel's operations in Mexico and time not on his side, he would do whatever he had to.

They pulled up into a side street an hour and fifteen minutes later, just next to the park entrance. The police were scouring through the house, and emergency personnel had just left the scene before Rob and Kyle arrived. Crime scene units were driving away in their big forensic vans. But one had stayed back. Detective Pérez was heading for a blue Ford Mustang parked in front of the house by the crime scene tape.

"That's him," Rob said. "That's the one I remember."

"Yeah, I see him," Kyle said. "What you going to do?"

Rob shifted the vehicle back into drive and waited for the detective to leave.

"We're going to follow him," he replied. "That's what we're going to do."

Pérez left the scene, and Rob pulled out behind him.

"If he makes us," Rob told Kyle, "just stay calm. Don't do anything irrational, okay?"

"You got it, buddy," Kyle replied.

Rob trailed the detective out of the neighborhood, down one side of a divided, four-lane highway outside of town.

"I wonder where he's going," Kyle said.

Rob pursued Pérez down the road and around a sharp curve, coming to a stop at an off-ramp intersection. They lingered behind him, a couple of car lengths back. The light turned green, and the detective took a left. Rob pulled out behind him, separated by two other cars. He didn't want to get too close and give them away before they could catch up.

Finally, the detective made a right turn into the driveway of a modest, middle-class home in the Mexico City suburbs. But he'd disappeared before the men got there. Rob stopped the truck behind a line of tall shrubs and palm trees in front of the house. They got out and sneaked along the blacktop driveway that pointed to the one-story house and a two-car garage.

"Don't pull your gun out," Rob said. "I don't want him to think we're trying to rob him or something."

They made their way down the drive and to the sidewalk that led up to the front porch steps.

"You just going to knock on the door?" Kyle asked.

"Yep. Why not?"

But as they continued toward the front door, they picked up a noise coming from behind. The men froze in place, and Rob was just about to turn around before the man addressed them.

"Don't move," the detective said in Spanish, holding his silver 45 Colt revolver on them. "What in the hell are you doing here?"

He wore a white cowboy hat, brown cowboy boots, a large, silver belt buckle, and an old-style Mexican tie, similar to those worn by old western cowboys in the United States.

Rob and Kyle, their backs to Pérez, held their hands high.

"Habla inglés?" Rob asked.

"Yes," the detective said. "I speak English. And you had better tell me what you are doing on my property before I split your head open."

The Messenger

"We came to talk," Rob said as he turned around slowly.

"Keep those hands up! Don't make a move, or I will shoot you!"

"I have a gun on me," Rob said. "But we are not here to cause trouble. We just need to talk, that's all."

Detective Pérez reached behind them and snatched both of their guns from their waist.

"What's this for, gringo?" he asked Rob.

"Protection," he said, smirking back at him.

"You know it is illegal for you to carry guns here?"

"So is drug running, prostitution, and sex trafficking," Rob countered. "Now, we only want to talk to you. Please, just hear us out."

The detective glanced at Rob and noticed the chain around his neck. He tugged at it from under his shirt, his ID tags hanging from the end.

"American soldier, huh?" he asked. "What are you doing down here in Mexico, soldier?"

He looked down again at Rob's name in silver.

"Robert Walker. Why are you here?"

"Let me put it this way," Rob stated. "We figured you were one of the few cops in this city or country who won't be bought by the cartels. Is that you, Detective Pérez? Or are you as dirty as the rest of them?"

The detective just stared at them. Rob had aroused his curiosity.

"That is correct, Mister Walker," he said, his wrinkled and scarred face pinching as he squinted at them. "Why is this of interest to you?"

"May we talk inside, Detective?" asked Rob. "Please, we

aren't a threat to you. We are just here for your expertise, nothing more."

Detective Pérez eyeballed them both. He had his doubts.

"Move," he replied. "Don't do anything stupid, gringo. I won't hesitate to shoot you."

The detective pointed them through the house entrance to a large living room just past the foyer.

"Have a seat," Pérez continued.

"Thanks," said Rob.

The detective took a seat on the couch across the coffee table from them.

"Before we begin, I have one question. How do you know who I am? Am I that popular? I don't think so."

"I've seen you on the news," Rob said. "You are very critical of the cartels, unlike many other Mexican police officers. You aren't bothered by their threats or cruelty. There's a lot of corruption down here. That I know. But it doesn't seem to faze you."

Pérez snagged an ashtray from the side table, setting it down in front of him, and lit a cigarette.

"Violence? Such is life here in Mexico, Mister. There's rarely anyone living here who hasn't been affected by it. Yes, I've been after the cartels for as long as I've been in this job. I've had friends, family killed for my trouble. So, naturally, I want to put them out of commission. But, as you said, crooked cops are a real problem in Mexico. Now, back to my original question. What are you doing down here?"

Rob just glared at the detective for a moment, steeped in thought. There was no getting around it. He had to tell him if he wanted his help. He would've found out, eventually. Rob looked over at Kyle as a kind of gesture of what he was about to say. Kyle understood him clearly.

"Look, Detective Pérez," Rob said. "I'm going to be straightforward with you. I was home on leave in New York from Afghanistan recently. My sister was hanging with some evil people up there. To make a long story short, Los Lobos Cartel members seized her and brought her down here. We are trying to find her before she's lost forever."

Rob reflected for a moment, wondering where Marianne was and what they were doing to her. He hung his head, troubled for her.

"By all means, please continue," said Pérez. "I'm listening."

"We were the ones who stormed that house yesterday, looking for her. We killed those people, Detective. We didn't have a choice."

Detective Pérez smiled, a cigarette hanging from the corner of his mouth.

"What do you do for the Army, Mister Walker?" he asked.

"We're with Special Forces. Scout, sniper team."

"Oh, I see," said the detective. "Well, you think I give a damn about the death of some cartel crooks, Mister Walker? I don't. You boys did me a service. These idiots have slaughtered more people than I can count."

"So you aren't going to turn us in?" asked Rob.

"Turn you in? Shit, I should give you a medal. You two saved many of those girls from dying a horrible death or wasting away on narcotics while the cartel milks as much money as they can out of them. But many of our so-called police don't need to know about this. Not everyone shares the same sentiment, you see? We have some perverse assholes working for us that would hand you over in a second. But I hope you find your sister. I really do."

"Oh, we'll find her all right," Rob replied. "I don't care who I have to kill. We will find my sister."

"What have you found out so far?" the detective asked.

"Well," said Rob. "While we were looking around, we found out the name of the leader and a few of his associates. It seems like they plan to sell her. That's as far as we've gotten. But they sent one of their men, evidently a marksman, to hit us."

"Is his name Marco?" Pérez asked.

"You've heard of him?"

He raised his button-up shirt and revealed a round scar in the middle of his chest.

"You could say that," the detective said. "He tried to kill me too. Lucky for me, I was wearing a vest. It hurt like a son of a bitch, let me tell you. The plate stopped it from going all the way through. But that man has a kill tally longer than my arm. He helped to grab my partner a few weeks back."

"By grabbed, you mean?"

"I mean they captured him, Mister, in broad fucking daylight."

Rob leaned his chin on his hand on the sofa armrest.

"Jesus...," he said.

"Why don't you get him back?" Kyle asked.

"Because," Pérez replied, "we don't have the resources. And I don't know who to trust anymore, hombre. Too many of our police officers have turned to make quick dinero. But I'll make a deal with you two."

"And what would that be?" Rob asked.

"If you help me save my partner, Detective Morales, I will assist you. I'll share intel with you. And I'll help you find your sister. And my partner will too, after we bust him out. But we have to hurry before they torture him to death. They have no reason to keep him alive any longer."

"Why trust us?" Rob asked him. "You just met us."

"That's simple, Mister Walker," he replied. "You need me. Otherwise, you wouldn't be here. And I need you too. Our needs favor one another."

Rob looked back at Kyle, and they both nodded in agreement.

"Okay, Detective Pérez. You know where they are holding him?"

"I do," he said. "I got the info from a confidential informant of mine. I was scouting the area on my own when I got called to the scene last night."

"All right," said Rob. "Agreed. We do this for you, and you help me find my sister."

The detective took a long drag from his cigarette and smiled. He produced their guns and set them by Rob on the table.

"Okay, then," he said, presenting a bottle of tequila from the bottom of the sofa table. "To a new unofficial partnership."

TWENTY-THREE

```
Durango, Mexico
```

They left the vehicle, tucked away among the creosote bushes a couple of hundred feet off a dirt road outside of Durango, a town in western Mexico. Rob and Kyle, gear strapped on, had followed Detective Pérez over a mile into the remote landscape until they reached a hilltop looking over an old, empty, and derelict factory in the middle of nowhere. The plant looked like it had been unused for some time. Overgrown vegetation, a rusty metal entry gate, and old equipment exposed to the elements suggested a place that had sat dormant for years.

Ghillie suit on, Rob took a knee, tilting his canteen back and taking a swig of water from it. The sweat dripped down the side of his head onto his shoulders. He wiped his eyebrow with his shirtsleeve and slipped his ghillie hood over the top of his head.

"Are you sure it's the right place?" he asked Pérez. "It doesn't look like anyone is here."

"Yeah, I'm sure," he replied. "My source said that he has a

cousin who is a soldier for the cartel. He has no idea the guy is working with us. But he followed him out here one night and saw them unload a large group from the back of a truck. Morales was not one of them. But he said they planned to move him to this site today."

"Well," Rob said, "if he shows up, we'll get him out of there. From where I'm sitting, the place looks deserted. But we'll stay here for a while and see what happens."

Rob and Kyle each removed their rucks and set them on the ground between them, positioned four hundred meters from the site. With his M4 set aside, Rob unfolded his sniper rifle and set it up on the high mound's edge and hit the dirt, bringing the gun tight into his shoulder. Kyle got down beside him with his binoculars as they waited for movement.

"Pérez," Rob turned his head and called out behind him. "Get back down and out of sight."

Detective Pérez's white shirt stood out like a sore thumb against the background. Pérez made his way back down the hill and hit the dirt. They waited there, looking through the glass and skimming the area for what seemed like a couple of hours. All remained still until they saw dust swirling above in rings across the flats. It was a caravan. They were cruising down the same road Rob and company had traveled in the opposite direction. Two of the five vehicles were narco tanks or modified, heavy steel armored Chevy SUVs with machine-gun turrets on top. These guns fired 7.62-millimeter, belt-fed rounds at up to nine hundred and fifty rounds per minute.

"Heads up," Rob said as he looked through the glass. "We've got a convoy over here. Holy shit! They have armored trucks with what looks like M240 Bravo machine guns mounted on top."

They watched as the vehicles stopped in front. A man got out of the truck and lifted the bent, vertical lift gate to allow the trucks to pass through. He lowered it after them. Pérez could just see them over the dense shrubbery he was lying between.

"We call those monstruos, or monsters," Pérez said. "If they are using those, they are protecting someone important."

The convoy sped up to the old structure. The trucks came to a standstill in front of a large, faded door. The men got out of their vehicles, holding AK-47s and Uzi submachine guns, favorites of Los Lobos.

"I never asked you," Rob told the detective. "What was your partner doing when they caught him?"

"We were investigating the disappearance of a couple of girls, sisters from Mexico City," he replied. "We had a lead which pointed us to the same operation you guys took down. The evidence we recovered beforehand indicated a place where they were moving them outside of the city. But Morales went off the rails. Our informant suggested somewhere we should look at. My partner said he needed to look into something else. Morales acted alone and didn't wait for backup, a reckless move."

"And then he was caught?" Rob asked.

"Yes," said Pérez. "With a warning. They sent a message saying they would crush us if we tried anything. My coward of a commander, Captain Domínguez, made us stand down. And he didn't even have the cojones to mount a rescue. Even the chief refuses to go against the cartel. We've been partners for eight years. He was the best man at my wedding. I can't just leave him, even though he did something so stupid."

"Do you know what Morales found out before he left?" Kyle asked.

"No, I don't," he said. "But we will ask him after I smack him for not listening to me."

They looked on as many cartel members jumped out of the truck, leaving the two machine gunners behind. Some of them started shouting as they opened the back of one truck, escorting a group of ten people chained together. Detective Pérez saw a familiar face in the middle of them. He was beaten and horribly bruised, but he knew it was his partner by how he walked.

"That's him," said Pérez. "The one in the center with his shirt ripped."

Another male figure got out of the black-colored SUV in the center of the convoy. He wore gold shades, boots, and a white Armani suit, sporting a custom, gold-plated AK-47 that sent a glint of sunlight in their direction.

"Shit," said Pérez. "That is Juan Luis, Los Lobos Cartel leader. What the fuck is he doing here?"

"Good question," Rob said. "But Morales is a cop, like you. They hate cops, right? My guess is Juan wants to speak to him. I wish I could put a hole in his chest right now. But they'd kill your friend for sure. They can't know we're coming, or these people are as good as dead."

Rob and Kyle followed their movement while they led the captives into the structure. The cartel men lashed them with canes and continued propelling them ahead. Many almost collapsed to the ground as they struggled to keep up with the chain around their legs. They disappeared as one man dropped the large pull-down door after them, leaving two guards outside to watch the entrance.

"As much as I hate to leave those poor people in there any longer," Rob said, "we need to wait until after sunset. Then we move under cover of night."

Rob kept his eye on the target but for the quick blink to relieve his sharp eyes. He held a four-inch distance from his right eye to the scope to capture a full-sight picture of the target. Rob was used to managing a long time behind the glass.

His longest sniper mission ever lasted almost seventy-two hours. He'd waited close to three days with no sleep in his sniper hide with his spotter on an Afghan mountainside. They were to eliminate an al-Qaeda lieutenant who'd ordered US-supported Afghan villages to burn in their AO (Area Of Operations) taking prisoners.

Special Forces and Special Operations snipers were a disciplined group. The mission was always a priority over everything else. Like Rob, most snipers were so dedicated to what they were doing, they'd even relieve themselves in their clothes, not wanting to risk losing their target. They were the 1 percent of 1 percent, something inconceivable to the average person.

Now the two were doing much of the same thing. But this mission had been personal from the start. Rob had to find his sister, no matter what.

A couple of hours had passed, and the men were getting ready to make their move. Kyle observed the guards outside, who were unaware that they were being watched. A few minutes later, Juan reemerged from the building, walking between two bodyguards back to his large Chevy SUV. He looked heated, swearing at his men as he climbed into the truck.

"Morales," said Pérez, shaking his head. "I'll bet you a case of tequila he's been fucking with them. Only Morales can make someone that angry."

"Is he really that brash?" Rob asked him.

"Yes," Pérez replied. "Yes, he is. I lost count of the times I saved his ass. But there is another side to him, a side many don't see. For all the dumb shit he's done, he's truly committed to what we are doing. I wish I could say the same for others."

"The guy must have big brass balls," said Rob.

"Something like that," the detective replied.

As Juan and the two security vehicles departed, Rob observed their movement, knowing his hands were tied for the time being.

"Damn it," Rob said. "He's getting away. I wish I could just end this fucker right now."

But he couldn't. Perhaps he'd have another shot. For now, he had to focus on the mission at hand. Left behind were two black Range Rovers and enough men to fill them. Rob detached one scope from his suppressed weapon, fixing the Leupold night-vision scope in its place on the Picatinny rail on top.

Detective Pérez slid back up next to them.

"Get behind the gun," Rob said to Kyle. "We need to synchronize our shots so they don't sound the alarm on us."

"On the glass," Kyle said, viewing the man to the left of the door.

"All right," Rob replied. "The one on the left is yours."

The tip of Rob's finger rested over the trigger. He went through his tactical breathing, inhaling deeply and exhaling, pausing for an instant. Without delay, Rob squeezed the trigger. He watched as his large-caliber bullet shot forward four hundred meters. It punched the guard in his chest cavity, jostling his body backward against the door and knocking him straight to the ground, leaving a bloodstain splattered on the door behind him. He was dead before he even hit the dirt. Kyle followed Rob's shot soon after, sending a round through the other guy's neck, blood spurting like a fountain from the hole. The shot had sent him tumbling back forcibly and slamming the back of his head against the wall before sliding to the earth.

"Targets down," Rob said. "Nice shot."

He just hoped nobody would wander outside and find their buddies lying there before the trio could make their way in. Rob took a glimpse around the building area. He saw no other guards outside.

"Let's move," he told them.

Rob sprang upward, placing his pack and the sniper rifle onto his back, and snatched up his M4. Pérez, with his black 45 Beretta, followed right after them, moving and stepping carefully to keep from making a racket as they pushed onward. But they had no idea that they were also being watched.

Rob detected a distinctive hissing sound that was unquestionable as they came out of the scrubs and onto the sizable area circling the target building. He glanced back at his partner, seeing the bright red oozing from his body as he hit the sand. It was apparent to Rob the shot came from a great distance. By the trajectory and where it hit, Rob knew what direction it had come from.

"Shit! Get down! Grab his legs, quick!"

He and Pérez pulled Kyle's body up and toted him to cover on the other side of the structure, beyond the weeds and out of the shooter's line of sight. It looked like the shot had entered the top of his vest just above his heart. It might not be fatal if they could get the bleeding under control.

"We need to stop it before he bleeds out!" he said. "Don't worry, partner, you'll be all right."

They spread him out over the ground behind an old broken-down truck. Rob took a pair of scissors from his kit and started cutting Kyle's bloody clothing away from the wound. He retrieved Kyle's medical kit and started applying sterile gauze, pressing with all his strength and attaching medical tape with his free hand. Rob took Kyle's hand, keeping it tight against his chest as he struggled against the intense pain, unable to lie still.

"Stay with us, brother," he said, squeezing Kyle's hand. "It'll be okay!"

"What are we going to do now?" Pérez asked Rob, rolling up a cloth and placing it under Kyle's head.

"I'm going in," Rob replied. "You are going to stay with him and out of sight. Stay low, stay behind cover, and don't pop your head up for a second, or it'll get shot off!"

"You're going in there alone?"

"Yes," he said. "You want your partner back, right? Just pack the wound and keep the pressure on it. Don't let him die, or I'll really be angry!"

"You are crazy!" said Pérez.

"Something like that," Rob replied.

Rob removed his sniper rifle and pack, left them next to Pérez on the ground, and swung his M4 up. He began shuffling forward, moving the weapon as an extension of himself, switching his aim with every shift of his body. Nobody inside that building had heard the muffled shot. Rob gripped the door latch on the building's left side, cracking it slightly. He slipped in unnoticed, inching his way through, taking cover behind a large wooden crate facing the building's center. It was a sizable shop-type room, with guards on all corners of a group of metal enclosures. For a minute, Rob snooped in the shadows.

There were six men, all possessing AK-47s and yelling obscenities at their captives. They were getting ready to beat them some more. In no mood to wait any longer, Rob set the rifle on top of the crate, a thirty-round magazine fixed in the magazine well. He began firing into the group. They hadn't seen it coming, nor were they prepared. Before they could fire a single shot, Rob had cut down all six of them. He made his way toward the cages, pivoting his body left to right, looking up the stairs that led to the second floor.

As he turned to the cages' front, a lone gunman came running down the steps, firing into the captives and Rob, striking him in his right shoulder just below his collarbone.

"Fuck!" Rob said.

He fired at the man, killing him and causing his body to plunge headfirst down the stairs, upside down on the floor as he hit bottom. Rob glanced left, seeing two captives killed by a string of gunfire. Rob aimed his rifle toward the sky, circling around to ensure no other guards were present on the upper floor.

He neared the cage, holding his injured shoulder with blood coating his hand. The containers were like prison-type cells bolted to the concrete floor. It must have been a holding area where the cartel kept their enemies before doing God knows what to them.

"Detective Morales? Which one of you is Morales?"

"That would be me," a voice replied from the back of the packed container.

"Your partner, Pérez, sent us to get you out of here."

"What?" he asked. "Who in the hell are you?"

"It's a long story. I don't have time to tell it right now. Stand back."

Rob shot the lock off and opened the container door.

"They hurt my buddy in the process. Follow me. I'll explain later."

Rob shot the locks off the other two pens, allowing the rest of the prisoners to escape.

"Go on!" Rob yelled at them. "You're free. Go!"

Rob herded them to the opposite side of the building, pulling Morales by his shirt.

"Come! We don't have a lot of time. And stay low. There's a shooter out there! Follow my movement and do not deviate!"

The detective followed Rob through the door to where Kyle was lying on the ground.

"Hey!" Morales called out to his partner. "I should've known you were behind this!"

Rob shoved Detective Morales to the deck.

"I said stay low. Keep your head down!"

Morales pressed against the ground between surrounding bushes.

"How is he?" Rob asked Pérez as he bent down by him.

"The bleeding has stopped," Pérez answered. "But he needs medical attention. We can take him to my house. My wife is a nurse. She can help him."

"Okay," Rob said. "We need to move, now!"

"Were you hit?" Pérez asked, seeing the blood on Rob's sleeve.

"I'm fine," replied Rob. "It's just a flesh wound."

"A sniper did this?" Morales asked.

"Yeah," said Rob. "And he's still out there. We need to leave before he repositions and gets a shot on us."

Rob glanced at the vehicles that were close to the warehouse door.

"You two grab him and follow me. Hurry!"

They trailed behind Rob as he went for the Range Rover nearest to them.

"Quickly! I don't want to give him another target!"

They scurried across the hundred-meter stretch as fast as they could go while carrying Kyle. Rob climbed into the driver's seat as Pérez and Morales spread Kyle across the back and jumped in alongside him.

"Shit!" Rob said when he noticed the keys weren't in the ignition. "Be right back!"

He took off in a sprint, quickly searching the dead guards by the front of the building.

"Hurry up, amigo!" Pérez shouted through the window.

Rob hit his knees, fumbling through multiple trouser pockets with both hands until he heard the distinctive sound of keys jingling. He yanked them out.

"Got 'em!" he said, running as fast as he could and jumping into the front seat.

Rob turned the key and slammed on the accelerator, spinning tires as he bounced over a pothole and out to the highway.

Suddenly, a large-caliber round shattered the back glass, just missing Morales's head as it struck the dashboard.

"Shit!" Morales shouted as he ducked down into the seat. "That was close!"

Rob swerved to the right, then the left, putting some distance between them and the shooter.

TWENTY-FOUR

```
Texcoco, Mexico
```

Rob waited in the living room of Detective Pérez's home in the Mexico City suburb, cleaning and applying a bandage to the wound to his shoulder. He was impatiently awaiting word from the detective's wife, Alexa, who was busy working on Kyle in the next room. Rob didn't want to gamble, bringing him to a hospital where they could track them down. And Pérez had convinced him that his wife knew what she was doing, having seen the same type of injuries at the hospital where she worked.

They'd been able to stop the bleeding beforehand. But Rob didn't know what harm the shot had done to his friend internally. Everyone in that room settled in pure silence for a period. Detective Morales had just finished rinsing the blood away from his savagely battered body and had stepped out of the shower. He was sitting, wearing shorts, a towel wrapped around him, and drying the water from his face. Now that they had some time to spare, Detective Pérez wanted to question his partner. Sitting across from Morales, Pérez stared him down, incapable of holding back his frustration any longer.

"What the fuck were you thinking?" he asked his partner in Spanish. "Not waiting for me, for backup? That was the dumbest thing you could've possibly done!"

Morales rolled his eyes at his partner.

"I had an instinct," he replied. "I got some information. I didn't have time to wait for you!"

"A lot of good that did. You got captured, you moron! They could've killed you! I'm your partner. You should have shared it with me. How can we work together if I can't trust you?"

Rob, not sure of what they were saying, interrupted.

"Enough, you two!" Rob said. "In English, please! I don't like secrets."

"Sorry, Mister Walker," Pérez answered. "My partner here is just being a clown. He says he had a lead, information that he neglected to share with me, his partner. He seems to think he's some one-man fucking army!"

Rob eyed Morales as he leaned against the wall.

"You know they would have killed you had we not shown up when we did," Rob told him, "so now is the time for you to talk."

"Who are you and your friend?" asked Morales. "How do you know my partner?"

"All right, Detective," he said. "Let me introduce myself. I am Sergeant First Class Rob Walker of the United States Special Forces. And let me be crystal clear. My spotter could've died, and I got shot rescuing your ass. Whatever you know, you'd better share it with us. These people have my sister. And I don't give a damn who I have to trample on to get her back! Do you understand me? As for Detective Pérez, he agreed to help us if we broke you out of there."

"Special Forces?" Morales questioned.

"Don't ask," Pérez told him.

"Well," Morales said, "I am very thankful to all of you."

"You're welcome," Rob replied.

"Now, partner," Pérez told him. "Just tell them what you know."

"Okay," said Morales. "Okay I have a source inside the cartel. He's been feeding me information about their human trafficking cell."

Morales paused for a moment to sip from a bottle of tequila. He lit up a cigarette to calm his shot nerves.

"Go on," Rob said to him.

"Okay," he replied, flicking ash into the ashtray on the side table. "I was trying to figure out where they were shipping the girls once they got them off the street. They were transporting them to that house in the city, the one across from the park. They get them hooked on drugs and high out of their minds. Some girls don't survive that. The ones who survive go to this place out in the Sonora Desert, well away from any populated area. Somehow they were onto me. They took me off the street, tossed me into a vehicle, and blindfolded me. Then they proceeded to beat the shit out of me."

"Did you find out where they were taking them?" Rob asked him.

"I have a vague location. The site is in the desert, about ten miles north of Sinoquipe. That's all I got before they caught me. I have no proof. But I think it was a police officer who ratted me out."

"Who do the orders come from?" asked Rob. "You have any idea?"

"All orders come straight from Juan," he said. "He's the boss and the only one who oversees the girls. It's become his primary focus."

"Why is that?"

"Greed," Morales said. "And power. He wants Los Lobos to be the number-one source for girls worldwide."

"That's pretty ambitious," Rob replied.

"Well, Mister," said Morales, "the man is crazy. And he is already the leader of the largest and most wealthy drug organization. They're the most prominent supplier of narcotics for both the United States and Canada. He's trying to branch out. Nothing is ever enough for him."

"We're going to make sure that doesn't happen. He fucked with the wrong family this time. But do you think he was wise to the information that you received?"

"I don't think so, Mister," Morales replied. "He would have killed me already, for sure. I think they had planned to beat it out of me before you showed up. But I never told them shit."

Suddenly, the door to the bedroom opened, and out popped Mrs. Pérez with a content smile on her face. Rob could only hope that it meant good news.

"How is he?" he asked her.

"Well," she said. "The blood has clotted, and the bleeding has completely stopped."

"Good," Rob said. "That's good."

"I removed the fragment. Our friend was lucky. One inch lower, and he probably would've died well before you guys got here. He is resting now. I would suggest he take it easy for a while, though."

"Is he coherent?" asked Rob. "Can he talk?"

"Yes, your friend is awake. But don't push him too much.

The shot badly bruised his chest, and it may be uncomfortable if he talks too much."

"Thank you, Mrs. Pérez," Rob told her. "Thank you so very much. I don't know what we would have done without you."

"You are welcome, Mister Walker," she replied. "You are most welcome. It is my way of thanking you for helping my husband."

Rob rose and cracked the door open. Kyle was lying on his back with no shirt, and his head leaned to the side. He was moving somewhat in bed, and Rob could tell that he was semiconscious.

"Hey, bro," Rob said as he entered the room and pulled a chair up beside the bed. "How d'ya feel?"

"Ugh," replied Kyle, speaking in a soft tone to keep his chest from rising too much. "Like a damn truck hit me."

Kyle covered his mouth with his hand as he began coughing laboriously. The look on his face was one of severe strain.

"Ah... fuck," he said. "Damn, that hurt."

"Mrs. Pérez was able to remove the bullet from your chest. You were lucky, man."

"I sure as hell don't feel lucky right now," Kyle said. "I feel broken."

Rob bent over Kyle and took his hand.

"You just need to rest here, partner. We got some solid intel from Morales. I'm going to move on it in the morning."

"Not without me, you're not," replied Kyle. "I'm not out of this fight, not by a long shot."

"Look, old friend. You need to take it easy. They almost killed you. I can do this on my own for now."

Kyle clutched Rob's hand tightly.

"Listen, man," Kyle told him. "I'm not dead. And I have never backed down from a mission in my life. I'm not starting now, either. We're in this together. I am not letting you go alone, and that's the end of it!"

Rob knew that Kyle could be headstrong. But his unquestionable allegiance to him as a friend and fellow soldier was a genuinely moving experience for him. Rob had never had a more loyal friend in his entire life.

"I'm not talking you out of it, am I?"

"Nope," Kyle replied. "Wild horses couldn't stop me. Besides, you would do the same for me."

"That's true," Rob said, pulling the blanket up over Kyle's body. "All right, brother. Just rest here for a while, and I'll be back in to check on you in a bit."

Rob moved his body closer and wrapped an arm around his friend, whispering in his ear.

"And thank you. Thank you for being here."

"Of course," replied Kyle. "Where else would I be?"

Rob left his friend to rest, closing the bedroom door behind him. While Kyle relaxed, he would prepare for what was coming next.

⋮⋮⋮

At a spot in the Sonora wasteland, Juan Luis stepped from his SUV, fancy boots kicking up dust as they hit the dirt. A phone to his ear, he adjusted his shirt collar and ran a comb through his long, shiny, black, pony-tailed hair. Juan had heard late the night before about his men's death and the breakout, some of whom were law enforcement and snitches. He considered them all sworn enemies of the Los Lobos Cartel.

"Marco!" Juan said into the phone. "I pay you to take care

of complications. How did you let this happen?"

"I got one of them," Marco said. "I know I did. But the other was running too fast. He went behind the building. By the time I switched positions, they were taking off. What could I do?"

Rob, being a skilled top-tier sniper, had known another shooter was targeting them. Once that first shot hit Kyle, he knew better than to give Marco a stationary target.

"What could you do?" Juan asked. "How about your fucking job? You idiot! And, about his friend, did you see the body?"

"No," Marco replied. "As I said, they left before I could get there."

"Yeah?" said Juan. "Yeah, you don't know shit! Don't let me see your fucking face, Marco, until you can do what I pay you to do. Otherwise, I'll just shoot you and take care of it, my fucking self!"

Juan was furious. He hung the phone up and slammed it down.

"Fuck!" he yelled. "You had one fucking job!"

"You all right, boss?" one of his guards asked.

"Yes," he replied. "Yeah, I'm just tired of fucking incompetence!"

He stuck the phone back into his pocket and, with his bodyguards, headed toward the front door of an old, tin-roofed building. His men opened the door for him. They wandered inside the long hall that ran from the front to the building's rear, cartel guards posted on both ends.

The place was primarily a brothel, with women and girls locked up in rooms and made to perform sexual acts on random men at all day and night hours. When they weren't working, they lived isolated, secured to the beds. Some girls stayed there indefinitely. They sold the prettiest in and out of Mexico for big money, some girls as sex slaves. Others were housemaids or both. The clients could do what they wanted with them. They were property, mostly paid for with dirty money.

"Ricardo!" Juan shouted out in his deep-toned voice. "Ricardo, get over here now!"

Ricardo was the guy Juan had put in charge of the girls in his absence. He handled operations, including bringing in new stock and managing a series of brothels and bars across Sonora, Mexico. It was the base for the cartel's human trafficking wing. And, knowing that making Juan angry wasn't wise, Ricardo would do anything to please him.

"Yes, boss?" he said, rushing out of one room to meet Juan in the hall.

"How is everything going here, Ricardo? Any problems?"

"No, sir!" Ricardo said. "Business is great. We can barely keep up with the demand!"

"Good, Ricardo. That is what I like to hear. Finally, someone I can depend on. That is a rare fucking trait these days. Some of these idiots are one stupid move from being dealt with."

"Thank you, sir," replied Ricardo.

"Listen, we've got another load of girls coming in tonight," Juan added. "I need you to meet them outside and pack them in here. I expect it to be a full house before the night is over. Stack 'em in tight. I don't care how many you have to put in one room. Just toss the bitches in like rag dolls!"

"Yes, sir," replied Ricardo. "Will do, boss!"

"Good," Juan said to Ricardo. "Now, where is that New York bitch at?"

"I put her in the last room on the left, boss."

"Excellent," said Juan. "She's my special merchandise. We need to get her ready for auction."

Juan was referring to a human auction, one that took place in secret in the basement of a high-class club in Sonora. Nobody outside of Los Lobos, their associates, and clientele knew much about the auction. Law enforcement in the US and Mexico had tried for years to uncover it. The cartel kept a tight lid on its whereabouts. Juan killed anyone in the organization who'd even think of disclosing the auction's location.

Juan strolled down the long corridor to the very last room on the left. He peeked into the tiny, square hole in the door, watching Marianne as she wiggled on the thin mattress. A wool blanket covered half her body as she lay on the bed, a chain around her wrist fastened to the metal bed frame. Marianne was semiconscious from the narcotics that were put into her body for days on end. The holes up and down both of her arms suggested drug needles that had pierced her skin. Most of the girls had become forced addicts. A drugged-up person was less likely to fight back.

Juan withdrew a metal ring from his belt loop and ran his fingers through the many keys that hung from it. He entered the correct key into the hole, the metal door squeaking as he tugged it open. Juan left it half-open, strolled toward her, and took a stool beside the bed. He stroked Marianne's hair, her back to him as she jerked around.

"I have big plans for you, sweetheart," he said to her, knowing she was too out of it to respond to him.

Juan stood and rolled her body over to face him. He pulled at her shirt to unveil her breasts underneath a white bra.

"Yeah. That is very nice. You're going to make me a lot of money, honey."

Marianne appeared to look up at him. Her eyes were bloodshot and dilated. She was far from able to see clearly or even understand what was happening around her. Her body began to spasm. Marianne's arms kept yanking at the chain like she was trying to break free. It was a reaction to the drugs. But Juan didn't care.

"What are you doing, you whore?" he asked.

Juan clutched her by the chin and slammed her hard, leaving a red handprint on her left cheek and knocking her head back against the metal headboard. Marianne began screaming gibberish at him, and Juan slapped her one more time, knocking her flat on the bed.

"Stop moving, bitch!" he said.

Juan held her down on the bed by her arms.

"Lie here and shut the fuck up!" he yelled. "And don't even try to get away, or I will kill you!"

Juan knew that Marianne couldn't understand him. But he was just too vile and coldhearted to give a damn.

"Someone is searching for you. And he is killing my men. I am guessing he's your brother. But he won't find you. I'll make sure of that personally and show him what it means to fuck with Los Lobos!"

"Everything okay, boss?" Ricardo asked, hurrying into the room.

"Yes, Ricardo," Juan said as he stood and walked toward the doorway. "Everything is fine. Get this bitch ready to go. She's getting too feisty. I expect you to handle that. I have other, more personal matters to tend to right now."

"Sure, boss," Ricardo said. "I'll take care of it right away, sir."

TWENTY-FIVE

Texcoco, Mexico
Next morning

Rob and Kyle tossed their things into the back of an old, maroon-colored four-wheel-drive Jeep CJ with a worn black canvas top that Pérez had lent them for the long trip. It was a fixer-upper he'd restored himself a year earlier but had seldom driven. The detective didn't want them to get stuck in the rigid Sonora Desert terrain. He knew that where they were going was full of loose sand and rocks, making anything other than a four-wheel-drive vehicle non-practical. Nor would it work if they were being pursued by Juan's cartel henchmen.

The Jeep had sat untouched in his garage for months, gathering dust. Pérez had been looking for an excuse to bring it out of its hole. Now he had one. Minutes beforehand, the detective had lifted the blue tarp that covered the vehicle. He'd checked the oil and that the lights were still working. Everything seemed to be in tip-top shape. Pérez had pulled the Jeep out, leaving it sitting at the end of the long blacktop drive.

Now, Rob and Kyle sat comfortably on the Jeep's brown leather seats, the soft-top windows zipped down. They set out rifles and handguns over their laps as they finished cleaning them and topping the magazines with ammo. They were getting ready to go to war, a war that had already begun.

Holding his long gun up and cleaning the excess oil from the metal, Rob dabbed a little onto the bolt, sliding it back and forth multiple times in a fluid motion. He drove the bolt forward a final time, forcing the bolt knob into the down position.

He began adding extra ammunition to each slot of the camouflage stock pack wrapped around the butt of his rifle. Rob stretched back and set the long gun behind him and inserted full rifle magazines into pouches attached to the vest lying beside him. Ghillie suits lay rolled up in the back. Each man's M4 carbine stood upright against the corners between their feet and the door, sniper rifles set on the back floorboard. Straps attached their packs to the roll bar in the rear.

Kyle slid a hand under his shirt to ensure the bandages were secured tight, where the round had exited and left a large wound on his shoulder blade. Pérez's wife had stitched Kyle up the night before, giving him all the antibiotics she had at home to prevent any infection. Kyle had found the cleaning and stitching agonizing. The area around the wound felt like someone had beaten him with a hammer, even with her gentle touch. Unlike lacerations, bullets, particularly large calibers, cause significant trauma to the entry and exit holes. They can take quite a while to heal. Kyle balked as he ran a hand over the dressing.

It wasn't Kyle's first time being shot. And he was well aware of the pain.

"Are you sure you are up for this, buddy?" Rob asked Kyle. "I wouldn't be offended if you sat this one out."

"I told you already. It stings like hell. And I'm a little woozy from the meds she gave me. But there's no way I'm letting you go at it alone, no matter how badass you think you are. So stop asking."

Rob turned the keys in the ignition.

"You're a tough son of a bitch," he told Kyle. "A shot like that would put a lesser man down. I appreciate it. But at least try to take care. I don't want to have to explain to your family why you got killed."

"Don't worry, man," Kyle replied. "I'm right as rain. You just concentrate on getting your sister back. Wherever she is, she's scared. That's all that matters right now."

Detectives Pérez and Morales wandered out from the house and met the guys on the driveway by the Jeep's driver's side. They'd gotten to know them a little on a personal level, and for what they did for them, the two were in their debt.

"Thank you for everything, Pérez," said Rob. "And thanks for the ride. I'll try to return it free of bullet holes, but I can't make any promises."

Pérez could appreciate Rob's sense of humor in a time like that. He appeared as cool as a cucumber. Inside, he had some reservations. But that was where they would stay.

"No," Pérez answered. "Thank you. And I do hope that you find your sister."

"I hope so too," replied Rob. "I hate to think about what she's going through. It makes me sick to my stomach."

"Mister Walker," Pérez added, "the cartels have brought nothing but pain and suffering to many people, in and out of Mexico. I pray that God gives you two the strength to punish them for what they do, destroying people's lives. And, whether you realize it, you guys are bringing hope to many people who lost it a long time ago."

"Thanks," said Rob. "We can use all the help we can get."

"There is one more thing I neglected to mention," said Pérez.

"What's that?" Rob asked.

"Auction," he replied. "I've heard from sources that there is some secret auction. Nobody knows much about it. But you might want to look into that."

"What? Why didn't you tell us about this earlier, Pérez?"

"I'm sorry, Mister Walker," he said. "I know nothing about it. It's just a rumor, really. If it is true, they keep it very hush-hush. But with all the confusion, it completely slipped my mind. I'm very sorry."

"I'm sorry too," said Rob. "Thanks for remembering, though. Just see what you can find out for me, please."

"Will do," replied the detective.

Morales roamed in front of his partner and leaned into the Jeep.

"I won't forget what you guys did for me and others," he told them. "And, Mister Branch, I'm sorry you got shot. But I'm glad you're okay."

"It was nothing," he replied. "It wasn't my first time being shot. It probably won't be my last, either."

Kyle was speaking the truth. In fact, he and Rob both had the Purple Hearts to prove it. Morales's demeanor shifted as he thought back to what Juan and his men had done to him.

"But," Morales said, "when you have the chance, please do not hesitate. Make these fuckers pay for what they've done. Kill them for me and everyone else they have hurt."

The Messenger

Detective Morales handed Rob a paper with a sketch of the place's approximate location, and he slipped it into his pocket.

"Thanks," Rob said. "That's the plan."

Rob put the Jeep into drive.

"All right, fellas," he told them just before driving off. "Wish us luck. We'll see you on the other side."

ⅲ

The Jeep came barreling over the hill. On the horizon, the fog hid distant desert peaks. The tiny town of Sinoquipe, one hundred miles from the Arizona border, finally emerged up ahead. It had been a long, twenty-four-hour drive. Rob and Kyle had slept a few hours in the Jeep at a campground midway through. They needed to be rested for what was to come.

Rob munched on a leftover burrito they'd had earlier that day for lunch. He turned the sharp curve on the two-lane road that passed by the west side of a town of fewer than four hundred people in the Mexican State of Sonora. The place was remote. There was no other town for miles around, and the only thing surrounding it was parched land on all sides with spots of light green vegetation and brown-colored trees with sparse green leaves. The flat scenery seemed to give way to rolling red dirt-covered desert foothills.

They had no plans to make a pit stop. Rob was in a rush to get to where they were going. The town was nothing but a blur as he shot by it to the spot Morales had marked on the map. But Rob wasn't going old school. With his handheld military-grade GPS lying between the seats, he'd planned to cross-reference the spot the detective had given him with real-time satellite imagery.

Rob monitored the Jeep's odometer. The information Morales had given him pointed a few miles north of Sinoquipe, a couple of miles out into the desert from the road. As the digits on the dash counted up and hit the estimated distance, Rob tapped the brakes, swinging right onto the road's shoulder.

"I think this is it," he told Kyle.

There was no road they could turn onto, just miles of open ground in either direction. Rob knew they'd need to go off road.

"Well," he said. "Hang on to your hat, buddy. It's going to get bumpy."

Rob turned the wheel to the right and slowly picked up the pace, kicking up fine, powdery sand and rocks into the roadway as they jumped the hill and crossed over bushes and small trees. They made their way out into no-man's-land, not another human being anywhere in sight. They drove out several miles, bouncing and rocking from the uneven terrain, and Rob came to a sudden stop. Kyle, GPS in his hand, examined the topography of the surrounding land. His eyes squinted as the bright sunlight reflected from the mirror, searching for traces of something man-made.

"You see anything?" asked Rob.

"Nope," he replied. "Just mountains and a whole lot of desert."

Kyle zoomed the satellite image in with his fingers.

"Wait, a second. I think I got something here. Look at this."

Kyle handed the GPS to Rob.

"That looks like something, all right," Rob said, studying closely. "It sure stands out between those hills, doesn't it?"

From what Rob could tell, it appeared to be a structure. And, from viewing the GPS, it was about half-a-mile northeast of their location. They didn't want to leave the Jeep too close and risk being spotted by guards. Out there, they could see a vehicle coming for miles. Rob shut the engine down and jumped from the Jeep. He went straight for the tailgate and their gear in the back. Pressing the button on the large igloo water jug and filling his canteen to the top, Rob took a sip of the cold water. He emptied a little over his head to cool off, water dripping down from his chin onto his tan shirt.

Rob stretched his arms high into the air, his colorful American flag and bald eagle tattoo appearing like a tear in his side beneath his top. He snatched his assault pack and opened it.

"Let's get ghillied up."

Both men stepped into their ghillie suits, pulling the pants up and tugging the top over their heads. Rob wrapped his leg holster around his right leg, inserting his .45 Glock. With his M4 and sniper rifle draped by slings over both shoulders, he was ready to move. The men began spreading a camouflage net cover over the Jeep and planned to leave it concealed until they needed to get the hell out of dodge.

"You sure you are up for this?" Rob asked Kyle.

"Man, we've already been through this. I'm good, okay?"

"All right," said Rob. "Let's see what we're dealing with."

The men began hiking over hills and through scrubland and sagebrush on the way to where the satellite image had guided them. The desert there was arid and stuffy. There were plants and vegetation, but only ones that grew with little rain, which that area hadn't seen in a while, it seemed. The afternoon sun was scorching and burned down on them as they made their way over one foothill encompassing a hidden valley below not seen from the road.

Rob peeked over the side as they made it to the top, past

creosote bushes and mesquite trees toward the bottom.

"Give me the spotting scope," Rob said.

Kyle released his pack to the dirt and recovered the scope, giving it over to Rob. He took a knee, peeping through the high-powered lens.

"Yep," he said. "There's something down there, all right. I can't see much past the trees, though. We need to move a little closer."

Kyle followed Rob further down the side of the hill. Rob dropped to the ground between the dry, withered foliage.

"Oh, yeah," Rob said as he glanced through once more. "Much better. I see a large warehouse-type building down there."

Rob removed his rifles from his back and set up his long gun out front, leaving the M4 set to his side as he fixed the bipod and flipped up the scope's dust cover. As he glanced through the glass, he found two guards standing next to a fence gate and a dirt trail cut by vehicle tires that seemed to lead nowhere. Many men were roaming across the grounds, AKs and submachine guns in hand. Morales had pointed out that he'd overheard a discussion about a shipment that was to occur when he was being held. There was also supposedly a meeting taking place that night with the Los Lobos Cartel boss, Juan Luis, in that exact spot. Rob and Kyle knew they were in for a long night.

"Get comfortable, partner," Rob said as Kyle set up next to him in the dirt. "We're in for a wait."

The men readied themselves with the best view of the grounds. If anyone showed up, they would see them coming from a long way off.

TWENTY-SIX

Sinoquipe
Sonora, Mexico

Hours had gone by, and Rob was ready behind the long gun, viewing the complex as the guards stood by the pole lights, generators humming noisily close by. They were talking to one another and smoking cigarettes under the half-moon sky. Conditions were ideal for a sharpshooter, weeds around them fluttering softly in the mild wind.

"You think she's in there?" Kyle asked, lying in the prone position by his friend.

"I don't know, man," Rob replied, spitting a dip to the side. "Let's hope so."

The men settled on that hill, watching guards out front and roving sentries stepping over their own footsteps around the perimeter. They'd already been there for a while, and Rob couldn't help but wonder if they had the right location. The time on his G-Shock watch showed half-past eight p.m. As Rob glanced past the guard shack by the entrance, he caught multiple sets of bright vehicle lights coming over a hill. They were racing over the semi-desert landscape in their direction. The flash was intense as it beamed toward them. It momentarily blinded him through his night vision. Rob removed it from his eyes.

"We have visitors," he said. "Coming from the west."

The convoy approached the entrance, and Rob got a closer look at them. It was five vehicles, two black Narco tanks, two black Suburban SUVs, and a flatbed semi-truck with a large box secured to the back. They slowed as the two guards waved them through.

"God, these people sure fucking love black, don't they?"

"It looks that way," Kyle said.

Four of the trucks pulled back around and parked in the yard's corner facing the front entrance gate. The semi backed up to a door at the front of the building, halting as the rear end bumped the rubber stop. The driver hopped out, engine still running, and opened the container.

"What do you think he's doing?" Kyle asked Rob.

"I have no idea," he replied. "Let's see what happens. It looks like they're about to load something."

Some men disappeared into the building as Rob, and Kyle watched. But, when they came back, they were poking and thrusting people forward, brown sacks over their heads, to the metal shipping container.

"What the fuck?" Rob said. "Looks like they're moving them."

Rob and Kyle both witnessed as they forced over twenty girls into a big metal box with a lock on it one by one.

"How are we going to know if Marianne is down there?" asked Kyle. "Their heads are covered."

Rob looked at every girl as they were each tossed into the back of the trailer. Then something got his attention.

"Wait, a second!" Rob said as he zoomed in. "That's her!"

"Where?"

"Right there," Rob replied. "The one that guard just shoved up the ramp. You see her?"

"How do you know that's Marianne?"

"The rose tattoo on her ankle! I'd recognize it anywhere. She got it at the same time I got my tattoo. We went to a tattoo parlor in Brooklyn together that day. I bought it for her birthday the last time I was home."

"Shit," Kyle said. "What are we going to do?"

"Poor Marianne," Rob replied. "I imagine she's scared out of her mind right now. Hold on. Let me think."

They watched and waited, knowing they couldn't act and risk the cartel killing her and the others.

"Where do you think they're taking them?" asked Kyle.

"I don't know," Rob said. "But we're going to find out."

They finished packing the trailer, and the driver climbed back into the cab, black exhaust smoke towering above as he released the air brakes and moved forward. The gun trucks and SUVs, filled with cartel men, circled the semi as they made their way through the entrance. Left behind were a few guards watching over the warehouse.

"Okay," Rob said. "Here's what we're going to do. We're going to get rid of these assholes, keeping one of 'em alive, so we can interrogate him."

"Why don't we follow them?" asked Kyle.

"Because," Rob replied, "they'll kill her if they spot us. We have to play this right. One dangerous move and she's gone forever."

Rob waited for the vehicles to fade into darkness. Once they were out of view, he rotated his sniper rifle toward the guards at the gate and touched his finger to the cold, metal trigger.

"Ready?" he asked Kyle.

"Roger that, brother."

Together, Rob and Kyle each got a solid sight picture of their targets.

Rob, inhaling lightly and watching the suppressed gun's rise and then the fall as he exhaled, prepared to shoot, pushing the remaining air from his lungs.

"Now," he said.

At practically the same time, both men pressed the triggers. The two guards out front fell straight to the earth under the glowing yellow light as blood spurted out from their backs. They'd hit the dirt almost concurrently, their AKs thumping to the ground as they dropped from their limp hands.

"Did anyone see them fall?" asked Kyle.

"I don't think so," Rob said as he examined the area, "but we got one moving that way."

The rest of the unknown number of men were inside or on the other end of the building. It didn't seem like the man had noticed his dead comrades yet, but Rob needed to put him down before he got too close.

"I got this asshole."

Rob, following him as he leisurely made his way toward the front, set his reticle on the guard's head. He let the round go. It tore into the side of his head above the ear, ripping his skull apart. The force of the .30-caliber round threw his body to the side as he fell, pieces of brain spattered across the ground.

The Messenger

"He's down," said Rob.

The large door at the front of the structure opened, white light flooding out as a dozen men started moving toward the center of the complex. One of them noticed the dead body and called back to the others.

"Damn it," Rob said. "We have a problem."

The whole place came alert as men shouted back and forth.

Rob peeked through the glass. He noticed a figure that seemed to stand out from the rest. He stood in the back of the others, wearing a camouflage suit and holding a black bolt-action rifle. Rob blinked to relieve his strained eye. But when he looked through again, the man had vanished.

"Shit."

"What?" asked Kyle. "What is it?"

"The shooter who got you," Rob said. "I think I just saw him. Come on, we need to move before he discovers us."

"How could you possibly know it's him?"

"It's just a hunch," replied Rob. "A feeling in my gut. I'm sure that's him."

As a trained sniper, Rob could imagine what he would have done in that situation. He presumed, if the shooter was skilled, he could tell what direction the shot had come from. The best thing they could do was change position. Kyle followed Rob as he moved low across the ground to another hill overlooking the warehouse's rear side. Lodged between a large bush and an ironwood tree, they kissed the dirt. The other men were out in the bush, searching for them. Kyle picked up his night-vision binoculars and began checking the compound's outer edges up into the surrounding hills.

"You see him?" Rob asked as he inched his weapon from

side to side, watching for movement.

"Nope," he replied. "Not yet."

"Fuck," Rob said as he saw a group of men drifting closer. "We need to deal with these guys first."

Rob left his sniper rifle, snatched his M4 from the ground, and performed a tactical roll down the hill. The cartel men walked in a gaggle as they rummaged through the bushes and dead brush, carrying AK-47s and handguns. Rob, lying across the dirt with his right elbow on a large rock, brought his M4 up. They both were masters of stalking and camouflage.

"Get ready, partner," he whispered.

Masked behind the hill, Rob rose to one knee. He flicked the weapon from semi-auto to burst and started sending a hail of bullets, three at a time, from his thirty-round magazine into their path. He didn't care where he hit them. They just needed to get them out of the picture before they figured out where they were. Kyle followed his buddy, dropping four of the men in a matter of seconds from his spot a few meters away.

A few got indiscriminate shots off, just missing Rob as he and Kyle continued firing into them. But one had struck Rob at the top of his vest. He fell backward onto his back.

"Fuck!" he shouted. "I'm hit!"

"How bad?" Kyle asked over his shoulder as he continued shooting.

"Ugh!" Rob said as he sat up.

He pushed the top of the vest away with his thumb and glanced down at the mark just above his ribs.

"Damn, it hurts like a bitch! But it looks like the vest took the brunt of it!"

"Good!" Kyle said, men still moving in their direction. "Get up here and help me!"

Rob boosted himself up with the butt of the rifle. His chest stinging like it was in flames, he sucked up the pain and began firing again.

One by one, the Los Lobos cartel cronies dropped to the ground. The only sign of Rob and Kyle was the thumping sound coming from their rifle muzzles. When it was all said and done, twelve bodies had accumulated around them.

"They're done," Rob said. "The fuckers."

Rob pulled up his ghillie suit top and unfastened the Velcro on his vest to take a quick look at the wound. He pushed the top of his undershirt down. The projectile had pushed through the armor plate and struck his chest, the tip just piercing the skin. Left was a golf ball–sized swelling over his rib cage. He refastened the vest.

"You good?" Kyle asked him.

"Yeah, man," he said. "I'm golden. It just burns like fucking hell. I'll be all right, I think."

"Good," Kyle said. "Because the shooter is still out there somewhere."

Rob carefully slithered back up the hill, keeping his chest from dragging across the ground by bracing with his knees and elbows. He peeked through the scope, feeling the foregrip of the weapon in his left palm.

"Where are you, asshole?"

Then Rob noticed a bright muzzle flash from the other side of the valley.

"Shit!" he said, ducking down as a shot kicked up dirt just in front of them. "I just saw him."

Rob moved a couple of meters to the right and scanned through the glass again.

"He's moved," he said as another rifle round pinged off

the ground beside Kyle. "Hit the dirt!"

Kyle snaked his way back a little way down the mound.

"Damn it," Rob said. "As much as I hate to say this, we're going to have to draw his fire so I can get a shot on him. I'll only have a second at him before he moves again."

"What did you have in mind?" Kyle asked.

Rob smacked him on the back and smiled.

"Give me your vest."

Kyle removed the vest over his ghillie top and gave it to Rob.

"Now give me your hat," Rob said.

Rob took the vest and the baseball cap and draped them from the barrel of his M4. He handed it back to Kyle.

"Here. Take this. When I tell you, hold that halfway up."

Rob moved to the left side of the hill and readied his rifle. He felt it securely in his grip as he held the glass to his face. His eyes fixated, Rob watched for the muzzle flash, hoping he'd take the bait.

"Now," he told Kyle.

Kyle held the vest up, half of it obscured behind the hill. Rob looked through the scope toward the other side, about eight hundred meters away. A muzzle flash got his attention as the round sailed across the field and ripped through the baseball hat, flinging it back onto the ground. Kyle lowered the weapon and vest.

Targeting where the flash had come from, a second later, Rob squeezed his trigger. He noticed a distant red spurt out from where the shot had impacted.

"I think I got him!" said Rob. "I saw his silhouette hit the dirt. Shit, man. That could've been your fucking head!"

Rob secured his gear and his pack.

"Come on!" he said.

The men sprinted across the way to the back of the structure. Up ahead, they noticed someone floundering across the ground like a fish out of water. Rob approached and got down next to him. It was Marco. And he was bleeding heavily, a gunshot wound to his lung and struggling to breathe—air bubbles leaked from the hole in his chest.

"So," Rob said, "you're the one they sent to kill us?"

Marco tried to speak, but Rob couldn't understand him.

"What was that, partner?" Rob asked as he went closer.

"You... will... die..." he sputtered.

Rob seized Marco by the collar and jerked his body upward.

"Where did they take them, asshole?" he asked. "Where? Tell me where they went!"

But Marco just snarled at him as he grew weaker. Rob realized it was a lost cause trying to get any information out of him. He took his black K-Bar knife from the black sheath fastened to his vest.

"Don't you worry," Rob said to Marco. "We'll send you some company very soon."

Marco tried to scream but couldn't manage to make a sound other than a slight moan.

"This is for my sister, my friend, and all the other innocent people you have hurt, you motherfucker!" Rob said.

Rob gripped the knife handle tight and sank it through Marco's throat just under his chin, blood gushing from his carotid artery, painting the sand around him red as his head fell to the side. Rob sliced the blade to the side, cutting Marco almost from ear to ear. He withdrew the knife and wiped the blood on Marco's sleeve.

"Let's go through this bastard's stuff. See if he's got anything of value. He knew something, or he wouldn't have been here."

They found a money clip with a large wad of US bills, a phone, and a bunch of random scrap paper in Marco's pants pockets.

"Take this," Rob told Kyle, handing over the stack of money. "He doesn't need it anymore."

Rob opened Marco's cell phone and glanced at his most recent message. He translated the most recent text using the internet on his phone.

The Americans will be there. Get rid of them, Marco. Reply to this message when it's done. Meet us at the Light Club when you're finished.

"How in the hell did he know we'd be here?" Rob asked.

Rob showed the phone to Kyle.

"Check this out," he said.

Rob knew the cartel would now chalk them up for dead.

"Watch this," Rob said.

Rob looked up the correct translation and typed it in Spanish: *It's done.*

"Now, they think we are history."

But only two people knew where they were going. Then Rob thought back to Detective Morales. He had a terrible realization.

"Oh, fuck!"

Rob picked up his cell again and phoned Detective Pérez. He put it on speaker.

"Pérez! You need to check your partner's home for bugs. I have a feeling they were onto him from the start. They knew we were coming!"

There was a brief silence on the line. Rob sensed that something was wrong.

"It's too late for that," Pérez replied. "I just walked in. He's dead, and they are sending some other detectives over here to investigate. They shot the poor bastard in the fucking head and wrote Los Lobos in his blood all over the walls. These people will stop at nothing! I'm sure it was payback for his escape and helping you. They wanted us to know who did it."

"What?" Kyle asked. "They fucking killed him?"

Rob pounded his phone in his hand.

"Damn it! I'm so sorry, man. I know he was your friend. I won't forget what he did for us, either. But how did they find where he lives?"

"I don't really know," Pérez said. "Maybe they followed us from the station. The cartel has infinite resources."

Rob felt a sickness in his belly as he recalled his previous conversation with Morales. He sensed the guilt of his death coming over him.

"I'm really sorry, Pérez," Rob said. "He was one of the good guys."

"Thanks," Pérez told him. "Listen, I need to go deal with this. But don't blame yourselves for his death. It's not your fault. They've been out for us for a long time."

"All right," Rob replied. "Thank you. Like I said, we're really sorry. Listen, though. Don't mention a word to them about us, okay? We don't need a bunch of cops on us right now. But, Pérez, you need to hide. They may come after you too."

"You got it, amigo," he said. "My lips are sealed. And, don't worry, I plan to disappear very soon."

Rob hung his phone up, feeling sorry for the detective and

Morales's family. They never meant for them to pay for what they were doing. But they'd make sure they punished Juan Luis and his associates. And now they thought Rob and Kyle were done for, out of the picture. But they needed to act soon, before the cartel found out the truth.

TWENTY-SEVEN

Hermosillo, Mexico

The men rode into the Sonora state capital late into the night, a city of hundreds of thousands of people in northwest Mexico and the hub of the Los Lobos Cartel's operations. The Jeep swayed into the parking lot as the music from that building echoed through the neighboring streets. Multicolored laser lights from the upper floor beamed down onto the road below. The disco ball spun around in circles from the ceiling inside. People on the balcony leaned against the stone railing, yelling in Spanish to friends and others below.

Limousines and fancy cars passed through the valet, drivers tossing keys to the attendants. The occupants walked toward the door, wearing expensive suits and brand-name dresses. EL CLUB DE LA LUZ (The Light Club) glowed in Spanish in bright, neon lights on the large sign on the roof above the door. Rob had gotten the feeling that this wasn't just an average neighborhood tavern.

"I guess this is where the Mexican elite hangs out," said Rob.

And he wouldn't be mistaken. Every corrupt politician, businessperson, or dignitary in cahoots with Juan's organization patronized the place. The Los Lobos Cartel owned the club, as they did most everything else in the city. Rob and Kyle were now in their backyard. Knowing they could be identified, the men brought items to help them blend in: black suits and fake mustaches Detective Morales had given them for the occasion. He'd known they would need them to keep from sticking out in that God-awful place.

"It's a good thing we stopped to clean up a bit, huh?" asked Rob. "Wouldn't want to smell like desert sweat."

"Yeah, no shit," replied Kyle.

They began getting dressed in the vehicle. Minutes passed, and they gave each other a strange look.

"So, how do I look?" Rob asked, mustache fixed above his clean-shaven chin.

"About as stupid as I do," Kyle replied, chuckling. "I mean, really, I have to say, I've never done anything quite so strange. And I hate wearing suits!"

"I do too," Rob said. "But just suck it up. We're dead, remember? If we look like we have money, maybe we can blend in with these crummy ass people."

Rob glanced across the way to the front door. He saw the bouncers frisking people as they walked in.

"Shit. We have to leave our guns here."

Kyle peeked over at the line to the door. They were checking everyone who came in.

"Fuck," Kyle said. "What are we going to do if the shit hits the fan? I don't want to go in there naked."

"I don't either," Rob said, "but we'll figure something out, I'm sure. We always do."

Both men stepped from the vehicle and prepared to move. A blanket in the back of the Jeep hid their camouflage packs.

"Wait," Rob said as he glanced down an alley to the right of the club. "On second thought, let's hold on to our guns. I have a better idea."

The men recovered their weapons and hid them under their suit coats. Leaving the Jeep on the far side of the lot, they headed for the street.

"Listen," Rob said as they continued on. "We can't go through the front. Too many people, and they are checking IDs. But I think we can find another way in."

"No shit, bro. So what's the idea, then?"

As they crossed the street between cars driving by to the valet pickup, they moved past the crowd of drunk partiers gathered on the sidewalk.

"Let's see what's back here," said Rob.

They both entered the blackened alleyway and melted into the dark at the side of the building, hugging the brick wall. Looking around the back corner, Rob found a single guard standing by the back door, smoking a cigarette and playing on his phone. The Mexican guard was a large man, arm muscles bulging from his short, black shirt sleeve. He looked like a gentleman who could take care of himself. But that didn't intimidate Rob. Past the door guard, a single yellow stretch Hummer stood as a status symbol for its owner, perhaps Juan himself.

It was gloomy behind the bar, a stark contrast to what it was like out front. The only light came from a single bulb above the back door. With black suits on, Rob and Kyle stood almost invisible in the darkness.

"Act drunk," he told Kyle.

Before he could ask why Rob was already on the move, Kyle kept up the performance as they careened and wobbled toward the door.

"Hola," Rob said to the guard as he tripped over his own feet.

Rob swayed side to side as he neared him.

"What are you doing back here, asshole?" the guard asked in Spanish. "This door is private. You use the front entrance like everyone else!"

Rob acted like he didn't hear him, even though he understood little of what he said.

"Hey!" the guard yelled at him as they got closer. "I'm talking to you!"

"Come... on... bro," Rob said. "I just forgot my keys."

Rob stretched a hand out to the private door. As his finger reached the knob, the guard caught him by the arm. Rob snatched the guard's wrist and twisted it hard in a quick move as he went down to the ground. The man tried to grip Rob's neck with the other. But Rob jabbed him in the throat before he could get another hand on him, sending him back to the pavement and coughing, hardly able to breathe. Before he could come to his senses, Kyle moved in, brought a leg up, and booted him in the jaw.

Rob got his suppressed Glock from inside his coat and touched it to the guard's temple, point-blank. With five pounds of squeezing pressure, Rob sent a shot into his head, keeping his reach to keep the blood from spilling onto his suit. The guard's arms fell to the side.

Seeing the outline through his black pants, Rob reached into the dead man's right pocket and found a set of keys.

"Jackpot," he said. "Hurry, grab his legs."

The Messenger

Hands seizing his appendages, Rob and Kyle moved the guard away from the building. They tossed him into a drainage ditch, watching as he rolled down the hill and into shallow water. The men hurried to the door, and Rob tried each of the ten keys. Finally, as he entered the last one, the lock clicked. He creaked the door open, and they slipped inside, unseen, into a long hall that led past the restrooms toward the front of the club. Rob adjusted his black coat.

"All right," he told Kyle. "Act natural. We're just here for the entertainment."

They both walked down the hall and turned left, then right, making their way to the bar, next to the dance floor.

"What will it be?" the bartender asked them in Spanish as they each took a seat.

Rob glanced up at him.

"No hablo español, señor!" he replied over dance music playing through the surround sound speakers over their heads.

"Inglés?" he asked Rob. "Good, good. What can I get for you?"

"Two beers, please," Rob said.

The bartender reached under the bar and came back up with two bottles, placing them both on the counter over napkins. They both started drinking, peeking back at the enormous crowd on the dance floor every few seconds. Rob and Kyle perched on the stools for just over half an hour, eyeing every person who wandered into the club. Rob couldn't help but wonder who worked for the cartel and benefited from the cartel's business. Minutes later, as Rob glanced to his right, he noticed a familiar face that he'd seen but never met in person. The man looked to be arrogantly and blatantly flaunting his wealth from head to toe, from the pricey suit to the jewelry he wore, the Rolex watch, and the shiny boots on his feet. But when Juan moved, everyone got out of his way. There was no doubt they all bowed to him.

Rob tapped on Kyle's feet with his shoe, trying not to make it noticeable.

"There he is," he said into his ear. "It's Juan."

They watched as Juan, with his entourage, marched past the parting crowd, out of the bar's customer side toward the back. Rob snatched his beer, and they moved over to a spot where they could see where he was going. He spotted Juan and his men heading for a locked door at the end of the hallway, a second guard opening it up for them.

"You see that?" Rob asked Kyle.

"Uh-huh," Kyle replied. "Sure did."

"We need to see what they're hiding behind that door," said Rob. "We have to get past that guard."

"Any suggestions?" Kyle asked as they watched people in the crowded club who were mindless of what was happening under their noses.

Rob stood by for a flash, glancing at the guard far to their right as they leaned against a pillar between the dance floor and the club entrance.

"Yeah," he said, raising his knife from his pants and hiding it under his long coat sleeve. "We shut off the power."

Rob skimmed the room and found a breaker box somewhat hidden behind a curtain at the side of the hallway. He tapped Kyle on the arm, and he followed. The men made their way down and stopped just shy of the hall entry.

"Get ready," he said.

Rob quickly pivoted around and pressed down on the main power switch, and the lighting and music abruptly went dead. People in the club began shouting and tripping over one another, unable to see where they were going. The men made a dash for the door.

A tussle ensued, the noise softened by a roaring and panicked crowd. Rob stuck the guard under his rib cage with his K-bar knife and twisted, causing him to die instantly, blood soaking his shirt. He and Kyle moved the guard through the darkness, discarding his body in the Janitor's closet by the back door. They slipped out and passed through the door just before the power began to flicker back on. Rob reached out and locked the door's deadbolt from inside.

"Let's hope they don't notice he's gone," Kyle said.

As Rob shut the door and locked it, they moved further in, spotting a staircase at the end of the empty hall.

"There's another floor here," said Rob.

They both rounded the winding steps and made their way down. As they came near the bottom, they detected a voice speaking over some kind of sound system. Doors were located every few feet, with God knew what going on behind them. They had to find out what was happening down there.

Rob cracked one door to take a look in. His jaw felt like it had suddenly hit the floor. He saw men sitting in a circular arrangement in private booths and a young girl, fifteen or sixteen, held in place by a woman speaking into a PA systems microphone. Nobody outside could hear what was happening through soundproofed walls.

"Shit," Rob said as he softly closed the door behind them. "So, it is true? It's a fucking human auction."

Before they could make another move, they heard footsteps hitting the marble floor and walking their way from the other side of the basement.

"In here. Hurry!"

They rushed into the only empty auction booth. Rob peeked through the tiny peephole in the door.

"Fuck," Rob added. "It's Juan. And it looks like he's headed back upstairs."

"Let's just hope he doesn't figure out what happened," replied Kyle.

They sat in the soundproof booth; the woman addressing clientele through the speaker above. It was a disturbing sight, girls being forced onto a stage, recognizably drugged, and sold like property.

"These people deserve death," Rob said. "What they do is a crime against humanity."

Rob and Kyle settled there for a time, watching as they sold them one by one, paid for by the wealthy elite scum of the earth. But just as Rob had doubts about his sister showing, the woman spoke again in English over the loudspeaker.

"Gentlemen, we always save the best for last. Our next and final product, a New York-born beauty, is sure to please anyone who purchases her. Bidding starts at one hundred and fifty thousand."

Rob looked up through the glass window encompassing the entire interior of the booth, noticing her long, brown hair flattened over the front and covering her face. They had dressed her up in a sparkling new dress. She stumbled over high-heeled shoes. The woman held her up to keep her from collapsing to the floor. She was obviously high, just like the rest of them. Then Rob spotted the rose tattoo on her ankle.

Bidding had already begun. And the price just passed one hundred and eighty thousand.

"Is that her?" Kyle asked. "Is that Marianne?"

Rob felt tortured at the sight of his sister in that state.

"Yeah," he replied. "It's her, all right."

The auctioneer continued over the speaker, "Do I have two hundred thousand?"

A dark character in another booth raised his paddle.

"Great, two hundred thousand. Do I have two hundred and ten thousand?"

Rob countered the bid.

"What the hell are you doing?" Kyle asked him. "We don't have that kind of money!"

"What choice do I have? They are about to sell her. I can't just sit here!"

The bidding had reached two hundred and twenty thousand. Rob held the paddle up once again. This time, another bidder raised his paddle and pushed the microphone button in front of him.

"Two hundred and fifty!" he said.

Rob lifted his paddle high before the auctioneer could respond to the bid and spoke into the microphone.

"Three hundred thousand!"

Rob waited to see if he'd have a counter bid.

"Three hundred thousand," the auctioneer announced. "I have three hundred thousand now."

But nobody else wished to counter Rob's offer. Rob released the microphone button.

"Sold to the number three gentleman for three hundred thousand. Thank you all for participating, and you can pick up your merchandise directly from down the hall. Have an excellent rest of your night."

"Great," Kyle said. "Now what? You don't have the money to pay for her."

"Of course not," Rob replied. "We burst in there and fucking take her."

He and Kyle left the booth and made their way down the hall to a lavish and extravagant room designed with money in mind. Expensive paintings covered the walls all the way around the circular room. Champagne flowed endlessly as people in high-end clothing sipped from crystal glasses. Opposite of them, a lady sat behind a counter, collecting money for recent purchases. Rob and Kyle stood fast, waiting for the crowd of people to taper down. Men escorted bought merchandise to a secret entrance elevator down the red carpet-lined passageway.

Twenty minutes later, as patrons worked their way to the exit, Rob walked toward the counter. As the lady smiled up at him, he removed his piece from his coat and pointed it at her.

"The last girl you sold. Her name is Marianne. Bring her to me now!"

The lady held her arms up and propelled herself away from the counter.

"Sir," she replied. "Please, there's no need for that! Whatever problem you have with your purchase, we can settle it!"

"Lady," he said, aiming for her head, "you don't understand. She is my sister. Bring her to me!"

"They are all someone's sister," she remarked. "Sorry, sir, sales are final."

All he was witnessing agitated Rob. None of those people seemed to object to girls being sold off like animals. But Rob didn't notice that someone had seen the dispute and was now right behind them. He saw the shadow on the floor. But, before Rob could turn to see who it was, he was whacked in the head by the pistol grip of a Colt revolver.

"Rob!" Kyle yelled.

He didn't react. The blow knocked Rob out as he hit the cold, hard floor, his Glock tumbling to the floor beside him. The assailant kept his gun on Kyle, so he couldn't move. He took Rob's gun from the floor and reached in the back of Kyle's pants for his, handing both to one of his men.

"Un-fucking believable," the man said as he crept up behind Kyle. "Why can't you motherfuckers just die?"

He pointed one of his men to the back of Kyle to secure his arms.

"My name is Juan Luis. I'm the boss, and it's nice to finally meet the two men who've been fucking up my world. You guys are good."

Juan grinned at Kyle and glanced down at Rob, flattened facedown across the floor.

"Maybe not good enough, though. I have plans for you two. It's just business, you see? And business needs to be treated with... how do you say... care? You two are coming with us! I will make sure you pay for sticking your noses where they don't belong."

One of Juan's men began tying Rob's hands and feet together.

"We're going for a little ride," Juan said.

TWENTY-EIGHT

Unknown location

Rob finally woke with his hands tied together with rope. He hung almost naked from a ceiling rafter, a blinding glare from above piercing his eyes and blurring his vision. He had no memory of getting there, or even the slightest clue of where he was. He had a burning headache from the knot on the back of his head.

"God, my fucking head."

Rob tried to focus his blurry eyes and rattled his head to get his bearings. The room was cold and clammy with no windows, just a brick wall all the way around. Rob felt weak. His arms stretched like they would pop right out of the socket.

"Where the fuck am I?" he asked himself, peering around the room.

Rob detected a moan coming from his left side. He carefully turned his head and saw Kyle dangling from the ceiling a few feet away, dried blood down the side of his head and his arm pooled on the cement floor.

"Kyle," he said to his friend. "Kyle, you okay?"

Kyle tried to speak, spitting up blood from his mouth.

"Where the fuck are we, man?" Rob asked. "All I remember is being struck in the head."

The impact to his head had impacted Rob's memory. He glanced at Kyle again and, as his eyes opened wider, saw the condition of his partner's face. It seemed they had beat him up pretty bad. One side was purple, like they had hit him with a blunt object.

"Jesus," Rob said. "What the hell did they do to you?"

Kyle's head tilted to one side as the pain appeared to be getting the better of him. But both men were SERE (Survival, Evasion, Resistance, Escape) trained, as all Special Forces operators were. They were not strangers to torture. This, however, was the real thing. They'd better figure something out soon if they wanted to get out of there alive.

Kyle started to talk, his expression suggesting suffering from each word he spoke.

"I-I have no clue... where we a-are," he stuttered. "They p-put... bags over our...h-heads. All I know is th-they started beating... the s-shit out of me. You were out of it."

Rob felt responsible for putting them in that position. He would never forgive himself if something happened to his friend.

"I'm sorry, man," Rob told Kyle. "I'm so sorry. I shouldn't have brought you here."

But Kyle was a tough guy. And he didn't want to hear it.

"Rob," he said, feeling the scathing burn with every move of his swollen lip. "Don't go there, okay? I would do it all again. So let's just find a way out of here, okay?"

Then, a light radiated down from the top of the wood

stairs as the door came open. They could hear multiple footsteps working their way downward. Out of the shadow at the bottom, Juan appeared in the light with three of his men. He flashed a cocky sneer at them as he got closer, stopping in front of Rob.

"Well," he said to Rob. "Look who's finally up. I thought you'd miss the party, sleeping beauty."

The guards behind Juan chuckled.

"As you can see," Juan said, "I did a number on your friend here. See, he wouldn't talk. So now he gets to watch while I do the same to you. What do you think about that?"

"Fuck you!" Rob yelled, spitting on Juan's fancy boots.

"Now, why would you do a thing like that?" asked Juan. "Normally, I would just kill you. But not this time. This is purely for my amusement. Neither of you will leave here breathing. We might as well have some fucking fun first! What do you say, cowboys? Want to test your resolve?"

Juan swiftly balled a fist and hit Rob as hard as he could in the gut, causing him to cough like he was about to spit up a lung.

"You like that?" Juan asked. "You fucking gringo!"

Juan drew his fist back and hit him even harder.

"How about now, tough guy? I can do this all fucking night!"

Juan fetched a 2x4 from the floor. He brought it behind his head and swung it forward with considerable force, cracking Rob right in his ribs. He tried to scream but couldn't breathe well enough to make a sound. A crushing agony rushed over him. His body went numb. Juan secured the piece of solid wood and moved to Kyle.

"How about I punish your friend some more? I'll beat him

senseless until he can't fucking move anymore, then I'll kill him right in front of you."

Rob and Kyle locked eyes. He wanted to get his buddy out of there. He sure didn't want to see Kyle tormented any longer.

"You lost," said Juan. "I sold your beloved sister to royalty after you fucks showed up. She is now on her way to his private yacht. She's gone. It is time you accept that truth. There is nothing you can do about it. It is over!"

Juan's phone began humming in his jacket. Eyeing Kyle down with the board still in his hand, he answered it.

"What?" he asked the caller. "What the fuck do you want now?"

Rob didn't know what the call was about. And he didn't care. He just needed an opportunity.

"Fuck, okay!" Juan said. "Don't move. I'll be right there!"

Juan ended the call and put the phone back into his coat.

"Looks like you two got a temporary reprieve," he said, laughing. "But I will be back. We'll continue this party later!"

Juan marched toward the stairs.

"It's not like you're going anywhere," he said, his loud, evil laugh sounding through the windowless room.

He began speaking in Spanish to his men as they went up the stairs. Juan left, leaving a guard at the other side of the door.

"Watch them!" Juan said to him in Spanish. "I'll be back later. And if they move or give you any trouble, kill them!"

Rob got the immediate sense that if he didn't do something, they'd never get out of that dungeon-like room. He needed to act fast.

Rob attempted to push himself up by his feet with his toes just touching the dirty floor. But he only moved an inch. Rob began tugging and yanking down on the rope around his hands, trying to get as close to the ground as possible. As he hoisted himself up little by little, straining as hard as he could against the rope, he felt a little slack.

"Just hang on, friend. We're getting out of this hellhole."

Finally, able to touch the bottom of his toes to the concrete, he bumped himself up, just boosting the rope over the hook hanging from the large wooden beam above. He fell straight down, hitting the floor and thumping his head hard against the concrete, hoping nobody had heard the noise.

"Fuck!" Rob said, jerking the rope and loosening it from his wrists. "Hold tight, buddy!"

With pain throbbing with every move of his body, Rob rose and wrapped his arms tightly around Kyle. Trying to ignore his own discomfort, he boosted Kyle as high as he could above the hook, but, unable to hold his friend's weight any longer, he cursed as Kyle's body fell down on top of him. His friend struggled to move. Rob untied him, tossing the rope to the side.

"Come on," he told Kyle. "We have no time to nap here. They'll be back any minute!"

Rob found their white dress shirts and black pants on the floor in the corner of the room. He nabbed them and tossed a set to Kyle.

"Here. Put these back on."

"How are we going to get out of here, Rob?" Kyle mumbled, pulling the shirt up over his head. "We don't even know where the fuck we are."

Rob took the rope that was around his arms from the floor.

"Behind the staircase!"

Kyle got behind Rob at the back of the wooden stairs, the only light coming from above where they'd been hanging. He picked up a piece of metal that he'd found lying near them.

Rob got up, launching it at the door, and crouched back down. The metal made a clinking noise as it hit the door and fell to the hard ground. Suddenly, the door came unlatched.

"What the hell was that?" the guard asked in Spanish. "What are you doing down there?"

Rob could hear the footsteps on the wood above them. The guard made his way down to the bottom, noticing the empty hooks and the ropes lying on the floor.

"No!" the guard said. "Where the hell are you, bitches? I will find and kill you, so stop hiding. You have nowhere to go!"

As soon as the guard put a foot on the floor, Rob charged him from behind. He wrenched the rope around his throat like a garrote. Rob popped it back as hard as he could, taking the guard down to his knees on top of him. Kyle moved in and stole the gun from the guard's holster as Rob squeezed the life out of him. He struggled, desperately trying to break free. The guard attempted to reach for Rob's head, but he just strangled him tighter. Rob let go of the rope, and before the guard could react, Rob grabbed his head and twisted it to the side. He heard a sharp snap of the neck, and the guard was gone. Rob rolled out from underneath his body.

Kyle tossed Rob the guard's gun, and they bounded up the steps. Rob peeked around the doorway, seeing a long passageway leading to their far left.

"Let's go," said Rob.

As they glided along the wall, they heard footsteps moving through from the other end. They dove into another room and waited for the guard to pass by. Rob stepped out behind him, raising the gun and sending a bullet through the back of his head. He sank to the floor with a crash, blood flooding from the gaping hole.

"Grab what you can!" Rob said.

They seized the guard's pistol and the AK-47 on his back. As Rob looked up, he saw a row of crates against the wall filled with AKs, handguns, and submachine guns, a treasure trove of weapons.

"Get that AK," Rob said. "And let's get the fuck out of this place before more show up!"

Snatching a few weapons from the boxes, they both took off running and neared another set of stairs that went almost straight up. The men fled up and through the big metal door above and into the black night. But, as they came to the top, four guards emerged from down a dirt pathway.

"They've escaped!" one of them said in Spanish.

"Shit," Rob said, taking a knee.

He raised the pistol as Kyle brought his AK up. The guards aimed their guns in their direction. But, as they prepared to shoot, both men mowed two guards down with a string of consecutive shots, dropping them into the brush along the trail. One of them was still convulsing on the ground. Rob stood over him.

"Here is a message for your boss, asshole!" Rob yelled at him, pressing the trigger and blowing half of his skull apart.

Rob spit on the body. The men left the dead guards and advanced forward.

"Where the fuck are we?" he asked Kyle.

"I don't know," he said. "But we need to put as much distance between us and this place as we can."

They scampered across the desert plain toward a highway in the distance, occasional headlights appearing around the bend.

"We need to find a ride," Rob said. "You have any clue

about what happened to my sister?"

"All I know," Kyle replied, his battered body fighting to keep up speed, "is that they sold her to a rich Dubai prince! I don't know his name or what he looks like."

"What about the yacht Juan mentioned?"

"I really don't know," Kyle replied.

"Fuck!" Rob said.

They both hoofed it as fast as they could to the road a few hundred meters away. Once they arrived at it, Rob bent down, trying to catch his breath and holding his throbbing rib cage. He thought for sure they broke one or more of them. As he lifted his shirt up, a black and purple bruise painted the side of his body. It was a pain that wouldn't soon wane away.

Rob stuck a thumb out to hitch a ride.

"We need to get out of here before anyone realizes we're gone."

As they stood, car after car passed by them, not even so much as a brake light. Twenty minutes flew by, and they were losing hope. Lastly, a tiny, faded red Nissan pickup pulled up alongside them, traveling east, chickens clucking and feathers drifting through the air from inside the partly covered truck bed.

"Ah, fuck," Rob said as the driver's brakes screeched just past them. "Finally!"

The vehicle reeked of chicken manure and cigarette smoke. The driver was an old Mexican man, seventies, with a short gray beard and mustache. He looked surprised to find someone on that lonely stretch of road that time of night.

"Where are you going?" the driver asked in Spanish as Rob ran around and met him at the driver's-side window.

The man noticed the weapons they were holding and

raised his hands.

"No, no, please!" he said in Spanish. "I have nothing of worth. I'm just a chicken farmer!"

Rob didn't understand him fully. But he knew why he was afraid.

"Inglés?" asked Rob.

"I speak a little," he said. "Please, no hurt me!"

"Good," Rob replied. "Relax, will you? We aren't here to rob you, Mister. We just need a ride."

AK on his back, Rob placed the gun he was holding into his pants.

"We mean you no harm," he told the man, showing his empty hands. "See? I'm putting the gun away."

Rob stood by, smiling at the man and waiting for an answer.

"Okay, Mister," the old man said. "Okay, get in."

He climbed into the front passenger side while Kyle slipped through the small opening to the back.

"I am Alonso," the driver said.

"My name is Rob," he returned. "And this is Kyle."

Alonso nodded at them, seeming a little too timid to let them in.

Rob knew they couldn't go back for the Jeep or their gear. There was no time to lose.

"Where are we?" Rob asked.

"Desert outside Hermosillo, señor."

Alonso noticed the bruising and marks on both of their bodies like they'd been in an ugly brawl.

"What happened you two?" he asked. "You were fighting?"

"Never mind that," Rob said. "Where's the closest boatyard?"

Alonso raised an eyebrow and paused as if he was thinking about the question.

"Ah," he replied. "Marina, boats?"

"Yes," Rob said. "You have any idea?"

Alonso reached into his glove box and retrieved an old map. He opened it halfway, and with a red ink pen, marked a spot on the Sonora coast.

"Here," he said.

"Good, Alonso," Rob told him. "Bueno, take us there, please, pronto!"

Noticing he wasn't wearing a watch, Rob took his off, offering it to the old man for his trouble.

"Here," he said. "You take us, and this is yours!"

Alonso glanced down at the watch with a smile that revealed his missing front tooth.

"Okay! Bueno, señor. We go!"

Alonso made a quick U-turn in the middle of the road. He drove away in the other direction, heading for Mexico's west coast.

TWENTY-NINE

```
Marina San Carlos
Sonora, Mexico
```

It was late into the night, a few hours past midnight. The Nissan pickup rolled up near the marina entrance under the bleak sky. Lightning flared high above the stormy sea waters. The rippling waves continually broke against the side of the jetties. The marina looked empty, with many watercraft tied next to the wooden docks. But they weren't ordinary boats. They were yachts that only the super-rich could afford, a grim contradiction to Mexico's average yearly salary.

"Stop here!" Rob said to Alonso.

Rob had noticed the secured, metal slide gate with keypad beside it. It was a private passcode entry. There was no way they could drive a vehicle in there without crashing through it.

"Gracias, Alonso," he added as they hopped from the cab. "Thanks for the ride."

"Welcome, señor," Alonso replied.

Rob placed the AK on his back. He and Kyle moved

onward, scaling over the chain-link fence as Alonso swung the truck around and drove out of sight into the night. The storm had picked up, pounding rain in from the side in the building wind.

"Shit!" Rob said to Kyle. "Let's hurry! Search every one of these boats!"

The men spread out and bustled down each dock, checking the crafts for occupants. The marina was expansive, with rows upon rows of large boats towering over them. It would take a while to search them all. But the chances of Marianne's buyer still being there were slim.

Rob jumped into one of the largest boats, a multi-million-dollar piece of construction large enough for a few families to live aboard. He searched beneath the harbor light, checking the deck, the living area, the galley. But there was no sign of anybody being there. With Kyle at the other end of the marina, Rob climbed out and went for the next one in line. But, as he turned around to leave, a bright flashlight blinded him from down the concrete walkway.

Kyle had hurried to meet Rob in the middle. As he approached, he noticed a short figure standing behind them, aiming a white light. He paused in place.

"You're not supposed to be here," the man said in Spanish. "This is a private marina."

The man was obviously a night watchman who'd been guarding the marina. Rob kept his hands up and backed away like he was planning to leave.

"Get out of here!" the guard said as he ambled closer to Rob. "Or I will arrest you for trespassing!"

The security guard stopped in front, holding the flashlight close enough for Rob to touch it.

"Leave, right now!" the guard yelled again.

Rob clutched the tip of the black Mag Light and tore it from his hands.

"No!" the guard said as he tried to pull the light back.

The watchman looked to be reaching for something by his belt. Rob clasped the metal light hard before the guard could remove it and smashed him over the head, causing him to drop to the ground. Before he knew what had hit him, the guard was out for the count. Rob turned the torch off and shoved it into his back pocket.

"Okay. Let's finish searching the rest of this fucking place."

Rob worried they may never find her, but he wasn't giving up. He didn't want to even think about not locating his sister. Rob continued searching desperately. His nerves were getting the best of him, causing his body to go numb from a mix of emotion and the pain his body was feeling.

While Rob continued probing, something far off had gotten Kyle's attention. He focused on a vessel on the horizon, somewhat lit up with lights shining from the sides.

"What?" Rob asked. "What is it?"

Kyle pointed out into the water.

"There!"

Rob turned around and saw the bow light of a large boat sailing away in the Sea of Cortez toward the open ocean.

"Come on!" Rob said. "That could be it!"

Kyle followed Rob as they moved to the farthest point in the marina. Upon examining closer, Rob saw something flailing in the wind above the boat's stern light. It was the yacht's flag, with its vibrant colors thrashing back and forth in the wind.

"That look like the UAE flag to you?" he asked.

Rob was pointing to the flag of the United Arab Emirates.

"Yeah," Kyle said, "it sure does."

Rob started scouring around the docks.

"Fuck! There has to be something around here. We need to get to that boat."

They raced up and down, trying to find something they could use in a push to chase the yacht. Just when Rob was about to break down thinking there was no way they'd find a quick ride in such an upscale Marina, Kyle called out to him from the other end.

"Hey!" he said. "Hey, I found something over here!"

It was a small skiff with an outboard motor tied to one of the older yachts. Rob jumped in with Kyle and untied the stern line, pushing away from the larger boat with his hands, and tried to start it. But it wouldn't crank.

"Damn it!"

With his muscles burning from the strain, he tugged on the cord again—still nothing. Rob pounded on the top of the motor.

"Fuck, come on!" he said. "Start, you bastard!"

He gripped the handle tighter and yanked it back even harder. Finally, the engine turned over and vibrated, spitting black smoke up into the air, the harsh wind off the water blowing it behind them.

"Damn, I was getting worried there for a second!" Rob exclaimed.

With no idea how much fuel they had, or if they could reach it, Rob turned the speed all the way up, and they started cruising after the massive vessel. Minutes went by. The tiny boat skipped and crashed into waves as they moved closer to the multi-level superyacht. The rain felt like hard pellets on the side of their faces as they drove forward.

The motor sputtered as they made it closer to the boat.

"No!" Rob said. "Don't die on me now, you bitch!"

As they continued to within a stone's throw of the vast yacht, the engine spit exhaust a couple more times. It died, leaving them dead in the water over the increasing swells.

"Fuck," said Rob. "I guess we're swimming the rest."

They took their weapons and dove into the water. Luckily for them, the firearms they had on their person could fire in and out of water. Unlike most firearms, the Glock handgun could shoot underwater because the gun used an internal firing mechanism instead of a hammer, as most pistols had. But it sacrificed killing capability at a lethal range of just five feet while submerged. However, firing the Glock underwater was extremely loud, because of pressure, compared to shooting on dry land.

They swam under the surface and rose just below the steps, grabbing the metal railing. The yacht was excessive, fit for royalty. It was so big, in fact, that it looked like a floating mini-mansion.

As they hung on, Rob overheard steps moving toward them from above. Glancing up from the side, it appeared to be one of the prince's bodyguards. And he was alone. The guard lit a cigar and took a sip of liquor from a clear glass. Rob slowly gripped the Glock and moved through the water to the open platform. Lunging up out of the water, he snatched the man by his black leather belt, tugging him back into the water as the glass tumbled down the steps and splashed. Holding the gun to his chest, Rob fired, the red-colored water moving by them as the boat sailed past. He sent his body down and away with his other arm as the yacht dragged them along. The guard sank behind them and disappeared into the depths.

They pressed forward, pulling themselves up onto the multi-million-dollar, multi-level yacht steps. They reached the aft deck and took cover behind a lounge table next to the deck's pool. From their spot, they could see shimmering lights and shadows moving along the walls up above. Rob sprang for a better position. Gazing up the steps to the extensive top deck, he got a glimpse of the prince's captain at the helm and a few guards around him, drinking and playing loud Arab music.

Just when the men were about to move up the stairs, one of the prince's men had rounded the corner and spotted them from behind. The man wore a white and red keffiyeh, a traditional Arab head covering.

"Hey, you!" he shouted in Arabic.

The man went for his gun.

"Who are you?"

Rob shot forward, grabbing the barrel as he brought it up. But the guard got a shot off before Rob could strip it from his hands. The bullet punctured the upper part of Rob's thigh, oozing blood down his black pants. Kyle had gotten a hold of the guy's arm, knocking the weapon from his hand and shooting him once in the neck. The guard went down, hitting his head on the side of the boat. Kyle heaved him over the side and dumped him overboard, his body splashing into the choppy water below.

"Shit!" Kyle yelled as he got down beside Rob. "Man, you okay?"

Kyle noticed the bloody wound to Rob's thigh.

"Yeah," Rob said, trying to boost himself off the ground. "I think so. But somebody had to have heard that shot. Get ready for company!"

"Hold on a second," Kyle said.

Kyle tore off a piece of his shirt and coiled it tight around the top of Rob's leg, tying it off in a makeshift tourniquet. A ruckus followed from above as the men ran to investigate. Rob strained up halfway, kneeling on his uninjured leg, and went for cover with his buddy behind a row of seats as the rain continued to pound the boat, their clothes soaked from head to toe.

The prince's men flew down the steps, keffiyehs on their heads and guns in hand, shouting to each other in Arabic.

"Spread out," Rob whispered to Kyle. "Let's hit them from two sides."

Kyle moved low along the extensive deck seating to the other side, his weapon ready for a fight. The guards moved in closer. When they advanced to within a few feet of their location, Rob signaled to Kyle. They both popped up together and started firing into the guards. Before they even knew what happened, the men ended in a bloody pile on the deck. Rob thrust up with the top of the chair, edging onward with his gun drawn.

"You sure you are good to move?" Kyle asked him.

"Yeah," Rob replied. "I'll live. Let's just move before they figure out what happened."

Kyle accompanied Rob as he hobbled up the stairs, moving along to the hatch that led to the bridge. The captain lowered himself in the corner, hands up and huddling against the bulkhead as they entered. He was not a guard, just someone the prince had hired to steer the boat. Rob held the gun to his head.

"Where is she?" Rob asked. "The girl! Where is she? Speak, damn it!"

But he acted like he didn't understand English.

"No English, Mister!" he said.

"Really?" Rob asked.

Rob leaned down in front of him. He snatched the man by the beard, removing his keffiyeh and pulling him by the hair.

"I'll ask you one more time, asshole," he continued. "Where is the girl? Answer me, or I'm going to send you to meet Allah!"

"Okay, Mister. All right, his highness is in the aft cabin, below deck. Please don't kill me!"

Rob released the man's head, holding the gun against him.

"See?" asked Rob. "I knew you could do it, Captain."

The captain's eyes bugged as he awaited his fate.

"But," Rob said, "this is a message to anyone who wants to rip young girls from their homes. Nobody who had anything to do with taking my sister is safe. None of you! And you can take this message with you straight to the afterlife, you fucking bastard!"

The man had a petrified look on his face, as if he knew he was about to die. Rob squeezed the trigger, watching as brains sprayed all over the cabin behind him. His body went limp as he fell back.

Rob reached for the controls and killed the engine in the middle of the water.

"Let's go get my sister," he said.

They left the bridge and exited the cabin to the rear, following along the dimly lit corridor. The yacht's interior was adorned in mahogany-paneled walls with solid gold accents and vivid paintings by renowned artists. Busts of past and current Dubai elite lined both sides of the hall. Suddenly, two guards came racing around the corner from behind, firing submachine guns from behind cover.

They vaulted out of the way, Rob landing right on top of his wounded leg.

"Fuck!" he shouted.

Rob rolled to the right on his stomach as Kyle took cover behind the wall opposite him. He fired back from the prone, striking one guard in the gut. The man fell, clutching his abdomen, and started to bleed out. Kyle discharged another round from behind the door, hitting the other guard square in the chest, and he slumped down to the marble floor.

"You all right, man?" Kyle asked Rob from across the hallway.

"Yeah," he replied. "I'm fine. The pain tells me I'm still breathing."

Rob had a sense of humor, even during gunfights. It's what kept him going and one thing Kyle admired about him.

"Let's move!" said Rob.

Rob pulled himself up by a lamp on the wall. They left one dead guard and another bleeding out and advanced to the yacht's elevator. As they entered, gold covered the interior walls, reflecting anyone who stood in front of it. To them, it was a crass sight. To a prince, it was a status symbol. The elevator jolted and beeped. It opened, and Rob took a quick look around the corner.

"On me," said Rob.

They advanced down another long hallway toward the back of the boat. Rob peeked into each room as they moved past, searching for more guards. They had no way of knowing just how many were on board. Then, two more of the prince's men shot out past one door. One of them grabbed Rob by the arm, trying to pry the gun from his hands. Kyle dashed for the other, springing forth and tackling him to the floor before the guard could fire.

Kyle pounded on his face while Rob subdued the other and pistol-whipped him with his own gun, flattening him. Rob stood over both men as Kyle jumped out of the way. Rob double-tapped each of them with four shots, one to the chest and one to the head.

"Come on, man," Rob said to Kyle. "Let's fucking end this."

Rob gingerly stepped over the two bodies, and they moved further down to the largest cabin on the boat. They circled the door, and Rob tried to turn the knob. It wouldn't budge.

"Stand back!" said Rob.

He shot the lock with the .45-caliber handgun, breaking it apart with a series of shots as pieces fell to the ground. Rob released the empty magazine and inserted his last one. He kicked the door open, and they entered the prince's cabin. As they marched forward into an empty room, they looked around.

"Where the fuck is she?" Rob asked.

"I don't know," Kyle said. "I don't see anyone."

Then Rob picked up a slight whimper coming from the other side of another door.

"Wait," he said, standing as still and quiet as he could. "You hear that?"

He pressed his ear to the door and heard what sounded like a weak cry coming from the next room. Rob gestured for Kyle to get ready. He stacked the door next to his buddy. Rob held his hand up as he started counting down quietly with three fingers.

1... 2... 3.

Rob jarred the door open, and they entered the room, guns focused ahead. It was a large, pompous bathroom with marble tiles on the floor and walls. The golden water faucets sparkled under the crystal chandelier light above. As Rob looked past the enormous bathtub, he saw her, Marianne. And she was being held, arms wrapped around her throat by Muhammad Ahsan, Dubai royalty.

Marianne looked wasted, confused. There was no telling what they had doped her up with to keep her from struggling. Whatever it was, it was working.

"Don't come any closer!" the prince screamed at them in English from the corner of the room. "Get away from me! I will kill her!"

Rob stood motionless, staring the prince down in contempt.

"You have my sister, your fucking highness," he said, his hand clenched in a fist around his weapon grip. "And I want her back!"

Prince Ahsan stiffened his hold on Marianne. He wasn't about to let her go willingly. He pulled her in closer to his head to shield his body. Ahsan didn't think they would shoot at him and risk hitting her.

"Unless you have lots of money," the prince added, "she is mine. That is how it works. I paid good money for her!"

Rob didn't care who he was or how much money he had. He wasn't leaving that boat alive.

"That's what I thought!" Ahsan said.

Rob relaxed for a second, glancing back at Kyle and then to Ahsan.

"I hate rich pieces of shit like you," Rob said. "You think

you can just buy anything or anyone you wish. Think you own the world? You don't. No amount of money is going to save you this time. And this is a notice to all who are like you. You aren't safe from me. Give Allah my regards, you fucking swine!"

Prince Ahsan started shouting at them in Arabic and English, tugging at Marianne's hair and holding her against him.

"Guards!" Ahsan shouted in Arabic. "Guards!"

But the prince was on his own. And, without his men to come to his aid, he was just another asshole in Rob's way.

"You hear that?" Rob asked him. "No, you don't, nothing. Nobody is coming to help you!"

Rob drew the Glock like a cowboy in a duel.

He sent a shot soaring past Marianne, missing her and cutting into the prince's head in a moment of concentration that seemed to occur in slow motion. It ruptured the top of his head apart, blood gushing out and slinging it back against the tub as his arms went lax, freeing Marianne's neck. She dropped to the side as Rob rushed in to grab her, catching her mid-fall.

"Don't worry, sis," Rob told her, not knowing if she realized who he was. "Don't worry. I'm here. Your big brother is here!"

Rob squeezed Marianne, a tear rolling down the side of his face as he wrapped his arms around her. He held his sister like he never had before, grateful they got to her before she became a statistic. He knew that Marianne would never quite see the world the same way again.

"Oh, thank God," he said, smiling back at Kyle. "Thank God we got her, partner."

The thunder roaring outside vibrated the yacht, rain pelting down against the deck. Rob and Kyle elevated

Marianne's fragile body, toting her out of the room and spreading her over the prince's lavish, gold-trimmed, king-size bed.

"You know how to drive a boat?" Rob asked Kyle as he covered Marianne with a blanket.

"Yeah," he replied. "More or less."

"Good. We need to get Marianne back to land as soon as possible."

Nobody had a clue what had just taken place on that yacht, giving Rob the element of surprise. They hadn't given them time to call anyone. And now, Rob had some unfinished business to deal with.

"Man," Kyle said to Rob. "You realize you just killed a prince?"

"Yep," he replied. "Fuck 'em. And anyone else like him. Watch my sister. I'll be quick."

"You got it," Kyle replied.

Rob cautiously made his way through the boat, ensuring there were no surprise guards left. He hauled bodies one by one to dump overboard into the shark-infested waters. Ahsan was the last. Rob tied his feet to a large metal chain he found and heaved him over.

"Good riddance, you fucking asshole," he said, watching as the prince sank below the surface. "You'll never hurt another girl ever again."

THIRTY

```
Culiacán
Sinaloa, Mexico
Next day
```

Rob had left Marianne with Kyle at a low-rent motel not far out of town, checked in under a fake name. His buddy was busy running IV fluids through her and flushing the narcotics from her system. Rob had gotten a ride to pick up the Jeep and their gear earlier that afternoon. But they couldn't leave just yet. Rob had one last job to do before he could have peace of mind.

He trusted his best friend to watch over Marianne until his return. Wanting the head of the snake, he was now on his way to the only mansion in the city. The property belonged to Juan Luis, Los Lobos Cartel leader. After all the suffering he'd caused his sister and other innocents, Rob would not allow him to walk freely any longer. Gripping the steering wheel hard and swerving around every car in his path, death to the king was the only thing on his mind.

He steered the vehicle over the shoulder near a wooded

area just off the side of the highway, hoping the night would hide the Jeep well. Rob eased out of the Jeep, feeling the last couple of days' gunshots and beatings, and removed his stuff from the back. His entire body felt worn and fatigued, an intense burn erupting from his leg wound. But he geared up anyway and headed into the woods roughly a mile away from the estate.

Just over fifteen minutes later, Rob came to a large, grassy area outside of the mansion's perimeter walls. Two guards stood at the front gate by a guardhouse and a black metal swing gate, chatting with one another and staring down the private driveway into blackness. Rob was just close enough to hear them talking. A single sentry roamed around the other side of the wall from the main yard, Uzi inside the brown leather shoulder holster over his button-up shirt.

Rob braced himself against a tall tree, wearing black clothing and hidden in the dark as he took a careful look around. He wasn't there for a gunfight. He wanted Los Lobos to know that they were no longer the aggressors. There was no place they could hide from his rage. Vengeance was about to come full circle.

Rob slithered along like a snake as the guard passed him by. As quiet as a mouse, he sneaked up behind the man, wrapping his arm around and holding a hand over his mouth, so he couldn't squeal. Not able to breathe under Rob's hold on him, the guard struggled. Wielding his long K-bar knife with a powerful grip on the handle, Rob reached around and thrust the blade into his chest, driving it deep into the guard's lung. His limbs went loose, and Rob slowly lowered him to the ground so the others wouldn't hear him fall. The guard's body jerked in the grass as his lights went out.

Rob left him there and moved up to the wall. He sprang from the ground and took the ledge with both hands, pulling himself up. Keeping his body against the top of the brick, Rob rolled over and dropped to the other side. He'd fallen to the grass without a sound and advanced forward, dipping behind a row of tall, green, manicured hedges.

A pair of Juan's men strolled by under the large house's overhang, puffing on Cuban cigars as he hid in the shadows. They were so close to him that Rob could smell their expensive cologne in the air. As they walked by and moved to the other side of the house, Rob removed the bag from his back and placed it on the ground beside him.

Earlier, he'd picked up several pounds of black market C-4 and a detonator that their Mexican detective friend, Pérez, had secretly swiped from the evidence locker at the precinct. Having used explosive charges in combat, Rob knew how they worked and the destruction they caused. He gathered a few blocks of plastic explosives from his pack, electric detonators inserted into each. Rob edged forth and arranged them in the bushes at the front of the building. He'd be long gone and out of the blast zone by the time they did their job.

Turning back and out of sight, Rob followed the wall to the other end of the property. As he neared the pool in the back of the villa, Rob sighted one of Juan's men walking across the tile patio, past the poolside furniture and the hot tub. Rob waited for him to move by.

Raising the suppressed Glock pistol from his trousers, Rob sneaked up behind him, placing a hand over his mouth. Rob touched the gun to the guard's back and pressed the trigger, the shot entering his body, exiting his chest, and leaving a large, bloody tear in his gray shirt. Rob boosted him up and set his body inside a large shed by the pool.

Rob pointed his weapon again, shooting out the light above the pool and seeing glass hit the concrete patio below. He removed a few more blocks of C-4 and scrambled to the side of the house. Looking about to ensure nobody was around, he set the charges along the center of the wall, at the bottom, and concealed behind the wooden walkway rail.

Suddenly, Rob detected noise from down the path. Three more of Juan's men turned up, and they were moving toward him. Rob hit the ground. Veiled by the home's greenery, he remained still. As they walked around the house and out of sight, Rob got set to make his move. He crouched and slid along the wall just outside the kitchen. Two additional guards sat outside in the garden, backs to him. Rob heard yelling coming from inside the house, and he took a quick glance through the kitchen window.

There you are, you shit stain, he thought to himself, seeing Juan sitting with a few of his men at the long, marble dining table. He had a phone to his ear as he savored a glass full of wine.

"I don't give a fuck!" Rob heard Juan shout over the phone. "Find them, or I'll have your fucking head on a stick!"

Rob watched Juan finish the call and slam the phone on the table. "Fuck!" he yelled to his men at the table as he bit into a piece of bread. "Do I have to do everything my fucking self?" Rob knew he was talking about them. It was evident he'd learned about the breakout and his men's colossal failure. But Juan had no idea what else was on the agenda that night.

Too late for that, asshole, Rob thought.

Rob inched forward under the twilight, planting the last few blocks of C-4 at the base of the kitchen wall below the large window. He fell back to where he'd come from and passed the pool for the last time as he made his way to the far section of the wall. He scaled back up and fell down to his knees on the other side. Springing to his feet, Rob headed into the dim woods outside the grounds and toward his waiting vehicle nearly a mile away.

A quarter of an hour later, Rob made it back to the Jeep. He jumped in, setting his backpack on the seat next to him. Rob reached into the outside pouch and retrieved the detonator. He grinned as he held the detonator in his lap, staring down the road behind him in the rearview mirror.

He pressed the switch on the detonator. In an instant, a massive boom rocked the hillside behind him as flames shot straight up into the air and over the tree line with incredible ferocity, vibrating the Jeep and the surrounding ground. The explosion propelled chunks of the obliterated estate high into the air like a volcanic eruption. Rob watched the glow in the sky behind him and lighting up everything around it. It was as if the sun had plummeted to the earth. Rob spun his tires in the gravel as he peeled away into the road.

"Enjoy hell, you fucking bastard," he said, tossing the remote detonator into the woods.

Rob saw the carnage getting smaller in his mirror with every passing second as he scrambled away from the scene. The blare of distant fire trucks sounded off from the other direction as he gained distance from the destruction. He was en route to pick up his sister and get her the hell out of that country.

▌▌▌

They'd pushed north across the Sonora Desert in the middle of the night. Marianne languished in the back seat of the Jeep for most of the drive. She was in and out and couldn't manage to stay awake for more than a few minutes at a time. Covered with a green wool blanket, her head leaned on the top of Rob's backpack. It was the next day, and it looked like the group had left trouble far behind them.

With Rob's foot heavy on the gas, the Jeep bounced over every sandy hill in their path. Rob glanced in his side mirror and suddenly noticed a vehicle hop the road and begin to gain on them from behind. He adjusted the mirror and took a closer glimpse, observing men with guns jutting out from the inside and taking aim at them.

"Damn it!" he said as he pounded a fist on the steering wheel. "I can't fucking believe this shit. Take cover!"

"What is it?" Kyle asked. "What's wrong?"

Rob pointed toward the back, and Kyle turned to see the vehicle racing up on the opposite side of the road.

"I think it's our cartel friends," Rob said. "Looks like they don't want us to leave. Looks like they want to avenge the boss!"

Kyle reached for his M4 on the vehicle's floor, yanking back on the charging handle and releasing it forward.

"We'll see about that!" replied Kyle. "How the fuck did they know where we were?"

Rob kept his foot on the floorboard, trying to keep them at bay.

"I don't know," Rob said. "But protect Marianne and don't let those assholes get close."

Marianne moaned incoherently as Kyle hovered over her, one knee on the back seat as he aimed out through the passenger window. Suddenly, a series of shots rang out from the assailant's vehicle, a gray Range Rover, and shattered the back glass, just missing him. Kyle ducked down quickly.

"Shit!" he yelled, rising slowly and peeking over the seat and through the smashed rear window.

Kyle punched through the remaining glass with the barrel of his rifle.

"Fuck these bastards!"

Kyle began shooting back as the cartel vehicle moved from side to side. Fire began erupting from the Range Rover, pinging off the Jeep's body and drilling the dashboard next to Rob. He continued driving, trying to lose them as he sank his head lower into the seat.

"Fuck this shit!" he said, glaring into his mirror once again and watching as the Rover shot up by them on the Jeep's driver's side.

Kyle pointed his weapon around the broken glass and sent a hail of M4 rounds into the side of the vehicle. But he didn't have a clean shot on them as they flew past him.

"I'm going to fucking end this right now!" Rob said.

The Range Rover's front end was almost even with them, and Rob got ready to make his move. He peered left and saw the passenger in the cartel vehicle pointing an Uzi in his direction. Rob knew they wanted to kill them and get Marianne back. But Rob would die before he let that happen.

"Hold on, man!" he shouted back to Kyle. "Hold the fuck on!"

Kyle grabbed the roll bar above his head with one hand, his M4 in the other. Rob gripped the wheel and swung it hard left, striking the Rover in the passenger door and causing it to swerve away from him. The passenger dropped the Uzi, and it fell through the window, bouncing off the blacktop behind them. Rob looked ahead and noticed a large billboard sign on the side of the road coming up fast. He squeezed the steering wheel once more.

His foot hard on the accelerator, Rob swerved again with all he had. The Jeep scraped and launched the Range Rover off the isolated stretch of road. The driver regained control and raised his submachine gun toward Rob.

"Shoot the tires!" he said to Kyle.

Kyle cracked the glass, pointing his M4 barrel through the window. With a series of shots, he popped one of the rear tires, causing the Range Rover to vibrate violently as the rim hit the pavement and sparked.

Rob swung back right, then a sharp left, striking the Rover hard and thrusting it off the road and into the dirt. The vehicle slammed into the sign at high speed as Rob veered right at the last second. Tangled metal rammed through the front windshield and into the Rover, severing the driver's head and stopping them in their tracks as the vehicle wrapped around the pole.

Rob slammed the brakes. The Jeep fishtailed off the dirt and skidded sideways, coming to a halt in the middle of the road. He glanced back at Marianne and Kyle.

"Fuck me," he said. "You guys all right? Anyone hurt?"

Kyle cleared his rifle and put it on safe, letting it down gently to the floor.

"Nope," he said, looking over Marianne as she lay on the seat. "Nope, we're good. Let's just get the hell out of this country before any more of these fuckers show up."

Seeing the top of the border wall barely visible behind the hill, Rob took a deep breath and put the vehicle into drive.

"Yeah," he said. "Sounds like a damn good plan to me, man."

Rob veered right and took the Jeep off-road for a couple more miles until they reached the house at the end of the dirt road. There appeared to be no one home from the outside. He stopped in front of the steps. They snatched up their gear, and Kyle, his arm under Marianne's, helped her through the unlocked door toward the back.

"Hello?" Rob called out, his pistol pointed outward. "Anyone home?"

But nobody answered. They hurried to the utility room, and Rob slid the heavy hatch to the side. He climbed down, supporting Marianne between them while Kyle helped her from above.

A lengthy sixteen-hour drive had passed. It was mid-afternoon as the three began making their way through the same tunnel the men had used to slip into the country. Rob was utterly worn out. But he refused to rest a moment until he got his sister back home safely. Kyle and Rob both had injuries and bruises all over their bodies. Bone tired, they had dealt with the bitter pain for days now.

They moved forward in the dark hole, Rob dragging his sister along as he held her hand. Her face was purple and bruised—the cartel had done a number on her for sure. Before, Marianne was a foolish teenager, blind to the dangerous world around her. Now, she felt scared, frightened, and would never be so trusting ever again. It would be a time before she got over the ordeal, if she ever did.

Clutching the bottom rung under Kyle, Rob grabbed Marianne's arm. He braced her feet and shouldered her up as she ascended the ladder above him. She was so weak, Rob had to support her with his arms to keep her from tumbling back down. Rob reached up and slid the hatch to the side. As they soared up and out of the opening, he shoved Marianne skyward. She fell into the desert sand, finally back on US soil.

"You okay, sis?" Rob asked her as he went up and squatted down beside her on the ground, grabbing her by the hand. "Marianne?"

A tear rolled down her battered cheek as she glanced up into the sun, the golden glare blinding her eyes. Marianne cried, her back slightly bent against the side of a cactus. Rob looked into her eyes with Kyle standing over them. She could speak clearly for the first time since they'd found her.

"What those barbarians did to me..." she said, shaking as she tried to fight back the tears. "You came for me, both of you. You saved me."

"Of course we did, sis," Rob said, on the brink of breaking down himself. "Why wouldn't we?"

Marianne wept, covering her reddened face in her hands.

"I swear, big brother," she said. "I'll never treat you and Mom that way again. I'll listen to you, I promise. I'm so sorry for the way I treated you!"

Rob stooped down and curved an arm around her, hoisting her up onto her feet while holding his burning bullet wound with his free hand.

"Let's go," he said, flinching. "Let's get you out of here."

They started trudging through the desert brush, making their way back to the small-town road. Bodies aching with every step, the trio slowly progressed closer to the meeting point, sweat pouring down their heads from the intense desert heat. Rob painfully supported Marianne, practically carrying her as they continued on. As the road came into view across the flat sand, a van appeared up ahead.

The vehicle halted at the side of the road. A woman shoved

the sliding passenger door aside and nearly stumbled over herself as she climbed out.

"Look who I found!" José yelled.

It was Louise. Rob didn't know it, but Kyle had organized with José to bring their mother down to meet them, and she'd taken the earliest flight out. Louise ran for her daughter as fast as her aged legs would carry her. She stopped in front of her, falling to her knees and hugging her tight around her waist. Marianne fell down into her mother's arms.

"Oh, you got my baby!" she cried. "You got her! Oh, my God, thank you so much!"

Rob's mind was finally at peace, thankful that his sister hadn't become another statistic in the cartel's savage game. He and Kyle saw as Louise embraced Marianne like she would never let her go.

"Mom," Marianne cried, tears dripping onto her olive skin. "I am sorry. I'm so sorry for not listening to you. I am sorry for being such a bitch. I promise you it will never happen again!"

Rob took them both by the hand and placed his arms over them.

"It's okay, little sister," he said. "You are safe now. Nobody's going to hurt you. What do you say we go home now, huh?"

"Yes, please," she replied with a cheery face, the first in a long while. "Please, let's go home."

Rob and Kyle were clearly in pain, walking alongside them as they started to cross the desert road. They couldn't hide the toll that recent events had taken on their bodies. Louise glanced back, noticing them both hobbling as they got closer to the van.

"Oh my God," Louise said to them. "You both are hurt!"

"We're fine, Mom," he replied. "Let's just go."

"Yeah, Miss Walker," Kyle added. "We're good."

"It doesn't look like you are good," she said. "We are taking you both to the hospital, now."

"No," Rob said as he put an arm out in front of her. "No, we will wait until we get home."

Rob's mother gave him a troubled look. She didn't like seeing her son in pain.

"Rob, please," she said. "You guys need a..."

But Rob interrupted her, nudging her forward toward the vehicle.

"Mom, no," he replied, itching to get them far away from that border town. "Nobody is dying here. We're fine. I promise we'll worry about it when we are home, all right?"

Rob opened the front passenger door and pointed his mom inside, closing her door behind her while bracing himself against the side of the van.

"Fine, then," Louise told him. "Just promise you'll take care of it."

"I told you, Mom," replied Rob. "We will. Kyle and I didn't get the worst of it, trust me."

They carefully hopped in and tossed both of their packs and weapons into the back. Rob helped his sister up into the seat beside him and slid the door shut as Kyle climbed in after them. José hit the gas, peeling out toward the highway on their way east. As he turned the knob on the radio, a news report sounded through the speakers.

Juan Luis, Los Lobos cartel leader, was found dead today with many other cartel members in what looks like the beginning of a new gang war in Mexico. They found severely burned bodies inside and around his residence due to a massive explosion felt and heard from miles away. As other cartels fight for dominance in the drug business, this looks to be another orchestrated attack from a bitter rival. Only time will tell who will come out on top in the Mexican drug wars, the criminals or the authorities.

In other news, a multi-million-dollar yacht was found in flames just off the Mexican coast. It appears to have been owned by a member of the UAE royal family. It's not yet known if these events are in any way related. We'll release more information when it becomes available. Thank you. This is Samantha King, KTAR news.

Rob held a hand on his hurt leg and grinned as he snubbed the pain and stared through the window, watching the yellow line blur past them on the Arizona desert roadway. It was another case of an immoral enemy who'd seriously underestimated his opponent. Rob had lived up to the Special Forces' motto, De Oppresso Liber, to free the oppressed.

THE END

WHAT DID YOU THINK OF THE MESSENGER?

Thank you for reading the first book in Rob's story. His journey continues in Retribution, book two in the Rob Walker series. Find out what happens when Rob puts his military career on the line for the truth - and pursues corruption across the globe no matter the cost.

Did you enjoy THE MESSENGER? Leave a review and let others know!

Don't forget to checkout book 2, RETRIBUTION

Visit www.johnetterleebooks.com to sign up to the newsletter

ABOUT THE AUTHOR

John is a retired US. Army combat Veteran, horse and animal lover, adventurer, and author. Joining the Army shortly after the September 11, 2001, terrorist attacks in the US, he served multiple tours overseas from 2003 to 2013. He was medically retired from the Army for an injury after being medevaced and sent to Landstuhl Army Medical Center in Germany in 2010.

Although John has always enjoyed writing, it wasn't until recovering from surgery that he began to take it more seriously. Writing has since become a passion for him, and he loves to share his stories with the world of book lovers.

John now lives in North Carolina with his wife Elizabeth, whom he met while stationed at Joint Base Lewis-McChord in Washington State in 2011. He is also a lover of cats. John and his wife share their home with a few beautiful Sphynx cats.

In addition, he studies the German language, and enjoys traveling, especially to Europe, and meeting new people. He loves hearing from his readers. Drop him a line anytime! Thanks!

MORE BOOKS BY JOHN ETTERLEE

Rob Walker Books:

RETRIBUTION
BLOOD RED
AN IMMINENT THREAT

Roger O'Neil Books:

THE COLD STORM

STRIKE POINT

Box Sets:

ROB WALKER (BOOKS 1-3)

FOLLOW JOHN

Facebook: jbetterlee

Twitter: JEtterleeWrites

Instagram: jetterleewrites

Sign up to John's mailing list and follow him @

www.johnetterleebooks.com

Printed in Great Britain
by Amazon